The house was buil[...] [...] moulded gable, su[...] [...] addition, Kate learned, and said to spoil the classical design. Wide steps led to its open front doors, shutters flanked the windows, and on each side were flowers in profusion.

There seemed to Kate, at first sight, a crowd of people at the front of the house – people and dogs; a crowd which resolved itself into a group of five once she had stepped from the car and brought them all into focus, and no more than two large, yellow dogs who leapt delightedly at Guy.

The Candlewood Tree

Barbara Whitnell

CORONET BOOKS
Hodder and Stoughton

First published in Great Britain in 1997 by Hodder and Stoughton
First published in paperback in 1997 by Hodder and Stoughton
A division of Hodder Headline PLC
A Coronet Paperback

British Library Cataloguing in Publication Data

Whitnell, Barbara
The candlewood tree
1. English fiction – 20th century
I. Title
823.9´14[F]

ISBN 0 340 61806 X

Printed and bound in Great Britain by
Caledonian International Book Manufacturing Ltd, Glasgow

Hodder and Stoughton
A division of Hodder Headline PLC
338 Euston Road
London NW1 3BH

With my thanks to Christine Alexander and Anne Dymond who dealt patiently with all my queries.

1

February 1961

It was a perfect morning. Later it would be hot, but now the sun was friendly, bathing the garden in a gentle warmth, the stillness broken only by the twittering of the sugar birds around the red-hot pokers in the flowerbed below the stoep.

Christiaan le Roux, Minister for Coloured Affairs in the South African Government, was conscious of a dawning feeling of optimism, the first for what seemed a long, long time. He wasn't out of the wood yet – he was well aware of that – but as he stood in the sunshine at the top of the steps, waiting for Eksberg, there was the undoubted feeling that disaster, after all, might yet be averted.

The strain of the past two weeks had been well nigh unbearable, and he had no idea, looking back, how he had been able to carry on. It had to be admitted that, in a way, Sonia's death had been a blessing, permitting him to be *distrait*, to act out of character. People had made allowances for him; and, as always, seeing things in political terms, it occurred to him that this apparent grief must surely have sent his stock up a little. The sympathy vote was not something to be ignored.

'How kind of you,' he had said huskily, again and again, as, eyes brilliant with unshed tears, he received the condolences of friends and colleagues. 'How very, very kind. Thank you so much.'

He had pressed their hands, smiling a brave but tremulous smile. Poor man, they were thinking. Poor, bereaved, brave man. He could see it in their faces. Maybe Sonia le Roux hadn't been the easiest of women, went their thoughts, but the marriage had seemed as successful as most and, despite all the temptations put in his path, Christiaan had stayed faithful. And I did, he thought, over and over, querulous in his self-satisfaction. I did stay faithful.

The truth was that Sonia's death had meant very little in comparison with the knowledge that Jan knew everything. Everything! Why else would he have rushed from the house like that, his face dark with contempt and rage?

The previous day, at Sonia's funeral, the boy had been friendly enough; well, perhaps 'friendly' wasn't quite the word. It was, to be honest, many a long year since the relationship could possibly be described in such terms. Still, they had greeted each other with subdued politeness as befitted the occasion. Sonia was, after all, Jan's aunt and the woman who had brought him up. Even though there had been coolness between them, too, he must surely have felt some regret at her passing. One did, on these occasions. But what a difference twenty-four hours could make! No politeness now, or any pretence of it; just incoherent accusations of treachery and heaven alone knew what else.

Jan had been searching Sonia's desk – for his birth certificate, he said; but Christiaan knew better. He'd been searching for evidence against him, that was the truth of it – and by God, it was clear that he'd found it. And now he knew everything – every sordid, squalid little detail.

Naturally, after Jan had left in a spurt of gravel and Christiaan had had a moment to collect his wits, he'd gone to Sonia's office and had searched through the top drawer of her massive desk which Jan, in his hurry, had left open, seeking some kind of confirmation of what he knew in his bones to be true.

It had felt strange to be there. This was Sonia's domain, and he had never intruded on her privacy; never, to be honest, would have been allowed to. Under the circumstances he had always felt it more dignified to maintain an air of complete indifference and though, from time to time, he had entered the office from where she conducted all the business of the vineyard, he had never been privy to the contents of her desk, though he knew she preserved records of the entire family, past and present.

Neatly, methodically, as she always did everything, she had kept envelope files containing every document, every certificate, every public statement pertaining to the person named on its label. She owed it to posterity, she was wont to say. The Lampards were one of the founders of the South African wine industry, and Gramerci one of the most important vineyards. Someone, some day, would want to write its history.

He had seen her cutting out newspaper articles and reports that concerned him and his burgeoning political career, but it was with growing despair that he found, as he searched the drawer with trembling fingers, that no file bearing his name was to be found there.

Jan had taken it; what other explanation could there be? The confirmation of his worst fears made him feel physically sick and for a moment he sank down on Sonia's chair staring at nothing, his mouth hanging open, unable to breathe or assimilate this numbing shock.

But wait, he cautioned himself, a flicker of hope returning. What had Jan said, exactly? Hard, now, to remember his precise words, for the moment he had mentioned the desk and its contents Christiaan had frozen with dread, so paralysed by the memory of the secret it held that he'd taken in very little. There'd been something about hiding the truth, something about collusion, all delivered with the kind of stuttering, incoherent fury that he'd thought Jan had outgrown long ago.

No, he hadn't heard much, but he'd seen Jan's disgust and could almost feel the searing contempt. It had left him sick and shaken, and standing at the foot of the steps that led to the stoep, he had clutched at the stone post to steady himself.

Why hadn't he thought of that letter – that damned and damning letter – for himself? Easy now to think that he should have searched for the incriminating evidence and destroyed it immediately after Sonia's death, not waited for so long as a day. But there had been so much to do here and now – the funeral to arrange, an important bill going through Parliament, caucus meetings he couldn't miss. There seemed, after all, no hurry. It had lain forgotten – well, almost forgotten – for twenty-two years, never alluded to, its presence ignored. How could he have dreamed that the boy would come like this, without warning, unforgivably searching through Sonia's desk without permission? Ludicrously, he found some relief in feeling outrage on Sonia's behalf at this invasion of her privacy before realisation of his own plight returned, redoubled.

Another few hours, he thought, as he stood at the top of the steps of the old Cape Dutch house waiting for Eksberg. Just another few hours and I would have remembered the bloody thing. All this would have been unnecessary, and Jan could have gone on his own, hot-headed, trouble-making way which would inevitably end in tears one of these days, without anyone else lifting a finger. His thoughts turned to his wife, so lately dead. Happy now, he demanded? Is this what you wanted – that this sequence of events should have been put in train? Anyone else would have thrown the evidence away long ago. Not Sonia.

Fear and bitterness remained, but he was used to acting a part and no observer seeing him on this summer Sunday could guess at the inner turmoil of the past weeks. He looked completely at ease, still handsome in spite of the fact that his abundant hair was now silver. His clothes were stylish, expensive, elegantly casual, his manner confident. Such a man, a stranger might think, would be a worthy prime minister.

And so I would, le Roux thought. So I would – if Jan permits. God, to think it all rested on what the boy might do, who he might tell!

But he must stop thinking of him as a boy, he told himself testily. Jan was a boy no longer, but a man, and an influential man at that in his own rabble-rousing way. He had changed altogether from the eager, sports-mad youngster who had in the past regarded his uncle as something of a hero. Then he had drunk in every word as if it were Holy Writ, boasting to his friends about being the nephew of a Member of Parliament. He had thought, then, that Uncle Christiaan was right about everything, but now that he had grown to man's estate he believed him right about nothing. And here I am, le Roux thought in desperation, so close to my goal. So close to what I have always dreamed of.

Ever since last May's Witwatersrand Agricultural Show when an assassin had attempted to put an end to Verwoerd's political career once and for all, there had been rumours regarding his possible retirement. Verwoerd, however, had returned to Parliament as vigorous and as long-winded as ever, and it was only in the last few weeks that Christiaan had given these rumours any credence. The Prime Minister's recovery hadn't been as great as people believed, it was said. His wife was pressing him to retire, and it was thought he was not unwilling.

This was heady stuff, the kind of news Christiaan le Roux had prayed for. An election was virtually certain later in the year, and who better than he to become the next leader of the party, and therefore the country? He was a long-serving minister, popular among the electorate, respected for his high moral tone and his determination to preserve the culture of the Afrikaner nation. He was not, perhaps, the first choice of all the differing factions in the party, but arguably everyone's second choice, which was far more important. And what's more, he had the backing of Cornelius Wenst – old, now, and retired from active politics, but still powerful, influential, recognised as a kingmaker. With Wenst behind him, le Roux would, until this moment, have backed his chances against anyone else's in government.

It was the thought of Wenst that had, in the end, prompted Christiaan to make the decision to send for Eksberg. No one liked Wenst; in fact there was probably no one in the entire country, Verwoerd not excepted, who did not fear him. He was a Boer of the old school; grim, humourless, and puritanical, with a face that looked as if it had been hewn from a slab of rock. He believed utterly in the necessity of *apartheid*; keeping white blood, more particularly Afrikaans blood, free from any taint of colour was his main preoccupation, even more so now that he was old than it had been earlier. He was also utterly incorruptible and for this reason commanded more respect than other prime ministers before him and certainly more than those that had come after.

What would his reaction be if Jan were to speak? God, it was unthinkable! And in the world at large there would be disgrace beyond imagining. It wasn't just his career. (*Just* his career, le Roux thought, with bitter amusement. Hadn't his career always been the most important thing in his life?) His entire life would be in ruins. He would be an outcast, laughed at by the whole of society, his private affairs picked over for the amusement of those who weren't fit to lick his boots.

He'd thought of appealing to Jan; humbling himself, throwing himself on the boy's mercy. He'd phoned him a number of times, but there had been no reply from his shack halfway up the mountain. He could be anywhere, doing anything, talking to anyone.

An appeal wouldn't have worked anyway, he told himself. Jan was a fanatic – why, think of all that he had said after Sharpeville! You could be forgiven for thinking that it was he, Christiaan le Roux, who had personally killed those sixty-nine blacks instead of the police, legitimately restoring order. In Jan's book, all Nationalists were in the wrong, and Christiaan more wrong than most.

Numbed by panic, he hadn't been able to eat or sleep. Colleagues spoke to him, but he was unaware of them; when unable to avoid making a speech in Parliament he uttered a few, lame sentences and sat down again, quite failing to make his point. Fellow Nationalists looked at each other in alarm and dismay and friends remarked that it was clear that le Roux had been hit harder by his wife's death than might have been expected for one so wrapped up in his career.

It couldn't go on. He knew he had to get a grip on himself, and what astonished him now was that he hadn't thought of the inevitable solution earlier. But when he did, Eksberg came immediately to mind as the man to carry it out.

A thug? Well, perhaps. It didn't do to look too closely into the methods the police were sometimes forced to use to maintain order. All he knew about the man was that he'd restored calm in a sudden violent dispute among the workforce, the year before the vineyard was sold. His methods had been too brutal, some said, but Christiaan hadn't agreed, and neither had Sonia. A few broken heads and as many arrests were a small price to pay for the peace that fell on the estate, in his opinion, and Eksberg had acted with commendable zeal and decision.

He'd said as much to the Chief of Police when he met him at a party soon after the incident. It was his attention to small details such as this that had made him popular over the years. Yes, the policeman had said. Eksberg was well thought of – a good, conscientious officer who would probably rise high in the force.

He'd laughed then. 'He'll need to rise,' he said. 'He married Connie Carmody, you know.'

'Pat Carmody's daughter?'

Everyone knew Pat Carmody, who had made a fortune in property development over the past few years.

'That's the one. She's pretty, but she's pampered, and I imagine she's demanding. She's not at all the kind you'd expect to marry an impoverished policeman.'

It was these words that le Roux suddenly remembered. Ruthless and hard up; Eksberg sounded ideal, just as long as discretion could be added to this description – which, it seemed, after a few enquiries, it could.

He had phoned the policeman at home to arrange a meeting, and – with some obvious mystification on Eksberg's part – it was agreed that he should come to Gramerci at eleven o'clock the following Sunday morning.

Thirty-six hours to wait! Looking forward then it had seemed a lifetime, but now, checking his watch, Christiaan saw there was only half a minute to go if the man was to be on time.

He looked around him and found that even at a time like this he was able to take comfort from the loveliness of his surroundings. The carefully tended lawn in front of the house, winding away out of sight beyond the oaks; the profusion of flowers, the distant blue hills that protected this most beautiful of valleys; all soothed his troubled spirit as no other sight ever could.

God's own country! How often had it been said? And never more true than now, with the scent of jasmine close at hand and the grape harvest in full swing at the far end of the valley.

He lifted his head from the contemplation of it as the first sounds of the car he had been expecting reached his ears. The drive was long and shielded by the ancient oaks and he knew it would be several moments yet before his visitor came into view. He straightened his back and put on his bright, eager, public face.

'Eksberg! Good of you to come,' he said, walking down the front steps to greet his visitor as the car at last came to a halt on the gravel in front of the house.

'My pleasure, Minister.'

He'd hardly had any choice in the matter! Gert Eksberg's smile was pleasant enough, but his eyes were wary. As a policeman he was used to working odd hours, but even so, informal meetings with a minister tended to be unusual, especially on a Sunday morning.

'Shall we sit outside?' It was, clearly, a question to which le Roux expected no answer, for he at once led the way through a plumbago hedge to the left of the house towards another, more private part of the garden. Here there was a table, with chairs angled to give the best possible view of the mountains, all shaded by a striped umbrella. The lawn, with more flowerbeds, reached as far as a row of hibiscus bushes, red and yellow and pink. Beyond them there was a swimming pool, glimmering in the sun.

'Would you like beer, or something stronger?' le Roux asked. 'Or wine, perhaps? We've always been very proud of Gramerci wine.' He smiled the famous le Roux smile – intent, it was clear, on striking an informal note from the start.

'Thank you, sir, but it's a little early—'

'Nonsense, man. It's never too early. And you're not on duty. This is just an informal chat. What'll it be?'

'Well—' Still Eksberg hesitated. 'Beer, then. Thank you.'

A white-clad servant was hovering at some distance and le Roux clicked his fingers to bring him closer, ordering beer for his guest and gin for himself. He sensed the policeman's wariness and uncertainty. He's like a cat, he thought. An alley-cat, all bone and sinew, tensed and ready to spring. Not bad attributes for a policeman, perhaps, though hard to see what could have attracted someone like Pat Carmody's daughter. Not that Carmody had any class, of course. Eksberg seemed polite enough, but even so one could somehow sense the ruthlessness; perhaps the Carmody girl appreciated that sort of thing.

Le Roux waved him to a chair.

'Do sit down.'

'Thank you, sir. I – er – was sorry to hear about the death of your wife.' It had to be said and Eksberg was glad to have been able to get shot of the matter at such an early stage, though in fact he had never met Sonia le Roux and had heard little that was good about her. A battleaxe, it was said.

'Ah, yes. Thank you. It was, of course, a merciful release. She'd been ill for some time, but the end came more quickly than we had expected.' Le Roux smiled sadly. 'I like to think,' he added softly, his voice faltering a little, 'that this garden is her memorial. She loved it so.'

'It's very beautiful.'

'Well, of course, it's not really at its best just now. You should see it in the spring.'

'Yes. It must be a picture.' How long, Eksberg wondered, would this polite chit-chat continue? The old boy clearly had something important on his mind, and he hoped he'd get to the point without too much delay. Connie had been spitting nails about his going out this morning, when they'd been asked to lunch with some of her swish friends at Muizenberg. She'd never forgive him if they were late, she'd told him, and he thought that she probably meant it. Still, he managed to smile across at le Roux, showing no sign of impatience. 'The view's pretty good, too.'

Le Roux nodded and lifted his head to survey the mountains.

'I've always loved it. I tell you, man, leaving this place for Pretoria every winter is a real wrench. I'm always glad when summer arrives and I can come back home. Of course,' he went on, acknowledging with a nod the tray of drinks that the servant put on the table between them, 'this was my wife's family home, as I'm sure you know. It broke her heart to sell off the vineyards, but she became incapable of overseeing them herself and it seemed the only sensible thing to do. There was no one to take over – no one in the family, anyway. Of course, she had hoped that Jan . . .' His voice trailed away and he dismissed the subject with an impatient flick of his hand. 'I don't mind telling you,' he went on, 'the money came in useful, too. It eased her last few years. God knows, the grateful nation pays its ministers little enough.'

Eksberg smiled non-committally, saying nothing. Try a police sergeant's salary, he was thinking, a brief picture of Connie coming to his mind; Connie, who wanted a new kitchen and a new car. And a new, enlarged patio. And new clothes. And a trip home to Ireland.

Le Roux was still maundering on about nothing.

'She was particularly fond of this part of the garden. *Gesondheid.*' He lifted his glass.

'*Gesondheid.*'

Eksberg sipped his drink. Surely, he thought, they would get down to business soon? His host, however, seemed in no hurry.

'We had a major row with Van Rijn when he bought the land,' he went on with a reminiscent grin. 'Apparently he understood from the survey that he would get all the land as far as that little rise over there, which would have included not only the pool but that line of jacarandas beyond it. My wife went crazy! They were her jacarandas, and she would go to the stake before she gave them up, she said. Who knew what Van Rijn might do to them? He could easily root them out to plant more vines.' He laughed again. 'She wasn't a sentimental woman, but she was sentimental about them, all right. And, of course, the candlewood tree.'

'Really?' Eksberg heard the lack of interest in his voice and hastened to atone. 'Which tree is that, sir?'

'I'm not surprised you don't know it. They're not very common in the Cape, but I gather they're tolerant of many different conditions.' He chuckled. 'Like me, it's a survivor, eminently adaptable.'

The policeman smiled thinly. For God's sake, get on with it, old man, he thought.

'It's that dark-leafed tree down there beyond the rose bed.' Le Roux pointed, and Eksberg, following the direction he indicated, nodded, even though he still had no idea which tree the old fool was talking about. As if it mattered! 'It's useless for shade because the branches grow so near the ground, but as you see, years ago someone cut away the low branches at the front, hollowing it out, as it were, to make a kind of bower. There's a seat inside. It makes a pleasant place to sit and my wife loved it, particularly when it was in flower.'

'Oh, that one. I see. Yes, it must be beautiful.'

Eksberg fought the impulse to look at his watch. If le Roux had brought him here simply to reminisce—

'Well—' Le Roux hesitated a moment. 'Well,' he said again, lifting his glass and squinting at its contents as if checking the colour of the slice of lemon it contained. 'No doubt you're wondering what was so urgent for me to bring you out here on a Sunday morning?'

At last!

'I confess I'm curious, sir.'

'It's a delicate matter. Intensely personal – which, I suppose, is why I've found it difficult to embark on it. I'm depending on your discretion.'

'You can rely on that, sir.'

'I'm sure I can. I wouldn't have approached you otherwise.' He put down his glass and looked at Eksberg. 'I also understand that five thousand rand might not come amiss.'

Eksberg was very still, his eyes narrowing a little, and for a moment no one spoke.

'Do you mind elaborating, sir?' he said at last.

Le Roux shifted a little in his chair.

'I – er – know that you're acquainted with my nephew,' he said. 'My wife's nephew, that is.'

Eksberg's mouth twisted a little.

'Big Jannie?' Like everyone else, he pronounced the name 'Yannie', the Afrikaans way. 'Well, yes. He is, as they say, known to the police.'

'He's a trouble-maker. You don't need me to tell you that.'

'No, sir.'

'He stirs up unrest wherever he goes, inciting the blacks to all manner of defiance, defending well-known criminals in the courts. And getting them off, half the time. Since Sharpeville, there's been no holding him.'

'He's trouble,' Eksberg agreed. 'We all know that.'

Le Roux took a breath, hesitating a moment.

'I want you to get rid of him,' he said at last, very quietly. 'And I mean get rid of him. Discreetly, but permanently.' He lifted the gin bottle that had been left on the table and poured himself another large tot. His hand, Eksberg noticed, was shaking a little. There was silence between them as he took one sip, and then another. He put the glass down on the table and stared at it without speaking for a moment.

'I don't imagine,' he went on, still apparently engrossed in the appearance of his glass, 'that you'd be averse to shutting him up, once and for all, would you? I don't care how you do it. God knows you could find a reason to arrest him and he could somehow meet with an accident in prison. Such things happen.'

Eksberg gave a grunt as if acknowledging a joke, but his eyes were unamused.

'Now and again,' he agreed.

'Or a car crash? Anything!' Le Roux looked directly at the policeman. 'Just get rid of him,' he said, a note of urgency in his voice. 'Quickly. I'll be very much in your debt if you can see to it as a matter of urgency.'

Eksberg returned his look assessingly. Was he looking at the next prime minister? There were many who thought so. It would, he reflected, be no bad thing to have such a man in his debt, and not just for the money, though heaven alone knew that would be welcome.

There was something else le Roux had in his power to give him – sponsorship to the Broederbond, that brotherhood open only to Afrikaners dedicated to the ideal of racial supremacy. It was becoming more and more obvious that such membership was a necessary qualification for high office, but so far he had known no one powerful enough to put him up for election. His father-in-law had no influence in this respect, being Irish and a Catholic. But le Roux could pull strings if he were so inclined – and here he was, promising undying gratitude! And for what? For ridding the country of a *skelm* who was nothing but a traitor to all white men, everywhere.

For the first time he gave a smile that was genuine.

'Minister,' he said. 'It'll be a pleasure.'

Le Roux drew a long breath and sat back in his chair.

'I'll leave everything to you,' he said. 'I don't know where Jan is at the moment, or what his movements are, but I'm sure you'll be able to find out. I shall be spending a couple of days in my constituency next week, but I'll be back in the office on Friday. Don't phone me there unless you have to.' He took a few sips of his drink, then looked again at Eksberg. He was relaxed now, smiling the boyish, mischievous smile that had won the hearts of all the matrons in his rural constituency for the past twenty-five years. 'We ought to give the project a code name,' he went on. 'How about—' He looked around him as if seeking inspiration. 'How about "Operation Candlewood" in the hope that both I and the tree continue to survive?'

Might as well humour the old fool, Eksberg thought as he returned the smile.

'Operation Candlewood it is,' he said.

It was winter in England, and as dreary a day as lowering skies and a bitter wind could make it.

Kate Newcott shrunk even further into the warmth of her sheepskin-lined coat. How she hated the cold! It was hard to remember, at a time like this, that once, long ago under an African sky, February meant high summer, sleeveless dresses and shady hats.

Enough, enough! She wouldn't trade the present for the past, not for a lifetime of summers, but this, surely, was the coldest, most miserable corner in the whole of North London – which, considering the fees charged by Moorcroft Close (Girls Prep., Boys Pre-prep., Headmistress: Miss J.D.Vereker, BA, NFF), seemed, to her way of thinking, less than equitable. Given that mothers – those, at least, who were unable to afford nannies or au pairs – were forced to stand on the pavement waiting for their offspring to emerge with only the earliest-comers able to park a car anywhere in the near vicinity, some form of shelter might, she thought, have been provided.

'Yet still we come,' she murmured, half to herself. She often asked herself why, though she knew the answer perfectly well. No state school could have provided a teacher/pupil ratio as advantageous as that offered by Moorcroft Close, nor a large rear garden to play in, well stocked with swings and climbing frames, nor the proximity to the Heath for nature rambles. The primary school serving the Newcotts' catchment area was a forbidding Victorian building providing the bleakest of alternatives, miles from the nearest blade of grass. It was for these reasons that she and Tom continued to meet the exorbitant fees – reasons, she assured herself, that had nothing to do with the undoubted fact that the other children came from backgrounds ranging from the mildly affluent to the positively aristocratic and without exception spoke with the right accent. She hoped they didn't, anyway. Such considerations smacked too much of her mother's discredited standards which she had prided herself on outgrowing years before.

It came as no surprise that no one among the gaggle of mothers took the smallest bit of notice of her muttered remark. Here, in this company, she always felt herself invisible, inaudible. All the others seemed to know each other so well; had all met, it seemed, at a cocktail party the previous night and would meet again at some other venue before the week was out. They swapped names of hairdressers and wonderful little women who ran up the most incredible clothes for next to nothing, and they screamed with laughter at talk of Ziggy who had been simply too, too outrageous the other night at the Swigget-Bloggs, and darling Nicko who really was the *end*, my dear, but *terrific* fun, one had to admit – and have you *seen* his new Maserati?

Her mother, despite the accents, would have dismissed them all as *nouveau riche*, not out of the top drawer – though heaven alone knew, she had scrimped and saved all her life and had nothing to crow about. Better *nouveau riche*, Kate used to think in those far-off days, than *vieux pauvre*, which seemed to sum up the fortunes of the Dearing family. Still, her mother would probably have been right about this lot – some of them, anyway. There seemed an air of desperate stridency about one or two which hinted at a lack of confidence. They tried just a bit too hard. Or was that just the sour grapes of advancing middle age?

With the nannies in a far more sedate, well-behaved gaggle of their own, Kate was aware that she belonged nowhere. The other mothers regarded her as old; and they weren't far wrong, she had to admit. She was, after all, over forty. Nearly forty-*six*, for heaven's sake! To this colourful, jaunty, never-had-it-so-good band for whom wartime worries and shortages were fleeting childhood memories, she must seem of a different generation altogether, as indeed must anyone who had actively participated in the six years of conflict. To this group, anything pre-1939 was ancient history, and anyone over forty positively senile. Whereas to her, before-the-war seemed only the other day—

She was doing it again, harking back to the past! What was wrong with her today? Hadn't life begun for her in 1945 when she'd met Tom? Never mind the rest. That was done with, forgotten; well, very nearly. Ninety per cent of the time she was the busy, contented wife and mother the world perceived her to be, thinking only of the present, preoccupied with the needs of Vicky and Mark. It was only sometimes, maybe in night-time hours when sleep was elusive and thoughts ran riot, or times like now – oh God, yes, times like now, when she caught a glimpse of a small, blond boy, totally unknown to her, yet so like that remembered image that her heart would be pierced with pain and she would be jerked back—

Shut up, shut *up*, she told herself savagely, forcing her eyes away from this stranger's son to search for her own children among the flood now pouring out of the front doors and down the steps, many clutching products of the art class. They all looked alike in that moment, the girls in round brown felt hats pulled low over their brows and held under their chins with elastic, the girdles of their tunics hanging below the hems of their overcoats. The little boys were even more disreputable with ties askew, long woollen socks wrinkled around their ankles and caps on the backs of their heads.

The nannies rushed to rearrange their charges, making them fit for Mummy to welcome home; while the mummies who were there claimed Nigel or Julian, Susan or Serena with off-hand, slightly *dégagé* amusement, trailing them off to the shooting brake or the Jag that was parked around the corner.

Vicky and Mark were inevitably among the last, mainly because Vicky – almost ten years old now, and over-protective – always went to the little ones' cloakroom to oversee Mark's preparations for the outside world. Never a wrinkled sock for Mark, aged five; never a crooked cap when finally, his hand firmly grasped in his sister's, he appeared at the top of the steps.

This, *this* is my life, Kate thought gratefully as she looked with love at the two children now descending the steps, going forward to meet and hug them, to admire Mark's picture of a house with four windows and a door in the middle dwarfed by a disproportionately huge figure with a pin head and enormous hands, captioned, in uneven letters, 'My Mummy'; to listen to Vicky recounting what

Gaynor had said to Marilyn and what Miss Longman had said to both of them.

She was surely the luckiest of women. After all, to how many was granted the beneficence of a second chance?

'You know Gaynor,' Vicky said, when much later Kate was cooking fish fingers for the children's tea. Gaynor was Vicky's best friend, the pretty, only child of wealthy parents, admired and envied and quoted on all occasions.

Kate wrinkled her brow, as if deep in thought.

'Now, let me see. Gaynor? Gaynor? It seems to ring a bell. Would that be Gaynor Greaves? Yes, now I come to think of it, I do believe I've heard her name once or twice before.'

'Oh, Mummy!' Vicky looked exasperated but even so she giggled, seeing the joke. 'Of course you know Gaynor. Stop being silly!'

'Me? Silly?' Kate shot a pained glance in her daughter's direction before looking back at the fish fingers lying limply on the grill pan. How long, she wondered, would the children's craze for this dubious gastronomic treat last? Was she doing the right thing to pander to them like this, or should she be offering other, more exotic dishes? One of the women outside the school had been talking of stuffed vine leaves and *taramosalata*, apparently accepted and enjoyed by her own children since a visit to Greece the previous summer, but she found herself unable to imagine Vicky's and Mark's reaction were she to confront them with such delights.

'I say, I say, I say,' she ventured. 'Why do fish fingers never wear gloves?'

'Mummy, you're not *listening*—'

'Sorry, love. What about Gaynor, then?'

Vicky appeared to hesitate. Kate looked at her more searchingly and saw an expression on her daughter's face that could only be described as one of acute anxiety.

'What is it?' she asked in a different voice. 'You haven't fallen out with her, have you?'

'No, but—' Again Vicky hesitated. 'I'm a bit worried,' she said at last.

Kate turned down the heat and left the fish fingers to their own devices. This sounded like serious stuff.

'Why, darling?'

'She said that her mummy was going to ring to ask you if I could go and stay with them for the whole weekend, very soon.'

'Well—' Kate looked puzzled. 'You'd like that, wouldn't you?'

'No, I wouldn't, actually.'

'Why not? You've been before.'

'Yes, but—' Vicky came to a halt, biting her lip. 'I don't want to go any more,' she finished after a moment, a sudden tremble in her voice. 'You won't make me, will you?'

Reassurance, Kate could see by her expression, was urgently needed.

'No, of course not – not if you don't want to. As if we would! You two haven't had a quarrel, have you?'

'"Course we haven't!" Vicky sounded outraged. 'Gaynor's OK. There's nothing wrong with her. It's just that her mum and dad are sort of – well, funny. Different.'

Kate considered this thoughtfully as she returned to the fish fingers, now browned and marginally more appetising. She divided them between the two plates and added spoonfuls of baked beans, her initial squeamishness at this fare long blunted by constant repetition.

Her acquaintance with Gaynor's parents, Roger and Caroline, was not close. The Newcotts had been entertained to drinks and had entertained in their turn, but it had been clear to both parties that there was little in common between them – in fact, Caroline Greaves hadn't bothered to hide the fact that she considered Kate and Tom laughable relics of a previous age.

Though only in his early thirties and appearing positively juvenile to Kate and Tom, Roger Greaves was employed in some senior capacity in a family banking firm in the City. They lived, complete with nanny and housekeeper, in an impressive house Roger had inherited from his grandfather close to Hampstead Heath to which Vicky had been bidden from time to time, usually to keep Gaynor company on a weekend when her parents were engaged in a more than usually hectic social round. Kate, privately, thought them among the most boring people she had ever met, but otherwise harmless enough.

'They always seem OK,' she said cautiously. 'Give Mark a call, there's a good girl.'

'You don't know them as well as I do,' Vicky pointed out, not moving. 'I don't think they like each other much. They were all right that time when they came here, but when they're at home, they argue and shout at each other and it makes me feel kind of sick inside. And Mr Greaves says really, really bad words,' she added, clearly hoping that this fact would prove the clincher.

Kate put the plates on the kitchen table and gently touched her daughter's cheek, stroking back her dark hair.

'That's a shame,' she said. 'It must be horrid for Gaynor.'

Vicky wrinkled her nose.

'She doesn't seem to mind. I s'pose she's used to it. But I'm not.'

'And I hope you never will be.'

'So you won't make me go?'

'Of course you needn't go, you goose – not if you don't want to. Didn't I say so? We'll think of a good excuse.' Kate held out her arms. 'Come here and give me a hug. And *then* go and tell Mark his tea's ready.'

Vicky enthusiastically did both, and nothing more was said on the subject until the meal was over when, very slowly and painstakingly, she was drying the dishes that Kate washed.

'Actually, I don't ever want to go away anywhere,' she said, with apparent offhandedness. 'Only holidays with you and Daddy and Mark.'

'You'll change your mind when you're older.'

'I won't,' Vicky assured her stoutly. 'Well, I don't think I will.' For a few moments she continued drying, saying nothing. 'There's a girl in Mrs Hayward's class called Amanda Duff,' she said at last with apparent inconsequence, 'whose mother said she was going to France for a week and she didn't come back and now she's married to a Frenchman and has a French baby. I expect they probably quarrelled, too – her and Amanda's dad, I mean.'

'Probably,' Kate agreed.

'Do you think Mrs Greaves will go off somewhere?'

'Darling, how would I know? It's possible, I suppose, but even if people quarrel, they often make it up again.'

'I'm glad you don't, anyway. You won't ever, will you?'

Kate grinned at her.

'Not seriously. And I promise you I won't have a French baby.'

Vicky giggled.

'*Sur le pont d' Avignon.*'

'Not even there.'

'Well, that's all right, then.' Vicky sounded more cheerful. She picked up a jug and proceeded to dry it with great care, her head bent. 'As a family,' she said thoughtfully, 'I think we're rather lucky, don't you?'

'I do,' Kate agreed, with equal solemnity.

Loud aeroplane noises reached them from upstairs where Mark was supposed to be undressing himself in preparation for his bath.

'Honestly, that boy.' Vicky tossed her head, amused, one woman to another, suddenly looking at least ten years older than she had a moment ago. 'Shall I go and see what he's doing?'

Kate stripped off her rubber gloves.

'I'll go,' she said. And as she went, she could hear Vicky burst into song.

'Walking back to happine-e-ess—'

That was more like it, she thought. Funny kid! Did she really think she and Tom would pack her off to the Greaves' if she didn't want to go? Who could tell what children thought? It was good to hear her singing, anyway. She would like nothing better than to be able to wave some kind of magic wand that would keep both the children secure and happy for the rest of their lives. If only it were possible!

The centre of her world they might be, but she readily admitted that Mark was infuriating when it came to baths. He objected strongly to getting in, but once in, was equally mulish about getting out. Tonight, having been well scrubbed all over, he had arranged several egg-cups along the edge of the bath and was intent on filling them with a pen-filler Tom had found and handed over to him. It was a slow and tedious process.

Kate tried coaxing.

'I've got a lovely warm towel waiting for you,' she said.

'Do you mind?' Mark, standing with his small, bare back towards her, looked at her over his shoulder, a pained expression on his face. 'I really have to finish this.'

'You'll freeze!'

'I'm *perfickly* warm.' He spoke firmly, turning back in an aloof manner to his egg-cups.

'Have you heard the story about the little boy who went for a walk and saw—' Improvising frantically, Kate looked round the bathroom, her gaze falling on a toy lying beside the door '—a fire engine? It was rushing along with its bell clanging—'

'Where was it going?' Mark, always enthusiastic about stories, stood with his pen-filler poised, the egg-cups apparently forgotten.

'To a shop,' Kate said, in a positive kind of way, as if this was something she had known for a long time, not a sudden inspiration.

'A sweet shop?'

'How did you know? It was the biggest sweet shop in the whole of the town—'

Mark flung down the pen-filler and clambered out of the bath, ready now to be enfolded in the warm towel. He had an amused and knowing look on his face that seemed to say that even though he recognised the ploy, he was ready to be entertained.

It was hard, sometimes, to remember that he was only five years old. There was something so mature and self-contained about his small, compact and beautiful person. For he was beautiful – it was not too strong a word. He had the dark hair and eyes and the smooth, peachy skin of a Renaissance cherub, no doubt inherited from the distant and allegedly aristocratic Italian ancestors that her mother had been so proud of, but with the added ingredient of something impossible to define. Charm, maybe.

And maybe I'm a doting, besotted, foolish mother and he's no more beautiful than other people's sons, Kate thought. It wouldn't, after all, be so surprising if that were the case. He had been born when she had almost given up hope of another child and could hardly believe her good fortune when she had given birth to a boy. Another boy.

She hugged his betowelled figure. At least he wasn't blond. She was glad of that – glad she could look at him as someone in his own right, without being reminded of that other she had loved and lost.

From below she heard the front door bang, and the sound of voices, laughter. Tom was home, and her heart lifted as it always did. It was a moment when she had no need to remind herself that life had, after all, been good to her. And at that moment the past was truly forgotten.

By seven thirty, Mark was asleep. Vicky, by virtue of her seniority, was granted an extra hour to watch a favourite television programme in the sitting room, which meant that Kate and Tom were, for once, able to sit down for a peaceful meal at the kitchen table.

'Did you know that the Greaveses fought all the time?' Kate asked, ladling a generous portion of Irish stew on to his plate. Tom was the sort of man who liked Irish stew and shepherd's pie and toad-in-the-hole. Just a plain, ordinary kind of bloke, he would have said – wrongly, in Kate's opinion. For one thing, he looked quite different from most other men in the street who, in dark suits and with umbrellas furled, stepped briskly along each morning, sleek as otters, to take the Tube to the City.

Tom, by contrast, was shaggy – a large man who wore cords and tweedy jackets and colourful shirts with hugely knotted woven ties. His hair was thick and curly and irredeemably tousled and he looked at the world through heavy, horn-rimmed glasses that were always falling halfway down his nose.

The neighbours, though rigidly conventional themselves, forgave him much because they regarded him as Arty; but more than that, they liked him. Everyone liked him. Kate, when she had first met him as a patient in the hospital in which she was nursing at the end of the war, had met no one like him; he seemed so kind, so easy-going. It seemed that nothing could dent his optimism and good humour – traits that had a lot to be said for them when life seemed almost more dreary after the war had ended than it was during the course of it.

He'd needed all the optimism he could muster in those early days when he was first starting out as an architect. He'd qualified before the war but the firm he had worked for had gone out of business so that there was no job waiting for him when he came out of the army. Instead he and Philip Smith, a friend from the old days, had gone into partnership, putting all their savings – hers, too – into their own business.

They'd been lean times, those early days; and even if she'd learned over the years that he was no saint – that it was possible, after all, for him to be dispirited and impatient and myopic about anything other than the business – she loved him still. That as the years went by he turned out to be a reasonably successful architect, able to provide a comfortable, if modest, life in an acceptable part of London, was an added bonus.

Amusedly, he quirked an eyebrow at her.

'Who says? Vicky? Has it ever crossed your mind to wonder what reports Gaynor takes home about us?'

'I can't say it has. At least she can't say we fight all the time, whatever else we might do.'

'No.' He took a mouthful of food and chewed appreciatively. 'Mm,' he said. 'This is good. Maybe we should,' he added after a moment. 'Fight, I mean. Just to demonstrate that it's not the end of the world and it's possible to make up afterwards.'

'Maybe we should,' Kate agreed equably, knowing it would never happen. 'Apparently Roger Greaves uses Bad Words, according to Vicky.'

'Really? So young, so clean-cut! I told you public schools aren't all they're cracked up to be.'

'Well, whether he learned them there or at his mother's knee, Vicky doesn't approve. She doesn't want to go there for the weekend any more.'

'Because of the bad words?'

'Because of the quarrelling. It clearly upsets her. She's so thin-skinned—'

'Like her father.'

Kate raised her eyebrows, but let this pass.

'All the mothers were talking about holidays today,' she said, suddenly remembering. 'Now is the time to book, apparently.'

'For where?'

'South of France. Spain. Greece. You name it. They were all trying to outdo each other.'

'Did you mention my rash and generous promise to take you on a day trip to Boulogne?'

'Strangely, no. I can't imagine why. Anyway, you made no promises, as far as I recall; just said it might be fun, one day, if your mother would have the children. Tom, couldn't we go to France anyway? I mean for a proper holiday. Brittany or somewhere. I'm fed up with Littlehampton.'

'Don't see why not. The only thing is—'

'What?'

He hesitated, looking at her with a comical expression on his face, his mouth pulled sideways as it always was when he was about to deliver some kind of surprise.

'I don't think we ought to book anything just yet. I heard a kind of rumour today that I just might be having rather a busy year.'

Kate, eating suspended, stared at him with dawning excitement. They had been waiting for weeks to hear the result of a competition that had been held for the design of a new shopping and residential development, in an area by the river which had long fallen into decay. It was a huge project, and one that had interested firms of architects not only from Britain but from all over Europe.

'Tom!' she whispered. 'Oh, Tom! You don't mean Shamley Hithe? Has something been decided?'

'Nobody knows for certain, but the word on the street is that they've split the project between Newcott, Smith and some Swedish firm. This could be big, Kate. This could be the kind of thing Phil and I have waited for. We should know very soon.'

'And you never *said*!'

'Nothing's certain. I didn't mean to say a word until I knew for sure, but I couldn't resist.' He grinned at her. 'The story of my life, really. I've never been able to keep any secrets from you.'

'Not even that Christmas you surreptitiously wrapped up that white sweater I'd admired in Jaeger's window, and left the Jaeger bag on the kitchen table.'

'Oh, darling—' He leaned across the table and gripped her hands in both of his. 'If we get this, you can have sweaters until they come out of your ears. And a fur coat.'

'I don't want a fur coat!'

'But you do! You always did!'

'In the past, maybe. It was a sort of symbol, I suppose. Now I'll settle for an Aquascutum. It would go down much better outside Moorcraft Close.'

'Oh well, that clinches it. How things change. Sad, really. Who was it said that the past was a foreign country?'

Kate sobered suddenly.

'I don't know,' she said. 'But whoever he was, he was right.'

2

No one knew where to find the man they called Big Jannie. He'd been in the Tsitsikamma reserve, Gert Eksberg found, defending a court case involving some old girl fighting an order to move to Ciskei. It hadn't been successful, needless to say. Eksberg's view was the same as that of the court; she'd been lucky to have notice of the removal, instead of having the government trucks arrive at dawn without any prior warning.

Big Jannie had left there some days before, it seemed, and had apparently melted into thin air. Discreetly, as ordered, Eksberg made enquiries, but discretion got him nowhere. There was no reply from his office, no reply from his house, and on Friday when le Roux rang him to ask what progress he had made with Operation Candlewood (taking, Gert noted, great delight in using the code word), he was forced to admit that he had made none at all.

'But I'm not worried,' he said reassuringly. 'He's obviously out of town, but he's bound to show himself before long. He always does.'

Le Roux grunted, not pleased.

'I did say it was a matter of urgency, man. I expect he's gone to ground in one of the townships – which as you are certainly aware is in itself against the law. I don't mind telling you I was hoping to come back to find the whole operation taken care of.'

'You did ask for discretion, sir. I can't exactly pull out all the stops.'

'Well, do what you can and report back to me over the weekend.'

Which, Gert thought as he hung up, was all very well. He still had his own job to do, and much as he would like, in view of le Roux's promises, to drop everything and concentrate on the so-called Operation Candlewood, the Minister for Coloured Affairs had made it very plain that nothing must be said to alert the top brass in the force to the hunt he had initiated. It was therefore a case of working extra hours to fit everything in, and Connie was not best pleased.

Late in the afternoon, when he happened to find himself in the office on his own, he made a few phone calls to known associates of Big Jannie, asking for news of him. He did not give his own name but pretended to be some anonymous associate from Durban, giving the impression that he was a friend, in sympathy with Jan's liberal ideas, part of the same fight. But either the friends were cautious, or they genuinely knew nothing, for none had any information to give him.

It was later still that he ran into Colin Vos in the middle of Longmarket Street, just outside the Marco Polo bar. Colin had, until recently, worked solely on the crime desk of the *Cape Town Courier*, but lately had been responsible for the occasional article covering lighter matters, published in the larger Saturday edition of the paper. The two were hardly friends, but their work had brought them together once or twice and it seemed quite natural to Eksberg that on this day when the temperature had reached ninety degrees he should take advantage of the chance meeting to offer the reporter a glass of beer. There was, he thought, a chance he might know something about Big Jannie.

'So congratulations are in order, man,' he said, when they were settled at a corner table.

'Why? What have I done?' Colin was both amused and puzzled.

'The Saturday column. Surely that means promotion? Next stop editor, eh?'

'Oh, sure! I'll make editor when you make Chief of Police.' Colin grinned. 'Which, no doubt, is when we shall see a cute little flock of pigs flying up Adderley Street.'

Gert raised his glass.

'Well, here's to it, anyway. Tell me, what's the news around town? Anything I should know about?'

'Surely I should be asking you that question? I've been stuck in court all week.'

'The Marais case?'

'That's the one.'

Piet Marais was accused of murdering his childhood sweetheart, Jeanie Swartz. They had been brought up next door to each other, and both were Coloured. But Jeanie, in view of the fact that her skin was exceptionally light, had applied for, and had received, white status, losing the dreaded 'C' for Coloured on her identity pass. It went without saying that in view of this, she had to lose Piet, too, for no white girl could associate with a Coloured boy; it was against the law.

'The bastard'll hang, no doubt about it.' Eksberg took a swig of his beer, not caring either way.

'You're probably right. But—' Colin sighed, looking unhappy. 'He's not anyone's idea of a killer, the poor little sod. I can't help feeling sorry for the guy.'

'What?' Eksberg looked outraged. 'He shot the girl, man!'

'I'm not defending that, but he was out of his mind with grief. Can't you understand how he must have felt? They'd been together for years, since schooldays, then suddenly the state decrees they can't marry.'

'Agh, you can't blame the state, man. The girl got ideas above her station, that's all. None of this would have happened if she'd kept quiet and accepted the status she was given.'

'Suppose it had been she who killed Marais, white killing black, instead of the other way round. I'll bet you anything it would have been dismissed as a crime of passion, with no talk of hanging.'

'Hey!' Gert tilted back his chair, grinning with amusement. 'Quite the little bleeding heart, aren't you, man? Which reminds me – you're a friend of Big Jannie, aren't you?'

Colin looked at him thoughtfully.

'Not exactly,' he said, at last.

'But you were at Varsity together!'

'So? Sure I knew him – at one time we both played rugger for the same team, until he went on to higher things. But friendly?' He smiled a downturned smile, as if at some private thought. 'No, I'd never go so far as to say we were friendly.'

'Bit of a hothead even then, wasn't he?'

'He spoke out against the system, yes. But it wasn't that. We . . . just weren't friendly, that's all. To be honest, politics weren't important to me then.'

'Best way to be. His kind of politics, anyway. You'd be wise to stick to that, in my opinion. So you haven't seen him lately? You've no idea where I can get in touch with him?'

Colin's instinct, sharpening with every year he spent on the newspaper, alerted him to a story. Casually, he picked up his glass.

'No to both. Why? What's he done now?'

Gert thought this over for a moment while he, too, took a sip of beer. Best, perhaps, to tell part of the truth.

'Le Roux wants to get hold of him,' he said at last. 'Some family matter, I gathered, so it's natural enough, but Big Jannie's gone to earth somewhere and can't be found.'

He'd waited a fraction too long before answering, Colin thought. Somehow it didn't ring true. And only the most racist newspapers referred to Jan as 'Big Jannie'. While the soubriquet seemed harmless enough on the face of it, it had always been used in a derogatory way by those who wished to imply that his physical size was in inverse proportion to his intelligence. Certainly the sneering way in which Eksberg uttered the words seemed to suggest that his intentions were far from good.

'Surely it's not your job to find him?'

Eksberg shrugged.

'Just doing a favour for le Roux, man. That's all.'

Colin still looked puzzled.

'Funny, though. I mean that le Roux wants to find him. Jan was almost certainly at his aunt's funeral just a couple of weeks or so ago, and you'd think they'd have got together then. Not that they ever saw eye to eye. I remember hearing Jan sounding off in the locker room—'

'He might have been at the funeral but le Roux doesn't know where he is now. Don't ask me what it's all about! I wasn't given any details. His aunt's will, maybe?' Gert looked at his watch. 'Agh – is that the time? My wife'll kill me.' He drained his glass and got to his feet. 'What's your status at the moment? Still fancy-free?'

Colin grinned.

'Intermittently,' he said. He stood up, too, holding his empty glass. 'Think I'll have another while I'm here. Nice meeting you, Gert. We must do it again some time.'

'Listen—' Gert took hold of his arm. 'If you happen to hear anything about Big Jannie's whereabouts, let me know, eh? From what le Roux told me, it sounds quite important that he should be found.'

'Sure,' Colin said, not meaning it. Something was brewing, and le Roux had got wind of it, was his guess. Another threatened revolt against the Pass Laws? Some kind of demonstration? Or was Jan preparing to defend some prominent member of the ANC in the law courts? He might be young, but he was an able lawyer, no one disputed that, even those who despised the fact that he had turned his back on the prospects of a lucrative career in order to devote all his efforts to defending those he considered oppressed or wrongly accused. This wouldn't be the first time he had raised official hackles.

On the other hand, he thought, his mind darting here and there in search of the story he felt certain was somewhere to be found, there was also the possibility that le Roux had other, more personal reasons for wanting to know Jan's whereabouts and the exact nature of his activities. More than one person lately had mentioned the name of Christiaan le Roux as a future prime minister, and a man with those sorts of pretensions would regard a nephew like Jan as the worst kind of handicap.

Left alone, he bought his second drink and took it back to the table. He didn't like Gert Eksberg, he decided. He seemed the archetypal South African cop as envisaged by the rest of the world – brutal, insensitive, not over-endowed with intelligence. He should go far, he thought dourly. The farther the better, as far as he was concerned. And though he could never describe himself as a friend of Big Jannie's, as Eksberg consistently referred to him in that sneering way, he knew very well with which of the two he would rather spend a convivial evening.

It wasn't Jan's fight for the underdog that had come between them at the University of the Witwatersrand. It was Nina Cambell – lovely Nina, whom he had loved but Jan had won.

He smiled, nostalgically. His first love! God, how it had hurt at the time! But over the past four years there had been other women, other loves, and now he felt no enmity for Jan, and nothing more than a reminiscent warmth for Nina. What, he wondered now, had happened to her? She and Jannie had never married, as far as he knew. He'd heard that she was teaching somewhere out of Cape Town – Paarl or Worcester, somewhere like that – but he'd had no direct news of her for ages. He'd be willing to bet, though, that her parents were still living in that little house in Wynberg. Nice people. Plain and honest and friendly, without pretension, and rightly proud of their daughter who had gone to university, unlike anyone else in the family. He grinned with inward amusement. Mrs Cambell had cherished quite a soft spot for him, he remembered. Unlike some other girl's mothers, it had to be said.

He'd spoken truthfully when he said that at university he had taken no interest in politics. He had been brought up on a farm in the Western Cape where life was simple, the old way of life unquestioned. The natives had been treated – as he had been – strictly but fairly. His father, as dyed-in-the-wool Afrikaner as it was possible to meet, had regarded his work-force as his family, to be punished if necessary, but also rewarded. That they all held him in high regard was obvious; it would not, even, be exaggerating to say that he was greatly loved.

He had built a school for the native children and badgered the authorities for a clinic to serve the area. There was, however, no doubt about who was in command, who was superior. Social integration was not to be thought of and it would never have crossed his parents' minds to ask a black or a Coloured man to dinner, no matter how educated he might be.

Which was, Colin had thought in the past, how it should be – amicable, but separate. It was only comparatively recently that he had become uneasy about certain aspects of Dr Verwoerd's policies. And even his father, who on the whole agreed with the Nationalist Party and thought that Dr Verwoerd had the right ideas, had protested about the law forbidding any gathering which included black and white together, even in church. Was this what Christ had taught? he asked; and Colin, though without his father's Christian beliefs, was forced to wonder with him at the necessity for these kinds of measures.

Then had come the horror of Sharpeville, which had thrown the government into a state of panic, sending it scurrying around like a chicken with its head cut off, passing laws left, right and centre; the African National Congress banned, a state of emergency declared, sixteen hundred people imprisoned without trial, and all because the police panicked and shot into a crowd of unarmed blacks intent only on peaceful protest. Sixty-nine killed, one hundred and eighty injured. Maybe, he thought as he brooded over his Castle beer in the Marco Polo bar, he should have listened to Jan more, back in their university days. In the light of what had happened since, it now seemed likely that his rival might have been hot-headed, but he sure as hell wasn't wrong.

Why was Eksberg looking for him now? The question nagged

at him. He didn't buy the line that le Roux had instigated the enquiry; there was something about it that didn't ring true. It seemed much more likely that the police were seeking him with even greater dedication than usual, and if so, maybe someone should warn him.

He finished his drink and left the bar. Nina might know where to find him – and the Cambell parents would know where to find Nina. It wouldn't take him far out of his way home, he thought, if he were to call on them.

He was right. The Cambells were still living in the same house, and neither they nor it seemed to have changed a bit, except that the wooden fretwork curlicue railings around the little stoep at the front looked as if they could do with a coat of paint. After the initial surprise at seeing him on their doorstep, they welcomed him warmly.

'Agh, man, it's been a long, long time,' Les Cambell said, shaking his hand. He was a small, wild-haired man with a wide smile. 'You just caught me on my way to choir practice.'

'So you still sing?'

Hennie Cambell clapped her hands and laughed aloud.

'Still sing? Could anyone stop him? He still plays his sax in the band, too – the Red Aces, they call themselves. You should just see them in their red shirts and white waistcoats with little red hearts all over them. Such bobby-dazzlers, they think themselves! They play all over the place nearly every Saturday. But come in, man, and sit down. The tea in the pot is still hot – you'll have a cup, won't you? And some cake? You used to like my cakes!'

'I bet they're as good as ever – but much as I'd like some, I can't stay, Mrs Cambell.'

He wanted to get in touch with Nina, he told them – and watched as a beatific grin spread over Hennie Cambell's face.

'It's just business,' he explained hastily. Mrs Cambell gave him a small push.

'Agh, you two were just lovely together,' she said. 'Jannie's a good boy, too, with a big heart, but he's not the kind to settle down. As the Good Book says, he's born to trouble as the sparks fly upwards.'

'Now, Hennie, you must leave the young ones to make their own mistakes,' Les told her, and she flapped her hand at him.

'I know, I know. Still, I can't help the way I feel. Nina's in Paarl, my dear. She'll be glad to hear from you, I'm sure.'

'Is . . . is Jan with her?'

Hennie shrugged her shoulders, lifting her hands palms upwards.

'Sometimes yes, sometimes no. She doesn't tell us much. He has a little house here in Cape Town but I don't think he spends much time in it, between you and me. What she gets up to is her business. I might not like it, but who cares what I think? Settle down, I tell her. Raise a family. But does she listen? Here – I'll write down her number for you. She'll be home next weekend for a couple of nights if you want to see her. Agh, man, why don't you come round? It would be like old times, eh? Come here on Saturday night. It's our wedding anniversary and we're having a party. Thirty-two years – not bad, eh?'

'Hennie, Hennie!' Les was laughing at her again. 'Maybe Colin has other things to do. Perhaps he has a new girl.'

'No. Not really,' Colin said.

'Well, there you are, man, come to the party! Our Margie is coming, and Steve, of course, and our grandson, little Barry, three months old – the first, but not the last, I hope. Did you know Margie was married? Steve's a lovely boy, doing so well—'

'Hennie, give the man a chance!'

Hennie reached up and gave Colin's cheek an affectionate pinch.

'Agh, I talk too much, I know, but it's so good to see you, man. I thought maybe you'd be married by now.'

Colin laughed and shook his head.

'Not yet,' he said. 'But I have got a date, and I must fly. I . . . I'm not really sure if I can make Saturday, but if I don't, many congratulations, and have a wonderful time.'

'Agh, man, come!'

'Thank you. I will if I can. It's been wonderful to see you. You look just the same—'

'Five years older, eh, man?' Hennie Cambell grinned at him, treating the years lightly.

'Just the same,' he said again firmly. And kissed her on the cheek.

Les, still smiling, stretched out his hand.

'Don't be such a stranger, man,' he said.

*   *   *

Nina answered at the second ring, as if she had been waiting for him. Waiting for somebody, anyway. No doubt it was Jan she had expected to call.

'Hallo?' Her voice was the same, low and musical as if she, like her father, were a singer. He remembered, suddenly, her light-hearted radiance; the quick tilt of her head when she was interested or amused.

'Nina? You'll never guess who—'

'Yes, I would.' She sounded surprised, but friendly. 'It's Colin, isn't it? I recognised you at once. How are you? What can I do for you after all this time?'

'It's about Jan,' Colin told her. 'Listen, I don't know any details, but I heard yesterday that the police are looking for him. I thought he ought to know.'

From the other end of the wire he heard an exasperated sigh.

'Well, thanks for letting me know, but the police are always looking for him, more or less. They like to keep tabs on him. Actually there's nothing they could charge him with at the moment. He's done nothing that anyone could object to. Not that I know of, anyway. As far as I know he's dropped out of sight for a while to do some research for a case he's taking on.'

'Well—' Colin hesitated, not wanting to alarm her unnecessarily. 'Maybe this doesn't mean anything, then. It's just that I was talking to a policeman today – Gert Eksberg. Maybe you know him?'

'I don't think I have the pleasure.' Nina's voice was dry.

'I gained the distinct impression that they're stepping up the campaign against Jan. They badly want to find him, for some reason. Something to do with le Roux, maybe?' Colin paused, but there was no reaction to this. 'I . . . I just thought he ought to know,' he said after a moment when Nina said nothing. 'You are in touch with him, aren't you?'

The silence continued for a moment.

'Sometimes I am,' she said guardedly. She seemed to be making an effort to speak normally. 'It's good of you to let me know, Colin, but really there's no need to worry. He's aware of the danger and anyway, he's leaving the country very soon.'

'Good! Where's he going?'

'We . . . we don't talk about things like that. It's best that way. You never know who might be listening.'

Colin felt the shock of her words. Was she serious? For all

that had happened lately it seemed unthinkable that the government found it necessary to take these kinds of steps to guard its security.

'OK,' he said. 'Just tell him to go as soon as he can.'

'I will,' Nina promised. 'And thanks for ringing. Actually I guessed something special was up. I had another call supposedly from a friend asking where he was, but I didn't recognise the voice so I didn't tell him anything. Tell me—' She seemed to brighten a little, to become aware of social obligations. 'How are you, Colin? I saw your article about education the other Saturday. It was good.'

'Thank you. Most of what I wrote about black education was cut—'

'You managed to get some good points in, even so.'

'Glad you liked it. Nina—' Colin hesitated. What would her reaction be if he told her he had been invited to her parents' house the following Saturday? What, indeed, was his reaction?

He told her, anyway, and she sounded welcoming. Or was that apparent warmth nothing more than good manners?

'I'm not actually sure if I can make it,' he said, giving himself a loophole in case he thought better of it during the course of the week.

'Do try,' Nina said; but afterwards, when he had put the phone down, he felt almost certain that she was simply being polite. Pity, really, he thought. She was a great girl. Still, he had, after all, done what he had set out to do and could now go on to enjoy the rest of the evening, which involved dinner with a decorative blonde, met in the course of duty only two weeks before. Diane, her name was, and she was gorgeous, he told himself. Absolutely gorgeous. He'd been looking forward to the occasion all week, but now, inexplicably, he found himself lukewarm about the whole thing.

He couldn't understand it.

It was a few days later that Gert Eksberg called round late at night to see Christiaan le Roux. The politician looked tired, he thought, and seemed on edge, as if the day in Parliament had been a trying one.

'England?' he said, glaring at Eksberg in a way that was at total variance with his normal manner. 'You're sure? How the hell did you let that happen?'

'It wasn't a question of letting it happen, sir. In spite of all my efforts, I only heard he'd gone after the event.'

'Your efforts weren't good enough, man.'

'He did all he could to cover his tracks, and we've been extremely busy at HQ. Everything's in turmoil.' As you bloody well know, Gert would have liked to have added. The state of emergency imposed after Sharpeville had been lifted for several months now, but this had not put a stop to crime or the atmosphere of unrest that pervaded the entire country. The police were as busy as ever.

'But you're sure of this?'

'Absolutely,' Gert said. 'I heard a whisper he was leaving the country and got on to the airports immediately, only to find he'd left just hours before. A passport officer at Jo'burg remembers him boarding. So your troubles are over, at least for the time being.'

Le Roux turned away, presenting a grim profile to the policeman. Behind it, his thoughts were racing. He would like to think . . . it wasn't that he relished . . . but no, it was foolish to assume that he was now safe. Jan was unlikely to keep quiet, wherever he was. Even this small delay might prove fatal. He could have shot his mouth off before leaving South Africa, and in England he was bound to go to the papers – perhaps, indeed, that was the main purpose of the trip! The English papers were only too ready to print anything remotely defamatory regarding South Africa, and even though the country was about to become a republic in a few short weeks, what the London *Times*, or even worse, any of the sleazy British tabloids published today, the *Cape Times* would publish tomorrow.

'I want him dead, Eksberg.' It was the first time he had put this quite so bluntly without use of euphemism, and he was conscious of a strangely painful feeling in the pit of his stomach as he did so, a feeling compounded of fear and recklessness and grief. Nevertheless, he went on, knowing there was no place for sentiment now – and who could blame him? For years now Jan had been nothing but a thorn in his side. His voice gathered strength.

'I want him out of my way for good, not just for the time being. Listen – everyone in both Houses is taking bets on an election before the year is out. Alive, my nephew is a constant embarrassment to me. You must see that!'

'Yes – yes, I do see that, sir. It's just that the fact that he's left the country somewhat complicates things.'

'Well, of course it does! I'm not a fool. Still, there must be a way. You could go over there.'

Gert drew a deep breath. How the hell was he supposed to leave

Cape Town now, with the townships still bubbling with resentment, only kept in check by relentless police patrols that cracked down hard at the first hint of trouble? The man was obsessed! Didn't he see the difficulties?'

'I don't honestly think my superiors would think much of that, sir.' His voice was commendably calm. 'I'm not actually due for leave, and anyway, as I said before and as you must be aware, these are troubled times. We need all the personnel we can get at Police Headquarters. I suppose,' he added, 'if I had your official blessing—'

'That's out of the question. I mustn't be involved. I don't want to be associated with this in any way.' Le Roux got up and strode around the room, absently picking up a folded paper and banging it down again. 'There has to be a solution!' Eksberg watched him, chewing the inside of his lip as he did so.

'A possibility did occur to me,' he said tentatively. 'But it means taking someone else into your confidence. And I'm afraid it would almost certainly be necessary to pay more.'

Le Roux turned and looked narrowly at him for a moment without speaking, then came and sat down again.

'Who are we talking about?' he asked.

'Charlie Van Niekerk.'

'And he is—?'

'A police lieutenant, and a family friend. My mentor, you could say. I joined the police because of him. After Sharpeville—' For a tiny, almost indiscernible moment, Gert hesitated. Charlie's actions on that occasion had caused the government to deem his removal from the scene greatly to be desired, and it occurred to him that this, perhaps, was not something of which le Roux ought to be reminded. On the other hand, this particular minister was unlikely to regard the incident as serious. Smoothly he continued. 'He was posted to the embassy in London. Security.'

For a few moments, though he kept his eyes on Eksberg, le Roux said nothing, but sat passing his hand over his mouth and chin as if in deep thought.

'Do it,' he said at last. 'Offer him a thousand rand—'

'A thousand? That won't be enough. He'll want at least as much as you're paying me.'

Le Roux thumped the arm of his chair with his clenched fist and glared angrily.

'Well, however much it takes. It doesn't matter. Just get the job done.'

Eksberg smiled.

'It will be, sir,' he said. 'It will be.'

Tom Newcott knew himself to be a fortunate man. He had a wife he adored, two lovely children, a satisfying job. Who could ask for more?

He had always enjoyed the company of women but had never found one he wanted to marry until he met Kate. He had been wounded in France, soon after D-Day. A spell in hospital in Normandy had been followed by further prolonged treatment in Southampton. There had been a Welsh nurse on the ward with blonde hair, a big smile, and a pneumatic figure, known to the others as Jonesy, who was greeted with wolf whistles whenever she appeared. But from the first moment he saw Kate, Tom barely noticed Jonesy's more obvious charms.

Kate, he had thought then, was a woman for the connoisseur. The purity of her profile appealed to his artistic nature; he derived the same kind of pleasure from it as he did from a graceful, well-proportioned building. Not that the building analogy was a good one on any level, for there was nothing cold or remote about her, and certainly nothing monumental where size was concerned – she was slight of build and neatly made. He had never seen eyes so ready to brim with infectious humour, or longed so painfully to touch a woman's skin.

He was on the ward long enough for tentative smiles to develop into conversations that became more and more important to both of them. He exerted himself to make her laugh, for her laugh was something else that delighted him. They found they shared interests, liked the same authors. He heard about her past; learned the reason why there were times when she looked so grave. And in return he told her of his ambitions for the future. One day, he told her, when the world had forgotten all this madness, he was going to design and build something that would be a lasting memorial – not to him, exactly, but to the future. Something beautiful to enhance the world for generations to come.

He almost dreaded getting healthy enough to leave hospital, but when the time came he found himself posted to Winchester, which pleased them both because it meant he was near enough for them to go on meeting frequently. By this time he knew that if he couldn't marry Kate, then he wouldn't marry anyone. It had seemed unbelievable that she felt the same.

Nothing had been straightforward, though. She had come carrying much baggage from the past and it had been all he could do to make her see that it was the future that was important, the past something to be consigned to oblivion. Neither of them was in their first youth; if they were to raise a family then there was no time to waste in chasing rainbows.

Hard times had given way to better, and even better. There had been, after the war, plenty of buildings for Newcott, Smith to rebuild and repair. Eventually they moved to bigger premises, took on more staff, achieving an enviable local reputation which might now, with the prospect of success in the Shamley Hithe development, be on the verge of becoming national. Even international.

'We could well know today,' he told Kate that Tuesday morning.

'I've got everything crossed! Best of luck, darling.'

'Don't count on it—'

'You'll ring?'

'The moment I hear. Whatever happens.'

It was one of Mrs Bishop's days. She came on Tuesdays and Thursdays, and was both quick and efficient at housework, her only failing being a tendency to recount, at great length, running battles that went on between herself and her neighbour who was, according to Mrs Bishop, the nearest to the devil incarnate that it would be possible to find on this earth.

It was not that Kate was unsympathetic, merely that she had heard it all many times over. Even as Mrs Bishop left her work to sit down at the kitchen table for the regulatory cup of coffee, she could feel herself growing rigid with boredom in anticipation, seizing upon almost any excuse that she could to escape without giving offence.

Thus it was that she greeted the sound of the telephone with relief, interrupting as it did a long account of how Mrs Bishop had found rubbish spilt in the alleyway separating the two houses. ('You could *tell* it was deliberate, Mrs Newcott. She knows I can't abide kipper, not at any price.') 'I think,' Kate said, rising from the table as slowly as the excitement bubbling within her would allow, 'that this will be my husband.'

But it wasn't, she found; it was Elaine Cody, her friend from nursing days.

They had worked together during the war, and even afterwards for almost five years, for she and Tom had needed the money, but whereas Kate had left the job with few regrets as soon as she became pregnant, Elaine had had no such distractions from her career. Her fiancé had been killed in Italy and she was only too thankful to keep on working at the job she loved. Now she was a ward sister at St Luke's Hospital in north London.

'Elaine?' Kate greeted her voice with delight. 'Are you free today? I hadn't realised—'

'No. No, I'm on duty.'

She sounded strange, Kate thought. Hesitant. She felt a twinge of fear. Tom? The children? The fact that she had seen all of them in the best of health so recently did nothing to prevent the feeling of panic.

'What is it?' she asked faintly.

'Don't worry, nothing's wrong. Not with Tom or the kids, anyway.'

Kate let out her breath.

'Well, that's a relief! But, hey, what do you think you're doing, then? Personal calls on duty? What kind of an example do you call that to all your underlings?'

'Just listen, Kate.' She did sound odd, Kate thought. Flustered, she would have said if it had been anyone else. But Elaine had always been a calm and serene kind of person – an ideal nurse, never ruffled even when all hell was breaking loose around her.

'Elaine, what is it? Are you all right?'

'Listen,' Elaine said again. 'I've been wondering whether to phone you ever since I came on duty this morning.' Kate heard the indrawing of her breath, the hesitation. 'This may be nothing. The last thing I want to do is raise your hopes, but I think maybe you ought to come over.'

'To the hospital? Why—?'

'Someone was brought in about four o'clock this morning. A young man. Twenty-five, twenty-six – that sort of age. He was unconscious and badly beaten up. He suffered a fractured skull among other things and he's still in a coma. It seems he was left for dead on waste ground down by the river.'

Kate's heart began to thump once more as if it knew something that was hidden from her conscious mind.

'Was it someone I should know?'

A moment elapsed before Elaine answered.

'We don't know his name.'

'Then I don't understand—'

'Kate, we don't know his name because he had no wallet, no ID. They must have been stolen, the police say, but there was something the muggers missed. He had your address on a slip of paper in the back pocket of his jeans. They're anxious to identify him so that they can inform his next of kin and I think they're bound to contact you before long, since your address is the only lead they've got. I just wanted to get in first.'

'Who on earth—?' Kate began, but Elaine was rushing on.

'There were a couple of other things. Look, it may be just coincidence, without any significance at all, but on the other hand I feel you should know. He was wearing a donkey jacket. The pocket of it had a torn lining, and down inside they found a coin, and an old, used stamp. Kate, they were both South African.' She paused for some reaction, which was not forthcoming. 'Kate? Are you still there?'

'Yes.' The word emerged as little more than a croak, and Kate cleared her throat. 'How . . . how old is he, Elaine?'

'I told you. Mid-twenties, we think.'

The right age, then. Not necessarily Johnny, though. She mustn't allow herself to hope—

Her head was spinning, her thoughts making little sense.

'Kate, there's an emergency being sent up and I've got to go,' Elaine said. 'Why don't you come over? He's in the neurological ward on the second floor. Ward Three. I'll look out for you.'

'Elaine—' Kate had suddenly managed to find her voice. 'Do you . . . do you honestly think—'

'I don't know what I think. Maybe the South African connection's no more than a coincidence. Maybe he bought the jacket from an Oxfam shop, or has the address because he's a burglar and your house is next on the list. How should I know? But on the other hand, it just could be Johnny, couldn't it? Or a friend he's asked to find you? I think you should come, anyway.'

'Can I come now?'

'Of course, if you can manage it. It's not visiting time, strictly speaking, but that hardly matters in a case like this.'

'I'll be over as soon as I can make it. The traffic's awful!'

'I know – and getting worse. Take it easy, now. Drive carefully. The patient isn't going anywhere. See you soon.'

St Luke's was an ornate, Gothic-looking building, long out-dated. There was a small, pot-holed area of waste ground behind it that did duty as a car park, but it was full, Kate found, having driven round it twice, gripping the wheel tightly, her arms aching with tension. In desperation she drove to a nearby street and left the car there, ignoring a prominent notice forbidding any parking whatsoever. What did such things matter at a time like this?

She hurried back to the hospital to find the entrance hall as busy as King's Cross station, with people coming and going, or just sitting, waiting for attention. A porter was pushing a wheelchair. Two doctors, white-coated, with stethoscopes round their necks, were talking together at the foot of the marble staircase.

'Excuse me—'

They stood aside, still talking, and she took the stairs at a run until she reached a half-landing where she forced herself to slow her steps. Calm down, she told herself shakily. There was probably nothing in it. How could there be, after all this time? Still, it was amazing how hope refused to die.

She forced herself to breathe slowly and deeply, and went up the rest of the stairs at a steadier pace, determined to appear composed and mistress of the situation when she reached the ward; even so, she found the size of it daunting as she stood in the doorway. The room seemed to stretch to infinity, beds on each side of it, but the sight of Elaine sitting at a desk in the centre was reassuring.

She was wearing the frilled cap that denoted her rank and was absorbed in writing, her head bent, but as if she sensed Kate's presence, she looked up and, laying down the pen, rose to come towards her. It brought home to Kate how long it was since they were junior nurses together, flouting authority, giving each other alibis, covering up small sins that would have brought down the wrath of staff nurse or sister upon their heads.

Now Elaine moved with assurance, as one who told others what to do. Only the red hair beneath the anachronistic bonnet seemed familiar, until she smiled and spoke, when it was possible to see that, after all, beneath all the starch and the frills and the fancy belt, she was the same person.

'He's in that bed over there,' she said, taking Kate's arm. 'Fourth down. We'll have to wait a moment. The nurses are just turning him – we do it every four hours, to relieve pressure.'

Kate nodded, her eyes turned towards the bed in question. She remembered the drill. He'd be on a drip, probably a catheter, turned regularly, closely observed. More than that, there was little anyone could do for coma patients. Except wait. And talk. It was considered important to do that, for no one could tell how aware an unconscious person was of the world around him.

'He's a big lad,' Elaine said, as they waited. 'The doctor said he'd stake anything he was a rugger player.'

Kate gave a breath of nervous laughter.

'If he's South African, that's more than likely,' she said. 'It's a religion over there.'

'They've settled him now. Come and look.'

Kate crossed the ward, her heart thumping wildly, the sound of it filling her head. For a moment, as if gathering her resources, she stopped at the foot of the bed. He was indeed a tall young man; broad, too. Like Guy? Like many South Africans, she had to admit.

She took a deep breath, then moved so that she could look at him. His head was bandaged, and his face discoloured, black and blue and yellow. She saw there was a cut over one eye and a row of stitches, and on his cheek a horrific contusion covered in yellow ointment. Even so, she could see the possibility of good looks beneath the injuries.

He had strong features with dark, winged eyebrows. His nose was large, but well shaped, his chin rounded, his face beginning now to show a trace of dark stubble. For a few moments she stood in tense silence, aware of Elaine standing a few paces behind her. Neither of them spoke. Then she gave a long, shuddering sigh and bent her head, and in a moment Elaine was there, taking her arm, full of comfort.

'Ah, don't – don't, love,' she said. 'I shouldn't have put you through this. Come to my room for a few minutes.'

'I'm all right,' Kate said, and looked again at the face of the young man, searching for something – anything – that she could recognise. She bit her lip and distractedly shook her head.

'I don't know,' she whispered. 'I just don't know.' And turning away, she wept.

'Come,' Elaine said. She took her arm and ushered her out into the corridor and into a small side room, scarcely bigger than a cupboard, furnished with a table and two chairs.

'I thought I'd know,' Kate said, when at last she was in control of herself and able to speak. 'I felt quite sure I would, even though he was only four when I last saw him. Not quite that, even.'

'Isn't there anything—?'

'He was a round, chubby little boy.' She gulped again, and wiped her eyes. 'Fair hair, and little button nose. No, no, I'm all right.' She took a breath to steady herself. 'You've seen the photograph, Elaine. You know what he was like. I must have been crazy to think I'd know him now. The truth is, I haven't a clue.' She gave a short laugh that ended in a sob. 'So much for the maternal instinct.'

Elaine reached to hug her.

'Oh, Kate, I'm so sorry. I shouldn't have brought you here like this, but I thought maybe you'd see some likeness. And I wanted to forestall the police. I should have realised what a trauma it would be.'

Kate gave a watery smile.

'You mustn't blame yourself. I'm all right now, really. I want to have another look. Is it all right if I go back to the ward?'

'Of course.' Elaine stood up. 'What about other members of the family – Guy's mother or sister, or your mother, come to that? You might see a likeness to someone.'

'He's not a bit like Guy,' Kate said quickly. 'I noticed that at once. But then, Johnny never was, not as a little boy.'

This time, as she looked at the young man in the bed again, she once more forced herself to be calm, shutting out the noise and the bustle that was going on around her – the whispered discussion between two nurses close by, the rubber-soled footsteps, the rattle of a trolley.

It was, she thought, the passivity that was such a barrier to recognition. Likenesses so often sprang from mobility; a smile, a lift of the eyebrow, the expression in the eyes. His mouth looked swollen, but even so she could tell it was nothing like Guy's mouth, which had been small; too small for the rest of his face, she had thought. Sonia, his sister, was different again, and his mother—

She paused. Went closer. Maybe there was something about the mouth that was reminiscent of Guy's mother—?

No. She didn't think so. Slowly she shook her head. She could see no definite resemblance to anyone, nothing she could pin her hopes on.

'What colour are his eyes?' she asked Elaine.

Elaine bent and lifted a lid.

'Blue,' she said.

Guy had blue eyes. So did she – well, blue-grey, it said on her passport. So did most members of both their families – except Peter, her own brother, who had quite exceptional eyes of clear, translucent grey.

'No,' she said regretfully, still looking at the young man. 'No, I can't see—'

She surveyed him lingeringly, top to bottom, then back again. Then suddenly she tensed.

'What is it?' Elaine asked her softly. 'What have you seen?'

For a moment she didn't answer; then she turned and Elaine saw that an expression of hope and delight had transformed her face.

'His hands,' she whispered, turning back to the bed. 'Oh, Elaine – look at his hands! I've only just noticed them. They're just like Peter's. I'd know them anywhere. The fingers are long, and the nails – look at the nails! They're kind of flattened with big half-moons.'

'Are you sure?' Although she was prepared to be encouraging there was nevertheless a note of doubt in Elaine's voice.

'Yes – yes, I am. They're the same, I promise you! For heaven's sake, I should know – Peter's my brother, isn't he? I've watched him a million times taking things apart and putting them together again. His hands used to fascinate me, they were so competent. So . . . so *sure*.' She became, suddenly, aware of her friend's scepticism and desperately she turned and reached for her arm. 'Don't you believe me?'

'Oh, Kate, I want to,' Elaine said fervently. 'I want to, so much. You could be right. On the other hand—'

'I am right, I know I am.'

'I just wish there was something else.'

'Well, it's something to go on, isn't it? The police could surely check—'

'I just wish—' Elaine broke off abruptly.

'Wish what?'

'That I hadn't raised your hopes.'

'You really don't believe me, do you?'

'I don't know. I don't want you to be disappointed, that's all.'

'But he had my address!'

'Someone could have given it to him. Told him to look you up. It happens, Kate.'

Kate turned towards the bed again, bending to lift the hand in question and to study it carefully once more.

'Peter's hands,' she said firmly. 'Why shouldn't hands be as individual as anything else? He's Johnny. I just know it.'

And speaking the words, she felt suddenly delirious with the joy of it. This was her son. After all this time!

'Come,' said Elaine. 'Matron will be doing her rounds soon, not to mention any number of consultants.'

'Can't I stay? I'd like to speak to them.'

'Better not. There's nothing they can tell you that you don't already know.'

'What's the prognosis, then? How long is he going to be like this?'

'Oh, Kate! You know as well as I do that there's no way of knowing.' Taking her arm, Elaine made as if to lead her towards the door, but Kate resisted the pressure.

'What actually happened to him?' she asked. 'Does anybody know?'

'Not really. He was kicked repeatedly in the head, we think, and there's a knife wound you can't see. No, no—' She spoke calmly in reply to Kate's horrified exclamation. 'He was lucky. It missed the vital organs. The head injuries are far worse. However, Mr Carstairs had a look at him when he came in – there's no better neurological man anywhere – and he was able to relieve a good deal of the pressure. He says there's no damage to the brain stem, so hopefully he'll make a good recovery. Maybe it will only take a day or two. He's young and strong, and that has to be in his favour.'

'When can I come and see him again?'

'Two thirty to four thirty in the afternoons, six thirty to eight thirty in the evenings.'

'I'll be back,' Kate said. She bent over the young man once more, touching his cheek, repeating her promise. 'I'll be back,' she whispered, and straightening up, she turned, smiling.

'Stop agonising over me,' she said. 'And stop reproaching yourself. I'm so glad you phoned! I tell you, this is Johnny – I haven't a doubt in the world. I'll be off now.' She gave Elaine's arm a shake. 'Take good care of my son, d'you hear?'

'I hear,' Elaine said, doing her best to smile. 'We'll all take care of him.'

Whoever he is, she added privately, as Kate walked away.

3

At lunchtime the phone rang again.

'Start thinking Aquascutum,' Tom said, without preamble.

Kate gave a shriek of joy.

'You've won the contract!'

'We sure have,' Tom confirmed.

'Tom, that's wonderful! Oh, what an incredible, beautiful day—'

'Isn't it, though? It's a breakthrough, Kate, no doubt about it. We're sharing it with the Swedish firm I mentioned, but that's OK. There's no conflict. We're going to meet the architect involved soon and I may have to go over to Stockholm for a few days. Hold on to your hat, Kate. I think we're due for take-off.'

'You deserve it. Both of you. I'm so pleased. But Tom, you'll never guess—'

'Listen, darling, I have to dash – I've got Sir Harold Matheson waiting to talk to me. He's the chap in charge of the whole thing and can't be kept waiting. I just wanted to tell you the news. Oh, one other thing! I may be a bit late tonight. Phil and I thought we'd go out for a drink or three, just to celebrate—'

'Oh, Tom! No – listen! I have to go out myself—'

But Tom had gone.

Mrs Nixon was perfectly willing to baby-sit. She lived two doors away on the top floor of a house that had been made into two flats and was usually happy to step into the breach, enticed not only by the money she earned but by the prospect of an evening spent in a home with central heating and a television set, neither of which amenities she owned herself. She was a motherly soul; cheerful, reliable, clean and sober – in every way the ideal baby-sitter.

Kate broke the news on the way home from school, and though Mark received it with equanimity, Vicky was distinctly put out.

'Mrs Nixon's boring,' she grumbled. 'And her false teeth wobble as if they're going to drop out.'

'Doesn't sound a bit boring to me,' Kate said briskly. 'It looks as if you're in for an evening full of suspense and drama.'

Vicky was unamused.

'Well, how long will you be?' she asked distantly.

'Only an hour or two,' Kate assured her comfortingly. 'Probably Daddy will be in before me.'

She'd already written an explanatory note to Tom in anticipation of this event, but to the children had only said that she had to go to visit a friend in hospital.

'Why do you have to go when we're home?' Vicky asked. 'You can go any old time.'

'Hospitals have visiting hours, and you have to keep to them. I couldn't go this afternoon, because I had to meet you. Oh, darling, do stop being so miserable about it! You like Mrs Nixon, you know you do. She lets you stay up much longer than I do.'

Kate could see in the mirror of the car that this consideration had given Vicky pause for thought, but it was a pause that lasted only a short time.

'Who's in hospital, anyway?' she asked, breaking in on Mark's attempt to tell Kate about Micky Crowe who had a fight with Jeremy Lee about the ownership of a Dinky toy, resulting in both of them having to stand in the corner.

'Different corners,' he explained, not wanting there to be any confusion. 'And Jeremy cried. Very loud.'

'Oh, shut up, Mark,' Vicky said crossly. 'Mum, who—?'

'A friend,' Kate said. 'No one you know. Auntie Elaine rang up and told me.'

'Is it someone you knew in the war?'

'Well—' She hesitated for a moment. To tell, or not to tell? No, she couldn't. Not yet. When they knew for sure who he was, when he was better, that would be the time. It wasn't as if they had any knowledge of their half-brother, after all. She had deemed them too young to understand, likely only to be worried by the thought that she had once had a son but had been parted from him. Vicky was such a worrier that she could well think it might happen again.

'Before the war, actually,' she said at last.

'Before I were born?' Mark asked.

'Long, long before.'

'*Was* born,' his sister corrected him fussily.

Kate relaxed. Vicky was back to normal.

She waited outside the ward with the others. They came in all sizes and shapes. A little grey lady with bent shoulders and a worn expression clutched a plastic bag. Clean pyjamas, Kate thought, guessing at the contents. And toiletries. I should have brought that sort of thing. Why didn't I think? I must ask what he needs.

Beside her, there was a plump, peroxided woman in a cheap fur coat accompanied by a plump, peroxided daughter with a vacant expression.

''E never should have *been* there,' the woman droned monotonously. 'I mean, 'ow often 'ave I said? "Don't do it, Fred," I says, day after day. "You'll get no thanks for it," I says to 'im – and now look where it's got 'im! 'E never should 'ave been there! Didn't I always say that, Dawn?'

Johnny shouldn't have been there, Kate thought. What was he doing, down by the river?

The waiting group swelled as others joined it, but at last the doors opened and everyone surged inside. Kate could see at once that there had been no change. He still lay there, bruised, silent, without expression.

Fred's wife and daughter had gone to the next bed and were unloading the supplies of cigarettes and other necessities they had brought him.

'Fred, you never should 'ave been there. Didn't I tell 'im, Dawn?'

Kate drew the curtains, shutting them out, shutting everyone out. She pulled up a chair beside the bed and, leaning forward, covered his hands with her own.

'Johnny,' she said softly. 'Johnny, it's me. Your mother. You were coming to see me, weren't you? You had my address, you must have been coming. Oh, Johnny, what did they tell you about me? It must have been bad, to stop you answering my letters, but you must believe me – I never stopped thinking of you. Loving you.'

She paused and looked at his impassive face. Was it, after all, familiar? His upper lip was indented, the mark echoed in the faint cleft in his chin. She could almost convince herself that, after all, he looked like the four-year-old Johnny, but on the other hand, without all that chubbiness, it was hard to tell. His face was undoubtedly thin. Aquiline. But there were the hands, she reminded herself eagerly. Even if every other feature was unfamiliar, even if no one else believed her, the hands, to her mind, were unmistakable.

'You are Johnny, aren't you? I know it. I'm certain.'

He can't hear, she thought despairingly. But I have to talk. Everyone knows that. And perhaps, underneath the unresponsive exterior, he's conscious of something calling him back to life.

A brisk little nurse drew the curtain aside and consulted the chart at the end of the bed.

'Everything all right in here?' she asked. 'We'll be turning him soon.'

'You don't mind the curtains—?'

'No, not while you're here. You'll see if there's any change. It would be a good idea to talk to him.'

'Yes, I know.' Kate smiled at the nurse as she whisked away about her business, but the smile died a little as she looked at Johnny once more. What should she talk about? Where should she start?

Where else but at the beginning?

It couldn't have been a better day for the annual fête. The Depression was far from over on that June day of 1934 and no one had much money to spend, but the sky was cloudless and the entire village was determined to extract the last drop of enjoyment from the occasion.

Kate, coming up to her eighteenth birthday, was wearing a voile dress in shades of pink that made her feel pretty – an event sufficiently novel in those days to lift her spirits, so making her prettier than ever. For once she didn't mind that the dress had previously belonged to her cousin Norah and that Auntie Gwendolyn had bestowed it in her usual patronising manner the last time that Kate and her mother had been bidden to Highlands for Sunday lunch.

Having grown up bemoaning the fact that she had failed to inherit her mother's looks, Kate was beginning, just recently, to feel happier about her appearance – reconciled, to some extent, to her dark, straight bob even though she had always longed for blonde curls. Her nose, longer than she might have wished (for wasn't her mother's little retroussé nose the kind that everyone admired?), somehow fitted her face better than it once had done, and her skin, with its peachy, Italianate bloom, had recently been openly admired. Not by anyone who mattered; still, it was a start.

Looks – the importance of, the absence of – had figured prominently in her upbringing. They were, it had been dinned into her by her mother for as long as she could remember, a girl's most important asset, particularly if accompanied by a cheerful smile and a vivacious manner, both of which were of even greater importance if the girl happened to be both genteel and penniless, as Kate undoubtedly was.

Kate's mother, christened Dorothy but known since childhood as Dotty, was one among the great number of well-born widows, impoverished, used to better things, who were ten a penny after the war. She had been brought up as a lady at Highlands in the county of Oxfordshire – a decaying but impressive house just over the county border, now occupied by her brother Reginald Viner, his wife Gwendolyn and their two daughters, Norah and Ethne.

In her day Dotty had ridden to hounds and been presented at court, but it had, even then, been something of a struggle for her father to maintain this way of life. When she met and fell in love with Captain Peter Dearing her parents had been dismayed, for the Dearings were even more impoverished than the Viners – added to which, nobody really knew much about them or where they came from. There was foreign blood in their veins, bequeathed by an Italian grandmother – no matter if she had been related to a count, she was still a Dago in Mr Viner's eyes – and the captain's father, a handsome, dark-eyed charmer, was said to be a bit of a bounder. Dotty was determined, however, and bowing to the inevitable, the Viners had at last given their permission and in the summer of 1912, the couple were married.

Fortune seemed to smile upon them at first. Less than a year after the wedding, Dotty gave birth to a baby son, also christened Peter. But by the time the gallant captain's daughter was born, the war had been raging for two years and he was among the many who would never return from France, and never, therefore, see the baby who was christened Catalina Francesca after his mother. Naturally, this folly was deplored by the Viners, but since the child was always known as Kate, her lamentable antecedents were rapidly forgotten.

Dotty and her children had continued to live at Highlands throughout the war, and even afterwards during her parents' lifetime. When her father died, however, and Reginald finally inherited

the family seat, it was made clear to her that from now on she must
make her home elsewhere. Reginald, who had done very nicely
out of wool during the war, being too shortsighted to serve in the
armed forces, magnanimously bought for her a picturesque dwelling
known as Chimneys in the village of Shenlake – a gesture regarded
as over-generous in the eyes of Gwendolyn, who persuaded him
that it was quite ridiculous of him to think he should pay for
repairs as well. After all, Dotty had her little legacy, carefully
invested, and a small pension, not to mention the trust fund set
up by her father for Peter's education. Thus it was that, delightful
as Chimneys appeared to the casual passer-by, the roof sagged and
pipes leaked and floorboards creaked ever more alarmingly.

In spite of this, Dotty regarded herself as one of the elite of
Shenlake society and comported herself accordingly. She never
seemed to lack admirers, but none were satisfactory enough for her
to marry them. Some already had wives in the background, others
had no visible means of support, still others had no pretensions to
breeding – and this, of course, was a factor Dotty found it impossible
to overlook. It was all too apparent that good men were thin on the
ground, so great had been the slaughter during the war.

Dotty's most faithful, and useful, admirer was Sir Randolph
Coningsby who owned Coningsby Hall. The Viners, in their heyday,
had moved in the same circles as the Coningsbys, but more recently
Captain Peter Dearing and Sir Randolph's son, John, had served
together, both men falling within a few days of each other.

It created a bond which Sir Randolph exploited to the full. He
was a bouncy, bearded little man who was said to have an eye for
the ladies. He certainly had an eye for Dotty, and, by association, for
the whole family. The odd salmon or pheasant was often delivered
to them, or flowers from the Coningsby hothouse, for Chimneys
lay conveniently close to the end of Coningsby Hall's drive; and
when the need for repairs became so pressing that even a casual
caller could not be unaware of it, such as the time the front gate
fell off its hinges, a workman from the estate would be sent to put
matters right.

In the village people commented on it, and were amused.

'You're in favour, and no mistake,' the village postmistress said
to Kate one day, weighing out humbugs. She had witnessed an
exchange of pleasantries between Kate and Sir Randolph and had
missed nothing – not the gift of a shilling, nor the solicitous enquiry

regarding Dotty's health. Expertly she twisted paper into a small cone and tipped the humbugs into it. 'Don't count on it lasting, though. One minute Sir Randolph's all over you, can't do enough for you, the next there's not so much as a "good morning".'

This was duly reported to Dotty who dismissed it out of hand. The woman was jealous, Dotty said, and Kate believed her, for Sir Randolph became almost skittish in her company and tended to describe her to others as a Plucky Little Woman. Kate had heard him, more than once.

And perhaps that's what she was. Dotty maintained her standards, was always bright and well groomed, and was implacably determined that her children should tread an easier road than she had done. Peter, of course, would go into one of the professions. Kate's only path to wealth, on the other hand, was to marry well, and preferably early. Education was deemed unimportant in her case, and and while old Mr Viner on his death had ensured that Peter could be sent to Cheltenham College, Kate was destined for Holmswood Manor, a private school in the next village, which was considered more than adequate for a girl.

There Kate had met Nancy Chalmers, each girl immediately recognising the other as a kindred spirit. In after years they agreed that neither of them would have learned a thing if the matter had been left entirely to the genteel Misses Greenhalgh, the joint headmistresses of Holmswood. Fortunately both girls were great readers, devouring everything that came their way, including (often secretly) the books that Mrs Chalmers borrowed from Boots Lending Library. All Kate knew of the magic of foreign lands, the romance of history, the complexity of human emotions, came from novels and the occasional foray to the cinema. All she knew of the opposite sex, as well. She loved her brother dearly, but since he was away at school, they saw each other only in the holidays. By 1934, the year that was to change seventeen-year-old Kate's life for ever, he was articled to a firm of accountants in London, and she saw him only occasionally.

Dotty read nothing but magazines, but they, too, yielded education of a kind. Nancy and Kate pored over beauty and fashion hints, and discussed at length the problems suffered by Troubled Brown Eyes of Bournemouth and her ilk. Much as the subject fascinated them, and long though they dwelt on it, they were both totally ignorant of the facts of life until at the age of fifteen

Nancy learned the truth from a visiting cousin who told her, as she later communicated breathlessly to Kate, All There Was to Know. Both girls were both suitably astonished, and not a little horrified.

'You'd have to love someone an awful lot to do *that*, wouldn't you?' Nancy said. Kate agreed with her, trying to picture that kind of closeness, emotional and physical.

'It would probably be OK,' she said, feeling a stirring of curiosity and excitement. 'If you loved them.'

'And if they loved you.'

Kate sighed. Nancy had put her finger on the problem. She could not, at that time, see anything in her appearance remotely likely to inspire a second look, never mind love. Even now, she felt far from sure that she would ever attract anyone worth knowing – anyone really handsome.

Such melancholy reflections apart, they giggled their way through the days – foolish, frivolous girls, encouraged to prepare for foolish, frivolous lives, a man of their own the only goal presented as worthwhile. It was, perhaps, no wonder that Kate longed passionately to fall in love.

She had no expectations that the village fête would provide anything more than a little light amusement on this lovely summer day. None had before. However, she and Nancy had been asked to take charge of the white elephant stall, and having nothing else better to do they had decided between them that it might be amusing.

Together they set out the stall, despairing at the junk they were supposed to sell, but as the afternoon progressed, business was brisk. It was during a lull that Nancy fell suddenly silent, right in the midst of recounting how Mrs Robertson from the dairy nearly had a fit when she saw on the stall, priced at one shilling, the vase she had given her sister for Christmas.

'Oh, my!' she breathed softly. 'Look over there, Kate. Who is that perfectly divine man with the Coningsbys?'

Kate looked and saw Sir Randolph and Lady Coningsby making their customary royal progress towards the stalls. Lady Coningsby was a tall, droopy figure who, mistakenly to Kate's mind, habitually wore limp clothes in dreary colours that made her merge into the background – which, as she and Nancy both agreed, seemed an awful waste of being a Lady and having lots of money.

Kate, however, had no eyes for her at this moment. Who would, when there was this Adonis of a man by her side?

'Heavens!' she said weakly.

Together, regardless of good manners, they stared in equal admiration and awe, until reminded of their duties by two small boys intent on buying a birthday present for their mother.

There was, thereafter, a small run on the stall and no time at all for conversation, though both girls glanced at the Coningsby party from time to time to see if it had come any closer. Then business fell off once more and they were able to discuss the matter.

'They'll get to us if they keep on coming this way,' Nancy said hopefully.

'I wonder who he is?'

'He looks just like a film star. Better than a film star. Sir Randy's always round at your place. Didn't he say anything?'

'Not a thing. Not to me, at least. Look – I think they're heading for the coconut shy.'

'Oh, *spit*! Now he won't come past this way at all. Oh, Kate, this is the story of our lives, isn't it? Nothing exciting ever happens to us. It isn't fair.'

'Wait – they're turning round.' Kate's heart gave a little bound and then sank like a stone because she could now see it was the sudden arrival of her mother out of nowhere that had caused the little group to stop in its tracks. Dotty was clearly visible, dressed in cream chiffon and a garden party hat, both second-hand from Auntie Gwendolyn but looking good, all the same. She could tell by the way the hat was going from side to side that her mother was being winsome. 'Oh, God,' she groaned. 'She's detached him from the Coningsbys. She's bringing him over here.'

'Well, I'm not complaining,' said Nancy, who seldom suffered from shyness. 'Now we'll know who he is and what he's doing here. What are you looking so sick about? You want to meet him, don't you?'

More than anything, would have been the truthful reply. It was her mother's involvement in the matter that made Kate yearn to crawl under the stall, knowing as she did the manner in which any introductions would be made; for ever since Kate had left school earlier that summer, Dotty's plans for her future had been made plainer than ever. She must, she assured her, get out and about and meet people.

'I do meet people,' Kate had protested. She had recently been taking a secretarial course in Oxford and had also gone to first aid lectures in the village hall, simply because the subject interested her and it seemed a useful thing to learn.

'I mean the *right* people,' Dorothy said crossly. 'What good are those wretched first aid village folk? For heaven's sake, Kate, you must see the importance of moving in the right circles.'

The unknown man lately in the company of the Coningsbys with whom Dotty was approaching ever nearer, talking with animation, looked to Kate as if he never stopped moving in the very best of circles, and it took no imagination at all to picture the way her mother's mind would be working. And by the time she had finished presenting him to her daughter, Kate was perfectly aware that the stranger would know it, too.

They were coming ever closer.

'He's *wonderful*, Kate,' Nancy said, managing to speak without moving her lips, already curved in a welcoming smile. 'Hallo, Mrs Dearing. Can we interest you in our wares?'

'Good afternoon, Nancy. Mr Lampard, this is my daughter's friend, Nancy Chalmers. And this is my daughter, Kate.'

The way Dotty managed, with the angling of her shoulder and a tilt of her flowery hat, to curtail the dazzling stranger's acknowledgment of the introduction to Nancy and deflect his attention to Kate was a masterly, if not very subtle, manoeuvre.

'Darling,' she said, her voice sweet as honey, 'I want you to meet Sir Randolph's great-nephew and the son of a very dear friend of mine.' Her eyes were telling Kate to smile, to scintillate, but Kate, grown woman though she might be, felt far less than her almost-eighteen years at that moment, far too shy to comply in the presence of this stranger whom she could now see looked even more handsome at close quarters than he had done at a distance. The combination of golden hair and tanned skin was devastating, not to mention the moustache and the chiselled features. His eyes were a clear, bright blue, amused and arrogant.

Kate's bones felt as if they had turned to water as she gave what she felt sure was a weak and tremulous apology for a smile. Nancy was right. He was wonderful, like no one she had ever met before in real life.

He lifted his hat and reached to shake hands.

'Guy Lampard,' he said. 'How do you do?'

His voice was clipped, his accent a little strange. But it must be *all right*, Kate thought, because otherwise her mother wouldn't be acting like this.

'Mr Lampard has just arrived from Cape Town,' Dotty said in explanation. 'He owns a vineyard there – isn't it exciting? He's visiting his uncle and he'll be here, off and on, for the whole summer. I'm just dying to hear more about the Cape, Mr Lampard, and I know Kate will be fascinated. You know, Kate, Mr Lampard's mother and I knew each other long, long ago, before either of us was married. Her family lived quite near to us when I was a girl – though of course,' she added hastily, 'she was some years older than I. Such a pity she hasn't come with you on this occasion, Mr Lampard. Is she keeping well?'

'Oh, quite well. Perhaps a little—' He seemed to hesitate. 'frail,' he finished.

'She was such a lovely girl, always the belle of the ball. And Kate—' Animatedly she turned towards her daughter once more. 'Do you know, I *think* I've convinced Mr Lampard that it's his public duty to come to the dance in the church hall tonight. After all, Sir Randolph usually looks in for a few minutes. Now do your part and tell him what fun it would be!'

Kate could neither breathe nor formulate any coherent speech. She continued to gape at the handsome stranger, sure she must look like the village idiot, knowing that Nancy, rightly, would never forgive her for not including her in the conversation, knowing her mother would, in due course, have much to say about her ridiculous shyness.

There was nothing she could do about it. Coming face to face with this man had set her foolishly immature senses in such a spin she couldn't have given her own name if called upon to do so. She clutched the table in front of her, for one moment fearful that she was going to faint. It was true, then. One's heart did stand still. Romeo had fallen in love with Juliet at first sight, but it could have been nothing like this. This was something much, much more cataclysmic.

'Would it be fun?' he asked, raising a mocking eyebrow in a way which Kate immediately recognised as being the height of sophistication.

She swallowed nervously, searching for a reply. It was the moment, she was aware, for a witty riposte – some amusing,

provocative line that would ensure that he would present himself
at the church hall that evening if only to get to know her better.
But how could she think of anything like that when her head was in
such a whirl? She took a breath, hesitated some more, swallowed
again, then at last managed to speak.

'Not really,' she whispered.

The date with Diane had not been a success. It wasn't her fault, Colin
conceded. Well, not altogether. She had looked marvellous which,
it became evident, was the only thing that had ever been demanded
of her. Conversation was clearly regarded as unnecessary, attempts
at humour greeted with a puzzled frown or, at best, a dutiful smile.
The only subject that induced anything approximating animation
was that of other girls' clothes, most of which seemed to give
material for scorn she didn't bother to conceal.

It had been his favourite restaurant, too, down by the sea at Hout
Bay. Wonderful food, wonderful atmosphere. Now, if he'd been
with Nina, he thought as he drove homeward having delivered
Diane at her parents' home in Rondebosch—

He shook his head, angry with himself. What was the point of
thinking like that? Clearly, she and Jan were still together. It was
just that talking to her again, hearing the way she said his name,
brought everything back. All the things he had kidded himself were
long forgotten.

Maybe he'd take the Cambells up on their invitation for Saturday.
Perhaps Nina was only being polite by saying he would be welcome,
but he shouldn't assume it. They'd parted on good terms, after all,
and she had sounded friendly enough over the phone.

He'd think about it, anyway.

4

Tom had come home in celebratory mood, full of excitement and anxious to share it with Kate, but instead of an equally celebratory wife, all he had found was Mrs Nixon and a note.

He had to read it twice to take it in properly; and not simply because of the alcohol he had imbibed. The whole thing was unbelievable! The fabled Johnny, turned up at last! Over twenty years without a word, even though Kate had written and sent cards every birthday, making sure he knew her address whenever she changed it. And now this!

'How can you be so certain it's him?' he asked Kate later – but gently, for she had arrived home at last, glowing with euphoria.

'Tom, I just *know*!' Kate said. 'Why else would he have had my address on him?'

'Well—' Tom hesitated, not wanting to prick her bubble but feeling the need to warn her of possible disappointment. 'There could be other reasons.'

'Name one!'

'When Megan went to Sydney she had several addresses on her.' Megan was his sister who had taken a trip to Australia the year before. 'People with relatives there pressed them on her. This could be a friend of Johnny's. You must face that possibility.'

'OK. I don't buy it, personally, but say you're right. Say this is a friend he's sent to find me. At least I'd be a step nearer to him, wouldn't I? It would mean he was anxious to be in touch. Oh, Tom! Be pleased for me.'

'Darling, I am. Honestly.' He went and sat on the arm of her chair and pulled her close to him. 'It's just that it would be such a hell of a let-down—'

'If it turned out to be someone else? Oh, why doesn't anyone believe me when I say his hands are just like Peter's? Look—'

She held out her hands, palms down. 'Hands are as individual as anything else about us, so surely it stands to reason that a certain type of hand can run in families?'

'I thought that was feet,' Tom said. 'Or noses, maybe. OK, OK, I'm sorry – I *am* taking this seriously, I promise. That's exactly why I'm worried about how you're going to feel if this chap turns out to be a stranger. I know just how much this means to you.'

Kate smiled at him.

'I know you do.' She leant against him, glad of his solidity, and made an effort to turn her mind to other things. 'And I know how much the contract means to you. I'm very, very proud of you, even if it does mean a proper holiday has to go by the board.'

'I might be able to get away for a bit. We'll have to see how it goes. If I can't, you could take the children down to the farm—' He broke off and laughed as he saw the look in Kate's eye. The relationship between his wife and his mother was excellent, but both he and Kate knew that this was only maintained by keeping visits short. 'Well, perhaps not,' he said. 'We could get away somewhere later on, I feel sure. Which reminds me, Phil suggested that it would be a good idea for the four of us to celebrate in style some time soon – maybe take a weekend break in that hotel in the New Forest where we went before. What do you think? You liked it there, didn't you? Mum would be glad to come and baby-sit the kids, or I could take them down to Sussex. She's always offering.'

'Go away?' Kate turned to look up at him, the smile dying, her face blank with anxiety. 'Leave London? Oh, Tom, I couldn't do that right now. What about Johnny?'

Some of Tom's enthusiasm died.

'Even if it is Johnny—'

'It *is*, Tom—'

'He won't be in a coma for ever.'

Kate looked exasperated.

'No, I know that. But we don't know what's going to happen, do we?'

She's right, Tom thought. We don't know what's going to happen, or how this unexpected turn of events is going to change our lives. Was that why he felt almost more frightened than pleased?

He wasn't particularly proud of himself, for he knew the pain she had gone through over the years. Suspected, anyway, for she had never said much and no one could fault her love and care for her present family, nor her pride in it. Still, there had been a couple of occasions when she had wept in her sleep, and once she had become upset over a television programme about South Africa, so he knew that she hadn't forgotten the past altogether; well, how could she? It would have been a traumatic experience for anyone, and no doubt there were those who would say he had acted wrongly in encouraging her to turn her back on everything that had happened. He'd had the odd twinge of guilt himself, on those occasions when she had shown her continuing grief, but on the whole he thought she had made the right decision when she had firmly closed the door on the past and concentrated on building a new life.

Now, seeing her joy, the guilt returned. Should she have gone back? Laid the ghosts? Seen her son once more, no doubt perfectly happy in his familiar surroundings, looking at her with indifferent eyes? As it was, the fair-haired little boy, perfect, without flaw, had been preserved in her memory, like a fly in amber. Suppose this same little boy, grown now to man's estate, fell somehow short of this perfection?

Later, in bed, he sensed her sleeplessness.

'Why don't you take a pill?' he urged her. 'I've got some, left over from that time I was ill—'

'No, I'm fine,' she said. 'Don't worry about me. Go to sleep.'

She was, she acknowledged, too wound up to sleep herself. It was as if those memories she had dredged up earlier were still milling around in her mind, still as real as if they had happened only yesterday. And there in the dark, she smiled to herself as she remembered her mother's reaction to the reply she had given to Guy when he had asked if the dance in the church hall would be fun.

Easy to smile now. It had been different then. Such a look of fury and frustration had come over Dotty's face that she had looked, for a moment, as if she were about to explode.

Amazingly, however, it had proved the right thing to say, for Guy had been amused and somehow his laughter had reduced the tension. She had laughed, too, and when later Sir Randolph and Lady Coningsby found their way to the stall, they had asked her to join their party, both for dinner and for the dance afterwards.

'I do beg you not to consider such a late invitation ill-mannered,' Lady Coningsby said in her fluttery yet pedantic way. 'We hadn't thought – but then dear Guy came a few days earlier than expected, you see, and we felt a little party might be—'

'My dear Florence, the young don't stand on ceremony these days,' Sir Randolph assured his wife heartily. 'This young lady and her charming mother will take the invitation in the spirit in which it's meant, I feel sure. Your mother has already accepted on your behalf, my dear, and we shall look forward to seeing both of you this evening.'

'Some people have all the luck,' Nancy said enviously, as the Coningsbys drifted off towards their Victorian monstrosity of a mansion, all but hidden now behind towering rhododendron bushes.

'My mother will be there, too,' Kate reminded her. 'You know what she's like. She'll probably say something that'll make me die from embarrassment.'

Nancy clearly thought any embarrassment was worthwhile and could be discounted.

'He's bound to dance with you,' she said. 'Why can't Sir Randy be sweet on *my* mother? Then we might have been invited as well.'

'I wish you had been,' Kate replied. But beneath the words, she was thinking something quite different. She was thinking that between the time when Guy had been introduced and the time when the Coningsbys had asked her to dinner, he must have said something to them – must have asked them, suggested it – oh, was it possible? Or was Nancy right in thinking the invitation wholly due to Sir Randolph's partiality for her mother? She wished she knew!

Imagine if Guy Lampard really wanted to dance with her! Imagine if he had felt something of the same attraction that had swept over her, the moment she saw him!

'What are you going to wear?' Nancy asked, bringing her down to earth.

At last she had slept, waking to the sound of the milkman, and the newspaper falling on to the doormat. Still only half awake she knew she was happy without, for a moment, remembering why; and then the joy hit her like a whirlwind. Johnny! He was actually here, in London, come to look for her. Naturally, his injuries were a worry; but he would be all right. Hadn't Elaine said so?

But suppose he wasn't? Suppose Elaine had been hiding the truth? Suddenly she found that all the happy certainty had gone, leaving her hollow with dread as she contemplated the prospect of losing him for a second time. She turned over on her back and flung her arm across her eyes, and for a moment she lay without breathing, rigid with fear.

Would it have been better, then, if she had never known? If Elaine had never made that phone call? If she had gone on for the rest of her life, trying to suppress the memory of that chubby, fair-haired little boy?

Slowly she exhaled, calmer thoughts prevailing. Elaine had said Johnny would recover, and she would never lie, not to anyone and particularly not to her. And from her own nursing experience she knew that, ill though he was, Johnny's injuries were relatively superficial. She'd seen far worse cases during the war make total recoveries. Hundreds of them.

Of course, there were others who hadn't made it. The fear was edging back, but resolutely she pushed it away. Think positive, she told herself. Johnny was going to be fine.

Her sleep, in the end, had been dreamless, but it had been a bitter-sweet journey that preceded it. How young she had been, how utterly foolish and gullible! Now, in 1961, girls of twelve or thirteen appeared more knowing than she had been when she'd met Guy.

Why on earth had he bothered with her? Well, she knew the answer to that now; had learned it, in fact, on the voyage to Cape Town which had been their honeymoon. Not that she had believed it then – well, not for more than a moment. She had been madly in love with him, unable to think anything bad of him, still utterly bemused by the fact that they were husband and wife, dazzled by her good fortune in being here, with him, sailing out to a new and exciting life in South Africa.

The wedding had seemed like a dream. Her mother was, naturally, ecstatic. Uncle Reginald had responded with unwonted generosity to the news of her engagement and had paid for a lovely dress – slipper satin, slinky over the hips and flaring at the hemline – and Lady Coningsby had lent her an heirloom veil of Chantilly lace with a little tiara to go with it, pearls and diamonds, so that she floated down the aisle of the village church on Peter's arm, clasping her bouquet of carnations and banksia roses, feeling like a princess.

The reception at Coningsby Hall was magnificent, little Sir Randolph apparently beside himself with delight that the two families were now joined in marriage. He had, in fact, demonstrated so much pleasure at the whole affair from the very beginning that there were those in the village who had slyly suggested that it had obviously occurred to him that, now related to Mrs Dearing by marriage, no one could raise an eyebrow at his frequent visits to Chimneys; and indeed, as if to confirm suspicions, he was not backward in suggesting that Dotty should accompany him when he drove the young couple down to London to catch the boat that would take them to their eventual home. No, no, he said to his wife. He wouldn't take the chauffeur. He enjoyed driving – and anyway, she might very well need the chauffeur's services herself.

There were flowers in the cabin, and champagne, and much excitement when finally they reached the docks and the MV *Dunnotar Castle* that was to take them to Cape Town. There was emotion, too, as Dotty wept – just as if this moment weren't one she had earnestly desired ever since clapping eyes on Guy at the fête.

'You will take care of my little girl, won't you?' she beseeched Guy. 'She's so young!'

'Oh, *Mother*—' Kate was overcome with embarrassment.

'You've no need to worry, Mrs Dearing.' No man could have looked more sincere than Guy, or more full of good intentions. 'She's safe with me, I promise.'

Eventually all non-passengers were ordered ashore, and Guy and Kate went up on deck to wave goodbye to them.

'What's the betting my dear uncle gets a puncture on the way home?' Guy asked. Innocently, eyes wide, Kate turned to look at him.

'Oh, I do hope not! Did you notice something wrong with the tyres, then?' The penny dropped and she blushed. 'Oh – oh, I see. Oh, surely not.'

'You are a funny little thing, aren't you?' He ruffled her hair, rather as one might fondle a puppy. 'Let's go below, shall we? I think there's some of that champers left. We might as well drink it before it goes flat.'

'It must almost be time to change for dinner,' Kate said. She had a number of new evening dresses among her trousseau and was looking forward to wearing them.

'Champagne first. Anyway, we don't dress the first night out.'
'Don't we? I didn't know.'

There were so many things she didn't know. Small things like not dressing for dinner, and big things like – well, bed, for one. After the wedding they had spent two nights in a hotel in the Cotswolds before driving down to the ship, and both had been simply terrible. She didn't know what she had done wrong, but it seemed that, after all, love wasn't enough. Guy had complained that she wasn't built right. She was too small, or something. Anyway, she felt quite sure it was all her fault and felt hopelessly inadequate.

He seemed, thankfully, to have forgotten all that now, however, and was looking at her with apparent approval.

'You're looking very pretty, actually. Marriage seems to suit you. Why don't you put on that blue dress you wore last night? That'll do very well.'

Guy wasn't over-generous with his compliments and Kate felt pleased by this remark. She wasn't at all sure, however, that she should have any more of the champagne, and made her half-glass last a long time. Even so she felt slightly dizzy when, clad in the blue dress and holding rather tightly to Guy's arm, she went down to the dining saloon where Sir Randolph had made sure of seats for them at the captain's table.

It was, Kate knew, reckoned to be an honour; but looking round at the elderly faces about her, she was not so sure. Across the way there was a table presided over by one of the other officers where there seemed to be several younger people and even a girl of around her own age. Someone's daughter, perhaps. She looked rather jolly, Kate thought, and wished, a little guiltily, that she could be over there, too.

Their newly married status was, it seemed, widely known, prompting fond smiles among their table companions and a certain amount of roguishness. One bewhiskered gentleman even essayed a mildly salacious joke involving bunk beds, causing his wife, a thin woman with iron-grey hair and no chin, to utter a sharp reproof. However, the same woman was forced to confine her disapproval to little more than a downcast look and compressed lips when the captain himself countered this with a rather long and rambling account of his own honeymoon, when mosquito nets and native bearers had apparently proved inhibiting.

Kate looked a little despairingly at Guy, and he winked at her.

He seemed to be telling her to cheer up, to be sociable, just as her mother had always done, and thus reminded of her obligations she turned politely to the elderly gentleman on her right, asking him if he knew Africa well. He did, it seemed, and was prepared to dwell on its charms at length, needing, much to her relief, little more than an occasional 'Really?' or 'How interesting!' to keep him going.

Much, much worse was to come, for Guy knew a number of people on board – had even travelled with some of them on his voyage to England – and when at last the interminable meal was over and they went up to the saloon to take coffee, these friends came over to be introduced to the new bride. Kate smiled and smiled, until her face ached with the effort. Her head ached, too, as a result of the unaccustomed wine, and she knew she would never be able to remember the names of half the people she met, or remember who was married to whom.

She thought them intimidating. They were so worldly, so sure of themselves, so . . . so . . . She searched for the right word and finally found it. So *grown up*, that was it. But then, so was Guy, and so must she be now that she was married.

'My dear child, what a pretty little thing you are,' said one woman. She was thin and blonde and nut-brown, already a little wrinkled around her eyes and her scarlet mouth. 'No wonder Guy pounced on you!'

'Steady on, Flick – I don't pounce,' Guy protested.

'No?' Flick, if that was her unlikely name, had a way of hooding her eyes in a disconcerting way, as if amused at something others could only guess at. 'Oh well, if you say so, darling. Didn't your family go over for the wedding? I'm sure they must have been thrilled to bits to hear of it.'

'Absolutely thrilled,' Guy said. He was smiling, but there was something in his manner Kate didn't understand. 'But as for coming to the wedding, Mother, as you well know, is hardly up to it, and Sonia's looking after things on the estate.'

And was very busy, no doubt, Kate thought, for Guy's sister had not even found time to send a telegram to wish them well. His mother, on the other hand, had written warmly, which had made her feel a lot more comfortable about leaving all that was familiar for a new life in another continent.

Flick abandoned the topic of Guy's family and sat down next

to Kate who felt, seeing the closeness of her scrutiny, like some biological specimen under a microscope.

'Tell me,' Flick said, 'are you *frightfully* good at deck tennis, Kate? I'm sure you are!'

'Oh, no. At least, I don't think so. I mean, I've never played, but I'm not very good at anything like that. I've absolutely no eye for a ball at all.'

'Really?' Flick opened her eyes very wide and then hooded them again, puckering her lips in a small, sideways smile. 'Then you probably won't mind if Guy partners me in the mixed doubles. We won the trophy on the outward trip, you see, and it would be rather fun if we managed to repeat our little triumph, wouldn't it?' She made no effort to wait for a reply, but looked over to the nearby bar, to which Guy had drifted with a few other men. 'Do you hear that, Guy? I have your wife's permission to partner you in the mixed doubles. She tells me she has no eye for balls of any kind.' She added something in Afrikaans which was, of course, incomprehensible to Kate, but made everyone laugh. Even Guy appeared amused, but he did have the grace to protest on Kate's behalf.

'Play fair, Flick,' he said. 'Kate doesn't speak Afrikaans.'

'Well—' Flick turned to Kate, smiling sweetly. 'That's just one more thing you're going to have to learn, isn't it? Tell me, do you play deck quoits, Kate?'

'No – no, I don't.' Kate gave a brief, embarrassed laugh.

'Bridge?'

'N-no.'

Flick pulled a comic face, raised an eyebrow.

'Oh dear! No eye for cards, either? How about golf? No, of course not! Even golf involves a ball from time to time.'

By now too demoralised to speak at all, Kate merely gazed at her with wide, despairing eyes. 'Never mind, my dear.' Flick's voice was cloyingly sweet. 'I'm sure you'll have the most lovely babies.'

'Shut up, Flick. You're being poisonous,' one of the other women said. Kate looked at her gratefully, trying hard to remember her name, and failing. She looked nice, she thought. Sympathetic.

'Do . . . do you all live near Gramerci?' she asked, making a determined, if hesitant, effort to be sociable. Gramerci was the name of the estate that belonged to the Lampard family. Kate knew that it covered many square acres in a district known as Constantia and that the house was old. She had no idea, however, where it stood in relation to other houses and estates. She very much hoped that Flick wasn't too close, but it was a hope that was quickly dashed.

'Brian and I live quite close,' Flick said.

'Brian?' Kate looked around her briefly. Had she met a Brian? She didn't think so.

Flick smiled.

'My husband. The absent Mr Masterson. We take our holidays separately. We find it eases the pain of marriage.'

'Oh!' Kate could find no reply to this.

'Helen's not too far away, either,' Flick added.

Helen – that was it. That was the name of the nice girl, the name she couldn't remember. Kate felt pleased that she would have at least one friendly face in the vicinity.

'Laurie and I live in Newlands,' said a thin woman in a red dress who clearly admired Flick and appeared to make a point of laughing at her jokes. 'We'll probably see quite a bit of each other.'

'How nice.' Kate smiled at her, hoping she sounded sincere but rather doubting it. A yawn caught her unawares. All she wanted to do, at that moment, was to run away and never see any of them again. Her headache was worse and she longed for her bed; yet in another way she didn't, because she could hardly go without Guy, and she was afraid he would start all that heaving and pounding again and that, once more, she would be a disappointment to him.

What was she going to do about that? There must be *something!* People couldn't go on and on for years, dreading every bedtime. It really was the most awful let-down because, loving Guy as she did, she'd been looking forward to what had been presented to her as a kind of mystic union. That's what the Church called it in the marriage service, anyway, and really it was the only term that seemed to make any kind of sense of it, but there was nothing mystic about Guy's activities which were simply painful and ultimately pointless.

She supposed she would get better at it. Or get used to it. One or the other. She wished there was someone she could ask about it, but of course there was no one. Even her mother had been vague and non-specific, telling her – at the last minute – no more than she already knew, which wasn't much.

When at last she and Guy reached their cabin, it came as a shock to realise that he was slightly drunk, slurring his words and stumbling a little as he took off his clothes. He seemed, at first, inclined to be more amorous than ever, but before anything could happen, he fell on to his bed and was immediately asleep, snoring slightly.

Glad as she was to settle, undisturbed, into her own bed, Kate nevertheless felt uneasy, as if she were sharing the cabin with a total stranger. She told herself that she was being ridiculous. What did a little drunkenness matter? Probably all men became tipsy once in a while. It wasn't anything to make a fuss about. Sir Randolph, it was said in the village, often took a drop too much, though she had to confess she'd never witnessed the effects of it for herself. It was just one of those things that wives had to get used to – and heaven knew, it was a small price to pay for marrying someone as marvellous as Guy.

Shipboard life settled down into a routine in which deck games of all kinds were a great feature. Even Kate was pressed to play. She did, once or twice, indulge in a game of shuffleboard with Mrs Cardew, one of their elderly companions at the captain's table, but was far too shy to do more, preferring to read or to watch Guy beating all-comers at anything he attempted. She and Jilly Markham, the young girl she had seen at the next table on the first night, gravitated together, being much of an age, but though Jilly was lively and amiable enough Kate found no meeting of minds when it came to books or humour or general outlook on life. She was, she admitted to herself, missing Nancy quite dreadfully.

Guy's friends, whom Kate had met that first night, came into focus and she now knew that Helen, the nice one, was married to Paul, and could be relied on to treat her in a friendly way, whereas Marcia, the thin girl who had worn the red dress and was married to Laurie, appeared to regard her with a kind of amused contempt. She, Kate learned, was English and a comparatively new arrival to Cape society – which might, one would have thought, have encouraged her to be sympathetic to this even newer *émigrée*. It did not, however. Kate suspected that she was still too busy ingratiating herself into this cosy little clique to have time for anyone else.

Flick, she learned, wrote the social column each Saturday in the *Ladies' Pictorial*, which seemed appropriate, given her inquisitive manner. She seemed friendly, but Kate detected an undercurrent of mockery, and didn't trust her. She was vivacious, into everything; she organised the games and was constantly table-hopping at meal times. And it was Flick, who, without a word to Kate (and with malice aforethought, Kate was certain), entered her name in the table tennis competition.

'My dear, good girl,' Guy had said with exasperation when she had protested. 'Don't make such a fuss! You can't pull out. Flick's gone to all the trouble of working out who plays who in the heats – honestly, darling, is it worth upsetting everyone? Any damned fool can play ping-pong! You must have had a go in your time.'

'Yes, but—'

'Don't be such a shrinking violet! You need to join in things more. Get to know people. I tell you, man, you're going to be damned unhappy in South Africa if you're not prepared to be sociable.'

'I am prepared to be sociable. You know I am! It's just that I'm awful at those kind of games. You've seen me—'

'So what? You'll be knocked out in the first round, but what does it matter? You'll have shown everyone that you're prepared to be a good sport. Come on now, cheer up!' He had put his arm around her and hugged her. 'I'll give you a few lessons, if you like.'

The 'lessons' had been a nightmare – a succession of nightmares, demoralising her still further and irritating Guy. Having shown her how to hold the bat, he had made no concessions to her inexperience and had slammed every ball on the table so hard that it was nothing less than a miracle if she were able to get within reach of it, still less return it.

'Well, I can see you haven't got much ball sense,' he agreed at last, tight-lipped but trying to make the best of it. 'Still, man, it's the taking part that's the important thing.'

His South African way of calling everyone 'man' – even the Coningsby Hall dogs had been so addressed – had amused her at first, but now, suddenly, she was angry.

'I'm *not* a man,' she said. 'And I can't play table tennis.' And in tears she had rushed back to the cabin.

He hadn't followed. He was going to, he explained later, but he ran into the du Toits and had been talked into a drink. Just as well, in his opinion. It had given her time to see how silly she was being about the whole thing, making mountains out of molehills, getting herself into a state about nothing at all.

He had ruffled her hair and kissed her, and she had apologised. And when the order of play was put up on the notice board she thought he was right, she had been silly, for in the first round she found herself drawn against portly Mrs Craig, a cheerful Scottish lady well past her first youth and clearly disinclined to take the match seriously.

'We'll have a grand wee knock,' Mrs Craig said comfortingly. 'And you'll beat me hollow, I've no doots aboot that.'

'I don't expect I will,' Kate said. But she was cheered nonetheless.

'There,' Guy said, hearing this exchange. 'That's the spirit. Winning doesn't matter.'

Which, Kate thought, was a little ironic coming from him, for he always played to win, no matter how trifling the game. At home, she had learned, he was a star on the rugby field, a champion at tennis, and had a sideboard full of golf trophies.

However, she was comforted and more or less resigned to her fate after this conversation with her future opponent; content, that is, until she found that Mrs Craig had gone down with some stomach complaint and had been forced to withdraw, which meant that Kate had been given a 'bye' into the next round and would be playing a girl called Minna Coetzee, muscular of body and terse of speech, who had been, so Flick gleefully informed her, the Cape Province junior tennis champion of 1932.

The prospect of attempting to play against her had revived all Kate's fears. The thought of it kept her awake at nights and haunted her days. Minna was bound to draw a crowd of supporters, and the prospect of the inevitable result was more than she could bear. Losing, as she kept on saying to a totally uncomprehending Guy, meant nothing to her. She didn't care if she lost. What she minded was the certain knowledge that she would fail to score a single point, that she would appear a figure of fun, that Minna would be hopelessly bored by the whole exercise, and that the game would end in her utter humiliation to the embarrassment of Guy and amusement of everyone else who happened to be present.

Still, there was no way out of it. She thought of feigning sickness but felt sure Guy would see right through her and would despise her more than he did already. Minute by minute, as nemesis approached, her misery increased.

It was while she was tying her tennis shoes with shaking fingers that it occurred to her that this was surely how the victims of the French Revolution must have felt as they tied their hair away from their necks and stepped into the tumbrils. Pointless to remind herself

that this was only a game, a pastime, meant to add a little light
entertainment to lazy days at sea. The match against Minna had
become a monstrous terror, a menacing obstacle beyond which it
was impossible to envisage life proceeding normally.

Guy had left her minutes before in order to go and place his bet
on the day's run of the ship, and she was alone in the cabin. Having
tied her shoes, she straightened up and caught sight of herself in
the mirror.

The face that looked back at her was deathly pale, her wide
eyes, blank with terror, giving her the appearance of a startled
rabbit caught in the headlights of a car. She was, in that moment,
incapable of thought, of reason. She just knew that there was no
possible way she could go through with this ridiculous farce. And
blindly, she fled.

She saw no one in her flight; no one, anyway, who was part of
her shipboard world. She avoided the games deck and raced by a
tortuous route to the deserted boat deck where lifeboats seemed to
offer salvation – different from that which was intended, no doubt,
but salvation just the same. Almost sobbing with relief, she climbed
into one, and there she lay, curled into a ball, hearing nothing but
the knocking of her heart, knowing that once again she had let
Guy down.

'Actually, I feel quite extraordinarily sorry for the girl.'

The words, accompanied by the scraping of deck chairs as the
newcomers to the deck settled themselves, came quite clearly to
Kate. She wasn't sure how long she had been cowering in the boat,
but it had been long enough to make her see her behaviour for what
it was: something to be ashamed of, the action of an imbecile. She
couldn't imagine what everyone would think, what Guy would say.
She knew she would die right there, on the spot, if anyone were to
discover her.

The voice she could hear only – surely? – inches away was
clipped and incisive and she had no difficulty in recognising that
it belonged to Flick. There was no help for it, then. She would just
have to stay there, not moving a muscle, until she and whoever was
with her decided to go.

'Oh, so do I! She's such a child, she can't possibly know what
she's let herself in for,' said an answering voice. An English voice,
no hint of Afrikaans. It was Marcia, Kate recognised, Flick's

constant companion, who hung on her every word, shrieking with laughter at her witticisms and apparently regarding her with slavish devotion – an attitude that Flick accepted as no more than her due.

'You can say that again. But then, do any of us? Marriage is a lottery, after all. Still,' Flick added, 'one can't help feeling that Guy's hardly drawn a winning ticket. What a little ninny, not turning up for the match.'

'It's such a rotten reward for all your efforts, Flick. Honestly, it's too bad. But at least it's given you a few moments to yourself.' Marcia yawned, then gave a long sigh indicative of great contentment. 'I say, it was a brilliant idea of yours to come up here. If I'd had to stand one more moment of that frightful Mrs Parmenter going on about the depravity of life today I don't think I could have borne it.'

'My dear, there's always one on every ship. It's an occupational hazard.' Flick spoke lazily. Her strange eyes would be hooded, Kate knew, and her mouth twisted a little in that odd, three-cornered smile. 'Thank God we seem mercifully free of do-gooders who insist on telling us how badly South Africa is run and how inhumanely we treat the kaffirs.'

'I expect they're all in third class.'

'Yes, they usually are.'

For a moment there was a silence during which Kate held her breath. Very, very carefully she moved an inch in an attempt to avoid something hard that was pressing painfully into her back. Then Flick spoke again.

'I give it five years, maximum,' she said. 'Though of course, you never know. There are wheels within wheels, I gather.'

'The Lampard marriage? Five years?' Marcia laughed, apparently finding this amusing. 'I'd call that optimistic. Personally, I'll be surprised if it lasts for two. I really can't imagine why he ever married her, can you?'

'Oh yes, that's simple enough. Money, of course. And the fact that he wants a son and heir for Gramerci.'

'Well, she may be able to produce a baby, but she hasn't any money. From what I can gather she's been brought up on the smell of an oil-rag. My dear, she doesn't know a *soul* of any importance – I quizzed her early on. I mean, she doesn't seem to have been anywhere or done anything. She hasn't even been presented.'

'Maybe not, but make no mistake – she has influential friends. Apparently Guy's old uncle, or second cousin twice removed or whatever he is, has got pots of money and he's apparently fond of the girl. He's taken a proprietary interest in the family for years, Guy says, and absolutely pushed her into his arms.'

'You're not telling me he married her to please his uncle? Come off it, Flick!'

'Really, he did! He wanted to keep the old boy sweet because the object of the whole visit was to touch him for some cash. On account, as it were. He hopes for more when the old boy pops his clogs, so he'd better make sure the marriage doesn't fall by the wayside before then.' Flick gave her lazy laugh. 'It'll be a test of his forbearance, won't it?'

'I had no idea he was as broke as all that. But then, I haven't known him as long as you have.'

'He's had a few disastrous years. I know everyone else has too, but Guy's father lost a lot of money in property speculation before he died and left massive debts behind him. That house of theirs is falling to pieces and they badly need new machinery. So that's why he married Little Miss Forgive-Me-for-Living. I gather it worked, too. The old boy coughed up quite handsomely.'

Marcia laughed again.

'Oh well, that explains a lot, I suppose. She's pretty enough, I grant you that – even so, you'd think he could have found someone with a bit more—' She hesitated, and it was Flick's turn to laugh.

'I know what you mean,' she said. 'She can't say boo to a goose, can she? I don't suppose she's been long out of the schoolroom.'

'And Guy's such an attractive devil—'

'Lousy in bed.' Flick was casually dismissive.

'Well, I wouldn't know about that.' In the brief pause, Kate could hear Flick laughing again. 'I wonder,' Marcia continued thoughtfully, 'if Greta knows?'

'That he's lousy in bed? She must do after all this time – but apparently she doesn't mind.'

'I meant about Guy being married, actually.'

'Oh, she's bound to have heard, one way or another.' This prospect seemed to afford Flick further cause for laughter.

'Poor Greta!' Marcia said, with unconvincing sympathy. 'She'll be awfully cut up, won't she?'

'Cut up?' Flick's voice soared with even greater amusement.

'Cut up? My dear Marcia, that's the understatement of the year. She's always regarded Guy as her particular property. It was all right for her to go off and get married, but she'll think it quite another thing for Guy to do the same.'

'A good thing, perhaps, that she and Neil have moved to Johannesburg.'

'It's only a temporary arrangement. They'll be back. Oh, hallo!' From the change in tone Kate gathered that someone else had arrived on the scene. 'Are you looking for anyone?'

'Kate. She's not up here, is she? She seems to have scarpered and we can't find her anywhere.' It was Jilly, hearty as ever.

'Not unless she's hiding in one of the lifeboats.'

Kate's eyes dilated with fear, but she relaxed as she heard laughter and recognised that this was meant to be a joke. Who, in their right mind, would hide in a lifeboat?

'I expect she's in one of the cabins. But Guy sent me to look for her, so if you happen to see her, will you tell her he's in the bar?'

'Sure,' Flick said. Kate heard her yawn. 'Maybe it's time we were in the bar, too,' she said, after a few moments' silence. 'How about it, Marcia? Are you ready for a quick gin?'

With no need to consider the question, Marcia agreed that she was and Kate could hear from the sound of fading voices that they had left the boat deck. Even so she waited a few more moments and only then very cautiously pulled the cover aside and raised her head. Yes, she was alone. She climbed out of the boat and went to stand by the rail, looking down at the churning water far beneath her.

She felt sick with misery, and cold down to the marrow of her bones, despite the sun. Suppose she jumped overboard – ended it all, here and now? For a moment it seemed an attractive proposition, but she knew she lacked the requisite courage.

Try as she might, however, she couldn't persuade herself that Flick was lying. It wasn't at all hard to believe that Guy had only married her to make Sir Randolph more kindly disposed towards him. It must have seemed, from that very first evening at the dance in the village hall, that the entire Dearing family held some kind of special place in his affections, not merely Dotty. He was like that. All or nothing. Everyone knew it.

All was now explained. It had always seemed unbelievable to her that someone like Guy could have looked at her twice, still less asked her to marry him; yet he had told her he loved her and seemed, at times, affectionate. Surely that wasn't all make-believe?

Perhaps if she tried harder to deserve his love – made more of an effort to respond when he fell on her at night? It was so awfully hard to know what she was supposed to do, and he never spoke, never seemed to want to talk about it or explain things.

Oh God – maybe she'd lost all chance of pleasing him, ever, by running away and hiding like this! He'd hate her now, and would be ashamed of her, and quite right too. She'd behaved like a stupid schoolgirl, and everyone in the entire ship would know about it. They'd laugh at her and feel sorry for him. And at this prospect she leant on the rail and cried as she had not cried for years.

Guy came looking for her at last, told of her probable whereabouts by one of the ship's officers who had noticed her earlier heading in the direction of the boat deck. She cried, then, with her face against his chest, clinging to him, feeling his hands stroking her hair, sobbing her regret.

'I'm sorry, I'm sorry. Can you forgive me? I was so stupid – I just couldn't face playing that match.'

It was some little while before she realised he was laughing.

'What a storm in a teacup,' he said. 'Brace up, man. Chin up, steady the Buffs, and all that.'

'You're not cross with me?'

'Not now. I confess the air was a bit blue when you didn't turn up, but then I saw the funny side and we all had a damn good laugh. You behaved like an idiot, no doubt about it, but Minna would have won anyway, so it didn't much matter. Come on – let's get you down to the cabin so you can powder your nose. Then we'll go and have a good stiff drink—'

'Oh, Guy, I can't go into the bar and face everybody, not with my eyes like this, not with everyone knowing—!'

He drew back and wagged a finger at her.

'A little less of what you can't do, if you don't mind, Mrs Lampard. You're my wife, remember.'

She kissed him again.

'Oh, Guy, I do love you,' she said. 'And I swear I'll do anything to make you proud of me. I will, really I will.'

'Just so long as it's not table tennis, eh?'

'I'm just no good at things like that!'

'That's a pity. For your sake, I mean.'

'There must be something I can do!'

'Well, don't worry about it now. When you get to Gramerci you'll have your hands full just being my wife.'

It was a prospect that seemed, just then, to dazzle her with unimagined joys.

'I was thinking,' she said as, having reached the sanctuary of the cabin, she studied her reflection in the mirror. Her eyes were red and swollen and her nose, she could see, was going to need more than a dusting of powder to make her feel ready to face the world.

'What?' Guy asked when she said no more. He was watching her as he smoked a cigarette, lounging in a chair with his legs stretched out in front of him. 'What were you thinking, darling?'

For a moment Kate hesitated, fiddling with her brush and comb, aligning them carefully against the edge of the chest of drawers.

'Guy,' she said at last. 'Can I ask you a question? Do you really love me?'

She could see in the mirror that he was staring at her, amused but puzzled, too.

'What sort of a question is that?' he said. 'I asked you to marry me, didn't I? It's not the sort of thing I make a habit of doing, I promise you.'

'I know that. It's just that—'

He got up from his chair and bent over her, nuzzling her cheek, taking little bites at her earlobe.

'Just that you can be such a goose, sometimes! Don't I know it? But you're such a pretty little goose, sweetheart, how could I help loving you?'

She turned and kissed him on the lips.

'Guy—' She paused, then took the plunge. 'Darling, I know we said we'd wait a bit before we started a family, but I was thinking, I don't really want to.'

He drew away from her a little, suddenly wary.

'You don't want children?'

She reached for him, laughing.

'Yes, yes, you idiot! I mean I don't want to wait. Why don't we start a baby now? Well, not *now*, exactly, but I mean as soon as we can. Oh, darling, I'd really like a baby. A little boy, just like you.'

'You would?' Guy was smiling again, surprised but undoubtedly gratified. 'You don't think it would be wise to wait until you're settled at Gramerci, and feel thoroughly at home there?'

Kate shook her head.

'No,' she said firmly. 'No, I don't. Not at all. I'm sure I'll feel at home absolutely right away, and I don't think waiting is at all a good idea.'

Not, she thought, with this Greta woman who, according to Flick, had some prior claim to him and might well be circling like a malevolent predator in the background. He wanted an heir, Flick said. Well, an heir was something that she could give him – she and no one else. It would ensure her place in his life, her place at Gramerci.

But of this she said nothing. Neither did she mention Greta, though she was full of curiosity about her. She'd meet her soon enough, no doubt.

Perhaps, she thought, as she picked up her hairbrush once more, she was learning discretion. Perhaps she was growing up at last.

Kate phoned Caroline Greaves to ask if Vicky and Mark could possibly go home with Gaynor after school, to be picked up from Hampstead no later than five.

'But do say if it's not convenient,' she begged. 'I shall understand perfectly.'

'Of course it's convenient, Kate! We always love having them.' Caroline was as meaninglessly friendly as ever. 'I shan't be here myself, but Nanny will be delighted. She adores your Mark and never fails to drop hints about how much Gaynor would love a little baby brother. They fall on stony ground, I'm afraid.'

'I'm awfully grateful, Caroline. Thank you.'

'I hope you're going to indulge in some madly exciting assignation! Heaven knows, you deserve a fling – oh, by the way, Kate, I've been meaning to ring you, actually. About Vicky coming for the weekend in a couple of weeks' time.'

Kate racked her brains for a reasonable excuse.

'She mentioned it. I'm really awfully sorry, Caroline, but it won't be possible. We – er – we might be going down to see Tom's mother in Sussex that weekend—'

'Oh, dear.' Caroline sounded genuinely taken aback. 'Oh, lor', that is a nuisance. You see, we have to go to a wedding on the Saturday and we rather hoped not to have to take Gaynor because children are really rather out of place at weddings, don't you agree?'

'She's hardly of an age to scream all through the service, surely?'

'No, no, of course not.' Caroline was not amused. 'It's rather that we'll probably go *on* somewhere and not get back till late, and Roger gets into such a state if he thinks we're neglecting the child. I mean, it's ridiculous, isn't it? I'm here all week – well, most of the time – and just because I want to go out for the day without her on Saturday he starts getting frightfully agitated about the whole thing. I managed to persuade him that if Vicky came, then Gaynor wouldn't miss us at all. Nanny was going to take them out to see a film in the afternoon – there's a Walt Disney thing coming to the Odeon. Are you really sure—'

'Really,' Kate said. 'I'm so sorry.'

She had opened her mouth to say that, in the circumstances described, Gaynor must certainly come and stay for the weekend with them until in the nick of time she remembered that this would reveal that all she had said about going to Sussex was pure fabrication.

'I wonder if we can find anyone else—'

Caroline sounded worried. Had Roger's Bad Words been worse than usual? Kate wondered.

'I do hope you find a solution,' she said, guiltily. 'But meantime, you are quite sure about this afternoon? Thanks so much. I really am grateful – a sudden emergency, you know how it is. I'll give the school a ring, so that they can tell Vicky not to expect me. And thanks again.'

'You're welcome,' Caroline said, sounding a little put out at the thought that Kate had not instantly changed any arrangements that might have been made. Or perhaps she hadn't believed the excuse. Kate disliked lying and was uneasily aware that she lacked any skill in the art.

Still, it was with relief that she put the phone down. This arrangement meant that she could now go and see Johnny in the afternoon instead of waiting until evening, which her every instinct said would be more acceptable to Tom. With the weekend looming, she wanted him in a particularly good mood. She hadn't yet worked out when would be the best time to go to the hospital on Saturday or Sunday, but one thing was certain – his co-operation would be vital.

A general feeling of elation was something she had almost come to take for granted over the past day or two, but as she turned to go upstairs, an extra, supercharged infusion of happiness flooded through her, numbing her with its impact. For a moment she stood still, her eyes closed, conscious only of its stunning impact. Thank you, God, she whispered. Oh, thank you, God.

She felt like singing an aria or turning cartwheels; but instead, after a moment, mindful of her duties but unable to stop smiling, she continued upstairs to make the beds.

5

'No change, then?'

Kate could see for herself that there had been none, but it seemed necessary to say something to the young nurse attending to the drip.

'No. He'll be like this for a little while longer, I should think.'

The nurse turned round and smiled. She had a pretty, pert face, and dark curls on which her cap sat jauntily, the combination creating an effect which, it occurred to Kate, must surely do nothing but harm to vulnerable male patients, particularly those suffering from heart conditions. 'Not that I know anything,' she added hastily. She gave a nod towards the bunch of early daffodils that Kate had brought with her. 'Pretty flowers.'

'Yes.' Kate looked at them, feeling the need to be apologetic. 'I know he won't be aware of them—'

'They'll be a lovely splash of colour when he wakes up.'

'That's what I thought.' Kate smiled, confirmed in her belief that all would, eventually, be well.

The nurse hurried away and, left alone, Kate stood looking down at the bed. Then she drew up a chair.

'Johnny?' She leant towards him, taking his hand in both of hers. 'Oh, Johnny, I am right, aren't I? I'm sure I am, even if no one else believes me. You are John Pierre Lampard. You were brought up at Gramerci, in Constantia. Such a lovely place! I thought I would be happy there for ever.'

She paused, her thoughts straying momentarily.

'Were you happy there?' she went on. 'I'm ashamed to say there were times when I hoped you'd be missing me. I'm sure you must have done, at first, but later—' She paused again. 'Well, you must have been happy. It was such a wonderful place for a child to grow up. So much space and light and freedom. And sunshine. And the candlewood tree! Oh, Johnny, did you play in the candlewood tree? You must have done! It was a perfect place for a little boy to hide. Perfect for me, too.'

It had been her sanctuary, she remembered. And with the memory came doubts. What had they told him about her? Nothing good, that was certain. Right from the beginning, Sonia had disliked her. Before she had any reason for it; before, even, they had spoken. Though she could have known nothing about her childish behaviour over the table tennis tournament, it was as if, at first sight, Sonia had recognised her as ineffectual and inadequate, and had despised her accordingly.

Most people had maintained a tactful silence regarding Kate's abandonment of the match. Only Flick saw fit to pretend, when she paused beside Kate and Helen as they sunbathed on deck the following day, that Minna had been shivering in her shoes at the thought of it and had been mightily relieved to find that Kate had given her a walk-over.

'Flick, shut up,' Helen said with a lazy good humour that yet had an edge to it. Adding: 'Don't take any notice of her, Kate. Malice is Flick's stock-in-trade. We all know she invents half the things she writes about.'

'Ah, but which half?' Flick asked, unperturbed. She perched on the deck chair beside them, as if to pursue the matter. 'That's what keeps you all guessing. Anyway, Ted O'Leary won't let me write most of the juiciest stuff. He likes me to stick to boring things, like Mrs van de Merwe appearing at the Ritz in her favourite shade of magenta with a fashionable scattering of sequins. I'm not allowed to say that Mrs van de Merwe, as always, looked like a whore on sailors' pay-day.' She looked at her watch and rose to her feet. 'Well, my dears, I must love you and leave you. I have a date with a rather delectable engineer. *Tot siens* for the moment.'

'Is that true?' Kate asked Helen after she had gone. 'I mean, about her inventing half of it?'

'Well—' Helen considered the matter. 'Not the stuff she writes, I suppose. As she said, Ted O'Leary – the editor – wouldn't want to lay himself open to any law suits, and it's a frightfully genteel kind of mag; but she does love to dish the dirt, and the dirtier the better. If she told me my husband was sleeping with my best friend, I would need at least three other sworn statements before I believed her.'

'Oh!' The note of relief in Kate's voice was clear, and Helen lifted her head to look at her more closely.

'Why? What's she been saying to you?'

For a moment Kate was tempted to confide. She had grown, lately, to like and admire Helen, who being in her mid-twenties was sufficiently older than she was to seem the fount of all wisdom. She was a girl of English extraction, but her husband, Paul, came from a well-known Afrikaans family in Cape Town, long associated with shipping. He had been at school with Guy and the two were great friends and golf partners. From the first Kate had found her friendly and supportive, an ally in an alien world, but even so, she decided not to share her secret. 'Oh, nothing really.'

Helen settled back once more.

'Well, whatever it was, I shouldn't believe it if I were you.'

Kate closed her eyes. Maybe it wasn't true, then. Maybe Guy hadn't married her to please Sir Randolph and get money out of him. In the cold light of day it did seem rather far-fetched. Maybe he really did love her.

For some time she was silent, letting this thought seep into her consciousness. The sun seemed like a warm, beneficent hand, soothing away her fears. After a while Helen spoke.

'I wonder if I can offer you some advice,' she said.

Kate opened her eyes and looked at her.

'Of course,' she said, a touch of wariness in her voice.

Helen hesitated for a moment.

'It's only . . . well, all I was going to say is don't let people walk all over you.'

Kate sighed.

'That's easy to say, but everyone seems so much more—' She paused, struggling to find the right word. 'I don't know. Sophisticated, I suppose.'

'Sophisticated?' Helen laughed. 'Rubbish! We're just brash. Full of our own importance.'

Kate remained unconvinced.

'Flick's sophisticated,' she said.

'Not in my book. She's as provincial as any of us. She just puts on a good act. As for her little hanger-on, Marcia, she strikes me as being more provincial than anyone else in spite of all her airs and graces.'

'My dear, *such* a crush at Ascot!' Kate said, in a Marcia voice.

'You'll never *guess* what happened to my ostrich feathers!' Helen countered, and they giggled together. 'But listen,' she went on after a moment in a quite different voice. 'I'm really serious. You must stand up for yourself.'

Kate sighed.

'I wish I could be like you. You know. Sure of myself. Sure of what to say and do.'

'You will be. Honestly. You're very young and everything's strange, but you've got an awful lot in your favour.'

'Have I?' Kate was genuinely astonished. 'What?'

'For heaven's sake!' Helen looked both amused and exasperated. 'Of course you have! Look at you – you're lovely! No, honestly, I mean it. And as I said before, you're young. Do you honestly think Flick wouldn't give her eye-teeth to be your age and have your face and your figure? She's like two pieces of board, back to back.'

'Being young isn't so wonderful.'

Helen slapped her lightly with a folded magazine.

'Snap out of it, for heaven's sake!' she said, laughing. She propped herself up on her elbows and looked at Kate lying next to her. 'But listen to me, Kate.' She was serious again, almost solemn. 'Let me give you a word of warning. You really must brace up if you're going to hold your own in the Lampard household. Sonia is quite different from Flick, but she's forceful. She likes her own way, and you mustn't let her have it. You must stick up for yourself.'

Kate opened her eyes and gave a shaky laugh.

'You make her sound terrifying!'

'I don't mean to frighten you.'

'Well, you're certainly succeeding.'

'Nonsense! Just remind yourself that you're the girl Guy chose to be his wife. No one else. Act as if you're sure of yourself, and have every right to be there, and everyone else will accept it.'

'Easier said than done.'

'Well—' Helen lay back in her chair again. 'It's up to you. Think tough. It's the only way.'

'I'll try,' Kate said earnestly. 'Thanks for the advice, anyway. Helen, we will be seeing each other when the trip is over, won't we?'

Helen looked amused.

'You won't be able to avoid me, even if you wanted to. Paul and Guy are good friends, always off together playing their little boys' games. And that's another thing. Don't ever forget that however young you are, you will grow up while Guy is likely to stay around seven years old. That's one of the facts of life your mother probably never told you.'

Kate laughed, more light-heartedly than she had done before.

'She didn't tell me any of them,' she said.

Somehow, after this conversation, things seemed to improve. Since the awful day of the match, Guy had been more attentive. Helen, he confessed, had taken him to task for being insensitive to Kate's natural shyness and diffidence – and he could see now that she was right. It was just that he had wanted her to join in and be part of everything that was going on.

She was only too ready to take her share of the blame.

'It wasn't your fault I was so silly,' she said. 'But you see, Guy, I'm not in the least bit sporty, and there's nothing you can do that will make me—'

'Agh, man, you're *you*, aren't you? The prettiest girl on board.'

'So you do love me? Even though I'm an idiot?'

'Kate, Kate!' He put his arms around her and rocked her, side to side. 'Of course I love you! Don't I prove it every day? And night?' he added, in a different kind of voice.

Kate smiled at him, not knowing how to answer this. If the regularity of his nightly onslaught proved his love, then she certainly had no cause to question it, but she did wish that there was more . . . more tenderness. Still, if this was the only way to get a baby, she supposed she would have to put up with it.

And with such proof of his love, Helen could be right about Flick, Kate thought. And right about other things, too; and calling on reserves of courage she didn't know she possessed, she forced herself to speak when previously shyness would have kept her silent. In astonishment, she found that people responded in a perfectly normal way with no indication that they thought her more stupid or trivial than anyone else. There were even times when they seemed to find her amusing – for the right reasons, not just because she'd said something silly; and when it came to the fancy-dress ball and ideas for a group entry were being discussed, her inventiveness was universally applauded and was instrumental in their group winning first prize.

Which was all very gratifying in the context of shipboard life.

She was conscious, however, now that she was thinking more clearly, of the way in which real life was miniaturised in this compact and claustrophobic world. In what other circumstances would a table tennis match cause such angst? Where else would bright ideas regarding knights and dragons and maidens lead to heightened esteem?

Everything, she could now see, was out of proportion, and even though, despite all Helen's good advice, the prospect of meeting Sonia still filled her with foreboding, she was anxious now to be done with the voyage and to start on her new life.

Especially was this true on the morning they sailed into Table Bay. Coming up on deck at dawn, she experienced, as she looked at the bay and the mountain and the pearly sea, a kind of humble gratitude that Guy had brought her to live in surroundings of such incredible beauty. Clutching his arm, everything else was forgotten as she stood and gazed and marvelled. Who, she asked herself, could fail to be happy in such a place as this?

It was her first intimation of the intense and all-consuming love felt by South Africans for the land that bore them. Guy's face was that of a lover reunited with his mistress as he leant over the rail in his eagerness to meet the moment when it would be possible to step once again on the beloved soil.

'There she blows,' he whispered under his breath, gazing at Table Mountain, its flat top softened by wisps of cloud – white and lemon and palest pink. 'Look, Kate – see those mountains on either side? That one's Devil's Peak, the other is Lion's Head.'

'For some reason I didn't expect it to be so green,' she said.

'This is spring. There'll be flowers in the meadows and lilies under the oaks at Gramerci.'

'It's beautiful . . . beautiful—'

'I told you—'

'I know, but I didn't expect it to be quite so wonderful.'

He turned and smiled at her, pleased at her pleasure, delight in his country making him seem more vulnerable than she could ever have expected. It seemed to her that they had at last found something they could share.

'This is the real beginning, isn't it?' she whispered. But Guy said nothing in return, and she doubted if he had even heard her. He had turned to the mountain once more.

*   *   *

After they had docked, officials came on board to carry out immigration procedures. It was while they were waiting in the smoking room to have their passports checked that something inspired Kate to turn her head and glance over her shoulder towards the entrance.

Other waiting passengers were behind her, but as she idly surveyed the scene the group shifted a little and she had a clear view of the doorway.

A woman stood there. She was tall and blonde, with hair swept up on top of her head, elegantly dressed in a lime-green linen suit, a green and white scarf knotted at her throat and a white straw hat the size and shape of a tea plate tilted over one eye. She looked, Kate thought, rather like a thoroughbred racehorse – lean and hard and sure of her own power. She felt the old twinge of envy for her obvious poise and sophistication, but it was only momentary. How could she envy anyone when it was she, Mrs Guy Lampard, who was embarking on this adventure? And who might (though this was so far from certain that she had said nothing and didn't really want to think about it) even now be carrying Guy's child?

This handsome stranger must have come aboard as soon as the ship docked, for she was certainly not one of the passengers, who were, by this time, all known to each other, at least by sight; but as, without haste, she surveyed the crowd, her gaze came to rest on Kate.

For a moment she seemed to be staring at her and, confused, Kate looked away; but a moment later, when she stole another look, she found the woman's eyes still directed towards her, studying her coolly and without expression. She seemed, then, to give a small, dismissive smile and looked beyond Kate and slightly to her left, where Guy was exchanging small talk with Paul de Vries.

Realisation came to Kate in a sudden flash. This, some instinct told her, was Sonia. She was as sure of it as if the name were written over her head in letters forty feet high. And she looked more formidable that she could ever have imagined.

Her nervousness flared into life again. How would she measure up? Would Guy's sister and mother approve of her? If only it was going to be she and Guy alone, together, just as it had been earlier on deck—

Sonia, she knew, was three years older than Guy. She was the clever one, Guy said with ungrudging admiration; the brains of the family, the one who really ran the estate and knew all there was to know about viticulture. She was also unmarried, lived at home, and excelled at all sports, just like Guy himself.

These factors, in themselves, were terrifying enough, without the stunning impact of Sonia in the flesh. Guy had shown her a photograph of his sister standing on the steps of Gramerci, but it was taken at some distance, her face was in shadow, and she had been wearing slacks and a wide-brimmed straw hat. She had looked perfectly ordinary then, perfectly approachable, nothing whatever like this glamorous, self-possessed creature now standing at the door of the smoking room. It was going to be just like meeting Flick and the crowd all over again, Kate thought, her heart sinking.

She pulled at Guy's sleeve to attract his attention, but he was busy arranging a game of golf some time in the future with Paul and frowned at the interference.

'Hang on, darling. I'm just—'

'Guy, look over by the door. I think it's Sonia.'

He turned and his face broke into a wide smile.

'Good Lord, yes! Hi, Sonia!' He waved at her. 'With you in a minute. How the hell did she manage that?' he asked, turning back to Paul. 'I didn't think anyone was allowed on board until after we'd been through immigration.'

Paul laughed.

'It'd be a brave man who'd stop her,' he said. 'Sonia does what Sonia wants.'

'That's true,' Guy agreed, and joined in the laughter.

Helen somehow materialised beside them, and took Kate's arm.

'Now remember all I told you,' she said in her ear. 'Straighten your back and stick your chin up and make her see you're a match for her any old day.'

'But I'm not!'

'I told you – think tough! Pretend you are, and you will be.'

Kate thought of this when finally the formalities were over and they were able to join Sonia outside the smoking room. How was she supposed to act when, instead of a sisterly embrace, Sonia merely looked her up and down?

'Really, Guy,' she said amusedly. 'What cradle did you snatch this one from?'

Kate's nervousness gave way to annoyance.

'I assure you I'm well past the age of consent,' she said stiffly.

'Sonia, behave yourself,' Guy said, putting his arm around Kate's shoulder and giving her a squeeze. He was smiling, though; not at all cross. 'Take no notice of her, darling. Her bark is a lot worse than her bite.'

Sonia laughed, snapping her perfect teeth at him.

'If you believe that, you'll believe anything.' Her smile, Kate thought, was not one that reached her eyes. 'Kate, I really don't know whether to congratulate you or not. Marriage to this rogue isn't going to be unalloyed bliss, but I wish you well. Now shouldn't we be doing something about your luggage, or do we stay here all day? I've been here ages, as it is. Dawn hadn't even cracked when I got up this morning.'

'Why didn't you send Joseph?' Guy asked. 'There really wasn't any need for you to come.'

'Of course I came,' Sonia said. 'You know I've been counting the days. I couldn't wait to meet my new sister-in-law.'

She glinted a smile at Kate as she spoke, but there was little about her manner that expressed any warmth. Neither was Kate particularly heartened, when finally they had collected the luggage, by the brisk manner in which she was told to sit in the back of the car while Sonia and Guy, together in the front, talked exclusively of people and events of which she had no knowledge.

Imperious was the word for her, Kate thought. Well, it was one word. She could think of others – like bossy and unfeeling. In fact, Kate thought, if anyone wanted her opinion, Sonia Lampard was rude. Damned rude. And as she nursed her simmering and quite uncharacteristic anger in the back seat of the car, she was amused to find that, after all, Helen's homily must have had more effect than she had realised, for only a few days ago she might have been cowed by Sonia's behaviour. Now it merely made her determined to stand up for herself.

Guy wasn't blameless, either. He hadn't spoken a word to her since leaving the ship – but then, she told herself, unwilling to think badly of him, of course he wanted to know everything that had been going on at Gramerci in his absence. It was only natural.

The view outside the window was enough to occupy her, in all conscience. They were high above the bay now, with the docks and the blue sea far below and the mountain somewhere above and behind, out of sight for the moment. Soon they were passing a large and impressive building. Hospital? University? She leaned

forward to ask Guy, but Sonia was in full spate so she sat back
again without speaking.

Now they were in a residential area, with impressive houses and
gardens, brilliant flowers, woodland – she looked from side to side,
and back over her shoulder at the mountain that had put in an
appearance again, its flat top shrouded now in a thicker veil of
cloud. Soon all this would be as familiar to her as the lanes around
Shenlake. It was an exciting thought, Sonia or no Sonia.

After they had been driving for twenty minutes or so, Guy
turned to her.

'Look down there,' he said. 'Those are Gramerci vines. That's
where they begin. They're budding now. Soon they'll be in full
leaf. And just round this corner you'll catch sight of Gramerci itself.
There – look – that's Gramerci.'

'Oh!' It was more an indrawing of breath than an exclamation.
'It looks lovely.'

'Is it what you were expecting?' Sonia asked.

Kate hesitated.

'I hardly knew what to expect,' she said. 'Guy showed me
photographs of the house, of course, but I had no idea what the
land around it was like.'

'So long as you're not disappointed.'

'It's beautiful! How could I be?'

'How indeed?' Sonia looked into the driving mirror and their
eyes met. She looked knowing and cynically amused. Why? Kate
wondered. What was she thinking? Did she imagine she'd married
Guy for the house and the estate? That they didn't truly love each
other? Well, she'd soon find out her mistake.

'It's lovely,' she repeated, more firmly.

'Nearly there,' Guy said, after a few more minutes. Kate felt
less brave now, more conscious of butterflies in her stomach. How
would she cope? Had it all been a terrible mistake?

In silence they turned into the drive where the oaks met overhead,
creating a dimly lit tunnel like the nave of a church. Then the oaks
thinned, they turned a corner, and there, apparently shimmering in
the sunlight, stood Gramerci.

Guy turned round, smiling.

'Welcome, Mrs Lampard. You're home at last.'

'Kate?'

Coming back from a long way off, Kate saw that Elaine was beside her. She gave a self-conscious laugh.

'Sorry. I was talking to him.'

'Good. That's what he needs.'

'Elaine, his eyes moved a bit, under the lids. That's a good sign, isn't it?'

'Excellent. He's going to be all right, Kate. But that's not what I came to say. The thing is, there's a policeman outside and he'd like to have a word with you.'

'I can't tell him anything.'

'No, but he'd like a word, anyway.'

Kate shrugged resignedly, picked up her coat and bag and gloves, and went with Elaine into the corridor. The policeman in question introduced himself as Detective Sergeant Baker, and he smiled at her in a friendly kind of way. He wore no uniform and seemed kind. Avuncular, even, though his eyes were shrewd.

'Is there somewhere—?' he asked Elaine.

'Yes, of course,' she said, and ushered them to the small room where she had taken Kate before, leaving them alone together.

'There's nothing I can tell you,' Kate said, before DS Baker could speak. 'This has just come out of the blue.'

'I believe you've identified him as your son, Mrs Newcott.' The policeman's voice was quiet, with a North Country accent.

'Yes. Well—' Hastily Kate back-tracked a little. 'I think he's my son. In my heart I think he is, but you see—' She drew in her breath and looked at him, trying to make him understand. 'Due to various circumstances that would be tedious to go into, I haven't seen him since he was four years old, so other people say I can't be sure. And I suppose,' she added, her voice failing a little, 'common sense is on their side.'

'He did have your address on him.'

'Yes.' Kate brightened again. 'I keep telling myself that.'

DS Baker smiled sympathetically.

'Whoever he is, I'm told he'll be round shortly, so then, hopefully, he'll be able to speak for himself. What's concerning us more at the moment are the thugs who beat him up. There's been too much of that sort of thing lately, in that particular area. Under the circumstances, I don't suppose you can tell us why he went there, or who he went to meet? There's a pub quite nearby and the theory is that he might have arranged to see a friend there.'

Kate shook her head.

'I can't tell you anything. I only wish I could.'

'You don't know the names of any friends he might have contacted?'

'No. How could I? I know nothing about him.' She saw the curiosity in the sergeant's eyes and lifted her shoulders helplessly. 'It's a long story,' she said. 'We were separated over twenty years ago and I'd resigned myself to never seeing him again. I suppose I always hoped, but without any real basis for it.'

DS Baker got to his feet.

'Let's hope he comes round soon and can give us all the answers,' he said. He went to the door and held it open for her. 'Incidentally, Mrs Newcott, what makes you so sure he's your son? Is there a family likeness of some kind?'

'Well—' Kate gave a nervous breath of laughter. 'Only his hands. It sounds so stupid, doesn't it? But you see, his hands are just like my brother's.'

The sergeant made no movement. She looked at him but saw no surprise in his eyes, no derision. There seemed, in fact, to be a sudden sharpening of those watchful brown eyes.

'How?' he asked.

She laughed again and shrugged her shoulders.

'Oh, just the shape of them. And the nails, the way they grow, with big half-moons. Unfortunately, my brother's in Canada, so I can hardly produce him to substantiate my claim.'

She preceded him into the corridor and quietly and deliberately he closed the door behind him and followed her, a step or two behind, not speaking.

'I have a thing about hands,' he said when they reached the stairs. 'Hands and walks. They're the most difficult things in the world to disguise. Many a criminal's been rumbled because of them.'

Kate turned and stared at him.

'You mean you believe me? That I'm right, and it's really Johnny in there? Oh, I wish my husband could hear you!'

He laughed at that and shook his head.

'I'm just a copper, showing off a bit. Still, you could be right, Mrs Newcott. We'll soon know, won't we? And if in the meantime you happen to be struck by inspiration as to who he might know in London or where he might have been going, you'll let us know, won't you? Those thugs need catching, that's for certain. They could have killed him.'

Kate, her mind still focused on his previous statement, had stopped listening. She continued to stare at him, eyes bright with renewed conviction.

'You believe me,' she said again. 'You really believe me.'

But DS Baker shrugged, said goodbye, and left without committing himself further. She was right, though, she told herself. She felt quite sure of it. He *did* believe her! She couldn't wait to tell Tom.

Colin had talked himself into going to the Cambells' party. He knew it didn't make a lot of sense – might, in fact, only awake lots of memories and feelings that were better left alone – but when it came to the point, his desire to see Nina again conquered his common sense.

He could hear, as he knocked at the door, that the party was in full swing. It was Hennie who came to let him in, and she opened her arms wide at the sight of him.

'Colin! Come in, man. I'm so glad you could make it. Nina. Nina,' she called over her shoulder. 'Look who's come. It's Colin.'

'So I see.' A slim girl in a pale, strappy dress detached herself from a small group of guests and came over to him. She was smiling, Colin noted thankfully, her chin narrowing to a point in the way that he had always found fascinating. She even gave him a light peck on the cheek in greeting. 'How nice to see you.'

'It's lovely to see you, too.' He stood grinning at her, suddenly shy despite his veneer of sophistication, still clutching the bottle and the wrapped box of chocolates that he had brought as a present.

'These, I take it, are for Mom and Dad?' she said, laughing at him, taking them from him. 'Or were you intending to hang on to them?'

He laughed, too.

'No, no, of course not. Happy anniversary, Hennie. And many of them.'

'Thirty-two years,' Hennie told him again, with pride. 'It's a long time, Colin.'

'And how I've put up with it I'll never know,' Les said, as he joined them, dodging a mock blow from his wife. 'Colin, man, good to see you again. Let me get you a drink. What's it to be?'

'Colin! It's great you could come.' This was Margie, Nina's sister, younger by two years, who had in the old days always indulged in flirtatious chat with him, both of them knowing that he had no eyes for any girl but Nina. Margie was a leggy blonde, cutely pretty, utterly unlike her elder sister. She had left school early and trained as a hairdresser, showing none of Nina's more cerebral pursuits. A living doll, Colin had always thought her – appreciatively, but with a touch of patronage.

'Margie!' It seemed only natural that they should embrace each other. 'What's all this about you being a wife and mother? Without a word to me! I can't believe it! I thought you were patiently waiting.'

'Agh – idiot!' She gave him a playful shove.

'Where's the baby? I wanted to see him.'

'He's upstairs on Mom's bed, dead to the world. He'll wake up before the night's out – that's one thing you can bank on, the little monster.'

Hennie pretended outrage.

'That's my grandson you're talking about, remember! He couldn't be a monster if he tried. He's an angel, straight from heaven, bless him.'

'You wouldn't think that at three in the morning!'

'Go on with you. He's an angel at any time of the day or night.'

Colin realised, with amusement, that nothing had changed since the years when he was a constant visitor. The Cambells still indulged in good-humoured mock arguments, pulled each others' legs, roared with laughter; all but Nina, who seemed like the still, sweet centre of this high-spirited family.

'Come and meet Steve,' Margie said.

'Agh, yes!' Hennie wasn't yet prepared to let him go. 'Such a lovely chap, our Steve. And done so well. Tell him, Margie – tell him how well Steve's done.'

'He's been promoted,' Margie said proudly. 'Just last month. He works at Verfelds, making radios, and he's just been made a floor foreman.'

'By Mr Gerard Verfeld's direct order,' Hennie said, fondly. 'The youngest man to be made a foreman in the history of the company.

And not only that – he plays the piano like a dream. Anything you can name! Just tell him the title and he can play it. We're so proud of him. Agh – here are the Nicholsons! Doreen, Derek – come in my dears. It's wonderful to see you after so long. Nina, see if Mrs Peschard would like a refill – she's standing there with an empty glass.'

'That's how I met Steve,' Margie said, while the party milled about them. 'He plays the piano in the Red Aces, and Dad brought him home one night.'

'Love at first sight?'

She smiled and nodded vigorously.

'You bet. Half a sight. Come on – come over and meet him.'

He did so, but not before he had met the Peschards from next door and the Van Rensburgs from across the street, and Pauline, who was a cousin of Les's, and the Van Rensburgs' son, Rudi (who, to Colin's way of thinking, was far too pleased with himself. What the hell did he think he was doing, pawing over Nina like that? Any fool could see she didn't like it).

At last he met Steve Dwyer and for a while they chatted, leaning against the wall side by side, glasses in their hands. He was a nice-looking boy, Colin thought; really, it was impossible to think of him in any other way, foreman or not. He had a round face, unruly dark curls, an attractive grin.

'Hennie's been singing your praises,' Colin said, smiling back at him.

Steve pulled a comic face.

'She does that, I'm afraid. Since this foreman business, anyway.'

'You've done well.'

'Maybe.' Steve's grin slackened, and he even sighed. 'Well, yes, I suppose I have in a way. God knows, we need the money, what with the baby and Margie not working any more.'

'It can't be easy, having older men under you.'

'Not always,' he agreed. Then he grinned. 'Nothing's perfect, is it?'

'That's true,' Colin agreed, thinking of George Porter, the faint-hearted editor of the *Courier* who never dared put more than a tentative toe in the water when it came to publishing something that might bring the government's wrath down on his head.

'Colin, you remember Doreen, don't you? And Derek?' Hennie was in front of him, two further guests in tow.

'Yes, of course.' Colin managed to smile at this pair who were, he vaguely remembered, somehow distantly related to Les. What he remembered quite clearly was the fact that they had been present on that terrible picnic.

They'd met, he and Nina, at a party in their last year of school and had been attracted to each other right away, soon viewed by their contemporaries as a pair, best friends as well as sweethearts. That they had both been accepted for the University of the Witwatersrand long before the date of their first meeting had been accepted as a happy accident, the hand of fate. In the light of their increasing love for each other, they looked forward to a new, more independent life away from Cape Town, but somehow things hadn't worked out that way.

The picnic at Cape Point had taken place on their second vacation when already Colin was fearful that Nina had changed towards him. They had walked to the lighthouse and had quarrelled on the way about Jan, a controversial figure on the campus, who seemed to Colin to be exerting an undue influence on her. Dismally he had sensed then that it was the beginning of the end. Now, six years on, he saw Nina looking at him and knew that she remembered, too. She looked both solicitous and regretful, he thought; but he knew it was the pain that she regretted, not the actions that had caused it.

The party moved on. There was a buffet that Hennie and Margie had spent days preparing, and toasts to be drunk, accompanied by execrable jokes. Steve made a speech that had everyone in tears of laughter. His was a great face, Colin thought. A merry face, with all the angles slanting upwards as if built for humour.

'Isn't he wonderful?' Nina said, standing beside Colin on the opposite side of the room.

'"A fellow of infinite jest",' Colin said, and she laughed.

'Funny you should say that. It's the phrase I often think of when I see him. I don't think Margie has a dull moment.'

Colin agreed, but a little absently. His thoughts had been running on another track. He had been thinking, not for the first time, what ridiculous laws his beloved country had somehow succeeded in dreaming up. There was Piet Marais, thrown into prison, awaiting execution, driven crazy with grief because he had the dreaded 'C' on his identity card and was therefore forbidden to marry his childhood sweetheart. Whereas Steve Dwyer, barely half a shade lighter when it came to outward appearances, could marry and prosper, with everyone's approval.

He conveyed his thoughts to Nina, who raised an eyebrow.

'Marais did kill the girl, after all.'

'That's what Eksberg said.'

'Eksberg? That policeman you mentioned? Well, he has a point. Also, it can't have been exactly love's young dream, can it? I mean, if she'd really loved him, she wouldn't have appealed against her classification, would she? She would just have kept quiet and stayed Coloured.'

'Eksberg said that, too. In different words.'

'Oh, lor'! I'm not at one with a cop, am I? I must be slipping.'

'Not from where I'm standing. You look marvellous, Nina.'

She smiled at him and dipped her head.

'Nice of you to say so.'

He felt ridiculously moved by the gesture; it was the old Nina, the Nina he had loved so much. He seized on the first subject that came into his head to hide his emotion.

'Margie seems happy,' he said.

'Yes.'

Nina's expression as she looked across the room at her younger sister seemed to Colin to have a touch of wistfulness about it. 'They're right for each other, she and Steve. Sometimes I think—' She broke off and glanced at him. 'Never mind,' she said.

'Don't be infuriating! What were you going to say?'

But there was no time to pursue the matter, for Hennie had swept down on them once more.

'Now what are you two talking about so seriously? Move over, now, there's good children. We're rolling up the rug for dancing.'

Obediently they moved over, the rug was rolled, and Steve, apparently without a care in the world, took his place at the piano, while Les went to fetch his saxophone. With Ronnie Peschard on drums, they burst into a medley of old favourites and the latest hits.

'You see now why we had to invite all the neighbours?' Hennie cried as she waltzed with Colin. He laughed and nodded. He saw only too well.

'Won't it wake the baby?' he asked.

Hennie shook her head.

'He's used to it,' she said. 'That child, he'll grow up with music in his bones.'

Perspiring, he danced with Les's cousin Pauline, and jived with Mrs Peschard from next door, but he was conscious throughout of Nina. She was doing her duty by the male guests, dancing with one after the other. At least, he hoped it was her duty. That bloody Rudi was becoming a pain, he thought, keeping a weather-eye on the young buck from across the road.

That's what he was like, a young buck – displaying, you'd say, if he were the four-legged kind; drawing attention to himself, standing beside the mantelpiece posed as if for a fashion photograph whenever he wasn't dancing with Nina. He made no attempt to do his duty by the older ladies. It was quite clear that in his opinion Nina was the only person in the room worth talking to.

And he wasn't far wrong, in Colin's view. She was like quick-silver, and prettier than ever with this new hairdo of hers. She used to wear her hair longer, but now it was cropped, curling all over her head. It suited her.

'It's my turn now,' he said, going over to her as the impromptu band fell silent for a moment, its members arguing amicably over what to play next.

'There isn't any music—'

'I'm just staking my claim before the red-hot lover springs into action again. Anyway, who needs music?'

Nina ran her fingers through her hair, lifting it up as if to let the air get to it.

'It's terribly hot,' she said. 'Let's go out to the stoep for a bit.'

Colin was aware of Hennie's beam of approval as he followed Nina outside. She had always welcomed him, always made much of him – which had not, he suspected, done his cause any good as far as Nina was concerned. He knew exactly what interpretation Hennie would put upon this joint escape, but even so wasn't about to refuse such an invitation.

They stood on the back stoep, side by side, leaning on the rail without speaking. The garden was bathed in moonlight. From behind them the band started up once more, and the less than romantic strains of 'Roll Out the Barrel' rang out from the house behind them.

'"Moonlight can be cruelly deceptive, Amanda",' Colin quoted in his best Noël Coward accent.

Nina laughed.

'I could think of more atmospheric strains to accompany it. Come on – let's go and sit out there for a bit.' She nodded towards a white-painted garden seat that stood at the far side of the tiny lawn. 'At least we'll be able to hear ourselves think.'

'You realise there'll be talk,' Colin said, tongue in cheek. Nina laughed at that.

'There's always been talk about me,' she said. 'About my foolishness in running around with a wild man like Jan, anyway.'

'Did he get away?'

'Yes. He left for London on Saturday night.'

'Good.' Colin looked at her thoughtfully as he sat down beside her. 'I must say, I thought you'd be married by now.'

Nina was silent for a moment.

'So did I,' she said at last, a little dryly. 'But Jan can be—' She paused, and sighed, thinking better of completing the sentence. 'He says he's not the marrying type,' she said at last. 'He says it's not that he doesn't think a lot of me, just that he hasn't really got room for marriage. I know what he means. He has a—' She hesitated a moment. '—a higher calling,' she finished.

'That sounds grotesquely pompous.'

She laughed at that.

'Not at all! Jan's the least pompous of men. No, that's not it. It's just that he feels—' Again she hesitated. 'He thinks they'll get him in the end. Something will happen. Another Sharpeville, some other crisis, with him in the thick of it. He doesn't know how it will come, from black or from white, but he's pretty sure that come it will. He doesn't want me to be involved.'

'Why would it come from blacks? I can see why some whites object to him, but why would blacks be out to get him? God knows, he's devoted his life to them.'

Nina laughed.

'What a simplistic view you have of the colour question, Colin. Don't you realise how some blacks hate white liberals? They see us as condescending – reaching down from a great height to elevate them to our level, which to them diminishes the importance of their own culture. It's logical enough, I suppose. They don't want integration. That, to them, is no more than a one-way street, with blacks trying to be pseudo-whites. They want nothing less than a black man's country. They want us out. Well, you can see the point, can't you? To them anything else is treachery, and someone like Jan, who has charisma and makes it seem that whites aren't so bad after all – well, he's no more than a focus for that treachery. They see him as a danger.'

'But he helps them,' Colin said. 'As a lawyer, he could earn good money, but instead he takes up all manner of cases – for love, I imagine. It can't be for any financial gain.'

'No, of course it's not. His aim has always been to defend non-whites who can't afford legal representation. He's heart and soul behind all their aspirations – but in all fairness, it has to be said that he doesn't go short. He came into money from some rich relative in England, and he maintains he has enough income from dividends to make legal fees immaterial. I'm not belittling him,' she went on earnestly. 'He does terrific work.'

'And you're equally committed?'

'Of course! Is there any other way to be? For a thinking person, anyway. Oh, I'm not as brave as Jan. I don't put my head above the parapet quite so much, but believe me, anything I can do to get justice, I will. I demonstrated at Paarl last year—'

'Over the Mafeking banishment?'

Colin knew about that, for it had been a *cause célèbre* during the latter part of 1959, dominating the papers for weeks. Mrs Elizabeth Mafeking, President of the Food and Canning Workers' Union, and by all accounts an exemplary wife and mother, had been sentenced to banishment far from her family and friends to a benighted part of the country without amenities of any kind, her crime that of refusing to carry her pass. Demonstrations and representations had eventually mitigated her sentence to a certain extent.

'There are more of us than you might think who hate the activities of this government,' she said.

'I can't say I'm wild about them myself. But be careful, Nina—'

'I'm always careful!' She sighed. 'Tell me, Colin – what do you think is going to happen when the Commonwealth Prime Ministers meet in London in a couple of weeks? Do you think they'll chuck us out? I can't see Verwoerd making any concessions, can you?'

'No,' Colin agreed. 'The knives are out for us, there's no doubt about it. But I can't see Verwoerd doing anything positive about it, can you? He'll just say "Yah-boo, sucks to you, we'll go it alone."' He paused for a moment, and laughed. 'It's dollars to doughnuts your mother doesn't imagine we're sitting out here talking politics.'

Nina laughed, too.

'I suppose there are other things. Back there inside, when we were talking about Margie and Steve, I was thinking how much more simple life would be if one could just ignore all the terrible things that go on and just get on with living.'

'Plenty do. I did myself, for a long time.'

'But not now?' She turned to face him and took hold of his lapels. 'Colin, I'm so glad everything's going well for you. I meant it when I said your Saturday column was good.'

'Come off it, Nina. It's superficial, non-controversial pap. I'm not allowed to say anything that'll rock the boat.'

'It's entertaining, though.'

Colin grunted.

'But it's not exactly the big time, is it?'

'Don't be so impatient! You'll get there.'

'Well, I want to be doing something a bit more significant by the time I'm thirty.'

'Political editor?'

'Don't take the mickey—'

'I'm not! Honestly! I think you'll make it.'

Colin looked at her, thinking how lovely she was; how she made all the other girls he had known since they had parted seem second-rate.

'You're taking a lot on trust, aren't you?' he said. 'I mean it's been so long since we had anything to do with each other that I could have become a fully paid-up member of the Broederbond for all you know.'

She laughed then.

'Not you,' she said. 'Even your non-controversial pap has lines to read between. Anyway, you've given enough hints. You hate *apartheid* as much as I do – admit it! Nothing so inherently evil can ever work.'

'You're right.'

'I knew your heart was in the right place!'

'To be honest, I'm not sure quite what my heart's up to. It must be the moonlight.'

'Come on!' She clearly wasn't going to sit and listen to this sort of dangerous talk. 'We ought to go back.'

Colin didn't move.

'Can we meet for dinner some time?' he asked. 'I could come over to Paarl. Please say yes. We were always good friends, weren't we?'

She stood up and stretched out a hand to pull him up beside her.

'Yes, we were,' she said. 'And are, I hope. It's good to see you again, Colin. I mean it.'

'So we can meet again? Soon?'

'I expect so. Give me a call. Now we really ought to go back inside.'

'You're right about that, too. Your mother will be calling the banns if we stay out here much longer.'

Nina laughed again.

'Don't mind her,' she said. 'She doesn't change, does she?'

Her small, pointed face was lit by moonlight, her eyes shining. Elfin was the word to describe her beauty, but it would take a braver man than he to use such a word to her face. She would hoot with laughter, say he was being sentimental, deride it as a cliché. Even so, he knew of no better description and was aware, as he looked at her, of a painful twist of longing.

'Nor do you, Nina,' he said.

6

Sunday, and the telephone shrilling at eight thirty in the morning did little to get Connie Eksberg's day off to a good start. She and Gert hadn't returned from Seapoint's most fashionable night-spot until close on four o'clock, and her head felt as if it were coming apart. Gert, whom she might have expected to answer the phone at its first ring since it was situated on his side of the bed, slumbered on. It was bound to be for him, she thought fretfully, jabbing him in the ribs. There were times just lately, and this was one of them, when she felt that marrying a policeman was just about the most stupid move she had ever made.

'For God's sake, answer it,' she groaned, as blearily he came to life.

He did so, more asleep than awake.

'Eksberg,' he said, dully.

'Have you heard anything?' Le Roux's voice was becoming irritatingly familiar. It sounded, Eksberg thought, as if he had been up and alert for hours. Or maybe he had simply not slept at all. Undoubtedly there was an edge of anxiety to his voice.

'Er, no.' Gert cleared his throat, desperately striving to sound at least half awake. 'Nothing definite, sir. There seems to have been some complication.'

He closed his eyes, unable, just yet, to cope with the volume and the forcefulness of le Roux's reply.

'There's no need to worry, sir,' he said, when at last the minister fell silent. 'I assure you it's all in hand.' He glanced over his shoulder at Connie. It looked as if she had gone back to sleep, but you never could tell. 'It's a little difficult to give details at the moment.'

'Come and see me later on,' le Roux snapped. 'Eleven o'clock suit you?'

Wearily, Gert closed his eyes once more. Vaguely he remembered making some arrangement the night before – a pool party at someone's house. Lunchtime. Today. Connie was not going to be pleased about this.

'I'll be there, sir,' he said.

In church that same Sunday, old ladies beamed at the Newcotts as they sat in their usual pew. The devoted couple, the pigtailed little girl, the cherubic boy. The ideal family. Such delightful people. An example to all.

Little do they know, Kate thought, trying hard to calm her troubled mind; and little, in fact, do I believe what happened – that Tom and I should have fallen out over Johnny! Funny that they'd spoken, not so long ago, about manufacturing the odd quarrel, just to show that it was possible to make up afterwards.

Probably, as quarrels went, it wasn't such a big one. Maybe it wouldn't even have registered on the Greaves scale. It was simply that they didn't go in for that sort of thing, and Kate found it upsetting. It probably wouldn't have happened, she told herself, if they hadn't had such a rotten night.

Unusually, Vicky had woken up and had twice come into their bedroom in a state of great distress. She'd had a bad dream, she'd told them, trembling and crying; and though the first time Tom had carried her back to her own bed and sat with her until she went to sleep once more, on the second occasion she was so upset that he moved into her bed and Vicky curled up next to Kate.

It was hardly a restful night for either of them, and the game of musical beds continued at dawn when Vicky woke up again and decided to move back to her own room.

'I wonder what on earth got into her?' Kate said, yawning, gratefully accepting the cup of tea that Tom had brought to her in bed. 'What can have upset her?'

'I can't imagine,' Tom replied, his dry tone implying the opposite. He climbed into bed beside her once more. 'Tell you what – why don't we get out into the country after church? Give the kids a breath of fresh air? The weather forecast was quite good.'

'Oh—' Kate's dismay was obvious. 'I was hoping to go to the hospital.'

'You went last night!' It had been something of a sore point, though Tom had said little at the time. He had always regarded

Saturday nights as something special meriting a better-than-average dinner and a bottle of wine.

'Actually,' Kate said, 'I was hoping that you'd come today, too, but I can't quite see what we'd do with the children.'

'Who we'd dump them on, you mean?'

She wasn't accustomed to tetchiness – did not, for the moment, detect the dangerous note in his voice. She laughed, briefly.

'Yes, I suppose that's what I mean. Just for an hour or so. I expect Mrs Nixon would come in—'

'Kate, this is Sunday. My free day. The children expect to see something of me, and I expect to see something of them – and surely, even you can see that whatever's the matter with Vicky isn't going to be helped by leaving her with Mrs Nixon?'

Kate turn to look at him, frowning.

'What on earth do you mean – *even me*?'

'Well, you have been a bit preoccupied lately.'

'Because of Johnny, you mean? For heaven's sake, Tom, this is my *son* we're talking about!'

'We don't know that for certain, do we? But we do know that Vicky is going through a particularly sensitive phase for some reason. She's worried. Are you aware that she's convinced herself that you keep going to the hospital because there's something the matter with you? She thinks you're going to die!'

'Oh, she doesn't. She can't.'

'But she does. She told me so, last night.'

'You convinced her otherwise, I hope.'

'I think so. I assured her you were visiting a sick friend, but I don't know if she believed me. I could tell she thought it very odd, and I'm not surprised.'

Kate sighed.

'What are we to do? I don't want to say anything specific yet.'

'Then maybe you should stop going to the hospital every spare moment until we know exactly who this guy is.'

Slowly Kate turned to look at him in astonishment, as if she could hardly believe her ears.

'Tom, this is my son. I'm sure of it.'

'You can't possibly be sure.'

'The policeman said—'

'I know what the bloody policeman said! You've told me a dozen times.'

'Well, I'm sorry to be so boring about it.'

'Oh, Kate!' Tom reached out to hold her, but she remained rigidly offended. 'Look,' he said placatingly. 'I'm sorry. I know how deeply you feel about this, but do look at it from the kids' point of view. They need you, too. I just don't think we should leave them this afternoon.'

'Your point of view, you mean.'

'That's not fair. They look forward to doing something special at the weekends, all of us together.'

'It would only be for an hour!'

'An hour *or so*, you said. In fact, it would take most of the afternoon, wouldn't it, by the time we got there and back? It's not on, Kate. I'm taking them out somewhere, and I really think you ought to come too.'

She picked up her teacup in silence and took a few sips before speaking.

'I'm not neglecting them, Tom, if that's what you're implying,' she said stiffly.

'No,' Tom said. 'I know you're not – at least, not in any material way. But I don't think you realise—' He paused and Kate looked at him defensively.

'What?'

He hesitated, his expression troubled, and when he spoke he had moderated his voice to make it more emollient.

'Darling, you're not really with us any more, are you? Mentally, you're somewhere else. Vicky's not dim – she knows perfectly well that something cataclysmic has happened to you. My view is that we ought to come clean and tell her the whole truth.'

'No!' Kate's voice was sharp. 'No,' she added more quietly after a moment. 'Whatever the circumstances, whatever the reason, I gave up Johnny. You can't expect Vicky to understand that, especially if she really is feeling insecure; though why she should, I can't imagine.'

'But if this really is Johnny—'

'Then we'll have to tell her eventually, I realise that, but there'll be all the excitement of a new big brother and maybe the whys and wherefores won't bother her so much.'

'Kate—' Tom's voice was persuasive. 'Give the hospital a miss today. After all, Johnny – or whoever he is – isn't going anywhere, is he? When he wakes up and knows where he is and who you are

– and who *he* is, for God's sake! – then you might be justified in spending so much time with him.'

'An hour a day!' Kate's voice was bitter. 'How can you grudge me that, Tom?' She threw off the bedclothes and got out of bed. 'All right. I see your point about the children, so we'll take them out this afternoon. But I'm going to the hospital this evening, no matter what. He needs me. I talk to him.'

'Well, lucky him,' Tom said sourly, as she headed for the bathroom.

The curtains were drawn around Johnny's bed when she arrived that evening, leading her to think that something had happened – he had got better, or dramatically, far worse. But it was simply that a doctor was looking at him.

'Oh—' She had hesitated. 'I'll wait, shall I?'

'It's all right.' The doctor straightened up. He looked young and unsure of himself, with overlong hair and a spindly moustache. 'I was just leaving.'

'How is he? Has there been any more movement? I distinctly saw his eyes flicker underneath the lids the other day.'

'Er—' It was the doctor's turn to hesitate. 'He's making progress. As much as can be expected.'

He left swiftly, and Kate smiled to herself. Doctors! She'd get more information from the most junior nurse. And someone, she thought, should tell that young man that his white coat wasn't as clean as it ought to be. Or his nails. Things had certainly changed since her day.

She moved to the bedside, the doctor forgotten. Tom was forgotten, too, or at least relegated to the back of her mind.

They had walked on the heath that afternoon, and the children had careered along muddy wooded paths, up hills and down, and Kate and Tom had walked and joined in their games, and more importantly had made friends again.

The whole incident, however, had given her pause for thought. It was true, she acknowledged, that she hadn't paid enough attention to Tom just recently. He was as excited about the Shamley Hithe project as she was about Johnny; bubbling over, one could say, and yet last night when he'd been enthusing about the need to preserve and renovate the run-down Georgian houses while opening up this little enclave to form part of the new and contrasting modern centre, she'd really heard very little. When she got back from the hospital, she'd ask for more details. Get him to draw a sketch. Ask some intelligent questions.

It would be so much easier for all concerned, she thought, when everyone accepted the fact that this was her son.

'Wake up, Johnny, and tell them,' she said, bending over him and gently stroking his face. 'Wake up now, there's a good boy. I want you to talk to me for a change.'

But still he slept, the bruises fading a little, the swollen mouth almost restored. A good-looking young man, Kate thought, as she had thought before. An arresting face.

She sat down and took his hand, as she had done before, and continued her narrative.

The house was built of white stone, with a central moulded gable, surrounded by a stoep – a later addition, Kate learned, and said to spoil the classic design. Wide steps led to its open front door, shutters flanked the windows, and on each side were flowers in profusion.

There seemed to Kate, at first sight, a crowd of people at the front of the house – people and dogs; a crowd which resolved itself into a group of five once she had stepped from the car and brought them all into focus, and no more than two large, yellow dogs who leapt delightedly at Guy.

He was equally delighted to see them, but managed, at last, to reduce them to order before introducing her to Joseph, who was, as far as she could gather, the chauffeur and general handyman. He was tall and broad and coffee-coloured, and having greeted her with grave politeness he at once took charge of unloading their luggage. Danny, a whippet-thin youth with an engaging smile, was immediately co-opted to help him, while yet another man in a battered straw hat, who had been sweeping the front steps immediately prior to their arrival, leant on his broom and gave them a gap-toothed grin.

A young girl whom Kate judged to be about fourteen or fifteen, her hair tied in two bunches, stifled nervous giggles as she bobbed her head towards Kate in a modified kind of curtsey.

'This is Rosie, cheekier than ever. *Voetsak*, you little minx!' Playfully Guy shooed the girl away and the giggles spilled over as she ran up the steps. 'And here comes Evalina!'

He opened his arms wide in greeting as one of the fattest women Kate had ever seen waddled down the steps, her pink dress covered by a snowy apron.

'Agh, man, good to see you, Mr Guy,' she cried, stepping into his embrace. 'You bin away so long, we all miss you. And dis your bride! Oh, she jes the prettiest lady!'

'Evalina's the most important person in the entire household,' Guy explained to Kate. 'She's married to Joseph – rules him with a rod of iron, isn't that right, Joseph? – and she brought us up, Sonia and me. What we'd do without her I can't imagine.'

'If she doesn't get back to the kitchen,' Sonia said coldly, 'we'll have to do without coffee. Breakfast seems hours ago.'

'You want breakfast, Mr Guy? I soon cook eggs and sausage and bacon, scrambled eggs the way you like 'em—'

'Thanks, Evalina, but coffee will be fine.'

'On the stoep.' Sonia threw the words over her shoulder as, back like a ramrod, she went briskly up the steps, her peremptory voice in marked contrast to Guy's affectionate tone. At the top, she turned round and addressed Evelina again. 'I suppose my mother is still in bed?'

'No, Miss Sonia.' Evalina was labouring upwards, breathing heavily, taking a little more time about it. 'I give her breakfast an hour ago and she up and dressed now. She so excited! I don't never know her so excited.'

'That's right.' A woman, tall and thin and faded, with silver-gilt hair, had walked out on to the stoep. 'Here I am.' She held her hands out towards Kate, waiting for her to reach the top. 'My dear,' she said, taking hold of both her hands and bending to kiss her, 'welcome to Gramerci. I hope you'll be very happy here.'

'Oh, I will – I'm sure I will. It's all so beautiful.'

'Guy – welcome home, darling.' Mrs Lampard remained holding Kate's hands but inclined her cheek to receive her son's kiss. 'Evalina's right – it does seem that you've been away a long time, but I don't begrudge a minute of it since you've brought back such a lovely young wife. Come along, my dear—' She slid her arm around Kate's shoulders and gently propelled her into the house. 'I'll show you your room before you have your coffee.'

It was a relief to be greeted in such an unequivocal way and Kate was grateful for it; yet there was something in Mrs Lampard's vague but patrician manner that was intimidating. (Think tough –

keep your back straight – be confident, she repeated in her head like a mantra.)

If this was her mother-in-law in an excited mood, Kate thought, what on earth was she like the rest of the time? There seemed a strange aloofness about her manner – a kind of vague, other-worldly detachment, benevolent but myopic, as if her surroundings weren't quite in focus. She reminded herself that Guy had remarked more than once on his mother's frailty. Though Kate had pressed for details, he had remained imprecise. Stomach trouble, she had gathered. A kind of general weakness. Maybe, she thought, it was ill-health that accounted for her remote air, as it surely must explain her pallor and the papery texture of her skin. Even so, it was possible to see that she must have been beautiful in her time. The belle of every ball, her mother had said.

It was dark inside after the sunshine. Kate had an impression of polished wood, glowing rugs, and the gleam of brass. An open door gave her a glimpse of a room with shabby, comfortable chairs and a huge fireplace.

Her mother-in-law led her past this and up a steep flight of stairs and along a corridor, where she threw open a door. 'This was my room when Guy's father first brought me here,' she said. 'He, too, was called Guy. It's quite the nicest room in the house.'

Kate turned to her in dismay.

'We're not turning you out, are we? Oh, we can't do that!'

'My dear Kate, I truly don't mind. In fact, if the truth be known, I welcome it. I've moved to a little cottage of my own just across the back yard. It was a storehouse that wasn't used much any more, so I had it renovated, just as soon as we heard Guy was getting married. I have my own sitting room as well as a bedroom and bathroom and tiny kitchen in case I don't want to come across the yard for meals. Believe me, I couldn't be happier.'

She drifted to the other side of the room and opened the window a little wider, giving Kate a chance to look around her. The room was large, and furnished with massive dark furniture, the wide, rather high bed covered with a white cotton bedspread. The walls, too, were plain, a bowl of roses on a side table the only splash of colour. The overall effect was one of solid but unadorned worth from another, earlier era. The sole concession to modernity was a wash-basin in one corner of the room.

Mrs Lampard indicated the bare walls.

'I took my pictures with me,' she said. 'I was fond of them and thought you would prefer some that appealed particularly to you. Pictures are such individual things, don't you agree? As you will see,' she went on, without waiting for a reply, 'there is a basin, but the bathroom is across the passage.'

'Thank you. You're very kind. It really doesn't seem right, though, that you should have to leave it like this, just because I've come.'

'It seemed perfectly natural to me, and indeed, I find it rather restful, being on my own. I'm more than happy to hand over the reins to you. You are the mistress of the house now.' This last statement was issued in a faraway voice, as unemphatic as if she were talking about about the number of towels provided.

This thought almost proved Kate's undoing, and her jaw dropped a little, but if her mother-in-law was conscious of her dismay, she made no comment on it.

'Someone will be bringing your luggage up shortly,' she said. 'You'll probably be glad of a chance to wash and tidy up a little.' Anxiously, Kate's glance went to the mirror. Was she untidy? Dirty? Should she change? 'Come down whenever you wish,' Mrs Lampard went on. 'You will soon find your way about, I'm sure. Sonia—' Her voice trailed away, as if whatever she had been about to say she had thought better of.

'There's a lot I'll have to learn,' Kate said humbly, when it seemed clear that her mother-in-law would say no more.

'And many willing teachers, I'm sure.'

Sonia? Somehow Kate doubted that she was among their number.

'My mother sent her best wishes to you,' she said hastily. 'She remembers you well.'

'She does? How very kind. Yes, of course, you mentioned in your letter that she thought we'd met . . .' Mrs Lampard's voice dwindled once more, as if it required too much effort to remember such distant events.

'That's right. You went to the same balls. Her name then,' Kate added, as Mrs Lampard continued to look blank, 'was Dorothy Viner.'

'Viner?' Kate knew quite well that she had mentioned the name in her letter too, but clearly the name evoked no memories in Mrs Lampard's mind. 'It was all so long ago,' she said vaguely.

The subject of Dotty being summarily dismissed, Mrs Lampard went on to other matters.

'By the way, my dear, I do hope you'll call me Lilian – until you can legitimately call me Ouma. Granny, that is. I thought it better to say something. The question was one of deep embarrassment to me when I first came to Gramerci as a bride.'

'You're awfully kind. I . . . I'll do my best—'

To call her Lilian? To fit into this family?

No matter what Helen said, she was terrified. Left alone, she acknowledged the fact and wished that Guy would come to give her words of reassurance, make her feel that at least he was on her side.

Which wasn't fair, really. Mrs Lampard – Lilian – was on her side, wasn't she? There was just something about her that was impossible to pin down, something not quite normal, not quite real. Perhaps she was seriously ill, even dying. That would surely explain her air of exhaustion.

Kate sighed, and went, in her turn, to the window. It looked over the front of the house, with a view of the drive and the front lawn and, to the left, a tall hedge covered in pale blue flowers. The garden seemed to continue beyond it, but she could only see glimpses of more grass, more flowers. Beyond that, the vines began, stretching on and on towards distant blue peaks.

There was a knock at the door, and she turned abruptly. Joseph and Danny had brought up her trunk.

'Rosie, she come soon to help unpack,' Joseph said.

'Oh, good. Thank you.'

It was all so feudal, she thought as she washed her hands and tidied her hair with the comb from her handbag. For a moment she stood and looked at herself in the glass over the basin, desperation in her eyes. How was she going to cope – with the servants, with Sonia, with Mrs Lampard? How would she ever bring herself to call her Lilian?

Think tough, she told herself without a great deal of conviction, and turning from the mirror, she went downstairs.

Her homesickness, those first few weeks, took her by surprise. Back in Shenlake she had often thought how wonderful it would be to get away from home and her mother's constant fussing, but now she found she missed the ease and familiarity of it all – the feeling that she was accepted and that she belonged. Here, she felt like a visitor, forced to be on her best behaviour at all times, even with Guy. Perhaps most of all with Guy.

Lilian had been right. The house ran itself, and there seemed no role for her. The office and winery buildings were to the back of the house, beyond the little cottage now occupied by her mother-in-law. On her first day at Gramerci, Guy had shown her the layout – the press, the fermentation tanks, the storehouses. He had taken her to Sonia's office, too. She had been sitting behind a massive desk but had looked up as she and Guy had stepped inside, making no reference to Kate's presence but speaking at once of crates that were ready for shipment, and arrangements she had made for their transportation to the docks.

'I've brought Kate to see the power-house,' Guy said, when this matter was dealt with.

'Oh? Well, do forgive me, but I really am terribly busy so now she's seen it, do take her away, there's a dear.'

'Perhaps later on I could help,' Kate said shyly. 'I have learned to type, you know.'

Sonia had given a tight little smile at the offer.

'How kind,' she said with obvious insincerity. 'I think, though, that I'm better off on my own.' And having spoken, she went back to her work without another word, the faint smile still on her lips.

Guy had pulled a face and ushered Kate out. She wasn't to mind, he said. Sonia was like that. He should have known better than to disturb her when she was busy – and as for helping her, well, it really was impossible for anyone to do that. Sonia kept all the records and managed all the correspondence. Her system was a mystery to anyone else, but although she never threw anything away and was totally fanatical about keeping the most insignificant letter or order, she knew where to lay her hands on anything at any time. No one else was allowed anywhere near her files. There really was nothing for Kate to do.

She decided to learn Afrikaans – an essential move, since Sonia was often moved to use it when she conversed with Guy in the evenings, even though she was perfectly fluent in English. A retired teacher, dour and desiccated, was enrolled for the purpose, visiting Gramerci three times a week for hour-long lessons. Kate found her teacher uninspiring and the language difficult. She sighed as she laboured over the copious amount of homework she was expected to get through; still, she knew it was something she had to do and she put all her effort into it.

For relief, and because there were still many empty hours to fill, she turned her attention to the garden. The part in front of the house, immediately visible to any visitor, was immaculate, the flowerbeds below the stoep and in the centre of the lawn colourful and well tended; but the smaller, enclosed part beyond the hedge with the blue flowers – now identified as plumbago – presented a rather different picture. Here there were beds that had become overgrown, many of the plants gone to seed. Kate fell upon it almost with relief, determined to restore it to its former beauty. She prevailed upon Guy to spare her an estate worker as an extra gardener and together they took it in hand; and in so doing, she found herself happier than at any time since coming to South Africa.

Though her homesickness was acute, she could not deny that the garden and its surroundings were more beautiful than she could have imagined. The glorious colour of the jacaranda trees had taken her breath away. They had flowered quite soon after her arrival, the month of November bringing into bloom the hydrangeas and agapanthus and roses, and lush foliage such as Kate had never seen. The candlewood tree was a particular delight, covered as it was with small white blossoms. She often sat on the seat within it during the hot afternoons, reading or writing letters.

'Who cut it away like this?' she asked Guy on one momentous occasion when he was sitting beside her – momentous because she seemed so seldom to get him entirely to herself. He had not let marriage change his life in any particular and most evenings found him playing golf or tennis or rugby. On Saturdays there was almost always a match of some kind. It was only on Sundays that they sometimes went out together, to one of the beaches or for a drive so that she could see surrounding countryside. And even then Sonia often elected to come with them.

'We don't know for sure,' Guy said. 'But we think it must have been my great-grandmother's idea. She laid out the garden, we know that, so it seems logical to suppose she ordered this to be done, too.' He gave a reminiscent chuckle. 'We used to love it when we were kids.'

Kate put her hand through his arm, feeling closer to him that evening than she had done for some time, touched by the thought of him as a little boy. She wished there were more moments like this.

'Our children will love it, too,' she said.

She knew the history of Gramerci – had very early been told of the way the Huguenot, Jules Lampard, had, in the seventeenth century, come to South Africa from France by way of Amsterdam to work among the vines for Mathinus de Groot, a Dutch farmer, and how he had impressed everyone with his knowledge and industry, especially Aletta de Groot, Mathinus's daughter. The two had married and produced sons, and it was from this stock that Guy and Sonia had sprung.

Kate loved the thought of continuing the line and was disappointed that so far there was no sign of this taking place. In her innocence, she had thought that once the decision to have a baby had been made, conception would follow at once, but another month had passed and her hopes had been dashed. Was there really something wrong with her? Love-making had become no more pleasurable than it had been at the beginning. Perhaps that was some kind of indication that she was lacking in some essential way.

Guy thought so, she knew – he had hinted at it more than once; yet here, away from the house in the shelter of the candlewood tree, he seemed happy in her company, and for her part she was able to relax, suddenly convinced that everything would turn out well in the end, all their problems somehow resolve themselves. Maybe Sonia would find a man and get married – even move away! On an evening like this, anything seemed possible.

'Hasn't Sonia ever thought of getting married?' she asked Guy, following this train of thought.

He gave a grunt of laughter.

'No one's ever been good enough for Sonia,' he said. 'She's had admirers, of course, over the years, but I don't think there's been one she's really taken seriously – oh yes, there was one! But he was something big in the mines and wanted to whisk her off to Jo'burg. She wouldn't leave Gramerci, so that was the end of it. I don't recall that losing him bothered her too much. She didn't show it, anyway – but then Sonia's a deep one. You never quite know what she's thinking.'

'No,' Kate agreed, her voice small, her hopes dwindling and dying. It was a depressing thought, that Sonia would be with them at Gramerci for ever. She held more tightly to Guy and leaned her head against his shoulder, wishing that they could stay hidden away like this. She'd just have to try harder to get on with her sister-in-law, she thought drearily, though sometimes she felt the more she tried, the more Sonia despised her.

From the beginning Kate had been aware of an expression of amused derision in her eyes, a look which seemed to imply that she was just an interloper who would never be one of the family. Two months on, she felt no more accepted. Except on the occasions when Lilian came over to the house to dinner, the conversation was always confined to matters concerning the vineyard, often conducted in Afrikaans, at least in part. Though she was beginning to understand a word here and there, she knew it would be some time before she could appreciate all the nuances.

Helen remained a source of comfort. They did not meet as often as Kate would have liked during the day, for Helen was involved in any number of charities and cultural events which took up her time, but she was usually present at the dinners and dances and parties attended by the Lampards. And there were *braais*, of course. *Braai*, Kate had quickly learned, was short for *braaivleis*, where food was cooked on fires out in the open – a mode of entertainment which was highly popular in South Africa, but totally new to her. Soon after her arrival they had given one at Gramerci for the purpose of introducing her to all Guy's friends. Most of the crowd who had been on the *Dunnotar Castle* had been invited: Flick Masterson – this time with Brian in tow – and the hateful Marcia, with her husband Laurie. And of course, Helen and Paul.

It was on this occasion that she heard the name of Greta mentioned again for the first time since arriving in South Africa.

Determined to be a good hostess, she had joined a group of women she barely knew in time to hear one of them ask another if it were true that Greta and Neil Carlton were returning to Cape Town. It was a question that was never answered, for another member of the group had frowned warningly at the speaker and begun, rather feverishly, to talk about a new dress shop, recently opened in Adderley Street.

'Who's Greta?' Kate steeled herself to ask Guy when everyone had gone.

'Greta?' Guy sounded innocent enough. 'Oh, just one of the crowd. She married a chap old enough to be her father.'

'Neil Carlton,' Kate said.

Guy looked at her briefly.

'That's right,' he said. 'Why the interest?'

Kate shrugged her shoulders.

'No reason,' she said. 'I heard someone talking about them, that's all. It seems they're coming back to Cape Town.'

'So I heard,' Guy said. 'Flick told me.'

She would, Kate thought bitterly, no more fond of the woman than she had been on board ship. Soon after Kate's arrival at Gramerci there had been a paragraph in the *Ladies' Pictorial*, penned by Flick:

'No prizes for guessing why Guy Lampard of Gramerci Estate, Constantia, wore such a proud smile on the voyage back to South Africa,' she had written. 'He was bringing with him his beautiful young bride, the former Miss Kate Dearing of Shenlake in Oxfordshire (picture inset), who no doubt will be as big a social asset in Cape Town as she was on the *Dunnotar Castle*. All Guy's many friends wish them well and will join your correspondent in welcoming this lovely newcomer to our shores.'

If the piece hadn't been written by Flick, and if she hadn't brought the *Dunnotar Castle* into it, then Kate might, possibly, have taken these sentiments at their face value. As it was, she wondered if the tongue in cheek was as obvious to everyone else as it was to her.

She was quite sure that Sonia was amused by the article, if no one else. She'd read it with her customary derisive smile that seemed to say that the thought of Kate as a social asset was the joke of the season – but perhaps, Kate told herself, she was being unnecessarily touchy. Sonia hadn't actually said anything.

She wanted to like Sonia, wanted it very much, for it was clear that Guy thought her wonderful. And she *was* wonderful, in many ways. She was so competent and capable, so knowledgeable about wines, yet at the same time always looked marvellous, even when she hadn't taken any trouble over her clothes and make-up. No one, Kate thought, could call her beautiful, or even pretty, but she was handsome in an indefinably glamorous way. She had style. And so much self-confidence! Kate longed to be like her, in this if in nothing else – but how could she begin to have confidence in herself when Sonia seemed to regard her as a child? She longed for the chance to prove to her sister-in-law that she wasn't entirely feather-brained and that she had, sometimes at least, something reasonably intelligent to add to the conversation.

Kate was the first to admit that her ignorance of the wine trade was total; how could it be otherwise? To her, a grape was a grape, but here the words Shiraz and Pinot and Gamay were bandied about, blends and casks – even corks, for heaven's sake! – were discussed with animation. From time to time, when the opportunity arose, she asked for enlightenment, but was seldom given any. Guy was too impatient to explain in any depth, while Sonia seemed oddly possessive about her knowledge, as if by sharing it she would lose power.

'If I were you,' she advised Kate loftily, 'I shouldn't bother my pretty little head about it.'

'But I'd *like* to know,' Kate insisted. 'It all sounds fascinating.'

It took her some time to realise that she had been damned for ever in Sonia's eyes on her very first night at Gramerci when, at dinner, she had expressed a preference for a light, run-of-the-mill Hock over the Cabernet Gramerci which was the estate's speciality but which proved too dark and strong-flavoured for her taste. From that moment on, Sonia regarded her as a hopeless case, with neither palate nor sense, fit for nothing but domestic concerns.

At least her fears regarding the running of the house had been proved groundless. Each morning she went to the kitchen after breakfast to discuss with Evalina the meals for the rest of the day – or, more accurately, to listen to Evalina telling her what she intended to cook. From time to time she made the odd suggestion, but on the whole it was a case of murmuring approval as Evalina expanded on Mr Guy's tastes – what he had liked as a child, how she had cooked this and that just the way he wanted it, how no one else could get it quite right.

She liked going to the kitchen, where Evalina's two little girls played on the step, and where Bokkie, her thirteen-year-old son, sat in the corner, reading his school books or teasing Rosie, his big sister. They spoke to each other in the *taal*, the Coloureds' version of Afrikaans, but both were equally at home with English.

Evalina was a happy woman who found much to laugh at, and her domain was a cosy and comfortable place, full of warm baking smells and the scent of spices. It was from Evalina that she learned that Lilian Lampard – Oumissus, as Evalina called her – had never been strong. Had never been, so Evalina said, *right* since the birth of Mr Guy.

'He more my chile than hers,' she said once. 'He like my own.'

Which was all right for her, Kate thought, but sad for his mother.

Kate saw very little of her mother-in-law, whom she was no nearer calling 'Lilian' than she was on that first day. She tended to wander, wraith-like, from her cottage to the main house and back again, seldom putting in an appearance before midday, and apparently occupying her time with knitting complicated garments in patterns that made Kate gape in honest admiration.

'You must choose something for yourself, dear,' she said, seeing Kate's interest. But she seldom appeared to finish anything for herself, let alone embark on work for someone else.

'She's in a knitting phase,' Sonia said with amusement, one day when Kate remarked on the work in progress. 'One has to admit she's clever with her hands.' On her lips, it hardly sounded like a compliment.

'She's artistic, too,' Kate said. 'She showed me some water-colours she'd painted.'

Sonia laughed.

'Terrible, aren't they? They were last year's craze. Mother never sticks at anything – which as far as her pictures are concerned is probably just as well.'

'I rather liked them,' Kate said; which was, in fact, the truth, but even if this had not been the case, she would have gone to the stake rather than admit it to Sonia. She was beginning to see Lilian as nothing more nor less than a victim, and she went out of her way to chat to her at every opportunity. Even so, there was never any hint of intimacy. Only once did Kate feel she had got within touching distance, and this was on an afternoon when they were taking tea together in the sitting room, having been driven from the stoep by a sudden shower. Eating a piece of chocolate cake with appreciation, Kate was moved to comment on Evalina's skill in the kitchen.

'I taught her how to make this,' Mrs Lampard said. 'And my mother-in-law taught me.' She gave a brief laugh, indicating with an inclination of her head the portrait which hung over the fireplace. 'That one up there. Old Johanna.' She paused before adding, in her strange, faraway voice: 'It was just about the only kind thing she did – for me, at any rate.'

'Oh!' Kate wasn't sure how to take this. She had always thought the woman in the picture looked somewhat forbidding, but it hardly seemed polite to say so.

'She didn't like me,' Mrs Lampard explained. 'Didn't approve of me.'

'But why—?'

'My dear, I was English. That was enough. Johanna honestly believed that the Afrikaner was chosen of God, superior in every way to the *verdomde* English, and that I would bring doom and disaster to them all.'

'How terrible!'

Lilian looked up at the picture again and gave a brief, unamused laugh.

'I suppose one must be fair,' she said. 'She had some good qualities. She was strong and determined and loyal.'

'But not to you!'

'She saw no reason to be. She had always disliked the British for what she saw as their arrogant attitude towards the Afrikaners. The Dutch were here first, you know – that's something no one can deny – and they've never forgotten it. They set up a victualling station at the Cape for ships *en route* to the Dutch East Indies in the early seventeenth century, but it wasn't until late in the eighteenth that the British seized the Cape to stop the French using it for their ships *en route* for India. There was trouble from the first, all culminating in the Boer War, of course, when it has to be said that the British behaved less than creditably. Johanna had an uncle who was killed in the fighting, and a cousin whom she claimed had been cruelly mistreated in a concentration camp, which of course made her hate them – us – all the more.'

'She could hardly blame you for that. Anyway, it was all so long ago!'

'Not to Johanna,' said Lilian. She sighed. 'And not really to me, I have to confess. I can remember soldiers going off to the Boer War when I was a child in England. They looked so heroic in their uniforms. I don't think it occurred to any of us that they weren't, perhaps, wholly justified. We thought God was on their side and that they couldn't possibly be beaten. And of course, in the end, they weren't, which did nothing to help Johanna accept an English daughter-in-law.'

'At least your husband can't have felt that way.'

Lilian smiled faintly but failed to comment on this.

'My dear,' she said. 'Do have some more of this cake. It really is delicious, isn't it? Tell me, have you tasted Evalina's *soet koekies*? They're quite wonderful – sweet biscuits that simply melt in the mouth. You must get her to make some.'

It was a determined effort to change the subject, but Kate was reluctant to leave it at that. She was, she felt, beginning to learn something important about her mother-in-law at last.

'Is . . . is Sonia at all like Johanna?' she asked hesitantly.

Lilian smiled faintly.

'Tell me,' she said after a moment, not attempting to answer the question. 'How do you get on with her? She's not the easiest person in the world.'

'No.' Was it rude to agree? Kate could think of nothing else to say. 'Well,' she said after a moment, 'I don't think she likes me much. I get the feeling she thinks I'm just a silly little girl.' She gave a small, self-deprecating laugh, but if she wanted reassurance she was to be disappointed.

'Of course, she adores Guy,' Lilian said. 'She'd resent any girl who married him, I dare say. Especially an English girl. You see, there is quite a lot of old Johanna in Sonia, I can't deny it.' She sighed. 'I wish I could,' she added.

In view of what had gone before, Kate found this less than comforting.

'We actually talked quite a lot,' Kate said to Guy, when later that night she was giving him an edited account of the conversation. 'Most of the time she says so little. I hope she doesn't feel she has to keep out of the way now that I'm here.'

Guy assured her that this was far from the case.

'Not at all! She likes you, she told me, but she's always been happy with her own company. And Larry's, of course.'

These last words were added with amused contempt, and Kate made no response to them. She found Larry Donoghue's position in the household rather puzzling. He was an artist who lived in a cottage on the far side of the estate once occupied by a manager, and he seemed to have a privileged position as far as Lilian was concerned, though Guy had made it clear he thought less than nothing of the man.

He had lived on the estate for four years, Kate learned. After Guy had taken over the running of the vineyards, a manager was deemed unnecessary and the cottage had lain idle until Lilian, in those days involved in her painting phase, had met Larry at an exhibition of his work. She had either been bowled over by his talent or suckered into paying over the odds for worthless daubs, depending on whose version she was to believe. Lilian herself naturally held the first view. Kate, though she had no real knowledge of art, thought his pictures odd but delightful. It was Larry's paintings that had been removed from the room occupied by Kate and Guy and now hung in Lilian's small domain.

On finding that he was looking for somewhere cheap to live, Lilian had offered him the empty manager's cottage. His tenancy, Kate could tell from various comments made both by Sonia and Guy, had been a bone of contention at the time, and irritation with the situation still surfaced occasionally, though it was clear that this was a matter on which Lilian would brook no argument.

The two of them seemed very close. Kate couldn't fail to see that though he never came to the main house, Larry visited her almost every day, walking into the cottage without bothering to knock or ring the bell. They must, she thought, be very good friends indeed. He was a small man with dark hair cropped close to his head, curious pale eyes and rather a sweet mouth. His skin was lined but for all that he had a youthful look about him and Kate found it impossible to guess what age he might be. He could, she thought, be forty or sixty, or anything in between. It wasn't out of the question to think that he and Lilian might be more than friends.

When she put this suggestion into words, Guy roared with laughter.

'Him?' he said. 'That little pervert? Oh no, my sweet, Mother's quite safe with our Larry. He wouldn't know what to do with a woman if she paraded naked in front of him.'

'Oh!' Kate, unaware that such a thing as homosexuality existed, looked bewildered. 'Well, I hardly imagined she'd do that.'

Guy laughed again, finding her ignorance amusing.

'Don't bother your little head about it, sweetie,' he said.

It was a few days later that Kate, driven by Joseph, went into Cape Town to meet Helen for a morning's shopping.

'I'm so tired,' she said to Helen over coffee at Stuttafords, 'of being told not to bother my head about things. What am I supposed to do all day? Oh, I've got the wretched Afrikaans lessons and there's the garden and people ask me out to coffee or tea from time to time, but it's only a way of filling time. I went to Marcia's yesterday – not because I wanted to but because I didn't have anything else to do. Suddenly, in the middle of hearing who was having an affair with whom, I wanted to scream! It all seemed so futile, so pointless – so boring! Everyone ought to have something to bother about. I mean, if you don't, there doesn't seem much point to living, does there?'

'No.' Helen looked at her thoughtfully. It occurred to her that less than three months of marriage was a very short time in which to decide there wasn't much point to living. It was clear to her, and had been clear for some time, that Kate didn't have nearly enough to fill her days and she felt guilty, knowing that she was in a position to remedy the situation. However, Paul had warned her not to get Kate involved in the charitable works which kept her busy outside the home. Guy didn't want her dashing about all over the place in less than salubrious surroundings, he said. She was too young, too impressionable.

Now, looking at her, Helen decided that she had gone along with this masculine conspiracy long enough.

'You must learn to drive,' she said decisively. 'Then you can get out and about more. You'll find all sorts of things you can do then – voluntary work, for one thing. Didn't you tell me you'd done a first aid course?'

'Yes, I did,' Kate said. She sighed a little. It seemed like another life, that class in Shenlake village hall – as if it had all happened a million years ago. There had been, she remembered sadly, quite a lot of laughter involved, especially when they practised bandaging. 'I didn't exactly qualify for anything, though.'

'Never mind. I've got a doctor friend who runs a clinic in District Six, an offshoot of the church, and I go there myself on Friday mornings for the mother and baby session. We could really do with some help.'

'I don't know if Guy—'

'Would approve? No, he probably wouldn't. Paul doesn't, either. You only have to mention District Six to have them going into fits.'

'Why? What's it like?'

Helen laughed.

'Noisy. Dirty. Crowded. Full of shebeens and whores and drunken sailors. In short, a slum. I love it!'

'Oh.' Kate hardly knew what to make of that.

Helen explained a little more fully.

'Seriously, it's indescribably awful – but there's something wonderful about it, too. A spirit – a feeling – I don't know how to explain it.'

'Is it safe?'

'I wouldn't set foot in it at night, but during the day it's fine.' She looked at Kate quizzically, head on one side. 'You know, I really think you ought to do this clinic thing. It would be an education.'

'I'd like to. And I'd like to learn to drive, too.'

Why hadn't she thought of that before? How wonderful it would be to go into Cape Town whenever she wanted to! True, Joseph would drive her now if she asked him, but she always felt guilty about taking him away from other duties unless she had some specific, grown-up reason for doing so. Today she had needed to visit the hairdresser – an errand which Guy had readily agreed was overdue.

'I can't imagine why Guy hasn't suggested it himself,' Helen said. 'This is a country where a woman needs to drive. I'll teach you, if you like.'

'Would you?' Kate looked at her with her eyes shining. But almost immediately she remembered Guy's strictures about women drivers – all women except Sonia, of course – and her enthusiasm died a little. The chances were that he'd want to teach her himself, which, in view of the disastrous table tennis lessons on board ship, was a prospect she found distinctly unnerving. On the other hand, he might dismiss the idea altogether – tell her she had Joseph at her disposal, she really had no need to bother her pretty little head about driving herself. She sighed once more. 'I'll talk to Guy,' she told Helen. 'I'd really love you to teach me, but—' She paused, and Helen laughed.

'But because I'm female he would think I'd teach you to grind the gears and drive on the clutch, not to mention accelerate out of side roads into the path of oncoming lorries. I know. I've heard it all.' She looked at Kate with affectionate amusement. 'You know, we South African women have to stand up for ourselves. Our menfolk tend to think we should be tied to home and hearth with pretty pink ribbons.'

Kate laughed ruefully, nodding agreement.

'Don't I know it! It's funny, though,' she added. 'Sonia seems to be an exception to everything. Guy regards her as some sort of superwoman.'

'Oh, Sonia!' Helen laughed, too. 'Sonia's a law unto herself. I don't imagine she's the easiest person in the world to live with. How do you get on with her?'

'You're the second person to ask me that in the last few days,' Kate said. 'I can only say what I said to Guy's mother. I don't think she likes me.'

'What was Mrs Lampard's reaction to that?'

'She didn't seem very surprised. She told me that she had a hard time with old Johanna, her mother-in-law, because she was English. She implied that Sonia felt the same.'

'It could be,' Helen admitted slowly. 'Some Afrikaners do feel that way. Historically the Cape is more Anglicized than the Transvaal because it was under British dominion for so long, sold by the Dutch East India Company for six million pounds, if you can believe it. A lot of the old die-hard Afrikaners couldn't take it – hence the Great Trek and the founding of the new republic in the Transvaal. The majority stayed in the Cape, though, and adapted to new ways. Or didn't adapt, I suppose, according to their nature. Old Johanna Lampard adapted less well than many, it seems, and Sonia's a chip off the old block.'

'Mrs Lampard said Johanna couldn't forget the Boer War. The British treated the Boers badly, she said.'

Helen pulled a face.

'I hate to admit it, but she's right,' she said. 'Farms were burnt, women and children were imprisoned in concentration camps. Twenty thousand of them died of typhoid.'

Kate's face twisted with the horror of it.

'*We* did that? Surely we didn't!'

'I'm afraid we did. You have to face it. But that isn't the only reason why some Afrikaners dislike the British on principle. They think that no matter how long they live out here, the English still talk about 'home', meaning England. Afrikaners see that as a lack of real commitment to this country. For them, 'home' is South Africa – nowhere else. And then there's the race question—' She paused a moment, while Kate looked at her enquiringly.

'Tell me,' she said.

'You see,' Helen went on, 'most Afrikaners feel that they are ordained by God to keep the blacks in subjection. And the Coloureds. They can quote the Bible at you, chapter and verse – Joshua, I think it is – proving that black men are the hewers of wood and drawers of water and that God has commanded that the races should live separately for ever and ever.'

'Guy and Sonia certainly think that,' agreed Kate. 'It seems so strange – I was asking Guy about it the other night, how it is that he can be so fond of Evalina and Joseph yet be so dismissive of blacks and Coloureds in general.'

'How did he answer you?' Helen asked curiously.

'Oh, he just waffled about God having made us all differently. The white man is genetically superior, he says. It's been proved scientifically. And as for being fond of Evalina – well, he's fond of his dogs, he said. He'd do anything for them – feed them well, look after their well-being, be devastated if anything happened to them – but he wouldn't expect them to represent him in Parliament or eat at the same table. I think,' she added hastily, seeing Helen's outraged expression, 'that he was kind of joking. Trying to shock me.'

Helen looked unconvinced.

'Maybe,' she said. 'But that's the way they all think, all Afrikaners. No, that's not true. Just most of them. Oh, I'm not saying that all Englishmen feel differently – we've already established that an Englishman can be as beastly as anyone else – but on the whole they have a less rigid outlook. They at least pay lipservice to the concept that all men are born equal and that one day this will be a country where we can all live together – black, white, Indian and Coloured – without barriers. Some of us even believe it.'

Kate made up her mind there and then.

'I'll come to the clinic,' she said. 'Whatever Guy says.'

7

Guy reluctantly accepted her decision to work at the baby clinic on Friday mornings, mainly because Sonia unexpectedly gave her support to the plan. It wasn't, Kate soon realised, that she thought there was any real merit in it, rather that she was afraid that her sister-in-law's boredom could reach the point where Guy might be tempted to find her something to do around the office.

'But if you must go to such an area, Joseph will drive you there and back,' he said. 'I don't want you attacked by some drunken *skolly*—'

'There's no need. Helen said she'd pick me up.'

'It's out of her way.'

'Oh, Guy! How can you say that? She only lives half a mile away.'

'Don't fuss, Guy.' Sonia spoke crisply. 'They're not proposing to stand on street corners or patrol at dead of night. Helen's been doing this for years, and she's never come to any harm.' Kate smiled at her, grateful for this unexpected support, but Sonia did not smile back. 'You should be aware of the dangers, though,' she said to Kate. 'Keep your wits about you, and don't wear any expensive jewellery.'

Kate toyed with the idea of saying that she'd actually thought of wearing a diamond tiara, but knew from experience that such flights of whimsy were lost on Sonia, who was totally devoid of a sense of humour.

'And for heaven's sake,' Sonia went on, 'take a hot bath when you get home. We don't want you bringing any nasty District Six bugs back here.'

Kate said nothing to this, but she and Helen laughed about it together on their way to the clinic the following Friday.

'Good old Sonia,' Helen said. 'She's priceless, isn't she?'

'I don't know what to make of her,' Kate confessed. 'I mean, she stood up for me over going to the clinic, but I think it must be the first time she's agreed with me about anything, ever since I came to Gramerci. Maybe she's getting resigned to me.'

'Hm.' Helen shot her a glance. 'How is Mrs Lampard these days?' she asked after a moment.

'She's all right.' Kate looked at her curiously. 'Why? What's the matter with her? Everyone asks after her health as if she's been ill, but she seems perfectly all right to me.'

Helen smiled at her.

'Well, that's good,' she said, not answering the question. 'Who knows,' she went on. 'Maybe someone will come and find the way to Sonia's heart. Sweep her off her feet. One can always hope.'

Kate sighed. There were times when she wondered if Sonia had a heart at all; but if she had, she thought, it was probably a hard, nobbly little thing, preserved in a cask of Cabernet Gramerci.

District Six was, as Helen had indicated, an assault on the senses. Hanover Street, the area's main thoroughfare, was choked with humanity and market stalls. Battered lorries blared their horns, blocking the road as shouting blacks unloaded wares.

'They all seem to be giving different orders,' Kate said, wonderingly. 'We'll never get through.'

'Don't worry. We will.'

It was hard to see how. The entire district seemed a jumble of sights and sounds; a mêlée of colours – the shrieking reds and pinks, lime greens and acid yellows of knitted berets or bandannas above black faces, of the shirts worn under drooping jackets designed for someone else. There were men in sharp suits, men in rags; they sat on the pavement, their feet in the gutter, playing games with dice, or in the shade of a shop's overhang, sleeping off their hangovers, waiting for the next. There were bicycles and chickens and cats and dogs. Women shopped at the stalls, their baskets filled with tomatoes, oranges, loquats, mangos, shouting to each other, back and forth. Somewhere a horn was shattering the air – a snoek-horn, Helen told Kate.

Slowly, slowly they inched their way along, turning soon into a lesser road, and then an even lesser one. Here squalid dwellings seemed to press in on them from either side, peeling plaster revealing broken bricks, some with rags at the windows, some with frayed curtains hanging over the open door.

There were children everywhere, laughing, playing, oblivious to the dirt and squalor. They stared at the car, some waving and shouting in recognition, a small bunch of them running after it. An old man sat on a doorstep playing a trumpet; another, clearly drunk, gyrating with arms outstretched on a waste piece of land, voice uplifted in song.

Helen grinned at her.

'You'll learn to love it,' she said. 'The clinic's just ahead of us – that brick building at the corner. There's room at the side to park the car, but I have to find a trustworthy-looking boy to guard it for a tikky.' A tikky was three pence; riches, Kate guessed, for a child in District Six.

Friday was the morning when mothers presented their babies for weighing and could, if necessary, see a doctor for advice. Some were given powdered baby milk at a reduced fee.

'But only on my say-so,' said the doctor in charge, a girl called Jane Ryder with bobbed brown hair and round spectacles who looked no older than Helen. 'It's a last resort. I preach the gospel that breast-feeding is best, especially in these kinds of circumstances when no one understands the first thing about sterilisation. So don't part with a tiny tin of it, Kate, without a little chitty from me.'

Christmas was approaching and, to mark it, someone had hung a few festive streamers from the corners of the room, meeting at the single light suspended from the middle of the ceiling. A bunch of balloons, half deflated, drooped overhead.

'Someone should blow those up,' Helen said. 'They look positively obscene.'

There was, however, no time for such irrelevancies. From the beginning they were besieged with mothers and children of all ages from birth to some that looked close on four or five. Kate was given the job of checking names and making a note of the weights, and also accepting the token payment from those for whom the milk was considered needful. It was a job that anyone could have done, she realised, but she didn't mind. It was enough to be there, among other people, doing something useful for a change and making sure she did it efficiently.

Her admiration of Helen, already great, grew by the moment. She knew most of the patients by name – remembered older children, now at school, and could ask about elderly parents. She joked and laughed and listened in such a way that no one could doubt that she cared about them, was concerned about their problems and anxious to help. She was knowledgeable, too, Kate could see. It was her job to deal with minor complaints and injuries, screening child after child before passing those with more serious problems to the doctor who would have been quite incapable, through sheer force of numbers, to cope with all comers.

The noise was incredible, with babies crying, toddlers shouting, mothers exchanging gossip, voices raised to make themselves heard over the din, thus increasing it still further. Smiling shyly, going about her job, Kate felt herself on the edge of things, a little battered by the sheer volume of it all.

'Well?' Helen said, as they edged their way homeward. 'Are you still in one piece?'

Kate laughed.

'It was hectic, wasn't it? But, yes – I survived it. In fact, I enjoyed it. Jane's wonderful, isn't she? I wish—' She paused, and laughed in a shame-faced kind of way.

'Wish what?'

'Well—' She laughed again. 'Just seeing her like that, doing such marvellous work, makes me wish I'd studied medicine. Which is crazy – I never even passed School Certificate! My school didn't go in for things like that, and what I know about science you could write on the head of a pin, but still I think I would have loved it. Maybe,' she added after a moment, 'I should have trained as a nurse.'

'Instead of marrying Guy?'

Hastily Kate denied this.

'No. No, of course not.'

She fell silent, her attention caught by the scene outside the window. Helen had brought the car to a halt to allow an ancient crone, dressed in rags, to cross the road. Matted grey hair fell almost to her shoulders and there was something wrong with her, some deformity, which caused her to creep sideways like a crab. She looked at them as she passed, baring toothless gums in a way that could have been a smile or a grimace. Kate suspected the latter.

'They must hate us,' she said unhappily as the car moved on. 'They have so little.'

'So little,' Helen echoed. 'And no hope – that's the worst thing.

I'm constantly amazed by the number who seem *not* to hate us, which isn't to say there aren't plenty who do. What's to become of this country, Kate? I ask myself that question all the time. Things seem to go from bad to worse.'

'Surely it's obvious that people shouldn't live like this?'

'Well, yes. You'd think so. But now, with the Depression causing so much hardship everywhere, there are masses of poor whites whose circumstances are almost as bad. Every bit as bad, in some cases. They'll take any job going – labouring, anything – so the situation of blacks and Coloureds just gets worse. There's nothing left for them to do.'

Kate thought this over.

'It's complicated, isn't it?' she said. Helen laughed, without humour.

'That,' she said, 'is something of an understatement.'

Over lunch, back in the more salubrious surroundings of Gramerci, Guy asked Kate how her morning had gone.

'Very well,' she said. 'I enjoyed it. I felt useful, for once.'

'Weighing babies!' Sonia looked amused. 'It's all a total waste of time, you know. These people will be back feeding them on tea and home-brew before they've left the clinic.'

'No, that's not true,' Kate said defensively. 'A lot of them want to learn about nutrition and hygiene—'

'And you, naturally, were able to instruct them?' Sonia smiled.

'No, of course not. Others did that. I just kept the records, but I could see how babies who were underweight not so long ago are thriving now.'

Sonia had no comment to make on this but turned immediately to Guy to speak of a large order for Cabernet Gramerci that had been received from England and the conversation progressed on accustomed lines, with Kate eating in silence, having nothing to add.

That afternoon she took a half-written letter to Nancy out to the candlewood tree to add a further instalment, mostly describing her morning at the clinic.

And though Sonia obviously thinks it's all a great waste of time [she wrote], it seems to me that we're doing a little bit of good, even if it's on a tiny scale. And it is a tiny scale, and not nearly enough, I'm quite aware of that. However,

*if I managed to find a way to build wonderful houses for
everyone, endow hundreds of hospitals and schools, solve the
employment problem and stop the snails eating the vines, I
have the feeling it wouldn't be enough for Sonia! She'd still look
at me as if I ought to creep back under the nearest stone.*

*I can't believe that Christmas is nearly here. I keep thinking
of what you and everyone at home will be doing – carols and
presents and decorating the church and all that. Peter wrote to
say he gave up a super invitation to his friend's house because
he didn't like to think of Mummy at home on her own without
me, but now she tells me that she's accepted an invitation to
Highlands for both of them, so what he's going to think about
that I can't imagine. Or rather, I can imagine it only too well!
Uncle R and Auntie G's idea of a jolly Christmas party is to sit
and eat their turkey in paper hats, solemnly discussing Affairs
of the Day and how young people these days are all going to
the bad, while Norah and Ethne sit smirking silently because
they know it's other young people they're talking about, not
them, horrid little goody-goodies that they are! Actually, I
don't know that it will be a lot better here when it comes
to Christmas dinner, but at least we have all been invited to
a party on Christmas night at the home of some old friends of
the family who live in a gorgeous house overlooking the sea just
outside Cape Town at a place called Muizenberg. It seems it's
a sort of tradition. They have a Christmas party every year
and ask absolutely everyone, and Guy very sweetly said I
could have a new dress for it because although I had several
new ones to come out here, I've worn them over and over.
I'm going shopping with Helen tomorrow to find one, but I've
already seen the one I want. I think. It's kind of misty blue
and a bit floaty, with diamante straps . . .*

'You look,' said a voice behind her, 'like the spirit of twilight.'

'Oh!' Kate whirled round to see Larry Donoghue standing behind
her. 'Oh,' she said again, this time on a note. She laughed.
'Is that good?'

'I think so. Twilight.' He appeared to savour it slowly. 'It's a
lovely word, anyway. Evocative.'

'I always associate it with clouds of midges. Though perhaps
spirits don't get bitten.'

'Not if they drink enough wine. Allow me.' He took her empty glass out of her hand. 'A few more glasses of this and any insect bold enough to bite will fall to the ground, dead drunk.'

'Well, in that case . . .' Kate, amused but slightly puzzled, watched him as he walked away. She had spoken to him before, but never at any length. Once she had taken her mother-in-law's mail across to the cottage to find him already there, sitting in one of the dainty, flower-sprigged armchairs reading the paper, somehow giving the impression of being completely at home. He had stood politely and welcomed her in as if she were the visitor and he the host. Of Lilian there was no sign and, oddly disconcerted, she had given him the letters and made an excuse to leave.

And only last week she had taken the dogs for a walk towards the hills and had turned a corner to find him painting the scene in front of him. She would have loved to have seen the result of his work, but assumed he would resent the interruption, so had passed on with a brief 'good morning', acknowledged by no more than a silent nod from him. Yet here he was now, not only showing a readiness to talk but displaying a marked sense of humour which, for some reason, she hadn't suspected.

'One doesn't usually see you at these parties,' she said when he returned.

'No.' He looked around him, his small, shrewd eyes taking in the scene. 'On the whole, I've forsworn parties. This one is different, though. I've known the Nelsons for a long, long time. In fact, years ago in Johannesburg, it was Grace Nelson who was instrumental in setting up my first exhibition. It wasn't particularly successful, but that's beside the point.'

'I love your work,' Kate said shyly. 'Though I've only seen the pictures you painted for Lilian.'

'I have another exhibition opening in a couple of weeks at the Sea Point Gallery, but you don't have to wait for that. Drop in to the cottage some time when you're taking the dogs for a walk.'

'I'd be afraid of interrupting you.'

'Don't worry about that. If you were, I'd tell you to go away and come back another time.'

'Well, if you promise to do that—'

'Certainly I promise. Hasn't Guy told you that I can be relied upon to tell the truth at all times? It's one of the things about me that he dislikes.'

Kate laughed uncomfortably.

'What on earth can you mean? I'm sure he doesn't—'

'Dislike me? Now, you know perfectly well that he can't stand the sight of me! I don't let it worry me, and I hope you won't let it worry you. Now—' He turned from her and surveyed the room where large french windows opened on to the terrace where people were dancing to the music of a band. 'Let's see who's among those present. Ah – Mrs Masterson, I see. What would any party be without her? And what, I ask myself, would any bar be without her poor, dear husband? Still, one can only sympathise. Imagine having to go home every night to that vitriolic little wasp.'

'You're pretty vitriolic yourself,' Kate said. Larry laughed.

'Dear girl, it's one of my few pleasures,' he said.

But Kate had stopped listening. She had caught sight of Guy, outside on the dance floor. It was no more than a glimpse – more, really, an impression. Guy, handsome and immaculate as ever, dancing a slow foxtrot with a woman she had never seen before. A woman in a jade-green dress, with dark curls falling to her shoulders and beyond. Among all the bobbed and cropped and shingled heads, she stood out, almost as if she were in fancy dress; and in that brief snapshot before they were obscured by other dancers once more she saw that they were not smiling or talking. They were just looking at each other.

Larry, beside her, continued talking, but he fell silent and looked at her curiously when she failed to answer.

'Is something wrong?' he asked.

'No. No, not at all.' She smiled at him brightly. 'I was just listening to the music.'

He lifted his hands, a glass in each.

'I'll get refills for these. Don't go away.'

Left alone, Kate looked towards the terrace once more. There they were again, gazing into each other's eyes in that peculiarly intense way. It was clear to the most casual observer that they knew each other far too well to indulge in exchanges of the bright, meaningless conversation that was common currency between strangers on the dance floor.

But then, whoever she was, she wouldn't be a stranger, would she? These were Guy's friends – the people, for the most part, that he grew up with. She wouldn't, Kate assured herself, be the slightest bit jealous, or even curious, if it weren't for the strangely trance-like way they seemed to be dancing, just as if no one else existed – as if they were somehow enclosed in a kind of transparent glass bubble, insulated from the rest of the world. With a sudden shock she realised that this must be Greta, and she put it to the test when Larry returned with the drinks.

'I see Greta Carlton's back,' she said.

'Yes. I've just been talking to Neil.' Was there something guarded in his manner? Kate wondered. Or was that her imagination? She looked towards the terrace again, incapable of turning her back on it completely. There they were again.

'Look,' she said. 'There she is. Isn't she lovely?'

Larry appeared to hesitate, as if reluctant to give his confirmation, but in the end he had no alternative.

'Oh, yes,' he said. 'She's lovely.'

Sonia, too, had seen Greta – had, in fact, been standing with Guy when the Carltons had arrived in the room at a time when Helen had whisked Kate away to meet some newcomer. And though she had little time for Kate, thinking her far too immature and unsophisticated for her brother, she was nevertheless conscious of a twinge of disquiet. It simply wouldn't do for Guy to take up where he left off with Greta. Suppose Kate got wind of it? Suppose she wrote home – or worse still, decided to break up her marriage? It would surely put paid to any hopes Guy might cherish of receiving a sizeable inheritance on Sir Randolph's death. She could understand the attraction Greta had for him, of course; but he ought to be more controlled, more self-disciplined. Gramerci was what mattered. It would be necessary, she resolved, to speak to him.

'Sonia?' She turned to find her host approaching her. David Nelson was a lawyer who had emigrated from England to South Africa many years before and married Grace de Wet, the daughter of a wealthy mine-owner. They had moved to Cape Town, raised a family, made some shrewd land deals, amassed a fortune, and were now among the grandees of the city, well respected by everyone. David still nominally kept an interest in the law firm of Nelson and Swart but was much in demand as chairman of this board or that, and could always be relied upon to underwrite charitable projects of which he approved, while his wife figured prominently in cultural activities. She was elegant, silver-haired and intelligent, her mildly liberal tendencies regarded, on the whole, as an endearing aberration. Both she and her husband were kind and generous hosts, both untainted by the arrogance that their wealth might have induced in them.

Sonia, though she respected the business acumen that had brought them to this point, was caustically amused by them and by their reputation for benevolent patronage. It was easy to be generous, ran her creed, when one was as wealthy as the Nelsons were. Easy to waste money on struggling artists and failed sculptors when the odd few hundred rand here and there made no difference at all. Even so, she was sufficiently aware of David Nelson's position in society to turn smilingly towards him as he spoke to her.

'David! What a lovely party, as always.'

'I was so sorry your mother couldn't come.'

'So was she. But she gets very tired—'

'It seems such a long time since we saw her. Grace is so fond of her. We must arrange for her to come over on her own one day. Lunch, perhaps?'

'I'm sure she'd love that.'

'And you? Are you enjoying yourself?'

'Of course! What would our Christmasses be without the Nelson party?'

David Nelson laughed but made no reply, turning instead to bring forward an unknown man who was standing a pace or two behind him.

'Sonia, my dear, may I present the latest addition to the firm? This is Christiaan le Roux, who has just come from Johannesburg to give us lustre. Chris, meet Sonia Lampard. Believe me, I quail every time I pour her a drink! What she doesn't know about wine simply isn't worth knowing.'

Sonia smiled coolly at the newcomer, extending her hand. He looked interesting, she thought, and very handsome. There was something about him that seemed to exude confidence. And power. Power had always been something of an aphrodisiac where she was concerned.

'How do you do?' she said. 'Welcome to Cape Town.'

He took her hand and bowed over it with old-fashioned gallantry.

'Thank you. I'm delighted to be here.'

Having effected the introduction – one which his wife, an inveterate match-maker, had urged upon him – Nelson excused himself and moved on to speak to other guests, leaving Sonia and le Roux to look at each other appraisingly.

'So you know your wines?' le Roux said, smiling.

'I flatter myself that's so.'

'Then, tell me—' Le Roux looked down at his glass. 'What's your opinion of the wine we're both drinking now?'

'My opinion?' Sonia looked amused. 'I think I'd prefer to hear yours. Can you identify it?'

'Not by name, I confess, but I recognise excellence when I come across it. But then I suppose one would expect David Nelson to make sure he provided the best.'

'Of course!' She gave him the brilliant smile that she was able to produce when the mood was on her. 'It's Cabernet Gramerci, from my own vineyard. Now look at me and tell me you didn't know that!'

'I'll look at you for as long as you wish,' le Roux said, with a charming mock bow. 'It's no hardship! But I assure you I had no idea.'

Sonia knew he had lied, but she thought no worse of him for that. Guy and his affairs were forgotten. It seemed a very long time since she had felt such an instant attraction to any man. The evening, she thought, might, after all, be more interesting than she had imagined.

After Larry had drifted off, Kate had been drawn to the terrace as if by a magnet, and once there, had joined a group of friends which included Helen and Paul. She had even danced once or twice, forcing herself to chatter brightly to her partners to the point where Paul remarked to Helen that Kate seemed in good form.

'You're crazy! She's putting on an act,' Helen told him shortly. 'Guy's behaving atrociously. Look at him! How does he imagine Kate must be feeling?'

Even Paul, great friend of Guy and always ready to defend to the death the rights of man as opposed to the rights of woman, had to admit that he was overstepping the bounds of good manners, to say the least. Indeed, it was clear to everyone that he had no eyes for anyone but Greta. Between dances, they either waited until the music began again, or moved to the little balustrade that edged the terrace, to sit, talking quietly together with an air of great intensity that seemed to shut out anyone who might approach them.

There was only so much that Kate could take and, numb with misery, unwilling to watch the spectacle any longer or to pretend she was unaffected by it, she left the terrace and went back to the drawing room. Sonia, she was glad to see, was for once taking no interest in her or in her brother but was talking to an unknown man in a way she had never witnessed before. She was smiling up at him, laughing – *preening*, for heaven's sake. Putting herself out to be charming.

At any other time Kate's curiosity would have been aroused by such unusual behaviour, but now she could concentrate on nothing but Guy's expression as he danced out there on the terrace by the light of the gigantic Christmas tree. Couldn't he see that others were noticing it, commenting on it? Looking at her sideways to see how she was taking it?

She made her way to the bathroom on the first floor and, locking the door, leaned for a moment with her forehead pressed against it, giving in at last to her unhappiness.

Greta Carlton was beautiful. Not just attractive. Not just ordinarily pretty. Beautiful. How on earth could she possibly compete with someone like that? Clearly Guy didn't think she could. Guy cared nothing for her; if he did, he wouldn't humiliate her this way in front of everyone.

She went to the basin and stared at herself in the mirror. Spirit of twilight! What a joke. Maybe Larry had meant she was dim and shadowy. That's how she felt, anyway. Dim and dull and—

She closed her eyes and gripped the basin, feeling suddenly faint, as if the world were slipping sideways and she was about to fall. There was a sound in her ears like rushing water, but through it she became aware that there was knocking at the door. She heard Helen's voice.

'Kate? Kate, are you in there? Are you all right?'

For a moment she was incapable of answering, but then slowly the room righted itself and she stumbled to the door, opening it to allow her friend to come in.

'Oh, Helen—' she said, unable to say more.

'You're ill!' Helen slipped inside and locked the door behind her once more. 'Here – come and sit down for a moment. You're as white as a sheet.' She put an arm around Kate's shoulders and, supporting her to a cane chair that stood at the end of the bath, she soaked the end of a towel in cold water and bathed her face. Then she filled a tooth glass with water and held it to her lips.

'I thought I was going to faint,' Kate said, normality beginning to return. 'I've never fainted in my life, but suddenly—' She broke off in mid-sentence and looked at Helen. 'Why did you come looking for me?' she asked.

'I saw you leave,' Helen said. 'I . . . I was just a bit worried about you, that's all.'

'Because of Guy?'

Helen gave her shoulders a squeeze.

'I knew how it must look to you, but you know Guy. He's not renowned for his sensitivity, is he? Never has been. He probably hasn't the first idea how much he's hurt you.'

'He doesn't love me, Helen. He can't do.'

'I'm sure that's not true. He's always been—' She hesitated and Kate finished the sentence for her.

'Mad about Greta?'

'No – I wasn't going to say that.'

What was she going to say, then? Miserably, Helen racked her brains to find the right words, the words that would be of some comfort to Kate. It was hard, in view of the fact that Kate had never spoken a truer word – Guy had always been mad about Greta. They'd known each other since childhood, and though they had monumental rows from time to time, each vowing that they would never speak to the other again, still it had seemed inevitable that the rows would be made up.

It was after just such a row that Greta had flounced off and married Neil Carlton – older, wealthier and possibly much kinder than Guy, whom Helen had always thought utterly self-centred.

'It's true they were always good friends,' she said cautiously. 'And they haven't seen each other for some time. I'm sure it's nothing more than that.'

'Are you?' Kate's voice was bleak. 'I think they were more than friends—'

'Well, maybe. Before you came along. But Greta's married too, you know, and Neil adores her.'

Kate said nothing to this. What was there to say? She had seen Guy's face for herself and Neil's feelings seemed immaterial.

'You look a bit better, thank heaven,' Helen went on. 'The

colour's come back into your face. You had me worried for a while.'

Kate made no comment, lost in her own thoughts. Then she gave a shuddering sigh.

'I . . . I just don't know how to cope with this, Helen. What am I to do? I know they had a serious affair. Flick said so—'

'*Flick* said so?' Helen gave a breath of derisive laughter. 'Oh well, then, it must be true. We all know that Flick tells the truth, the whole truth and nothing but the truth.' She gave Kate a small shake. 'Listen – Guy behaved badly out there and I'm not going to defend him, but my honest opinion is that the last thing he wants to do is break up your marriage. He's probably had too much to drink. He'll be really sorry and repentant tomorrow, mark my words.'

'He's not drunk,' Kate said stonily. 'I know when he's drunk.'

'Look – half the men in the Cape were crazy about Greta when we were all kids together, and no doubt Guy was the same as the others. It was you he married, though, wasn't it?'

'Only because—' Because of the money, she had started to say, but even to Helen she could not bear to admit to such humiliation. 'Because she was married already,' she finished.

'Yes, she was. And to a very rich man. Greta knows which side her bread is buttered on, believe me. Guy's just a little diversion as far as she's concerned. Come on! Powder your nose and put on some lipstick and let's go down and show the world you're a match for Greta Carlton any day.'

'If only I could believe that!' Kate was as despairing as ever, but she made the effort to get up from the chair and go to the mirror again. 'I look terrible,' she said, peering at her reflection. 'Oh, Helen—'

'Powder!' Helen said briskly, pointing an authoritative finger at her.

When the repairs were finished, Helen linked her arm in Kate's and marched her towards the stairs. Halfway down, where a curve in the staircase gave them a view of the wide hall and the room beyond, they stopped for a moment as if by mutual consent. Guy, it seemed, had at last left the terrace and was standing with Paul by the open double doors that led to the drawing room, engrossed in conversation. Helen laughed.

'You see?' she said, nodding in their direction. 'It's golf now, not Greta. And I know damned well which Guy thinks is more important. I don't suppose he has any idea how seriously you were taking that little show outside – he certainly wasn't!'

Kate managed, then, to smile, just a little. Together they went down another step or two before Helen came to a halt again, pulling on Kate's arm so that she was forced to face her. 'Hey!' Her voice was low but full of suppressed excitement. 'I've just thought. That funny turn of yours in the bathroom. You couldn't be pregnant, I suppose?'

Such timing! Kate, over two decades later, smiled with caustic amusement. If anything had been designed to deflect Guy's attention from Greta, then prospective fatherhood was it. He had turned, suddenly, from the kind of husband who considered his wife a kind of optional extra to one who treated her like a piece of precious Dresden china, monitoring her welfare every hour of the day.

Having longed for more of his attention, Kate now found such an excess of it stifling, though, conscious of contrariness, she did her best to accept it graciously. The worst thing was his renewed objections to her visits to the clinic.

'But all I do is write in a ledger,' she protested. 'Honestly, Guy, it isn't a bit tiring and I do love it so. I can't sit for the next eight months sewing fine seams!'

'You could catch something – something that would damage the baby.'

'On the other hand, I could pick up some useful information about child care. I don't know the first thing about looking after babies.'

'You won't need to. We'll get a good nanny. Evalina will know someone.'

'But I don't want a nanny. Well, only for the laundry.'

'Nonsense! Everyone has a nanny.'

'But *I* want to look after him! Or her,' she added as an after-thought.

Guy ruffled her hair.

'It'll be a him,' he said. 'No doubt about it.'

'You mustn't be disappointed if it's a girl.'

'It won't be. How about calling him Randolph? It would please the old boy, wouldn't it?'

Kate wrinkled her nose.

'I don't like it much. I know what would probably please him

more. He'd be thrilled to bits if we called him John, after the son
he lost. I would, anyway! It's a much nicer name.'

'Ye-es.' Guy thought this over, his smile broadening as he did
so. 'You're right, man.' He turned to her, full of eagerness. 'My
great-grandfather was called Jan Pierre Lampard. We could call our
son John Pierre officially – Jannie to us.'

'Johnny,' said Kate. Guy patted her hand.

'We'll see,' he said.

'Guy, about the clinic – please don't make me give it up just yet.
It can't possibly do any harm. Please, Guy.'

'Well—'

'*Please*, Guy—' She sounded like a child, she thought. Just like
the child she'd seen in the local store yesterday, pleading for a
lollipop.

'Well, maybe for a month or two,' he said grudgingly. 'But I
don't want you taking risks.'

'All right,' Kate agreed. 'Just for you, I'll postpone my run up
Table Mountain, and stop the Olympic training.'

He looked at her, a frown drawing his brows together.

'What? I had no idea—' he began.

'I was joking,' she said, patiently.

Miles away in time and space, the rain that had been falling since
dawn seemed to gather in intensity, beating against the kitchen
windows. Kate sat at the table, clasping her coffee mug with both
hands, conscious of the numerous chores that were clamouring for
her attention but disinclined to tackle any of them.

Was it possible that Johnny could hear and understand all those
reminiscences she was spilling out, day by day? Was it even right
that she should dredge up the past like this? Perhaps not. Perhaps
this was all more for her benefit than his. She had refused to think of
it for so long, had kept it hidden, blanking out the screen the moment
any part of it occurred to her. There was, undoubtedly, a feeling of
sweet relief to be able to bring it all into the light of day.

At least she'd redeemed herself with Tom, in part at least.
She'd carried out her resolve the previous night, encouraging
him to expand on his plans to the point where she had grown
enthusiastic herself, despite her own preoccupations. It had been no
hardship. It was an exciting project. Shamley Hithe had once been
a vibrant part of London and Tom was on fire with enthusiasm for

making it equally attractive again. It was impossible not to rejoice with him at the fulfilment of the dream he'd always cherished: to build something important and memorable.

But agreeing to leave London was another matter. He had mentioned the idea of a weekend away once more and had looked disappointed when she temporised. Why couldn't he understand that she couldn't go away just now? It wasn't like him.

The doorbell rang, shrilling through her thoughts, and she went to answer it. On the doorstep she found Detective Sergeant Baker looking very wet indeed. For a split second she stared at him.

'There's news?' she said. Then she collected herself. 'Come in – you poor man, you're soaking.'

'It's coming down in stair-rods! Look at me, I only walked from the car to the door. Yes,' he said over his shoulder as, having wiped his feet on the doormat, he shrugged himself out of his raincoat. 'There's news. Oh, sorry – I've dripped on your carpet—'

'Never mind, never mind! What news?'

'You've been right all along. The man in hospital is without doubt your son. John Pierre Lampard.'

'Oh!' For a moment Kate covered her face with her hands, and when she looked up her smile was tremulous. 'I knew it, I knew it! How did you find out? Come into the kitchen and tell me all about it. I was just having coffee. You'll have some, won't you?'

Baker accepted the offer and followed her to the rear of the house.

'It was really quite easy,' he said. 'I merely assumed you were right and acted on that premise. We were able to confirm that someone of that name entered Britain on a flight from Johannesburg on 18 February. On the immigration form he gave his destination address as a private hotel in Earls Court, but nobody there remembers him in any detail. He only stayed for one night. One of the receptionists thought he might have gone off in a taxi the following day, but she didn't strike me as a particularly reliable witness.'

'So how did you identify him?'

'I made enquiries at the embassy to see if anyone there had seen anything of him, and I discovered that although they weren't aware he was in England and had no idea of his recent movements, your son is rather well known back in the old country. He made the headlines, it seems, when he was picked for the Springboks rugby tour of New Zealand a few years back, but before the tour he opted out on principle because of the team's racist policies. There was a woman in the reception part of the front foyer who remembered all about it. She was very aggressive, very indignant, as if he'd done something quite unforgivable, rather like Edward VIII giving up the throne.'

'Being picked for the Springboks is far more important than that,' Kate assured him.

'So I gathered. Anyway, this woman said he's a qualified lawyer now, renowned for defending every malcontent known to man. Well, anyone whom he regards as being persecuted by the race laws, anyway.'

'Well, good for him,' Kate said softly.

'She said she'd read somewhere that his name was really John, but that everyone called him Jan. She managed to find a back number of a newspaper with a photograph of the team – before your son resigned, presumably. It left me in no doubt at all that the man in the back row was the man in hospital.'

Kate gave him coffee and sat down opposite him. For a moment she rested her head on her hand, elbow on the table, and there was silence between them as he drank. Finally she looked up with a smile, shaking her head helplessly.

'I'm in a whirl,' she said. 'I was sure I was right, but having it confirmed like this—'

'We still don't know where he went after Earls Court or how he got to the place he was found. There's a day and a night unaccounted for. Where was he in the interim, and where's his luggage? Did someone take him there or did he go with some purpose in mind? He could easily have been killed, they told me at the hospital.'

Kate shuddered.

'Don't!'

'I can't help wondering if it was more than just a straightforward mugging. I gather he was brought up by his aunt who died quite recently – the woman at the embassy seemed to know all about it. That was in the paper, too. It seems her widower is something very high up in the South African Government. Minister of something or other.

'Christiaan le Roux. He was just an ordinary Member of Parliament when I knew him. I didn't know Sonia was dead,' she added. It was, somehow, unbelievable. Sonia! She was always so strong and forceful. 'She wasn't old,' Kate went on. 'No more than fifty-eight, if that.'

'What side is this le Roux on?' Baker asked. 'Is he in favour of *apartheid*?'

'Oh, yes!' She spoke with feeling, remembering his enthusiastic support, all those years ago, of the National Party; remembering the nights when she had sat there, hardly able to bear Christiaan and Sonia's smug assumption that *apartheid* represented the only way forward for any right-thinking people. Argument had been useless, though occasionally, goaded beyond bearing, she had tried to put another point of view. Always she had been dismissed with scorn as nothing but an ignorant *rooinek* who knew nothing of the people or the culture.

'Oh, yes,' she said again. 'There was never any doubt about that.'

'Then the activities of your son must have been an embarrassment to him.'

'I suppose they were. You're not suggesting that he was responsible for—? No, I can't buy that. Christiaan would never do that. God knows he had his faults when I knew him. I hated his politics, but I wouldn't ever have said he was a violent man, whatever his beliefs. And he was always fond of Johnny.'

'Maybe your Johnny had other enemies. I could tell from the attitude of the girl at the embassy that he was hardly her favourite person.'

Kate thought this over, a worried frown on her face.

'Feelings run high in South Africa, it's true. They did when I was there years ago, and I imagine it's worse now. But even so—'

She fell silent, appalled by the possibilities.

'No point in seeing conspiracies where none exist,' Baker said. 'I was just exploring different avenues. As I said before, that particular part of London has seen quite a number of muggings lately. The borough council is putting more street lights around the place and the local police are keeping more of an eye on it, so hopefully things will improve. I'd like to get my hands on the villains, though.'

'I hope you do!'

'Well, Mrs Newcott—' He brought the flat of his hands down on the table-top with a smack. 'I must go out into the cold hard world again. Thanks for the coffee.'

'You're most welcome. Thank you for coming to tell me the news. I can't wait to let my husband know.' She rose to usher him out, and had opened the front door before a disquieting thought struck her. 'Suppose,' she said hesitantly, 'that it *was* attempted murder, not a mugging. Might he not still be in danger? Whoever wanted to get rid of him could try again.'

Baker smiled reassuringly.

'In a busy ward? I don't think so, Mrs Newcott. Those nurses are keeping a very close eye on him. He's probably safer there than anywhere else in London.'

'I hope you're right,' Kate said, uneasily, and after he had gone, she did not rush for the phone to give Tom the news, but instead stood in the hall, suddenly beset by fears for Johnny's safety.

Was Baker right? How could anyone be sure. Yes, the nurses were keeping a close eye on him, but the hospital – any hospital – was like an ant-heap, with people coming and going all the time. No one's eyes could be on him every moment of the day.

The matter of whether she and Tom should go away for a weekend was decided for her now, once and for all. The moment that Johnny was conscious, she would bring him here. She could look after him as well as any hospital. Of course, it would all have to be explained very carefully and sensitively to the children . . .

She bit her lip, her determination faltering a little. Explaining things to the children was something she had refused to dwell on, but the problem had to be faced – sooner, it now appeared, rather than later. Heaven alone knew what they would make of it all, or how they would feel. Excited at the thought of having a new big brother in residence, she hoped. On the other hand, Jan would need a lot of attention. She would have to work very hard to ensure their noses weren't put out of joint.

She had no worries about Tom, though. He was the kindest man in the world and once he knew for sure that this really was Johnny, then he would be just as thrilled as she was herself. Well, maybe not quite *that* thrilled, but perfectly happy to welcome this needy stranger into his home. It would be a chance for all of them to get to know each other, to become a family. She felt quite confident that Tom would see it that way, too.

He was not available, however, when she phoned. He was in a meeting, the secretary said. She'd get him to phone back when he was free. Kate thanked her and went back to the kitchen to make a belated start on her daily chores, no more inclined to tackle them than before.

Was Johnny's arrival in England anything to do with Sonia's death? she wondered. (Sonia, dead! She still found it difficult to take in.) Was it love and respect for her that had kept him from answering all those letters she wrote over the years, so that now he felt released from obligation? It was hard, somehow, to imagine Sonia inspiring that kind of love in a child. Respect, yes. That was possible. But love?

You're being unfair, Kate told herself as she looked at the kitchen floor, debating whether or not to mop it. Just because you had no affection for her, it didn't mean others were the same. Guy, after all, admired her above all other women, and Christiaan had apparently stayed with her all these years despite his initial reluctance to commit himself.

She'd leave the floor to Mrs Bishop, she decided. She didn't feel like doing it today. Tomorrow would do. Idly she made herself more coffee.

Christiaan le Roux. Kate remembered him as she had known him back in 1934. He'd been the catch of the season – handsome, charming, and debonair. Successful, too. David Nelson thought the world of him, and so did everyone else. She hadn't been present to see Sonia walk down the aisle on his arm, but she guessed there could have been hardly a woman in Cape Town who wasn't green with envy.

'But not I,' Kate said aloud. 'Not I.'

8

Kate suffered no more fainting fits and very little sickness during those early months of her pregnancy, though she quickly learned to keep well away from the fermentation tanks which, at this time of the year, hubbled and bubbled as the grapes were shovelled into their insatiable maws, causing a heavy, sickly smell to permeate the entire cellar area which proved her undoing on a couple of occasions.

She seemed, in these early days, to bloom with contentment, enjoying the novelty of Guy's attention and the comfortable feeling that at last she was doing what was expected of her.

'You look marvellous,' Helen told her. 'Like someone made for motherhood.'

It was just like her to be able to say that without bitterness, Kate thought. Helen herself had had a series of miscarriages and was beginning to come to terms with the thought that she might never carry a baby to full term; nevertheless she seemed genuinely delighted on Kate's behalf.

Sonia, too, had never been so amenable – though this, Kate knew, had nothing to do with her condition but rather with the fact that Christiaan le Roux was now a constant visitor to Gramerci—'spreading his charm around the place as thick as butter', Helen remarked on one occasion when she had been subjected to a large helping of it.

'It seems to work,' Kate said. 'Everyone likes him, and certainly Sonia has been a lot nicer lately.'

'Is marriage in the air?'

'Heaven knows. I'd like to think so.'

'Well, even if it is, don't bank on Sonia moving out. I can't see her ever giving up running the estate. I think Christiaan would be more likely to move in here.'

'Guy runs the estate!' Kate said, with mild outrage; but she knew in her heart that what Helen had said was true. Guy's first love was his blasted sport, which took precedence over everything. It was the reason he was away from home so much, even now; his excuse for going out in the evening, so often leaving her to face Sonia – and quite often Christiaan, these days – on her own. It wasn't, of course, that golf or rugger was played by the light of the moon, but that it was only natural, so Guy said, to stay on for a drink with the boys. Her pregnancy had caused him to limit his activities to a certain extent, but he saw nothing amiss in going out several times a week and had given her a sharp answer, pregnancy or no pregnancy, when she tried to talk him out of it.

Kate was aware that Gramerci would die without Sonia. Guy was capable of overseeing the physical work – the pruning, the harvesting, the checking of the sugar ratio, the cleaning of the big oak vats. The work, in short, of a manager. It was Sonia, however, who possessed the palate and the flair that could detect the most minute deterioration in quality; and it was Sonia who developed the overall strategy – who arranged sales and shipping and made the decisions that Kate, now that she knew him better, realised that Guy would have found difficult.

He would never have brought himself, as Sonia had done, to invest so much money and effort in the growing of the Steen grape, now the basis of Gramerci's most successful white wine. He had argued, as many had done before him, that in the warm air of South Africa the grapes became over-ripe too quickly, losing all subtlety and bouquet. It was only Sonia's perseverance in ensuring the grapes were picked as they ripened and that the fermenting vats were kept cool and closed, never allowing contact with the air to disperse the bouquet, that had brought success.

'You're much too cautious,' was one of the accusations Sonia threw at him; but then, just as often, she would accuse him of being a gadfly, hopping from one project to another, managing on the way to avoid responsibility.

Kate knew what she meant. She was beginning to realise how difficult he was to pin down, how little he wanted to be deflected from his own concerns by those of others. Decisions would be postponed, promises forgotten. On one matter, however, he never wavered; he hated Larry Donoghue, which was something that, from time to time, ruffled the surface of the calm waters in which Kate now found herself.

'He's nothing but a pansy-boy,' he said disgustedly when she tackled him about it. She frowned at him, uncomprehending.

'Because he's an artist, you mean?'

'No – *not* because he's an artist! Because he's a dirty little pervert.' And this time, annoyed by her disapproval, he spelled it out for her. She stared at him in amazement.

'How very odd,' she said faintly.

'Odd?' he said. 'What do you mean, odd? It's disgusting! How my mother can stand him anywhere near her, I can't imagine. I'd run him off the property if I could, but legally it belongs to her. For the moment.'

'There's no harm in him,' Kate said, placatingly. 'He's very easy to talk to. You might like him if you tried it.'

'Like hell I will – and I don't want *you* talking to him, either. You're not to go anywhere near him – do you hear me?'

Guy, usually so easy-going, so full of smiles, was taut with purpose and for a moment Kate said nothing. She had, as Larry suggested, called in at the cottage and had been shown his pictures, most of which she liked a great deal. In particular, an Impressionist-style painting of boats drawn up in Fish Hoek at sunset had caught her fancy and she had hoped to persuade Guy to buy it for their bedroom, still largely unadorned.

She had also fallen in with Larry one day when she walked with the dogs. They had sat for a while in the vine-growing foothills looking over towards False Bay, and with the distant ocean glittering in the sun, they had talked peaceably, without strain, of art and England and life in South Africa.

'Perhaps he can't help being the sort of man he is,' she said, at last.

'What?' Guy, who felt that the last word had been spoken on the subject of Larry Donoghue and had dismissed him from his mind, looked up from the paper he was reading in surprise, a frown on his face.

'Larry,' Kate said. 'If he's made that way—'

'Of course he can help it! He's a filthy little queer.'

He returned to his paper, unaware of the momentary look of shock and revulsion that his words had caused. He also seemed unaware that she had given no undertaking to carry out his instructions to have nothing more to do with Larry Donoghue. She picked up her book and tried, unsuccessfully, to take up the story where she had left off. It was hard to concentrate when she was so angry.

There was now no chance of her taking the driving lessons she had hoped for. Guy had put his foot down firmly, and since he had – albeit reluctantly – agreed that she should carry on at the clinic for a few more months, she said no more on the matter, resolving that as soon as the baby was born she would renew her campaign.

Her tasks at the clinic remained as humble as ever, but she enjoyed the involvement and became fond of Jane Ryder, the young doctor who was in charge. There was a scrubbed, schoolgirlish look about her, emphasised by her round steel spectacles and the hair which hung like dark curtains on either side of her face, but she was not quite as young as she appeared, Kate discovered. She had already worked in a busy Liverpool hospital for several years before coming out to Cape Town.

'I wish she could be my doctor,' Kate remarked at lunch one day. Now over four months pregnant, she had that morning been for a check-up with Dr Grobler, who had attended the Lampard family in all their ills for more years than anyone could remember. From the first she had taken a dislike to the man, thinking him brusque and impersonal and altogether too puffed up with his own importance.

'Dr Grobler knows what he's doing,' Guy assured her. 'There's to be no second best for my son.'

Kate had hardly been serious in her desire to be attended by Jane, knowing as she did that her time was already more than fully occupied in her mission work and that she took no private patients. Still, she was mildly exasperated by Guy's assumption that she was less competent than the arrogant Dr Grobler.

'Jane wouldn't be second best,' she pointed out. 'She's very well qualified. And experienced. And conscientious.'

'If you say so.' Guy's smile insinuated that he was not convinced. 'But tell me, if she's as good as all that, why does she spend her time doctoring kaffirs, eh?'

'She wants to do something worthwhile with her life—'

'Oh dear, oh dear!' Guy laughed at this foolishness, turning his eyes to heaven. 'If you believe that, you'll believe anything, man.'

'Why should you doubt her?' Kate's irritation was mounting. 'There are people who feel like that. I can't see what's so funny.'

Sonia, smiling in sympathy with Guy, attempted to explain.

'Experience shows,' she drawled, 'that doctors who can't get a decent job elsewhere suddenly become *Kaffirboeties*. One sees it all the time. You'll learn, my dear.'

'I expect she came to catch a husband,' Guy said. 'She'd probably heard that South Africa was full of virile men.'

'She came to work,' Kate said. Guy laughed.

'If you say so.'

'I do say so,' Kate muttered childishly, feeling both outraged and impotent, just as if she were back in the schoolroom, perfectly aware of the amused glances that Sonia and Guy exchanged behind her back.

Guy was even more amused when, only a few days later, they ran into Jane with a girlfriend at the cinema – the bioscope, as Kate was learning to call it – where they had gone to see *A Farewell to Arms*. He was polite enough while introductions were performed and pleasantries exchanged, but later, when he and Kate had left Jane and her friend below and gone to take their seats upstairs, he could hardly restrain his mirth.

'Well, my God, no wonder she hides herself away in District Six! You'd have to go way out in the *bundu* to find a man desperate enough to take her on. She was behind the door when looks were given out, man, that's for certain.'

Kate was indignant.

'How can you say that? She has a sweet face, and the nicest smile. I think she's lovely! She's so kind and funny.'

'Funny's right,' Guy said. 'I agree with you there. Funny peculiar! But lovely? Don't say expectant motherhood is affecting your eyesight!'

'Looks aren't everything,' Kate muttered, as the lights dimmed and the curtains parted. She attempted to settle down to watch the film, but Guy's remarks had upset her and her attention kept wandering.

It was only later she realised that indignation on Jane's behalf was only half the reason for her inattention. The other was the sudden crystallisation of a thought that had been building gradually. Guy had, she now saw, only one yardstick for measuring women. Men could look any way they chose, just so long as they were good sports, bought their round, and had no time for namby-pamby pursuits like art or music. (His comments on the son of one of his mother's friends who had gone to England to become a ballet

dancer had taught her many words she had never heard before.)
For a woman, however, looks were the only things that were of
value, with domestic skills coming a poor second, and all other
accomplishments – with the possible exception of an ability to play
games – dismissed as unimportant, even faintly risible.

It was so much a reflection of her mother's attitude that, though
it irritated her, she was not much surprised by it. It was only later
when they had returned home and Guy was asleep beside her that she
identified a new worry. She was already beginning to thicken quite
markedly around the waist, and he had teased her about it more than
once. Would his new-found pride in prospective fatherhood keep
him as attentive as he was now as the months went by and her
waist expanded to gigantic proportions? It was hard to imagine.

She bemoaned her increased girth and lack of clothes to cope with
it one morning when she was sitting with Lilian in the candlewood
bower one late afternoon.

'You must contact Mama Lou,' Lilian said.

'Who's Mama Lou?' Kate asked.

'A dressmaker I've used quite often in the past. She's so clever
with her needle, she'll run you up some dresses in no time at all.
Mind you, it's a long time now since I've sent for her. I've so many
clothes that new ones seem a gross extravagance – and in any case,
all my cupboards are full. Still, she'll help you if she can, I'm quite
sure. I'll write her a note and get Joseph to deliver it.'

Kate thanked her, but checked with Helen the next time she saw
her, just to make sure that the garments produced by Mama Lou
would be of the kind she would want to wear.

'Well, she used to be very good,' Helen said. 'She's made for
my mother in her time, but her hands are so crippled with arthritis
these days that she's had to give up. She has a daughter, though –
she's run up things for Jane. I remember she was talking about her
one day. She's very good, I believe.'

Kate looked doubtful.

'I'm very fond of Jane, but she's hardly fashionable—'

'Don't you believe it! I know she doesn't bother what she wears
most of the time, but I've seen her looking marvellous when she
really makes an effort. I met her at a wedding once and hardly knew
her, she was so stylish. When you see her next time, ask her how to
get in touch with this girl. She'll know.'

Her name was Dora, Jane told Kate the next time they met.

She worked in the OK Bazaar, but she took in sewing as a sideline.

'And she's good and very quick,' Jane said earnestly, eyes gleaming behind the round spectacles. I can't recommend her highly enough. Dora Botha, her name is. You'll find her on the glass and china counter.'

It was early evening on the following Saturday when Guy, whom Kate confidently expected to be at the club for the next couple of hours at least, decided to come home early.

He came pounding up the stairs, throwing open the door of his bedroom, to be shocked by the sight of a complete stranger awkwardly perched on the edge of the silk-covered armchair. She was dressed in a pink-striped dress and had a heart-shaped face and hair in a tight roll around her head, a white straw hat with a turned-up brim set very straight on top. She was young and she was pretty. She was also Coloured.

'What the hell—' Guy stopped in surprise and scowled at her.

Hastily the girl stood up, hands clasped in front of her, eyes wide with consternation.

'Sorry, *meneer*. I am very sorry. *Mevrouw* Lampard told me to sit down and wait—'

Kate appeared behind him, holding a tray on which was a cup and saucer, a pot of tea, a jug of milk.

'Guy, what are you doing at home? I didn't expect you for ages.'

Guy turned round, still scowling.

'Who's this, and what's she doing here?'

'This is Dora Botha, the daughter of Mama Lou who used to sew for your mother. She's come to see if she can alter any of my clothes so that they're fit to wear, but the poor thing's been on her feet all day so I just popped down to get her a cup of tea—'

'You did *what*?' Kate had never seen him look so angry.

'I told her to sit down and take the weight off her feet for a minute. For heaven's sake, Guy, look at her! She's only a little slip of a thing—'

'I'm sorry, *meneer*,' Dora said again. She looked as if she were about to burst into tears. 'I tried to tell her—'

'Well, get out now,' Guy said roughly. 'And don't come back.' He advanced into the room and began unbuttoning his shirt. 'I've never seen such bloody effrontery,' he added in a furious undertone, as if to himself.

The girl would have left – indeed, by her expression she could not wait to do so – but Kate put the tray down on the bedside table and caught her by the arm.

'Don't go, Dora,' she said, more calmly than she could have thought possible. 'My husband is about to leave.'

'The hell I am!'

'Dora's come all the way out here after putting in a full day's work at the store so that she can do some sewing for me. I'd be very pleased if you'd give us a chance to get on with it.'

She still sounded calm, but was aware of the anger pounding away in her head, not on her own behalf but on Dora's, whose only crime had been to do what she had been told. His face tight with rage, Guy stared at her; then, to her surprise, he strode out of the room without another word, slamming the door behind him.

For a moment the room seemed to reverberate with his anger. The two girls – much of an age, Kate guessed – stood silently; then Kate gave a nervous laugh.

'Don't let the tea go to waste,' she said, turning to pour a cup.

'Better if I go, *mevrouw*—'

'No! Why should you? Sit down, Dora, and have some tea while I change. Goodness knows if you'll be able to do anything. I'm getting so horribly fat, but it's in a good cause, I keep telling myself. I wanted a baby so much, but was beginning to think it wasn't going to happen. And now it has, and I'm so excited!' Kate chattered feverishly in her attempt to banish the ugly echoes and put Dora at ease. 'Here you are. Do you take sugar?'

She handed the cup to Dora, who had little option but to take it; she stood as she drank, however, her eyes wide with nervousness over the rim of the cup.

Kate looked at her for a moment, and when she spoke again she was more in control of herself.

'I'm really sorry about all that,' she said softly. She gave another little laugh in which there was little humour. 'I expect my husband lost at golf, or something. His manners aren't normally as bad as that. I . . . I do wish you'd sit down!'

Dora put down the cup with only half the tea gone.

'If you yust show me de dresses, *mevrouw*—'

'Very well,' Kate said, seeing that she was unable or unwilling to relax.

No more was said as she paraded her small store of dresses. There were two, Dora said, which could be successfully let out, but of course this was only a temporary solution. *Mevrouw* would need several more dresses soon.

'I know, I know,' Kate agreed. 'I'm not looking forward to being so huge.'

'A skirt maybe is good,' Dora said. 'Wid de different tops, hanging loose.'

'Yes, of course! And you will make them?'

'Maybe I bring pictures when dese dresses are ready. My momma has dem.'

'Thank you. I'm really very grateful.' For a moment Kate hesitated. 'Would it be best if I came to your house?' she asked. 'I could get someone to drive me.'

Dora was quick to agree.

'Maybe yes,' she said. 'You come any time – Mama Lou can measure and pin, and I'll sew. We live on Gysbert Street, down by Wynberg Station. The other side of the line,' she added, unnecessarily. 'Number eight.'

'I'll come,' Kate said. 'Tuesday morning.'

And Guy can say what he likes about that, she thought defiantly.

He had plenty to say when, after seeing Dora off the premises, Kate went into the drawing room where he was sitting in an armchair, smoking furiously. At the sight of her he stubbed out his cigarette in an ashtray, grinding it flat with the force of his anger.

'And now,' he said, 'perhaps you'll explain why my wife sees fit to sit a little Coloured chit down in my bedroom and serve her tea in the good china. What the hell were you thinking of, Kate, waiting on her like that?' Kate sat down opposite him and for a moment or two said nothing. 'Well?' he snapped.

'I had no idea you'd be home so soon,' she said. 'Why were you, Guy?'

He brought the flat of his hand down on the arm of the chair.

'Answer me, will you? How could you have been so bloody stupid? Haven't you learned anything since you've been here?'

His vehemence frightened her. Suddenly he looked like a petulant stranger. His mouth, always his weakest feature, was distorted in its anger.

'I saw no harm in it,' Kate said. 'She was tired, Guy. The bus broke down and she had to walk part of the way – and as I told you, she'd been on her feet all day. She looked exhausted.'

'I don't begrudge the girl a cup of tea! You should have sent her to the kitchen.'

'Rosie showed her straight up to the bedroom. I was already there, you see—'

'So why not tell Rosie to fetch tea?'

'Because she'd gone by the time I—' Kate suddenly rebelled and jumped to her feet. 'Stop it, Guy! Stop quizzing me like this. What does it matter? I went to fetch the tea because it was the quickest thing to do. It wasn't a question of waiting on her.'

'Just don't do it again.'

He got out of the chair and walked towards the door, but she caught hold of him, pulling him to a halt. Her heart was fluttering and her head felt light with anger.

'And that's the end of it, is it?' She could hear her voice trembling. 'There's nothing more to be said? Well, I was brought up to believe that it was the worst of manners to embarrass a visitor and I think you behaved atrociously. You upset me and you upset Dora.'

He stood and looked down at her, his mouth set in a sneer. Then he relaxed and gave a short laugh.

'I upset Dora? Well, I *am* sorry! Listen, man – you'll just have to learn our ways. You were lucky it was me saw what you were up to, and not Sonia. She'd have gone mad. You don't ask Coloured people to sit down in your home, still less run around after them like they were royalty. The sooner you get that through your head, the happier you're likely to be. OK?' He didn't wait for a reply, but pulled his arm free and chucked her under the chin in a gesture that she assumed meant the incident was forgotten.

'Now I'm going upstairs to get changed,' he went on. 'And then I'm going out. I met an old schoolfriend at the club, visiting from Kenya. Nick Barend. Paul and Nick and I used to raise hell here together years ago. We haven't seen him for ages, so Paul and I agreed to meet him for drinks and dinner at the Mount Nelson. Sonia's out with Chris, I suppose – but you don't mind an evening on your own, do you?'

Kate looked at him, not returning his smile.

'I'll welcome it,' she said.

Colin, on the road to Paarl, sang along to the car radio. He was feeling extraordinarily pleased with himself. He had handled this suggested assignment well, he thought, subtly manoeuvring his editor into suggesting Paarl as a suitable place to begin his investigations into the past, present and future of the wine trade, when he could so easily have been directed to go to Franschoek or Stellenbosch – or Constantia, come to that.

But Paarl was where Nina lived and taught, which meant that Paarl was where he wanted to be. There was, of course, nothing in the world to stop him phoning her to suggest a date any day of the week. It was only an hour's drive from Cape Town, after all, and he'd be prepared to drive a lot longer and further than that to see her again. But being able to say that he would be there on business all day Tuesday—'and oh, by the way, couldn't we meet for dinner?'—seemed so much more casual. Less revealing. Less . . . He struggled for the word. Less importunate. That was it.

He didn't want to importune her – make her feel that he was badgering her, taking advantage of Jan's absence, even if that was exactly what he proposed to do. And for his part, he didn't feel so bad about it. It was his opinion that Jan should have married the girl long ago if he was set on keeping her for himself.

But Jan had a higher calling, Nina had said, apparently resigned to the fact that she came second to the cause of freedom. What, Colin wondered, was Jan actually like these days? He had always been single-minded, always charismatic and capable of swaying a crowd – unless, of course, it happened to be a crowd made up of racist fanatics like the ones in Johannesburg that night when all hell broke loose. Anyone could have told him that he was being foolhardy, speaking on the emotive subject of the Group Areas Act in this stronghold of Afrikanerdom; and as if that wasn't enough on its own, he'd invited an African to share the platform with him. No matter how much sympathy one might have with the cause, only a fool could imagine that the occasion would pass without trouble.

Colin had gone just to make sure that Nina was all right. It was at the time, he remembered, when he still had hope, still thought that it might possibly be Jan's politics that attracted her – the song, not the singer, as it were. And thank heaven he had been there, for it was he who had sheltered her and managed to get her out of the hall when students of the far right persuasion had rushed the platform, faces contorted with hatred and fury, overturning chairs and scattering the crowd as they brandished their sticks and their *sjamboks*. To them – the respectable, God-fearing sons of middle-class, law-abiding parents – Jan Lampard was little short of the Antichrist, preaching against the word of God who had, in his wisdom, laid down the sacred law of segregation.

Colin had blamed Jan – not for speaking his mind, which was every man's right, but for encouraging Nina to go with him into this lion's den where violence was virtually certain to result. He had said as much to her when they were sitting in his car outside the hall, both of them shaken by the ugly scenes inside. He had held her trembling body and called Jan a fanatic and other, far worse things, until she had belaboured him with her fists and screamed at him to stop. Jan was a hero, she'd said. A man with ideals who wasn't afraid to stand up and be counted. Unlike others, who couldn't and wouldn't see that their beloved country was a pariah in the eyes of the world, flouting justice and human rights and . . . and . . . and—

She had run out of words, he remembered, and, blinded by tears, had fumbled at the car door in her haste to get away from him and back to Jan, now being manhandled out of the hall with his shirt torn and his hair wild, blood pouring from his head. The police arrived then, too late to prevent the demonstration but in time to restore some kind of order.

It was the beginning of the end; the end of the Nina years. For a while she had barely spoken to him, but then, as if she had on reflection understood that his intemperate words were born out of fear for her and not hatred of the cause she supported, she had unbent a little and become more friendly.

'No hard feelings?' she'd said when, right at the end of their university career, they had found themselves together in a queue at the cafeteria and had, by mutual consent, shared a table.

'No hard feelings,' he'd agreed; and they'd talked of the future – of her sudden, road-to-Damascus conversion to the idea of teaching, and of the decision he had to make regarding the *Cape Town Courier*'s offer to give him a kind of apprenticeship as a reporter.

'The money's peanuts,' he told her, 'but they say they'll send me to Europe for six months, just to travel and get a wider perspective on world events.'

She'd been amused at that.

'You need it,' she said. And she'd been right.

He'd learned so much during those six months. He'd talked to everyone who would talk to him and had been forced, even as he attempted to defend South Africa's politics, to re-examine his own thoughts and beliefs. And then, just before his twenty-first birthday, he had come home to find the country in the throes of the 'blackspot' crisis, exemplified in the total destruction of Sophiatown, the home of more than sixty thousand Africans, Coloureds and Asians, many of whom owned the title deeds to their own property, valued by them, however mean and dilapidated such property might appear in the eyes of the authorities. All had been bulldozed, the residents moved away, and a new town had been built for the white workers of Johannesburg. 'Triomf', it was called. Colin could see no reason for triumph, but at least it concentrated his mind wonderfully. He might not be a zealot like Jan, prepared to risk his job and his comfort and the approval of his parents by tilting at windmills and being thrown into jail at regular intervals, but he now had no doubt on which side of the fence he stood.

'Do you think,' he said to Nina when, his duty on the wine estates done and his notes made, he sat opposite her in the town's best restaurant, 'that in our lifetime we will be able to bring anyone, of any colour, into a place like this?'

'We've got to believe it.' She paused in attacking her steak. 'Jan believes it.'

'He does?'

'Sure he does. I had a letter from him yesterday.'

'Oh?' Colin looked at her enquiringly. 'How's he enjoying England?'

'He didn't say. It was written on the plane and posted at Heathrow.'

'Oh,' Colin said again. It was, he thought immediately, the action of a lover, but he began to doubt this when Nina put down her knife and fork and reached for her handbag.

'You can read it if you like,' she said, holding out the folded sheets of paper across the table.

He hesitated, frowning.

'Are you sure? It doesn't seem—'

'It's not personal. Not much, anyway. Read it.'

'All right. If you say so.'

She was right, he found, about it not being personal.

> 'So here I am,' [he had written, after a few general remarks regarding the flight,] 'miles above our beautiful, stricken country, leaving it for the very first time. In some ways I already feel myself a stranger, looking at it with a stranger's eyes, even though I'm South African to my very backbone.
>
> Why is it, do you think, that the likes of you and me can see its faults so clearly when others can see no spot or blemish? Perhaps it's the sheer beauty of the place that puts their senses in a spin, like a glorious piece of music or poetry.
>
> But no one can stay blinded by beauty for ever, and sitting here next to a voluble lady who I know is waiting for me to lay down my pen so that she can continue telling me about her cute grandson, I feel unaccountably optimistic about the future. Don't ask me why! Maybe it was the sight of the city and the veldt as we took off and soared away from it. For whatever reason, I was filled with a feeling of elation.
>
> Everything must be well, Nina. It has to be! When? Maybe not for years. How? No idea! A charismatic leader, maybe – though I can't think of any of our current crop of politicians who would fill that particular role, can you?
>
> I know we all go up and down, one day thinking that things will change, the next that nothing ever will. Maybe tomorrow will find me in the depths of despair, but I wanted to share this particular moment of certainty with you, with whom I have shared so many good things, and will I profoundly hope, share many more. Because, Nina my love, I do want us always to be friends – always, always, no matter what should befall.
>
> Dinner is about to be served, so this is all for now. Take care of yourself and think of me kindly.'

The signature seemed to lurch a little as if the plane had hit a pocket of air at that point, but it was not for this reason that Colin came to the end of the letter with a puzzled look on his face. Why no proper ending? he wondered. Not even a childish 'love from'. Just the scrawled 'Jan', tilting upwards.

He handed the letter back to Nina.

'That bit about staying friends,' he said. 'Do I take it that you and he are finished in any other sense?

She clicked her tongue in irritation.

'Oh, Colin! That wasn't the important bit. It was the rest I wanted you to read. Jan's weird feeling of certainty that everything was going to be all right.'

'Yes, well . . .' Colin resumed eating. 'He was always an emotional type, wasn't he? I suppose we all have these bursts of hope from time to time.'

'It was more than that. He must have felt pretty strongly to write that letter.'

'Like he said, he'll probably be back to earth tomorrow. I don't give much for the chances of any would-be leader, charismatic or otherwise, getting the better of the Nats, do you?'

'*Colin*! We mustn't think like that. That's why he wrote the letter – don't you see? We've just got to keep on working and hoping. We must never give up.'

Her earnestness was appealing and Colin longed to reach out and touch her.

'You're right,' he said. 'But come on – come clean about the rest of it. Are you and Jan still together? I – I need to know, Nina.'

Nina said nothing, concentrating for a moment on her salad and the last of the French fries. Then she looked up at him.

'We . . . we decided we weren't going anywhere,' she said hesitantly. 'We had a row. It was a trivial kind of thing really, all about him not wanting to commit himself to taking me to the wedding of some mutual friends.' She gave a rueful laugh. 'I think he has a kind of phobia about weddings. He goes into a kind of spasm at the very thought of them. But the fact it was a wedding wasn't important. He hates to be tied down – to commit himself to a time and a place. I should be used to it, but somehow this particular occasion seemed a kind of test case. It seemed to me that if he wouldn't commit himself to being free on that particular Saturday, then he'd never be able to commit himself to anything. Anything to do with me, anyway. I suppose you could call it the final straw. But just as he says in the letter, we've been through a lot together and we'll always be friends. I couldn't possibly excise him from my life, just like that.'

Colin looked at her for a moment without speaking, then he gave a mirthless grunt of laughter.

'So there's just a little loophole left,' he said. 'I might have expected it. I can't see him letting you go.'

'Can't you?' Her expression was unreadable, her eyes mildly quizzical. 'Well—' She took a sip of her wine, hesitating a little. 'You're wrong, Colin. Although it was I who did the letting go, I don't think there's any doubt that it came as a relief to him. I'd become a habit – a problem. Oh, sure – he was in love with me at one time, and he's still fond of me, but any kind of happy-ever-after is out of the question. He has other things on his mind.'

'Did you actually speak to him before he left?' Colin asked. 'Could he throw any light on why le Roux wanted to get hold of him?'

Nina shook her head.

'We barely touched on it. He always clammed up whenever his family was mentioned, and as he was leaving anyway it didn't seem important.'

'It was probably nothing much.'

He was happy to dismiss the subject. They'd spent enough time talking of Jan, he felt. It was hard now to remember the alarm that Eksberg's enquiries had triggered in his mind. Why wouldn't le Roux want to contact his wife's nephew? Eksberg had probably spoken nothing but the truth when he said it could be something to do with Sonia le Roux's will. He'd over-reacted, he told himself.

The important thing was that he was here, with Nina. They had both changed, of course; had moved on, grown up. They met, now, almost as strangers, and it wouldn't do to assume they could pick up where they left off. On the other hand there was undoubtedly still a spark between them; on his part, anyway. On hers, too, perhaps. Surely he wasn't imagining this feeling of . . . what? Sympathy? Fondness? Ease, anyway.

Whatever it was, it was something to build on. He wasn't going to give up easily, now that he'd found her again.

Operation bloody Candlewood, Gert Eksberg thought, as he drove along De Waal Drive on his way to Constantia. He was beginning to wish he'd never heard of it, or of le Roux and his schemes, money or no money, Broederbond or no Broederbond.

He was getting nothing but complaints and accusations from all sides these days. Connie seemed to moan endlessly. He was neglecting her more than ever, she said; and as if that wasn't enough, the boss had wiped the floor with him that morning, accusing him of not having his mind on his work; and then, to

cap it all, le Roux had been on the blower just as he was about
to leave and go home – on time, for once – demanding that he put
in an appearance at the house on the instant.

The tone prepared him for the reception he received as he arrived
at Gramerci. Gone were all the smiles that had been the order of
the day on that first visit. Gone the pressing invitation to a drink,
the polite chit-chat. Now le Roux's only conversation was a terse
query as to what the hell was going on.

'What kind of a fool have you got over there?' he demanded,
once the two men were closeted in the study together, le Roux
on one side of a desk and Eksberg on the other. The minister's
face looked thinner, Eksberg thought. Older. There was no doubt
he was under great strain.

'Van Niekirk's no fool,' Eksberg assured him. 'I give you
my word on that. It wasn't his fault that the first strike mis-
fired and he's as angry as you about it. He phoned me at home
last night.'

'So what's his next move?'

'He's been trying to get someone into the hospital, but apparently
that isn't as easy as it sounds. They managed it once. It was last
Sunday evening when there seemed to be fewer nurses around than
usual. The guy he hired dressed in a white coat and borrowed a
stethoscope from somewhere. He got right to the bedside but before
he could do anything, visitors started flocking in and he had to leave.
It's not made any easier by the fact that your nephew's in a ward
with at least a dozen other beds, and the nurses are up and down
all the time.'

'He can't still be unconscious?'

'It seems he is – was yesterday, anyway.'

'Maybe nature will do our job for us.'

'Maybe.'

'But we can't rely on that. Your man had better move fast before
Jan comes round.'

'Don't worry. He's going to.'

'I hope,' le Roux said, his voice suddenly sharpening, 'that you
and your friend are discreet on the phone? No word of this must
get out.'

'Don't worry,' Eksberg said again, this time getting to his feet,
intent on ending the interview. 'Charlie's at least as concerned with
secrecy as you are, you can be sure of that. We don't give anything

away. No names, no specifics. What he said to me would make no sense to anyone else.'

Le Roux got up from his desk and, going to a tray in the corner of the room, poured himself a large measure of brandy.

'I just hope he makes sense to himself,' he said.

9

On the evening that Kate visited Johnny knowing without doubt that he was her son, Tom was there, too. He stood to the side of her, half a pace behind, and as he looked at the young man in the bed and then at his wife, he was aware of complex emotions. Shame was one of them. He'd had no right to encourage her to turn her back on the past, the way he had done. Seeing her face now, he knew that he had failed to understand the half of what she had been through.

She turned, saw his expression, and, giving way to tears of joy, she buried her face against his shoulder. He held her close, moved almost to tears himself.

'It's all right, love,' he said softly. 'He's going to be fine.'

She smiled and sniffed and searched for a tissue in her coat pocket.

'I know,' she said, dabbing at her eyes. 'It's just that all this time, when I was telling everyone he was my son, I was crossing my fingers at the same time. Now I don't have to. It really is Johnny, and everyone believes me. Most important of all, you believe me!'

'Oh, darling, I'm sorry—'

'No, no.' She patted away his apology. 'It doesn't matter now. I just wish—' She broke off and leant over the bed again, laying her hand on her son's face. 'It seems such a long time for him to be unconscious. I know it isn't, really. Elaine keeps quoting case after case of young men in a coma much longer than this, who've been up and winning Wimbledon and climbing the Matterhorn in no time flat. She says he's showing various signs of coming out of it soon, and I know she's right. I've recognised them myself.'

'When he does, we'll bring him home,' Tom said. 'We'll look after him.'

She flashed him a smile so brilliant that it made him blink.

'Oh, we will, won't we? I knew you'd agree. He'll be safer with us.'

Tom made no comment. She had told him of her suspicions and fears and he had given his reaction. Her imagination was running riot, he told her. No civilised government would countenance violence like this, not even South Africa.

She had raised her eyebrows.

'Who said they were civilised?' she asked.

Such a beautiful country! She hadn't, actually, seen much of it, not nearly as much as she would have liked. She had longed to see the Drakensberg Mountains 'One day,' Guy had promised, but that day never came. There was always too much work to be done, or some other urgent reason why it was impossible to leave Cape Town – a match of some kind to be played, a team practice he could not avoid.

So instead she had been taken to beauty spots that were close to home: Hout Bay, False Bay, Muizenberg, Camps Bay, Fish Hoek and Cape Point. She had explored Kirstenbosch and climbed the mountain, and had loved it all.

The trip she looked back on with most pleasure was one she and Johnny had taken to Hermanus with Helen one long weekend when their menfolk had gone away for a three-day golf match.

'You'll love it,' Helen assured her. 'And it'll do you good to have a change of scene. Johnny will adore it, mark my words.'

He was eighteen months old, a handsome, sturdy child – and brighter than average, Kate felt quite sure. He could say any number of words now. The thought of having him entirely to herself, if only for three days, was one that appealed to her greatly.

They planned to lie in the sun and swim in the sea, but these plans were largely foiled by the wind that whipped up the waves and tore the hats from their heads and blew sand into their eyes; but even so Kate enjoyed every moment of the short time away from Gramerci. There was something about the wildness of the ocean and the magnificence of the coastal scenery that made her feel as if prison doors had opened. She said as much to Helen, but then caught herself as soon as the words were out of her mouth.

'That's an awful thing to say,' she said, laughing. 'Gramerci is hardly a prison.'

'Of course it isn't,' Helen agreed. 'I must say, though, that this place seems to suit you. You're looking awfully pretty.'

'I wish—' Kate said.

'Wish what?' Helen prompted when she said no more.

'Nothing,' said Kate.

Helen did not persist. She had no need to. She thought she knew at least some of the things that Kate wished.

Despite the disclaimer, there was a distinct feeling of prison doors clanging shut when Kate returned to Gramerci, even though she had, by this time, learned to drive and thus had more freedom. Paul, Helen's husband, had been her official teacher. Guy, who at first had said that he trusted no one but himself to teach her properly, had nevertheless given up after the second disastrous lesson which had ended in temper on his part and tears on hers; however, it was Helen who, in secret, had given her subsidiary lessons and to whom she felt most of the credit was due for liberating her in this way.

Even so, she was aware of an undeniable feeling of claustrophobia every time she drove up between the oak trees towards the house, as if some all-powerful presence there was waiting to smother every ounce of individuality she possessed. Johnny – whose name had been a cause of controversy almost from the day of his birth – was a sunny, healthy child, beloved by everyone. His birth, Kate felt, might have been expected to result in Sonia's recognition of her right to be part of the family. It hadn't happened like that.

Lampard babies were left to cry; they had the intelligence, Sonia said, to learn very quickly that crying had no effect, and that they would be fed four-hourly. Particularly, Lampard babies did not wake in the night, loudly demanding additional snacks.

In vain did Kate protest her willingness to get up several times a night, if necessary. Guy refused to allow it. A few bad nights, he said, and the baby would be quiet thereafter. Silently Kate wept as he held her down; but it had to be admitted that he appeared to be right. Johnny *did* learn to go through the night without a feed – but at what cost, Kate asked herself? At what cost to her, as well as to him?

Her wants and opinions were brushed aside. Sonia – who had never had a child of her own and as far as Kate knew had never been exposed to any – seemed, nevertheless, to know all there was to know about bringing up a baby, just as she knew all there was to know about everything else. And Guy, naturally, took her part.

Even Dr Grobler, appealed to by Kate in desperation, told her that she worried too much.

'Maybe that's why our cricketers beat your cricketers,' he said jovially, flashing a man-to-man smile in Guy's direction. 'We breed them tough in South Africa, Mrs Lampard.'

Kate prayed for Christiaan le Roux to get to the point and ask Sonia to marry him when, hopefully, he would whisk her off to some other place of residence. And even if marriage did not result in Sonia's removal from the scene altogether, she would, surely, have other things to occupy her mind? Maybe even a baby of her own.

There was, however, no immediate answer to her prayers. Undoubtedly, Sonia was in love with Christiaan; at least, Guy seemed to think so. He had never seen her like this with anyone before, he said – adding that if Christiaan had any sense at all he'd give in sooner rather than later, for Sonia always got what she wanted in the end and was like a tigress if thwarted in any way.

'But is he in love with her?' Kate asked him. Guy smiled at that and shrugged his shoulders.

'Your guess is as good as mine. He seems devoted, doesn't he?'

Kate said nothing. She wasn't at all sure about Christiaan. He often dined at Gramerci, as much at ease as if he were already a member of the family, and constantly escorted Sonia to social events. In the eyes of the world their official engagement appeared to be regarded as only a matter of time, yet clearly no proposal of marriage had taken place.

'There's something . . . something *slippery* about him,' she said to Helen. 'He smiles too much.'

'I know what you mean,' Helen agreed. 'He's too good to be true. Still, it's not our opinion that counts, is it?'

'I just wish he'd pop the question and put her out of her misery.'

'Sonia's the kind of person who only wants the unattainable,' Helen said. 'So maybe the fact that he isn't swooning at her feet is part of the attraction. That and the fact that he is so divinely handsome he makes Clark Gable look like an also-ran.'

'He's handsome all right,' Kate agreed. 'But doesn't he know it?' She'd changed, she realised, from the girl who had almost swooned at her first sight of Guy at the village fête. Looks were beginning to seem to her like the least important thing about anybody.

She had given up the baby clinic three months before Johnny was born, instead redoubling her efforts to learn Afrikaans. Her original teacher had given up through ill-health and she had been all too ready to let things slide; however, she asked around and found a sweet old *predikant*, long retired, who was happy to give her lessons. It was altogether a happier association than she had experienced with her previous teacher, and she felt, with satisfaction, that she was making progress at last.

Even these lessons went by the board when Johnny was born, however, and for some reason she felt reluctant to begin them again. Instead, encouraged by Jane, she waited until the baby was six months old and she was no longer tied by breast-feeding and then signed up for a preliminary nursing course. Guy was both astonished and disapproving, but she stood her ground. It was only part-time, she said, and Rosie was capable of looking after Johnny for a few hours.

'But why the hell—?' Guy had demanded.

'So that I can be more useful at the clinic.'

'And I suppose the good doctor suggested this?'

'Yes, she did,' Kate said firmly. 'And I thought it an excellent idea.'

When the course was over she found herself anxious to take up her duties again, and having done so, was delighted to find that her studies, elementary though they had been, had increased her confidence. Her respect and affection for Jane Ryder grew with every week that passed, and she was sad when she applied for a job in a prison hospital in Port Elizabeth.

'My God,' Guy said when he heard of her new appointment, 'when mass attempted escapes are reported, we'll know what caused them. But what's going to happen at the clinic? I suppose another *Kaffirboetie*'s been found to take her place?'

Kate made no reply to this. The term *Kaffirboetie* meant, literally, 'Little Brother of the Africans', but it had become an expression of contempt which she disliked intensely; however, she had no intention of giving Guy the satisfaction of arguing with him on the matter. Any protest, she knew from experience, was a waste of emotion.

Since the Dora episode, which had upset her far more than Guy ever knew, she had realised that if she were to continue to live as his wife in his house, she would have to do so according to his rules, accepting him for what his upbringing had made him. It was not that he was unkind. For Evalina and the Africans that worked on the estate he felt real affection, and it had to be admitted that this was reciprocated. 'My boy,' Evalina called him, and Kate soon learned that he could do no wrong in her eyes. Her bewilderment at this apparent inconsistency grew. Guy would go into the kitchen, joke with Rosie, dip his finger into Evalina's mixing bowl, playfully duck to avoid a blow – yet she knew, because he had told her, that he had thrown away the cup that Dora had used. Playful he might be with his own servants, but he had no time for those who filled the natives' heads with dreams of equality.

With a few meritorious exceptions, all others of his race and upbringing were the same – totally incapable of seeing the racial situation from any perspective other than their own. Kate knew now that harmony between them could only be maintained if she bit her tongue and refrained from argument.

Still, Guy wasn't as anti-British as the others, she told herself. Sometimes he laughingly protested when Sonia denigrated the entire British race, pointing out that they were half English themselves.

'Don't I know it,' Sonia had said bitterly. 'I've been trying to live it down from the day of my birth.'

And Guy had laughed at that, too.

Kate still loved him, even if she didn't agree with everything he said. He was so handsome and popular; the most attractive man at every gathering they attended.

'You must be so proud,' an elderly lady had whispered in her ear just recently when she had been present to see Guy go up to receive his monthly medal prize at the golf club. And Kate, seeing him so tall and bronzed and handsome, so amusingly self-deprecating in his acceptance speech, could only nod her head in smiling agreement.

'I always think,' the woman had continued, her voice tremulous with emotion, 'that your husband is the very . . . the very *epitome* of young South Africa. He's a credit to his country, my dear. You're a lucky young lady.'

Kate had nodded and smiled once more. She *was* lucky, she told herself. Only a romantic fool – as, admittedly, she once had been – would really imagine that any marriage could exist without the odd disagreement. She was sure that she and Guy were as happy as the next couple.

Even so, there were days when she felt herself to be superfluous to requirements, her views totally disregarded, and on those days it seemed to her that if she were to go her departure would pass unnoticed. As a wife, Guy could replace her many times over – and replace her, she was well aware, with a nice, conventional South African girl who was in agreement with his views and played a good game of golf. Sonia would be only too pleased to take over as mother.

It was on one such day, after a particularly blatant piece of interference from Sonia concerning punishment for what she considered bad behaviour on Johnny's part but which Kate saw as normal for a child of two, that she was provoked into pouring her heart out to Larry, whom she met, as she often did, in the hills surrounding his cottage when she was out with the dogs. She had taken little notice of Guy's order not to speak to him and though she had never been to his cottage again, still their friendship had grown.

Larry had seen her distress and had guessed the reason for it.

'Get out while you're young,' he said. 'They're not your sort of people, Kate. Cut your losses and run.'

'That's an awful thing to say! You can't run away from a marriage just like that.'

'There's such a thing as divorce,' Larry pointed out. 'I'm divorced myself.'

'Are you?' Diverted from her own problems for a moment, Kate looked at him with interest. If he'd been married in the past, did that mean that Guy was completely wrong about him? It wouldn't be the first time, after all. On the other hand, maybe his peculiar preferences were the cause of the breakdown in his marriage. 'I'm . . . I'm sorry.'

He was smiling, as if he knew her thoughts and was amused by them.

'No need to be. Some marriages are better ended.'

'Maybe,' Kate conceded. 'Not mine, though. I couldn't leave Johnny and I couldn't take him away. It wouldn't be fair on Guy. I know he really loves him even if I don't always agree with everything he does. And anyway,' she went on after a moment's pause, 'there are practical difficulties. I couldn't earn a living. I've no qualifications, I'm only half educated. In fact I'm utterly useless, with no talents at all.'

'I don't believe that, not for one moment.' Larry sat down on a fallen log and patted it, inviting her to sit beside him. 'No money and no qualifications, maybe. But no talents? That's just nonsense. You don't know what they are yet, that's all. How old are you, anyway? Not quite twenty? My darling girl, you're a babe in arms!'

'I was a babe when I married Guy, that's certain.' Kate gave a bitter little laugh. 'I had no idea that I was going to have to marry his sister as well. If only she would leave us alone!'

'Tell him,' Larry urged her.

'Make him choose?' Kate looked at him, biting her lip. Then she shook her head. 'I daren't. He wouldn't choose me, you know. He'd choose Sonia and Gramerci.' She sighed, then shook her head in disgust at herself. 'Oh, hark at me! Take no notice of me, Larry – today started off badly and I'm just feeling low. I know I'm lucky to be living in such comfort in such a gorgeous place. And I do still love Guy, you know. Leaving him really doesn't enter into it.'

'Well—' Larry stood up, ready to go back to his own concerns. 'You must do what you think best. I'd just say one thing to you when you're pondering your future. Look what the Lampards did to Lilian.'

He lifted his hand in farewell and began to move away in the direction of his cottage, leaving Kate beside the log looking after him.

'Hey – don't go for a minute,' she called out, wanting to know more. But though he turned, smiled at her over his shoulder and waved his hand again, he kept on walking away from her without another word.

Kate's relationship with her mother-in-law had remained friendly but remote. She had, apparently, been delighted with the arrival of Johnny, bringing with it the status of 'Ouma'. But though she liked, sometimes, to sit with Kate in the candlewood tree, watching as he kicked on the rug spread on the grass, or later took his first steps, she was never anxious to take a more active part. Not for her was there any question of involvement in his day-to-day care.

Fortunately there was no need for it. Rosie had been appointed as nursery maid and was devoted to him, often allying herself with Kate in an unspoken conspiracy against the more severe rules laid down by Sonia.

At least Lilian was not severe. Vaguely benign would most adequately describe her attitude, Kate thought; and there was no doubt that she seemed to be getting more vague as time went by. Days passed without Kate seeing her at all, for she took more and more to having meals in her own cottage. Sometimes Kate paid a friendly call, but though Lilian was never less than politely friendly in return, neither did she give the impression of being particularly pleased by the visit.

Guy, who out of a sense of duty sometimes dropped in to see her in the evening, invariably came back in a foul mood, raging at the latest sayings or doings of Larry, who remained as constant a visitor as ever.

'But just think, darling,' Kate said soothingly on one such occasion, 'he must be a great comfort to her. After all, she doesn't seem to have any other friends.'

'She did have,' he said angrily. 'She had a load of arty-farty friends, but she's alienated all of them. Even the Nelsons. She was very close to Grace at one time, but she never sees her now. She never sees anyone but that filthy little—'

'Did you know he'd been married?' Kate said, forestalling the inevitable description. 'He's divorced.'

'I'm not surprised.' Guy laughed. 'What woman could stand him?'

'Well,' Kate said, unwisely, 'your mother, for one.'

Guy had blazed with anger at this.

'Her brains are addled,' he exploded. 'She's not fit to run her affairs. I ought to have power of attorney, that's the truth of it. I've a damn good mind to ask Christiaan if it can be arranged. Grobler would back me up, I'm sure of that.'

'But why?' Kate frowned at him, bewildered. 'She's perfectly capable of managing her own affairs, and you know it. I don't understand why her friendship with Larry bothers you so much.'

'You don't, do you?' Guy gave a derisive laugh. 'You really don't see the point! Doesn't it occur to you that she could make a will leaving the cottage to Donoghue? She still nominally owns the land. And not only the cottage,' he went on. 'She could leave him money – money that we badly need! That's what he's aiming for, of course, smarming around her like this as if he really cared two hoots about her welfare.'

'He's fond of her, I'm sure,' Kate protested. Guy laughed again.

'My God, man, you are so green! I wouldn't trust Larry Donoghue as far as I could throw him. Something's got to be done. I'll talk to Christiaan. See if he can advise anything. He's a lawyer – it's time he sang for his supper,' he added, happy now that he had decided on a definite course of action. He went to pour himself a drink.

Kate, busy mending a small pair of striped dungarees, looked at him with the needle poised for a moment, a frown on her face.

'It doesn't bother you,' she said at last, 'that anything you do against Larry would make your mother very unhappy?'

Guy, glass in hand, turned to stare at her, uncomprehending.

'That's the trouble with women,' he said after a moment, shaking his head as if the female mentality were a closed book to him. 'They get so emotional.'

Colin was out of the office when the news came through. He had been in court all day, not returning until late afternoon when, quite by chance, in coversation with the sports editor, he learned that Jan Lampard was in hospital in London.

'Unconscious,' Don told him. 'The victim of a mugging, apparently. It'll be in tomorrow's paper.'

Colin stared at him in horror.

'How bad is he?'

Don shrugged his shoulders.

'Dunno. It was Craig Summers who told me. He should have the details.'

But details, Colin found, were thin on the ground. Craig Summers, who had been given the task of writing up the story, had no information regarding the gravity of Jan's condition. All anyone knew for certain was that Jan was unconscious in St Luke's hospital, London.

'Presumably we'd have heard if he was on the critical list,' Summers said.

Colin's suggestion that he should phone the hospital met with a marked lack of enthusiasm.

'Does it matter?' Summers asked. 'It'll probably be spiked, anyway, for lack of space.'

'He is Christiaan le Roux's nephew, you know.'

'Yeah, well—' Summers remained lukewarm. 'There's the Marais murder trial taking four columns, which means moving the piece about the union trouble in Durban to page two. It's going to be a tight fit. I'll have to see how it goes.'

'What did you say the hospital was called? St Luke's, was it?'

'That's right. Hey – you a friend of his, or something?' As if scenting a story, Summers looked up and pointed his thin nose in Colin's direction.

'Just a friend of a friend,' Colin said.

It was important, he felt, that Nina should be forewarned if there were the slightest chance that she might read the news in next morning's papers, and he tried to phone her as soon as he reached home. There was no reply – neither then, nor half an hour later when he tried again, nor on the next three occasions.

The evening was sultry, following weeks and weeks of blazing sunshine and a hot, dry wind that had devastated the gardens of suburbia. Now the wind had dropped and heavy clouds were building. There seemed no air at all.

Colin sat on his small balcony overlooking a street, quiet now that the shops were shut and the office workers had gone home. He poured himself a cold beer, and as he drank it he thought about Jan.

Did the mugging have anything to do with the fact that Christiaan le Roux was anxiously looking for him before he left the country? It was, he thought on reflection, unlikely; but not impossible. By no means impossible. He could easily have contacts in London who would carry out any dirty work required of them – but then again, would le Roux really commission the death of his nephew simply because he was an embarrassment to him? It seemed a bit rich, even for an ambitious politician.

Maybe it was just a mugging, plain and simple. A visiting holiday-maker, a stranger in a strange land, drifting away from the respectable part of the city by mistake. It could happen anywhere. And surely, if murder had been intended then Jan's attackers wouldn't have left him before making sure they'd carried out their orders?

But they might have thought they'd done so. They could have underestimated the toughness of their quarry. Jan's head was hard – he'd proved that many times over, not only on the rugger field but on other fields of battle when police batons had rained down on him, and outraged citizens had wielded chairs.

Passing the telephone on his way to the kitchen for another beer, Colin paused and tried Nina's number once more. There was still no reply; but instead of continuing to the kitchen he stayed where he was, looking thoughtfully at the phone.

Overseas calls were expensive, and his salary ill equipped him to make them. On the other hand, there was Nina. She was still fond of Jan, no matter that they weren't together any more. She would be out of her mind with worry, not knowing any details, not knowing, even, if Jan were still alive.

Nina's feelings, he realised, not without some surprise, meant more to him than anything else. He gave a brief grunt of amusement which ended in a wry laugh as he dialled Overseas Enquiries.

This surely had to be love.

Tom drove one-handed back from the hospital. The other hand was clasped firmly round Kate's.

'We must tell the children,' he said. 'They need to know. Anyway,' he went on, glancing briefly at the look on her face. 'Vicky's going to guess something. You look as if a lifetime of Christmasses have been rolled into one.'

'Do I?' Kate laughed. 'Well, maybe just half a lifetime. When he comes round and we can talk – that's when I'll hit the jack-pot.'

Pray God he comes up to expectations, Tom thought, still wary. It wasn't, however, the kind of reflection to lay before Kate on a night like this.

'Larry said once that I should have to look to Johnny for my happiness,' she said.

'How old were you? Eighteen? Nineteen?'

'Twenty by then, I think.'

'Even so—' Tom frowned. 'It assumes a pretty bleak prospect for a girl, doesn't it? Not that Johnny didn't bring you happiness – then, anyway – but all life was in front of you. You might have expected there'd be more.'

'And there was, as it's turned out. I've been lucky.'

'Me too. You know,' he went on after a few moments as they waited for the traffic lights to change, 'I don't think I ever heard what happened to Larry.'

'Oh, you must have done! I'm sure I told you.'

'Maybe I forgot.'

'Maybe you did. He played such a big part. A strange man, Larry, but incredibly kind. No one gave him any credit for it. Guy and Sonia, they never could see why he took such an interest in Lilian. How important he was to her. They never believed it was out of the goodness of his heart – that he didn't have his eye on the main chance in some way. He didn't, though. Whatever his sexual proclivities, he was a good man.'

It was his sexual proclivities that did for him, though. There was, undoubtedly, a certain femininity in the way he moved and a look of girlishness to his features – even the bone structure of his neat little skull looked as if it might more happily belong to a woman – but never, as far as Kate was aware, did he entertain men friends at the cottage or behave in any way that could have laid him open to any charge of promiscuity or obscene behaviour. Guy, however, was homophobic to a degree. He felt, he told Kate, physically sick whenever he saw the man, and he would do anything to remove his hated presence from Gramerci land.

When Guy asked for Christiaan le Roux's advice and help in getting power of attorney over his mother's affairs he was met by expressions of doubt. There seemed, Christiaan said, no good reason in law why he should do so. Lilian was perfectly *compos mentis* – vague, of course, and a little eccentric like many elderly ladies, but far from senile. If she were to contest the proposal, then Guy would have no hope at all of instituting such an arrangement.

'But maybe,' he went on thoughtfully, 'you could think of some way of getting Donoghue out? Am I right in thinking that if he were discredited in her eyes to the extent that she gave him his marching orders your troubles would be over?'

The four of them – Kate, Guy, Sonia and Christiaan – were sitting on the stoep drinking gin slings. It was very hot. The garden seemed to swim in an impressionistic haze of colours, and tiny emerald-green sugar-birds darted among the flowers just below them. While Christiaan had been talking at some length about the requirements for powers of attorney and giving reasons why Guy would be unable to procure it, Kate had allowed her attention to wander, diverted by the antics of the birds; but at this suggestion, she sat up straight in her chair.

'No!' she said, indignantly. 'No, Guy! You can't do that.'

'Why not?' Guy asked mildly, laughing at her vehemence. 'Sodomy's against the law. Let's get the bastard put away.'

'You can't!' she said again. 'Oh, Guy – you can't. You have no proof at all—'

'Christiaan might find some.'

'But think of your mother,' Kate begged him. 'He's her friend!

She'd be lost without him. Honestly – it would be like . . . like a bereavement. After all, she has no one else—'

'Well, really!' It was Sonia's turn to laugh, but clearly she was more outraged than amused. 'I must say I think that's rather rich, Kate. No one else? With Guy and me living here? Whatever right do you have to say such a thing? Why, there never was such a good son as Guy. He's always looked after her devotedly, and only has her welfare at heart. This dependence of hers on a wretched little pervert like Donoghue is hardly something to be encouraged.'

Kate refused to back down.

'Guy's worried about what she might leave Larry in her will, that's all.'

'That's only part of the story.' Guy's expression was one of outraged innocence.

'But you said—'

'I don't want her to leave land and money away from Gramerci, that's perfectly true. Not for my sake, though. Only for the business. You'll agree with me there, Sonia, won't you? We can't allow a jumped-up little nobody like Donoghue to weasel his way in for the sole purpose of feathering his own nest at Gramerci's expense.'

'Of course I agree with you.' Sonia looked at Kate unsmilingly. 'I know we can't expect you to understand how we feel about the land, Kate, but it would be like cutting out our hearts to give a foot of it away to the likes of Donoghue.'

'I do understand,' Kate said hotly. 'Of course I understand how you feel about Gramerci. It's just that Lilian would be so dreadfully upset.'

'Well!' Sonia smiled once more, and did her best to moderate her voice to the kind of honeyed tones that she so often employed in Christiaan le Roux's company. 'We shall just have to be extra kind and thoughtful towards her, won't we?'

Kate said nothing, subsiding into a sceptical silence. And Sonia suggested that *my* statement was rich, she thought. When had she ever been kind and thoughtful towards her mother?

No more was said on the subject in Kate's hearing, and she cherished the hope that it had died a natural death. Christiaan le Roux went to Durban for a few weeks in connection with a protracted court case, and it was Easter before he came again bearing an Easter egg for Johnny, silk scarves for Kate and Lilian and gold earrings for Sonia.

Still no ring, Kate thought; and seeing the fleeting expression of expectation on Sonia's face as she accepted the small, square jeweller's box, moderating immediately into a look of polite pleasure as she realised it was the wrong shape, she felt pretty sure her sister-in-law had the same reaction, even though she thanked le Roux prettily enough.

There were a number of social events to occupy the weekend, including a *braaivleis* at Gramerci on Easter Saturday to which all the usual set of friends had been invited. Greta was to be there, but her presence didn't worry Kate unduly. These days Guy paid no more attention to her than he would have done to Helen or any other of their circle; rather less, in fact.

The devotion he had shown towards Kate preceding and immediately after Johnny's birth had moderated now, but he still gave every appearance of being a loving father and a faithful husband, whatever their differences in private. Kate suspected that Sonia had given him a dressing-down following his behaviour at the Nelsons' party the Christmas before last. Certainly there had been no repetition of it. What Greta's husband had thought of that incident was not on record, though he couldn't, surely, have been unaware of it. However, if it had angered him then, he had certainly put the incident behind him now, for he was always genial in his dealings with Guy – which must surely mean that she had over-reacted in being so upset about it. Helen had been right. Greta and Guy were old friends, that was all.

Kate couldn't help feeling a little wary of Greta, though. She was so spectacularly lovely, so beautifully and expensively turned out at every gathering she graced. It was impossible not to feel gauche and slightly sub-standard in comparison – but, Kate felt, she held one trump card which Greta did not possess, and never would. Johnny!

So full of paternal pride was Guy that Johnny could never throw a ball without being hailed by his father as a future Springbok, or plunge into the smallest pool without his assuring anyone near enough to listen that the boy knew no fear. Didn't know the meaning of it! There never, to hear Guy talk, had been a child so intelligent, so gifted, so handsome. Or so tough. Toughness, to Guy, was the most prized attribute of all, and it was the reason that he upheld Sonia in every argument regarding discipline. Tough little boys, in their opinion, took their punishment like men.

Kate was sometimes irritated by this constant emphasis on toughness and was anxious to encourage the more sensitive side of Johnny's nature. There were arguments with Guy on the subject, but even so never, ever, did she have any doubt of Guy's love for his child. It gave her a sense of security. She felt quite certain that he would never risk his marriage for the sake of a fling with Greta, or anyone else.

It had rained heavily just before Easter and Good Friday dawned cool and cloudy. Vague plans had been made for a day out at the beach, but in view of the weather they were shelved and Guy, astonishingly, opted for a day at home. Even more astonishingly, he agreed to accompany Kate and his mother to the morning service at the little grey English church. Kate's delight at this was increased a thousandfold by the knowledge that Sonia and Christiaan had gone out for the entire day and would not be returning until night.

For once she felt they were a real family. Johnny behaved well, looking about him with saucer eyes, flirting outrageously with the lady in the pew behind, standing on the pew seat during the hymns, hymn book upside down, singing – fortunately in a muted voice – something that to Kate bore a distinct resemblance to 'The Grand Old Duke of York', one of his current favourites.

He went to sleep during the sermon and, when the service was over, he allowed Guy to carry him outside to the accompaniment of smiles of admiration from the feminine portion of the congregation. Outside, after the service, they surrounded Guy, who proudly accepted all the compliments that came his way. Kate stood by, happily smiling, wishing that it could always be like this.

Lilian had lunch with them, then retired to her cottage to rest. Watery sun emerged in the afternoon and, taking advantage of the weather, Kate went outside with Johnny. There were protea seeds ready for sowing and the first bulbs pushing their shoots through the earth, encouraged by the rain.

'Come and look,' she called to Guy, who was beginning to look less enchanted with his quiet day than he had done earlier. Without a match to be played, a ball to be hit, he seemed, to Kate, to be at something of a loss. 'Look, Guy – what are these?'

He sauntered over, hands in his pockets, and, staring down, shrugged his shoulders.

'God knows,' he said. 'Lilies, or something.'

'Isn't it odd that they grow in autumn and not spring?'

But Guy was not listening. He'd discovered a ball hidden under a low branch of the plumbago bush and had picked it up.

'Come on, old man,' he said, throwing it to Johnny. Crowing with delight, the little boy scampered after it and made a good attempt to throw it back. 'There, look at him, Kate!' Guy was practically crowing himself. 'He's got terrific ball sense. Here, catch this, you little Springbok.'

Kate abandoned the bulbs and stood for a moment, watching them. She was smiling. We could be so happy here, she thought. Just Guy and Johnny and me. We could have more children, build a proper life. Guy would settle down—

Please God, she said to herself as she turned back to her gardening. Please God make Christiaan marry Sonia and take her away somewhere, and make Guy love me and please, please make everything all right.

The following day the clouds dispersed altogether and the *braaivleis* took place under a starry sky with only the lightest of winds to fan the flames. Larry, needless to say, had not been invited, but Lilian, elegant in black, put in an appearance and seemed to be enjoying herself in the company of her old friends, David and Grace Nelson. Kate, looking at the house with the lights streaming from doors and windows, hearing the voices and laughter of friends, felt again the same wistful longing for the happiness that was surely to be found here – quite close, but just out of reach, it sometimes seemed.

'Ah, the mistress of the house,' said a silky voice. Kate turned to see Flick smiling at her in that strange, ambiguous way. Kate smiled back, not afraid of her any more.

'Flick – hallo! Welcome to Gramerci. The drinks are over there, by the side of the steps.'

'I can wait a moment or two, darling. I'm not that much of a tippler.'

'Oh, I didn't mean—'

'I adore your dress.'

'Thank you.'

'That colour must be fashionable this season. I've just seen Greta Carlton in one just the same sort of shade. Look – there she is, talking to Guy.' She smiled and waggled her fingers in greeting. 'Such a gorgeous creature, isn't she? How can any of us compete?'

Kate continued smiling.

'How indeed? Excuse me, Flick. I must go and welcome Marcia and Laurie. Do go and get a drink.' And why not put a little arsenic in it, she added silently as she moved away. Not that Flick's barbed remarks bothered her in the slightest, she assured herself – but even so, she could not avoid a quick look in the direction in which she had seen Guy and Greta only a moment before and was undeniably relieved to see that Guy was now walking towards her with Greta nowhere in sight.

She liked Marcia no more now than she did on board ship, but hoped that she gave no sign of it. Nevertheless it was with relief that she was able to turn from her to greet Helen and Paul who had arrived just a few moments later. Behind them, awaiting his turn, stood Christiaan le Roux, charming smile at the ready.

'Must talk soon,' Helen whispered over her shoulder as she and Paul were drawn into the party. 'I've got something to tell you.' She grinned widely as she spoke. It was good news, then, Kate thought as she turned to le Roux. Could it possibly be—?

'Kate! How delightful you look.' Christiaan took her hand in both of his. 'I'm so glad the weather was kind.' He turned to Guy, who had just joined them. 'Hallo, Guy. Just the man I wanted to see. Did Sonia tell you I had some news for you?'

More news? Kate was aware of Guy's brief glance in her direction.

'She mentioned something of the kind,' he said. 'Later, eh, man?'

She might have taken more notice, Kate thought afterwards, had she not been so intrigued by Helen's look of excitement. There was only one piece of news she could think of that could bring such an expression of joy to her face.

'Well?' she said, when under cover of the band hired for the occasion she drew Helen aside into the shadow of the plumbago hedge. 'Tell me! Is it—'

'A baby,' Helen said. 'At last! Isn't it wonderful? I'd given up hope of ever being able to have another.'

'Oh, Helen! I'm so pleased.'

The two girls hugged each other, laughing in their delight.

'I've got to hang on to this one,' Helen said. 'Dr Grobler says it'll be my last chance. I must rest, he says, which is an awful bore, but I don't care. I'll do anything.'

'You'll be just fine,' Kate assured her. 'Oh, Helen – I couldn't be more pleased.'

Later, in bed, she told Guy.

'Isn't it wonderful?' she demanded.

'Mm.' He was undressing, putting his pyjamas on.

'Didn't Paul say anything?'

'What? Oh, no. He didn't mention it.' He went to the window and drew the curtain aside, standing for a moment to look at the night sky. He was smiling when he turned back to her.

'Good party, wasn't it?'

'I thought so. People seemed to enjoy it.'

Guy chuckled.

'I enjoyed it, anyway. Christiaan put the finishing touch on it for me.'

'Oh, yes!' Remembering, Kate sat up a little straighter against the pillows. 'What was it he wanted to say to you?'

Guy laughed again.

'He's done us proud,' he said, climbing into bed beside her. 'Come up with the perfect reason to get rid of Donoghue once and for all. Would you believe that he's got a sworn affidavit from a shebeen-owner in District Six saying that friend Donoghue has frequented his premises for years for the sole purpose of picking up boys? Kaffirs, of course. Now what do you say about him?'

Kate stared at him.

'I don't believe it,' she said.

'It's a criminal offence, you know.'

'I don't believe it,' she said again. 'I think the two of you cooked it up between you. He's much too fastidious for that.'

'Fastidious? Him?' Guy roared with laughter. 'I'm afraid you're wrong, my love. We've really got him now. Either he gets out or we turn him in.'

'Guy, that's despicable! Larry Donoghue is an educated, cultured, talented man, and your mother's fond of him. You can't believe this of him! She certainly won't.'

'She's misguided. And so are you. Go to sleep, Kate. It's been a long day.'

Kate ignored this. She had never felt less like sleep.

'Lilian's not going to think much of you if you succeed in dragging him into court, is she?' she said bitterly.

'It won't come to that.' Guy sounded weary of the subject. 'Donoghue won't want this to come to light. He'll be out of here before the count of three, mark my words. Now, please, can we get some sleep?'

'You can, if you like,' Kate said stonily. 'I'm too angry to sleep.'

'Well, please yourself!'

With that, Guy turned over on his side, his back towards her, and said no more.

10

What was she to do for the best? Larry was her friend; she could hardly bear to go to him and tell him what Guy proposed to do. On the other hand, if he were forewarned, might he be able to fight it in some way? Get his own lawyer, maybe?

In the end she decided it would be kindest to tell him, and consequently she went to the cottage the very next morning.

She found him engrossed in his work, but on this occasion she had no hesitation in interrupting him, even though he scowled at her at first and made no bones about it not being the right time for visitors. However, as, very hesitantly, she told him of Guy's intentions, his expression changed. He became first bewildered, and then furiously angry.

'There's not a word of truth in it! The bastard's out to ruin me.' Savagely he flung down his brush and took a few wild and random steps around the room he had converted into his studio.

'No – no, Larry, I don't think it's that. He wants you out of the cottage.'

'And away from Lilian – that's it, isn't it? He thinks I'm a bad influence.' Larry gave a loud and mirthless laugh. 'Bad influence! That's a good one. Doesn't it enter his thick head to wonder why she's stopped drinking?'

'Drinking!' Kate stared at him.

'You must have known. Surely Guy told you.'

'No, never. I've never seen her take so much as a glass of wine, not in all the time I've been here.'

'Because of me. *Me!* I know what it's like, Kate. I was an alcoholic for years – still am, I suppose, but the difference now is that I control it instead of the other way around. When I met Lilian it didn't take me long to see she had the same problem. I've helped

her. Encouraged her. Talked to her for hours when the craving was
more than she could bear.'

Kate was still looking at him in horror.

'I had no idea,' she said. 'But surely Guy and Sonia must
realise—'

'Yes, of course they know. But do they care?' He gave another
bitter laugh. 'The answer to that is no, not as long as she keeps out
of sight and doesn't disgrace them in front of their friends. She has
been known to.'

'I had no idea,' Kate said again. 'Surely—'

'Guy and Sonia are as self-centred as each other.' He swung
about the room, not giving her time to speak. 'They were brought
up by their father and grandmother to think that the Lampards are
the centre of the universe. It never occurred to them that it was
the bloody Lampards themselves that might possibly be the reason
Lilian started drinking in the first place.'

'But *why*?' Kate asked. Larry took out a cigarette, lit it, and began
to smoke in short, angry bursts.

'You should know,' he said at last, very quietly. 'Loneliness,
I imagine, and a sense of inadequacy. A feeling that she never
measured up. Lilian told me she hadn't been married a year before
her husband told her he'd been tricked by her beauty into making
the greatest mistake of his life. It was an aberration, he said. A
moment of madness. She was never made welcome. Her children
were taught to despise her—'

'No!' Kate's whispered denial was no less forceful for being so
faint that Larry could barely hear her.

'Remind you of something?' Larry asked savagely, rounding on
her. 'Can you see yourself in a few years' time?'

'No,' she said again, louder this time. 'I wouldn't let it happen.
I've got more pride.'

Larry made no reply to this, but walked outside to the small
terrace which lay beyond the french windows of his studio and
stood on the edge of it, his back towards her. After a few moments
she followed him.

'"Earth hath not anything to show more fair,"' he said, in a voice
totally devoid of expression.

'"And only man is vile,"' Kate said. 'Oh, Larry, please fight
this. I only told you because I thought it would give you time to
think – time to form a plan of action. As soon as Guy told me

about it, I was certain the whole thing was thought up by him or Christiaan or both of them, I knew it wasn't true. There are heaps of others who'd think the same. Think of Lilian! What's she going to do without you?'

For a long moment he smoked in silence. Then he shrugged his shoulders.

'I don't know what she'll do,' he said. 'But I'm no hero, Kate. I'll be sorry to leave her. I've grown fond of the funny old dowager over the years, but I've struggled for years to make my mark professionally and I have to put that first. I'm nearly forty-five and I have the feeling that it's now or never. Maybe you're right – if I fought this I might emerge with my reputation intact. On the other hand, I might not. No smoke without fire, people would say. And they're right! Yes, I'll come clean! I am a homosexual – a pansy, as Guy would undoubtedly put it – but that's my cross, not anyone else's. What do you think it's like for me and others like me, living in a place like this, knowing that something I have no control over is enough to put me in jail?'

'Oh, Larry! I'm so sorry.'

He turned and looked at her, a bitter little smile on his face.

'Yes,' he said. 'I know you are. None of this is your fault. It isn't true, you know. I mean about the shebeen and the boys. I've been more or less celibate for years. Work seemed the only possible thing.'

'It simply isn't fair. I wish you'd stay.'

'I can't. There's too much at stake.'

'What will you do?'

'Go to America. New York. As a matter of fact, I've been thinking about it for some time. I have a friend there. A dear friend. He wants me to join him. Really, it was only the thought that I was getting known at last that held me back. And Lilian, believe it or not. And all this, of course.' He swept his arm from left to right, encompassing the hills and the silver-trees against their background of darker firs. 'This is my home and it's hard to imagine living anywhere else. You know,' he said after a moment's pause, jerking his head in the direction of the house behind them, 'you could do worse than move in here. You and Guy and young Johnny. It might give you a slim chance of happiness, and it's not a bad little place.'

Kate shook her head.

'Guy would never leave Gramerci,' she said. 'I cling to the hope that perhaps Sonia will, one day.'

'When she marries le Roux?' Larry gave a breath of laughter. 'He's proving a little reluctant, isn't he? Which doesn't altogether surprise me. Sonia knows some influential people and I have no doubt he likes to be seen around with her, but he's not enough of a fool to make a lifetime commitment to a bitch like that.'

'I still wish you'd stay and fight,' Kate said.

For some time Larry said nothing and she became hopeful that he was, after all, reconsidering his future. But all he did was throw down his cigarette and grind it out under the sole of his shoe.

'I'd better get on,' he said. 'Take care of Lilian, won't you?'

In a month he was gone, and the little house stood empty. Guy had laughed heartily at her tentative suggestion that a home of their own would be rather nice. Leave Gramerci? he said incredulously. Live in that poky little place? That would be the day!

Kate increased the frequency of her visits to Lilian's cottage and made frequent offers to take her out – to town, or for country drives, or to visit friends. Sometimes she accepted the invitations, but more often than not she said that she preferred to stay at home.

It was rare indeed that she came over to the house for the evening meal.

'Surely we should persuade her to come?' Kate said to Guy. 'She hardly sees anyone these days. It can't be good for her.'

'Don't worry about her,' he said easily. 'She's always been a bit of a recluse. She likes to listen to her gramophone records, and the odd talk on the radio. She knows she's free to come over here any time she wants.'

'That's not the same as making her feel that we want her, is it?'

'Well, face it, darling, she is a bit of a blight, isn't she? I mean, Sonia and I like to chew over the day's events at dinner and she makes no secret of the fact that she's not the slightest bit interested. She doesn't understand the half of it. I must say, I'm proud of the way you've buckled down and learned Afrikaans. Mother never did.'

'She tried, she said.'

'Not so you'd notice. I don't honestly see why we should be made to feel guilty because we want to talk business instead of indulging in idle chit-chat about nothing in particular. Mother's always been like that,' he went on. 'Never taking much of an interest in the really important things.'

'I wonder why?' Kate asked, a note of savagery in her voice. 'I'm sure you gave her all the encouragement in the world.' But Guy merely smiled vaguely in her direction and was gone.

The maternity clothes that Dora had made for Kate three years before proved so successful that she had recommended her to friends and employed her on several occasions since, but never again did their meetings take place at Gramerci. Instead Kate drove herself to the little shack on the wrong side of the tracks where Mama Lou herself still managed to measure, pin and tack, albeit with increasing difficulty. It was Dora, however, who supplied the undoubted flair. Not only did she sew well, but she was skilled in other ways as well.

'You jest draw a picture and my Dora can make it,' Mama Lou assured Kate early in their acquaintance. 'Me, I could sew good and make damn fine dresses when I had de fingers to do it, but I got to have de pattern. Not my Dora. She's real clever, my Dora.'

'She's done this beautifully,' Kate agreed, looking at the skirt that was finished and ready for collection. 'Tell her I'm really pleased with it, won't you?'

Mama Lou nodded and grinned, revealing gums only sparsely occupied by yellowed fangs. She was a thin woman with frizzy grey hair, her shoulders bent, her hands distorted with the arthritis that now prevented her from doing the fine work she had enjoyed in the past, but there was a sweet good humour about her that made Kate enjoy her company.

Dora herself, who had seemed so shy and self-effacing at Gramerci, was quite a different girl at home, and bloomed still further as Kate got to know her better. Her appearance was different, too, out of the uniform she wore for work. With her hair tied in a loose knot, pulled forward a little to frame her face, and clothes that accentuated her small waist and pert breasts, she was positively eye-catching, but even so there was nothing loud about her dress but rather a stylish elegance. She knew what suited her and had confidence in her natural flair for fashion. As she grew to know Kate's tastes, she often suggested small changes and touches of her own which always

proved, to Kate's mind, more becoming than the original would
have been.

'You should have your own business,' she said on one occasion.
'You're wasted in the OK Bazaar.'

Dora had laughed at that.

'Maybe one day I get to Stuttafords,' she said.

That day seemed a long way off on the occasion when Kate went
to see Mama Lou with her latest proposal for an evening dress,
sketched more to cheer herself up after Larry's departure than to
fill a pressing need.

'Come in, come in,' Mama Lou said. 'I just check your meas-
urements, *mevrouw*. You look like you lost weight to me.'

'I have, a bit,' Kate agreed, coming inside. 'I can get into most
of my old dresses now, so I feel a bit extravagant having a new one
– but I couldn't resist this material, Mama Lou. Isn't it lovely?'

'Oh, so pretty!' Mama Lou said, stroking the flowered silk with
her misshapen fingers as Kate took it out of its wrapping.

'And I made a few sketches,' Kate went on, delving further. 'I
don't know what Dora will think of them. She might have a few
ideas of her own.'

'Ideas?' Mama Lou laughed. 'Oh yes, my Dora have ideas.'
She seemed amused by the idea. 'Come in, *mevrouw*. You're as
welcome as de flowers in spring.'

The shack was small and crowded with cheap furniture, but it
was spotlessly clean, crocheted mats on small tables and a larger
fringed cloth of vivid pink material embroidered in purple and green
covering the larger central table on which stood an ornate pink china
pot full of ferns. On the mantelpiece a new picture of the two young
princesses, Elizabeth and Margaret Rose, caught Kate's eye.

'That's new,' she said.

'Dora bought it, from the Bazaar. Lovely children, eh, *mevrouw*?
I so glad deir daddy going to be king. I don't have no time for dat
Simpson lady. Dat Edward, he did right to up and go.'

'Oh, I agree,' said Kate.

'It's a lovely picture, right enough.' Mama Lou opened a drawer
and produced her tape measure. 'But not so lovely as my Tiffy, eh,
mevrouw?'

'Oh, not nearly,' she said.

Tiffy, as she had been told many times before, was Mama Lou's
husband who had been killed during the last month of the war. He

had reigned alone on the mantelpiece before the advent of the two princesses, staring a little blankly from his frame with his mouth slightly open; a solemn, upright man in uniform.

'Yust one month,' Mama Lou said, shaking her head as she put the tape around Kate's waist. 'Yust one month, *mevrouw*, and he would have been home with me.'

'You were never tempted to marry again?' Kate asked.

'Never, never, never. Never no one come up to my Tiffy. A lovely man.' She sighed heavily as laboriously she wrote Kate's waist measurement in a notebook and turned her attention to her bust. 'War is a terrible thing, *mevrouw*, but nothin' I say could stop him goin'. He had to do his duty for the sake of the King.' She sighed again. 'I wish he never had that moustache, though. Yust one picture I got, and him with a moustache. He never had one when we married, before he went away, so dis is like him and not like him, if you get my meaning.'

'Life must have been hard for you,' Kate said. Even if Mama Lou had not already told her, she knew all about life without a bread-winner.

'We manage,' Mama Lou said, measuring the skirt length and breathing heavily with the effort it cost her. 'We got dis house. Tiffy was a builder by trade, and he built it himself, brick by brick, before ever he axed me to marry him. So, plenty worse off dan me and my Dora. I got my house and I got my memories.'

However, when some days later Kate called again to discover Dora's reaction to her sketches, she found a far less sanguine atmosphere. Mama Lou's mouth was set in a grim line and she barely spoke in reply to Kate's conversational gambits.

'Is something wrong?' Kate asked Dora when her mother had left the room for a moment. 'Is Mama Lou's pain bad today?'

Dora hesitated a moment.

'It's not dat, *mevrouw*,' she said at last. 'It's de house. Dey say we got to get out.'

'Who says?' Kate asked, appalled.

'De man in de garage next door.'

'But if you own the house—'

'My father built it, dat's true, but dey say now he never had no proper title to de land. He say he goin' to pull it down and build a petrol station.'

'That's terrible! *Did* he have title?'

'We got a document, but de garage man, he say it ain't legal. All dese years we live here and he say it ain't legal!'

'That's just terrible,' Kate said again. 'I can't believe it.'

'She tell you de news, den?' Mama Lou said, coming in from the back. 'What you tink we should do, *mevrouw*?'

'I don't know. Have you had legal advice?'

'I ask de Indian down de road. He a lawyer. Trained. Dere's a board outside his house to say so. He says maybe dey're right but he got to get other advice, which will take more time and more letters. I tink he yust making a long yob of it so he can charge me more – and I can't pay such fees. Me and Dora, we don't know where to turn.'

'Oh, Mama Lou, I'm so sorry. I wish there was something I could—'

She stopped short. Christiaan le Roux! She didn't like the man – never had, and now, since the Larry affair, she liked him still less. Still, he was a lawyer, and heaven knew, he'd had enough hospitality at Gramerci to make him feel a little in her debt. Perhaps he might consider redeeming himself, at least in part, by putting his professional skills to good use for once.

'You think of something might help, *mevrouw*?'

'I don't know, Mama Lou. Maybe. I know a lawyer,' she went on incautiously. 'He's a friend of the family. I'll have a word with him and see if he's got any advice.'

Mama Lou's eyes brightened.

'A proper white lawyer! Now dat would be something! Maybe you bring him here to see Dora and the documents? She de clever one – she understand dese things. Not like me. I don't read English too good.'

'I don't know if he'd do that,' Kate said, already wishing she had said nothing, at least until she had spoken to Christiaan. 'He's a very busy man. Maybe if Dora went to see him . . .' Her voice trailed away. It was hard to imagine Christiaan taking kindly to any of this. 'I will try,' she promised, 'but don't get your hopes too high.'

Christiaan, she reminded herself, was busier than ever now that he was interesting himself in politics. He still practised law several days a week, but was now actively nursing the constituency of Wachsfontein, a busy farming area to the north of Cape Town. Weekends at Gramerci were not now quite so frequent.

An opportunity to raise the subject came the following Saturday, however, when they were both among the guests at a formal dinner given by David and Grace Nelson.

Grace had long been known as one who espoused liberal causes and Kate was secretly amused at the way Christiaan moderated his opinions in conversation with her. She, of course, presided at the foot of the table, the formidable Cornelius Wenst at her right hand, Christiaan on her left. Next to Christiaan came Kate, and on her other side, a young actor who was beginning to make a name for himself in the South African theatre.

She had recently seen him in Shaw's *Man and Superman* and was a little in awe of him and his exceptional talent, relieved to find that at closer quarters he was quite ordinary – even a little dull; though she was uncomfortably aware that the fault was probably hers. She had seen so few plays that it was hard to find common ground, until he mentioned that he had been in England only a month before, whereupon she found herself full of questions for him.

'Suddenly, I'm homesick,' she said to him.

'It was damned cold,' he assured her.

'But snowdrops, you said!'

'The snowdrops were fine. It was all the dirty slush in the London streets I didn't like so much.'

London had never been familiar territory to Kate, but suddenly she longed for it, slush and all. For all of England, in fact. Talk of snowdrops made her think of the patch of them by the front gate of Chimneys, and the smudgy bare branches of the trees in the lane. Would she ever see it again? Surely one day Guy would want to take a holiday, if only to see Uncle Randolph – to protect his investment, as it were.

She was aware, suddenly, that their hostess had turned to Mr Wenst, who until this moment had talked exclusively to the woman on his other side, the widow of a bishop, who looked almost as stern and formidable as he did himself. The consequence of this was that Christiaan, on Grace's left, was forced to engage Kate in conversation, however unenthusiastically he might regard the prospect. It occurred to her that as far as Dora was concerned it was probably now or never, and with some reluctance she abandoned the actor.

'How goes the political campaign?' she asked him.

It was going well, he told her. Only last night he had addressed a packed meeting and received numerous pledges of support.

She smiled and congratulated him. Buttering him up, she thought guiltily, for she had long ago realised that they were unlikely to find many points of agreement, in politics or anything else. The subject of Nazism in Europe had come up at dinner at Gramerci not long ago, and while she knew little about it and consequently felt unqualified to speak on the matter, her every instinct was to distrust it. Christiaan, on the other hand, spoke of it at length in approving terms. Hitler was a man with the right ideas, he said. He knew the importance of racial purity, just as the Afrikaners did.

'But,' Kate had said tentatively, vaguely remembering a newspaper article she had skimmed through recently, 'hasn't he been very cruel to the Jews?'

Christiaan had laughed at that.

'He has the right ideas,' he'd repeated.

She pushed this from her mind and forced herself to flirt with him a little.

'I hope the good people of Wachsfontein realise how lucky they are to have you in the running,' she said. 'But when you're elected, you won't forget all your friends and admirers in Cape Town, will you?'

Careful, she warned herself. Don't go too far. He must know that you've never been among those admirers. He gave no sign, however, of finding her behaviour out of character and raised his eyebrows at her, smiling his charming smile.

'As if I could,' he said. 'I've made such good friends and met with nothing but kindness since I've been here.'

'You're a popular man.' Kate smiled at him. 'And always welcome at Gramerci, as you well know. I'm afraid there are times when you might feel that you're a bit *too* popular with Johnny! He can be such a pest sometimes, but he does love to play with you.'

This, she consoled herself, was at least true. Christiaan seemed genuinely fond of the little boy.

'He's a great little chap. A credit to both of you.'

'Thank you.' Kate smiled again, inclining her head to one side to enable the white-clad servant to remove her empty plate. 'I wonder—' she began; then she bit her lip and shook her head. 'No, that was naughty of me! I was going to ask for your help, but I shouldn't bother you—'

'Nonsense, nonsense!' In a thoroughly expansive mood, Christiaan allowed his wine glass to be filled by another servant.

The bishop's widow having engaged Cornelius Wenst in conversation again, Grace turned to Christiaan once more.

'Do tell me your nonsense,' she begged, smiling, her expression animated. She's fallen for him too, Kate thought with astonishment. Intelligence, common sense – all count for nothing. What *is* his secret?

'I was saying I mustn't bother Christiaan,' Kate explained. 'My dressmaker – a Coloured girl – is in a spot of legal trouble. She can't afford proper advice, of course, but knowing how kind you are, Christiaan, I wondered if you—'

'Christiaan,' said Grace, laying her hand on his arm, 'is quite the kindest and most charming man my husband has ever invited into the firm! I'm quite sure he'll give a few moments of his time in a good cause. Isn't that right, Christiaan?'

His hesitation was only momentary.

'Of course,' he said heartily. 'I'd be glad to help. Send her along to see me at the office on Monday afternoon.'

'What time?' Kate was intent on pinning him down.

'Oh, latish. Five, five thirty.'

'You'll still be there? You'll wait for her? Not leave early, or anything?'

He laughed, his eyes slightly less warm.

'My dear Kate, you have such a passion for dotting the i's and crossing the t's, you should be a lawyer yourself! Yes, I'll be there – probably until much later than that.'

'Good! Her name is Dora Botha. You won't forget?'

'Of course he won't forget,' Grace said soothingly. 'Christiaan, dear, write it down. Dora Botha.'

Making the best of it, Christiaan produced his diary from an inner pocket and turned to the appropriate page.

'Dora Botha,' he said as he wrote. 'Five thirty. There. Are you happy now?'

'Thank you, Christiaan,' Kate said, smiling at him sweetly once more. 'I knew I could count on you.' And thankfully she turned once more to the actor.

'But what did the hospital actually *say*?'

Nina sounded desperately anxious, Colin thought gloomily. Distraught, even. Both he and she were surely fooling themselves if they really thought that there was nothing but friendship between her and

Jan. And where had she been all last night? And more important,
who with? It had been after midnight before he had abandoned his
attempt to get hold of her, and he'd been equally unsuccessful first
thing the next morning. He had been forced, eventually, to phone
the school and had left a message asking her to call as soon as
possible.

'Just what I said. That he was unconscious, but stable and as
comfortable as can be expected.'

'That's what they always say! It doesn't mean a thing.'

'Well, at least he's alive.'

'Yes, well . . .' She sounded as if this were poor comfort. 'We
have to hang on to that, I suppose. Colin—'

She paused for a moment, and he could hear the muffled noise of
children playing, the odd shout of laughter. It was the mid-morning
break, she'd explained, and the Head had allowed her to make the
call from his office.

'What?' he asked.

'You don't think—? No, it couldn't be.'

'Something to do with le Roux?'

'Well, something to do with the unknown person who phoned
me before Jan left. The one who wanted to know where he was.
He kind of gave me goose-pimples. I felt quite certain then that Jan
was being threatened in some way, but by whom I had no idea. I
can't help wondering—'

'I can't help wondering, too. But surely, Nina, the odds are on
this being a mugging. He'd been robbed, the original story said.'

'Well, it would be bound to look like a mugging, wouldn't it?'
She paused again. 'I wonder,' she went on after a moment, 'if his
mother knows.'

'His mother?' Colin sounded puzzled. 'I didn't know he had one.
I mean, I knew the le Rouxs brought him up and I assumed he was
an orphan.'

'Well, you assumed wrong. His parents were divorced and it was
left to his aunt and uncle to look after him. He'd found his mother's
address, though, and was determined to look her up.' A bell rang,
somewhere in the distance. 'That's the end of break. Look, I must
go, Colin. I'll be home on Friday.'

'Can I see you then? Can we have dinner?'

'Call for me at seven thirty,' she said, adding, before Colin's
heart was able to do more than give a preliminary bounce of

joy: 'I'll want to know absolutely everything you've been able to find out.'

'Seven thirty,' Colin promised.

It had been difficult for Christiaan le Roux to contact Gert Eksberg, but finally he had tracked him down.

'Have you seen the papers?' he shouted.

Eksberg's reply was monosyllabic, giving nothing away to any listening ears.

'Come and see me.'

'I can't. I'm about to leave for Kraaiffontein.'

'I must speak to you! Come here first.'

'This is urgent police business. I should have left ten minutes ago. Believe me,' he added in a lower, more conciliatory tone, 'I'd come if I could. As it is, I can't promise to be with you at all tonight. I'm tied up in court this afternoon, and tonight my wife and I are going out to the theatre. It's our wedding anniversary.'

He could hear le Roux's ragged breathing at the other end of the line. The old fool's going to pieces, he thought. He hasn't the stomach for this kind of thing.

'This is more important than the theatre. You've got to come.'

Momentarily, Eksberg closed his eyes. More important than the theatre? Le Roux should meet Connie! He hunched his shoulder, shielding the phone, and spoke quietly.

'I'm afraid that's out of the question. As I told you, it's my wedding anniversary and this is something that's been planned a long time. I can't possibly get out of it.'

'Later, then. After the theatre.'

Eksberg sighed, considering the matter.

'All right,' he said at last. 'I'll try. It won't be before eleven thirty, though.'

'I'll be here,' le Roux said, and put the phone down.

A colleague cocked an enquiring eye at Eksberg as he did likewise.

'Who was that?' he said. 'Sounded like an assignation to me. You're not playing away, by any chance?'

'Not by any chance,' Eksberg assured him as he made for the door. 'I was talking to a tree expert,' he added over his shoulder.

The other policeman laughed, shrugged his shoulders and shook his head. Eksberg was a deep one. He'd never known quite what to make of him.

Le Roux had no need to look at his diary to know that he had a Broederbond meeting that night: Friday, 17 February 1961. Nine o'clock. No matter. He would have to cancel it, make up some excuse. A migraine, perhaps – no, no, not that! A migraine might give people the idea that he was subject to such things, liable to be out of action at important moments, which was hardly the right kind of attribute for a prospective Prime Minister. A stomach bug was a better idea. In fact, it was brilliant! The previous night he'd dined with de Groot, one of the leading Broeders – he could say he must have eaten something that disagreed with him; that way it would be de Groot offering his apologies, not the other way round.

But whatever excuse he came up with, it was utterly essential that he meet with Eksberg as arranged. That short piece on the inner page of the *Courier* had shaken him more than he would have believed possible.

The High Commission in London was mixed up in it now, and the British police. Dispatching Jan here, where he had enemies by the score and where he himself was beyond suspicion, was one thing. A violent end was virtually inevitable for a trouble-maker like him, one way or another. But having him murdered in a strange country by hired assassins was something else again. The police might find that the trail led back to South Africa – to him! Something was going to have to be done – some damage-limiting exercise—

God, where was it all going to end? He should never have trusted a junior officer like Eksberg. The whole thing had been botched from the beginning. He should somehow have contacted Jan himself – talked to him, thrown himself on his mercy. Now he had to face the possibility of being unmasked as a murderer, as well as everything else.

The worry of it was driving him crazy. He was losing his grip, drinking too much, shaking like a leaf. Somehow that short report in the *Courier* – seeing Jan's name in print, seeing him described as the nephew of Christiaan le Roux's late wife – had brought the magnitude of the risk home to him. He hadn't thought it through properly.

It was the hired assassin angle that really frightened him. He had no idea who they were. They bore him no allegiance. How could he possibly tell if they could be relied on? If they would keep their mouths shut? These were questions that had tortured him all day and would, he knew, continue to torture him all night if Eksberg didn't do something about it.

He must have looked at his watch a thousand times between ten and eleven that evening. Eksberg was late. Maybe he'd forgotten. No, not that. He wouldn't forget. He'd give him another half-hour before he rang his home; meanwhile he poured himself another drink.

In England, the nine o'clock news had come to an end and the weather man was talking about cold fronts and rain spreading from the west.

Kate hadn't heard a word of it.

'Tom,' she said, 'I can't help worrying.'

Tom got up to switch off the television.

'What about?' he asked.

'Johnny, of course. He could still be in danger, you know. If someone were really determined, they could easily get into the hospital.' For some reason she was unable to get out of her mind the young, untidy doctor she had seen on Sunday evening, though she knew she was being illogical. The fact that she hadn't seen him before or since meant nothing; duty rostas changed, she told herself. Doctors came and went, and they didn't all look like Dr Kildare.

Tom looked at her with sympathy and tried to calm her fears.

'He's well looked after, darling—'

'I know that! But there are always times when nobody's about. He's so helpless, so vulnerable.'

Tom, unable to think of words of comfort, fell back on the practical.

'How about a nightcap?' he suggested.

'That would be nice.'

She was not comforted, however – not even by a glass of best Napoleon brandy. She had taken only a few sips when she put it aside as if she'd come to a decision.

'I'm going to phone Elaine,' she said. 'I'd hoped to see her today to ask her to ensure that the nurses were even more vigilant than usual, but she wasn't around. It won't hurt to have a word with her. I know she's not on duty now, but she won't mind.'

'Good idea,' Tom agreed absently, reaching for a pencil with which to do the crossword. 'It'll put your mind at rest.'

'Call it off?' Eksberg stared at le Roux in astonishment.

'That's what I said.' Le Roux reached for the phone, picked up the receiver and held it out to the policeman. 'Ring your friend now. Tell him it mustn't happen. Well, get on with it, man!'

'I can't do that,' Eksberg said.

'Of course you can! I'll pay. I'll pay what I promised. All of you. Just stop the whole thing.'

'I can't.' Eksberg looked at his watch. 'It's too late. It's gone nine thirty in England. I already spoke to Van Niekirk and he said everything was arranged for tonight. His man is taking the place of an orderly. He's got the uniform, knows the drill.'

The colour drained from le Roux's face, and he looked older and more drawn than ever, with no trace now of his former good looks. For a moment he looked helplessly at Eksberg, his mouth sagging, then he sat down heavily in a leather chair, groping for the glass on his desk. It was empty.

'Shall I get you another, sir?' Eksberg asked, politely. Wordlessly, le Roux let him take the glass.

'You could try to get hold of him,' he said hoarsely. 'Just try. It may not be too late. Something might have held them up—'

Eksberg shrugged his shoulders wearily and, still holding the glass, lifted the phone. He spoke to the operator briefly, then replaced it again.

'Hopeless,' he said. 'There's a five-hour delay.'

It was, as the weather man predicted, raining once more as Kate made her way to St Luke's on Thursday morning. She had not slept and though there had been no adverse word from the hospital she continued to feel apprehensive. At least she was able, by some miracle, to find a parking space quite close to the entrance. A good omen? Cheering though it was, she didn't dare regard it as such.

There were as many people as ever in the entrance hall where the passage of their wet shoes had tracked dirty marks all over the marble floor. Kate hurried through to the stairs and went up to the ward, arriving a little out of breath at the second floor. She could see at once that the curtains around Johnny's bed were closed. Her feeling of apprehension grew, though she told herself that of course there was a perfectly good reason for it. He was being washed, or the doctor was with him—

But when she arrived and pulled the curtain to one side, all she saw was an empty bed, freshly made, the pillows untouched by any patient's head, the pristine sheets drawn taut.

Her mouth went dry and for a moment she clung to the curtain, incapable of movement. Something terrible must have happened—

'Kate?'

She turned to see Elaine approaching her; neat, authoritative, in charge. And smiling!

'He's perfectly all right,' she said at once. 'Don't look like that.'

'Where is he?' Kate asked.

'Come with me.' Seeing her shock, Elaine took her arm and led her through the ward to the far end and a further door. 'He really is all right,' she said. 'After you phoned last night, I came back here and had him moved to a side ward and told the night staff to keep a special eye on him. It seemed the safest thing to do.'

Briefly Kate closed her eyes and let out her breath in a sigh of relief.

'Thank God,' she whispered. 'I thought . . . I thought—'

'I know what you thought! I was hoping to catch you the moment you arrived but suddenly there was a bit of a panic elsewhere.'

'And he's all right?'

'He's fine,' Elaine said. Kate looked at her narrowly.

'I know you, Elaine Cody,' she said, with sudden suspicion. 'There's something you're not telling me.'

Elaine grinned at her.

'Sister's privilege,' she said. 'Go on in and see for yourself.'

She opened the glass door of the narrow cubicle and Kate went through. Johnny was lying in the bed, the back of his head towards her; but at the sound of her entrance he turned to look in her direction, blinking sleepily. Then he smiled.

'Hallo,' he said.

11

It was several weeks before Christiaan le Roux came again to Gramerci, for he was much taken up with pursuing his political ambitions. There were influential people to meet and meetings to attend.

'Poor man,' Sonia said, reading an account of a meeting with union representatives. 'It must be deadly for him. He doesn't seem to have had a moment to call his own recently.'

And probably no moments at all, Kate thought, to do anything about Mama Lou's problems. One could certainly understand if this were so. She had heard from Dora that Christiaan had listened to her story and looked at the documents she had produced. He would write to her, Dora said, when the matter was settled; but by the time Kate collected her new dress the outcome was still unknown. With so many other things occupying him, it seemed more than likely to her that the whole affair had slipped his mind. Maybe she could find some tactful way of reminding him, she thought.

On his next flying visit, however, she found that she had misjudged him. Far from forgetting, he had brought the whole matter to a satisfactory conclusion.

'The chap was pulling a fast one,' he told her. 'He had no more legal right to that land than I have. I wrote a letter that put the fear of God into him.'

Kate was genuinely grateful and thanked him warmly.

'Pretty little thing, isn't she?' he added.

'And a good dressmaker, too. I am grateful, Christiaan. It was really good of you to take the trouble.'

Kate was aware, as she spoke, that Sonia was looking less than pleased, her finely shaped brows brought together in a frown. Perhaps, Kate thought, it was the reference to the 'pretty little thing' that had annoyed her.

'What's all this about?' she asked. Kate told her. 'Well!' Sonia had been reclining lazily in her chair on the stoep, but at this she lifted her head and looked at Kate with outraged astonishment. 'Really, Kate, you do take the cake! Do you honestly imagine, with all he has to do, that Christiaan has the time to bother with this kind of thing?'

'I was glad to help,' Christiaan said, smiling benevolently. 'Members of Parliament do that kind of thing. Hopefully, it's something I shall have to get used to.'

So maybe that was it, Kate thought. He'd seen it as a necessary part of his duties. Maybe they could all look forward to a new and selfless Christiaan le Roux in future, if his political ambitions were to be realised.

Sonia subsided once more but not without another annoyed glance in Kate's direction. She was not in the best of moods that day, for this was no more than a flying visit on Christiaan's part. He had to go back to Wachsfontein that night, he said. There was a dinner at the home of Theunis Van Doorn, an important member of the Nationalist Party – the party he aspired to represent. It wouldn't do to miss it, he assured her. It was a damned nuisance, but just one of the hoops he had to jump through in the cause of furthering his career.

She was hardly mollified when, later in the week, there was a picture in the *Ladies' Pictorial* of Christiaan, taking his place on the dance floor of a Wachsfontein hotel and smiling with great charm at Miss Stephanie Van Doorn, an eighteen-year-old *ingénue* in a frothy white dress. For perhaps the first time ever, Kate felt sorry for her sister-in-law, for the occasion depicted here bore little resemblance to the rather boring dinner party Christiaan had allowed them to think he was expecting. However, she had enough sense not to show her sympathy.

Wine harvest time had come round again, with the sickly, sour smell of the fermentation tanks heavy on the air. It was hot and still, with not a breath of wind; but not for long, Kate knew, for she had learned that come what may, from time to time during the summer the south-easter would roar up from the sea, scouring the valley and tossing the trees, sending down showers of leaves and twigs and acorns and driving dust clouds for miles. The Doctor, it was called, as if it blew away all the germs and bugs it found in its path; but in spite of that, she did not welcome it. It seemed so dry, so pitiless. It made her head ache and her skin shrivel, and her thoughts turned with longing to the green softness of an English spring – to primroses on the banks along the lane and fields full of lambs.

She was always glad when The Doctor died away and once more the beauty of the valley and the distant blue hills came into its own again. Always, after the wind, it was still and airless as if the force of it had left the entire world exhausted. Kate felt listless, half asleep, and even Johnny seemed to have less energy than usual; but then came news that jerked her out of her lethargy. Sheltered in the candlewood tree, she wrote to her mother:

> I am so thrilled to hear that Peter and Nancy are getting engaged. My brother and my best friend – what could be more wonderful? I had gathered, reading between the lines of Nancy's letters, that she was seeing quite a bit of Peter in London, but I had no idea things had got this serious. I am sure you are pleased. Nancy is such a darling and you were always fond of her.
>
> Actually, I had a letter from her by the same post, telling me the news for herself. She says they hope to get married next spring, and she wants me to be matron-of-honour! Oh, if only I could! It gives me a whole year to work on Guy. The trouble is that your spring (our autumn) is the really busy time of year and I can't see him agreeing to leave Gramerci then. Perhaps I could come on my own and bring Johnny! He'd make the cutest page-boy!

'I just couldn't be more pleased about it,' she said to Guy when later he joined her on the stoep for tea.

'Mmm?' He had picked up the newspaper to glance at the headlines. 'Oh, yes. It's great news.'

'You liked her, didn't you?'

'Who?'

'Nancy, of course. We always said we would be each other's bridesmaids, and I kept my side of the bargain. Guy – *Guy!* Do listen! Couldn't we go? The three of us? We haven't had a proper holiday since we've been married.'

Guy laid the paper aside with considerable ostentation and the air of one sacrificing much in order to pay attention.

'When is this wedding?'

'Next spring. I told you.'

'You mean this time of year?' He laughed. 'You're crazy, man! You know I can't go then. Later, maybe. Say July or August – but even then I was hoping to get on with the new buildings. I can't really spare the time or the money.'

'Suppose—' Kate began; but then she stopped. Suppose I went on my own, she had been about to say, but common sense had intervened. Such a suggestion would need careful timing. She'd been a fool to mention the trip at all, really, when at breakfast that very day he'd been going on about the necessary repairs and extensions which were all going to cost more than he thought.

'Suppose you go on your own,' he said, taking the wind out of her sails.

'Oh!' She looked at him in astonishment, eyes round and bright, not believing her ears. 'Oh, Guy! Wouldn't you mind?'

'Why should I?' He smiled at her, reaching for the paper once more. 'You've been a good girl – done your best to fit in. I know it hasn't always been easy. You deserve your reward. Besides,' he went on, turning the pages to find the comic strip, 'you'll be coming back, won't you?'

'Of course I will.' She went to him and kissed him, and he ruffled her hair, just as he had done in the beginning when he had been demonstrative in his affection.

'Of course you will,' he said.

You could have knocked me down with a feather when Guy actually suggested it himself [she wrote to Nancy]. He really can be so sweet. So yes – I will be your matron-of-honour and I am so excited about everything I simply don't know how I'm going to wait a whole year. And if you should, by any chance, want a cute, golden-haired page-boy who just happens to own rather a fetching little sailor suit, I just might know the perfect candidate.

I simply can't get over how sly you've both been, though! Not a word about romance or falling in love. Not a hint that you were even harbouring the tiniest, remotest, most infinitesimal thought about getting married! Just accounts of films you've seen together and rambles in the Surrey countryside. I thought we vowed, a million years ago, that we were going to tell each other EVERYTHING!

Dotty sounds delighted at the prospect of having you as a daughter-in-law. What do your parents think? I hope they're equally pleased and feel sure they must be, for Peter is a good chap. Kind and thoughtful and generous, and if a sister says things like that, then they have to be true.

One thing in your letter bothered me, though. Does he really think there's going to be a war? I read enough of the paper every day to know that Germany is rearming and behaving in an aggressive kind of way, but no one I know really believes that it will come to war. Not on the same scale as the last one, anyway. When one remembers all those millions of men killed on both sides the last time round, one has to believe that mankind has learned SOMETHING! The contemplation of it happening again is surely more than anyone can bear. Even Herr Hitler!

So I hope Peter's wrong – but at least it seems to have focused his mind and persuaded him that now is the time to settle down, so it's not all bad. I do wish I were not so far away from you all! What shall we do about my dress? Should I wait until I get home, or will you send me the pattern and material so that I can get it made out here? I have a perfectly wonderful dressmaker . . .

Had she misjudged Christiaan le Roux? Kate's mind, seduced by the heavy, scented warmth and the song of birds that came to her in the depths of the candlewood tree, wandered away from her letter and along the track suggested by thoughts of Dora. He was such a busy man, and yet he had taken time from his other concerns to deal with the Bothas' troubles.

Poor Sonia! She would be thirty next birthday. It seemed, to Kate, quite incredibly ancient, particularly if one was an unmarried woman, yet to start a family.

It was a thought she voiced to Guy that night in the privacy of their bedroom, after they had made love. Such an occurrence was not frequent these days and since, when it happened, it was still a brief and unsatisfactory experience, Kate was not too unhappy with this state of affairs. Tonight, however, he had come back from the club in a mellow mood and because she was still overwhelmed with gratitude at his generous offer, she had been compliant, even welcoming.

Afterwards she lay with her head on his shoulder, his arm around her as, contentedly, he smoked a cigarette.

'Do you think they'll ever get married?' she asked him.

'Sonia and Christiaan?' He exhaled smoke, slowly and sensuously. 'God knows! He's certainly taking his time.'

'You'd think,' Kate went on, 'that he'd be just as anxious as she is. I mean, a married parliamentary candidate seems much more worthy and settled than a bachelor. I can't imagine why he doesn't ask her at once, can you? He's really awfully good with Johnny. You'd think he'd welcome the thought of a family of his own.'

'Maybe that's the trouble,' Guy said, after a moment. Kate turned her head to look into his face.

'What do you mean?'

'Well—' He hesitated a moment. 'Sonia can't, you see. Have children, I mean. For heaven's sake—' He removed his arm and took her by the shoulders, giving her a little shake. 'Don't ever let on that I told you. She's very sensitive about it.'

'But why—?'

'She was ill, years ago. Ten years ago, at least. Had to have all the equipment taken away.'

'How terrible!' Kate stared at him, aghast. 'What was wrong?'

'It was cancer – but not a word to a soul, Kate. Least of all to her. Promise?'

'Yes, of course!'

'The word was never spoken, not to her. She knew about the effects of it, of course – I mean that she could never have children – but everyone skated round the actual cause. She was so strong, so good at sports, any kind of illness seemed a weakness to her. Something to be ashamed of. Especially something like this. I mean – cancer! It's not the sort of thing you talk about, is it? It was Mother who told me and she made me swear not to mention it.'

'Poor Sonia!' Kate turned to rest her head against him again, looking up at the ceiling. 'How terrible! Is she all right now?'

'Yes, I think so. I suppose she was lucky.'

'Well, yes, if it saved her life. But not to be able to have children! I just can't imagine . . .' Kate's voice trailed away. 'You think she's told Christiaan, though?'

'Perhaps. I don't know. It would explain his reluctance to marry her, wouldn't it?'

Not if he loved her, Kate thought, but for some reason she did not want to put this into words.

'Most men want a son,' Guy went on after a moment. 'I know I did.' He kissed the top of her head. 'You've done me proud there, man.'

'They could adopt,' Kate said.

'It's hardly the same, is it? I mean, what do you know of a strange child's background?'

'What do you know of Johnny's background?' Mischievously, Kate looked up at him again. 'Did I ever tell you about my seafaring great-grandfather who married a girl from Timbuktu?'

'No!' There was, for a second, genuine concern in Guy's voice, a tensing of his muscles, but then he realised she was teasing him and he relaxed once more. 'Don't say things like that, man. Not in South Africa. Coloured blood isn't something to joke about.'

'Well, we don't really know, do we? We've all got four grandparents, and sixteen great-grandparents, and thirty-two great-great-grandparents. Can you honestly tell me you know what they all got up to? Maybe,' she added unwisely, 'one of your ancestors had a little fling with—'

'Shut up!' Guy's mellow mood had gone as if it had never been. 'Don't *ever* say that! You can see the family tree in the old Bible, it's all down there in black and white. Good Huguenot stock—'

'I was joking,' Kate said, a little shaken by the force of his reaction.

'Well, it was a pretty poor joke.'

'You're right. I'm sorry.' She sighed. It had been a tasteless thing to say. 'And I'm really, really sorry about Sonia,' she added.

It explained a lot of things, she thought, as she lay there with her eyes wide open, long after Guy had gone to sleep. But if Christiaan truly loved her . . .

She sighed again. Who was she to talk of love? The more she thought of it, the more it seemed that she didn't know the first thing about it.

Helen's pregnancy was advancing without problems, though she was forced, on the strict instructions of her doctor, to give up all her outside activities and rest a great deal.

'He says I have to take care,' she said. 'And I know he's right.

He keeps dinning into me the fact that this is my last chance, so I couldn't bear to lose this one.'

'Wouldn't it be nice if it were a girl?' Kate said. 'Then she could marry Johnny and our dynasties would be united.'

'Paul wants a boy. For myself, I simply don't care, just so long as it's healthy. And grows up with the right ideas.'

'Which are?' Kate asked her. They were sitting on the shady terrace of Helen's house, Johnny happily occupied with watering the flowers, filling his small can from a tin bath full of water. Since he spilled most of it on his journey to the flowerbeds, it was an activity that seemed likely to take him a considerable time. Both Helen and Kate had sewing to do, but neither was showing much enthusiasm for it.

Lazily, Helen laughed at Kate's question.

'You ask me that? You know the answer as well as I do.'

'Yes, I do,' Kate admitted. 'And it's something that worries me. I don't like the idea of Johnny growing up with Lampard opinions and Lampard prejudices. It's all very well for me to listen to Sonia and Guy – and Christiaan, of course – laying down the law about how the country should be run. I just sit there very quietly and think my own thoughts. But what hope has a child, being force-fed those kind of racist views day after day?'

'De Vries opinions and prejudices aren't any better,' Helen said. 'You should hear my father-in-law's views on Jan Smuts! I won't go so far as to say he's pro-Nazi, but he'd string up Slim Jannie before Hitler, any day of the week. He got us into the last war, he said, and he'll get us into the next if we're not careful. And what quarrel have we with Hitler? All he's done is voice what any good Afrikaner believes in his heart; that racial purity is the most important thing in the world. What have the Jews ever done for us? Etc., etc., etc.'

'But he's such a nice man!'

'I know.' Helen's smile died. 'I'm very fond of him, even if we do have the most terrible arguments sometimes. We almost came to blows over the repeal of the Cape African Franchise last year.'

'But he's a Christian,' Kate said. 'A pillar of the church.'

'Yes, he is. There's a verse in Acts that I quoted at him the other day: something to the effect that God made the world and all things therein and hath made of one blood all nations of men to dwell on all the face of the earth. Or something similar. I've probably got it wrong, but that's the essence of it.'

'What did he say?'

Helen was silent for a moment, and Kate waited, anxious to hear the answer. It was something that had always puzzled her. How could a practising Christian embrace the concept of separate development?

'He said,' Helen said at last, 'that I'd only quoted half the passage. That it went on to say that God had determined the bounds of man's habitation. Which means, he said, that every race has its own boundaries – not just physically, where they live, and so on, but mentally as well. And when I was unwise enough to say something about all men being brothers, he said, well, yes. Of course they are. But nowhere does it say that all brothers are equal in the sight of God. Look at Cain and Abel. Or Jacob and Esau. Not to mention Joseph and the wicked brothers that sold him into slavery. Believe me, one starts quoting scripture to my father-in-law at one's peril. He's always got another quotation that proves just the opposite.' She laughed with rueful amusement. 'Paul's mother is more on my side,' she said. 'And she's as Afrikaans as they come, which proves the folly of sticking people into little boxes.'

'Maybe,' said Kate, 'if the worst happens and there is a war, it'll take everyone out of their little boxes and shake them up.'

'So that when everything gets back to normal, attitudes will be different?'

'Oh, I hope so!' Kate looked towards Johnny, still playing with the water. He was sitting with his legs straight out in front of him, a chubby, sun-bronzed little boy with a floppy white cotton hat on his head, singing happily to himself. 'It has to be different,' she said. 'It just has to be.'

But Helen said nothing, making it plain that she could find no words of encouragement.

'I always thought of you as Johnny,' Kate said to her son. 'I even managed to persuade your father to call you Johnny. He and Sonia were always pro-Jan.'

'It seems a bit strange.'

He was sitting up now in a chair beside the bed, the bandage gone, wearing a hospital dressing gown and beneath it the pyjamas she had brought in for him.

'Next time I'll bring a dressing gown—'

'No, really, you mustn't.'

'Of course I must. I want to.'

He didn't argue but just looked at her, blinking a little.

'I'm sorry if I seem a bit—'

'No, no. You're fine,' Kate hastened to assure him. 'You're bound to be a bit sleepy – a bit disorientated. Your memory will come back, you know. It's not at all unusual to have forgotten what happened just before the accident.'

'Accident?'

'Mugging. Whatever it was.'

'By the river, you say?'

'That's where you were found, beaten half to death.'

He shook his head.

'I can't remember a thing about that! Why on earth would I have been there? I wonder if that's where I was staying.'

'It doesn't seem likely. It's not a very salubrious part of London.'

'Well, I've stayed in not very salubrious places in my time. But somehow—' He screwed up his eyes as if desperately trying to remember. 'Somehow I think I went somewhere halfway decent. I have a dim recollection of a flight of steps and a huge mirror with a fancy gilt frame.'

'Don't try to force it. It'll come.'

He looked at her, forcing a smile.

'It's weird,' he said. 'Ten days out of my life that I know nothing about. He shook his head wonderingly. 'And you were here every day, they tell me. That was good of you.'

'*Good* of me?' Kate stared at him. 'For heaven's sake, Johnny—'

'Couldn't you try Jan?' he asked gently. 'It feels more familiar.'

'Jan.' She smiled at him. 'It'll take a bit of getting used to.

'So will a lot of other things. Things like having a mother like you! When Sister Cody told me you'd be in this morning, I tried to imagine what you'd be like, which was pretty impossible because I'd never even seen a picture of you. I suppose I must have been told how young you were when I was born, but even so you've taken me a bit by surprise. I imagined someone middle-aged. You could be my sister.'

'Well, hardly.' Kate felt sure she must be blushing. 'But thanks, anyway.'

'What do I call you?'

Kate laughed.

'It's a little late for Mum, isn't it? Kate will do nicely.'

'Kate, then. I'm sorry I look such a fright.'

'You look better than you did. Your hair will grow and the bruises will soon fade. They'll take the stitches out any time now, I imagine. You'll be back to normal before you know it.'

They were strangers, Kate thought, circling round each other, doing their best to seem at ease. She was smiling too much, making party conversation. Well, of course they were strangers! What did she imagine it would be like? They had to get used to each other, just as if they were new acquaintances.

'What *do* you remember?' she asked him. He frowned, thinking about it.

'The plane,' he said. 'Arriving. It was pretty late. I took a taxi to a hotel and it cost me an arm and a leg. I remember that perfectly well. Someone back home had recommended the hotel I stayed in, but it wasn't very good. I remember thinking, sod this, I don't want the Ritz but I'm not so broke I have to stay anywhere quite so crummy. So after one night I went—' He paused, screwing up his eyes in thought. Then he shook his head once more. 'That's what I can't remember,' he said. 'Somebody I talked to recommended this other hotel, but who that was or which hotel, I have no idea.'

'Don't worry about it. It'll come back to you in time. Nobody ever remembers everything all at once, not after a bash on the head like that.'

He sighed and closed his eyes, suddenly looking weary.

'I'll leave you,' Kate said, getting to her feet. 'You need all the rest you can get.'

His eyes flew open.

'You'll come back?'

She hastened to reassure him.

'Yes, of course I will! Shall I help you back into bed?'

'Thank you.'

She took his arm and he stood up cautiously, wincing a little, and for the first time she realised how tall he was. Well over six feet, she thought. Even taller than Guy.

She looked up at him and saw what his previous stillness had prevented her seeing before. There was something of Guy in him, after all. Something quite elusive, incapable of being pinned down, but there just the same; a movement, an expression. But there was the strength, too, that Guy had so signally lacked. As she looked into his face a sudden rush of emotion brought the tears to her eyes.

'I'm sorry,' she said, turning away from him. 'It's just that . . . just that—' She took a deep breath, steadying herself. 'Sorry,' she said again. She did her best to smile at him. 'Just that you'll never know how I've longed to see you and touch you and know that you were alive and well. I think I can truly say that never a day passed in all these years without my thinking about you.'

For a moment he looked down at her, frowning, biting his lip. I've ruined it, she thought. Embarrassed him. Grief was like a stone in her stomach. She'd thought a hundred times how she would play this scene, and this wasn't at all the way she had planned. Sentiment must be avoided, she'd told herself. No young man appreciated it, especially in this case. He had, after all, taken over twenty years to acknowledge her existence. Weeping all over him would undoubtedly make him want to avoid her for another twenty.

His mouth was working a little as if he wanted to say something but couldn't find the words; then with a sudden, jerky movement he put his arms around her and they clung together.

'That's a hell of a lot of days,' he said huskily.

'Don't go,' he said when he was back in bed. 'Not yet. There's such a lot to talk about.'

'I don't want to tire you.'

'I'm OK. Really. There's something I have to tell you.'

'What's that?'

'I . . . I just didn't know about you. Honestly. I didn't know a thing about the letters and the birthday cards, and all the times you wrote to Sonia giving your change of address in case I wanted to find you. You never gave up, did you?'

'Never,' Kate said. 'You mean Sonia kept them from you?' She frowned, finding this incomprehensible.

'Every last one. But she didn't throw them away, for some reason. She was always a great hoarder. I was looking for my birth certificate after she died, so that I could apply for a passport. I'd had a copy but managed to lose it somewhere and needed to get my hands on the original – so I did something I'd never have done when she was alive. I went to her desk to look for it myself. It was incredible! She had a row of files in her drawer, all named.

Every Lampard for the last three generations, plus a kind of family history, and the history of Gramerci. The woman was obsessed!

'Inside mine were all sorts of things, as well as the birth certificate. School reports, certificates I'd won for swimming, cuttings from the newspaper about various sports I'd taken part in. And there was a separate, foolscap manilla envelope stuffed full of your letters and cards. There they all were, preserved for posterity. There was one you sent on my sixth birthday. It had a big six on it, and a train full of toys, and you'd written, "I wish I was on this train and it was puffing all the way to you," and underneath you'd put a row of kisses.' Jan bit his lip and paused for a moment. 'It got to me, I don't mind telling you. Sonia didn't go in much for that sort of thing.'

Kate looked down at her hands, finding it necessary once more to struggle for composure.

'Why . . . why would she have kept them all, then?'

Jan shook his head.

'I have no idea. Except – well, I wondered if she intended me to see them one day. It seems the only logical explanation. Maybe it salved her conscience, the thought that she was only concealing your interest in me for the time being, but that the time would come when she would reveal all. Maybe she thought it would unsettle me while I was growing up – though, hell, I've been grown up for a long time now. Really, I've no explanation.'

'She must have told you something about me.'

'Just that you hated South Africa and couldn't stand living there. That you went away and left me and my father—'

'That's not true! None of it's true!'

'I know that now. At least, I know some of it.' He gave a brief laugh that was almost a sigh. 'I'm afraid I gave Christiaan a bad time. The day I went to the house, he was out. I'd have asked about the birth certificate if he'd been around, but as he wasn't, I went over to Sonia's office and looked for myself. Christiaan came home just as I was leaving after finding out you'd been writing to me for years, and I was just so mad I really let him have it. I'm afraid,' he added ruefully, 'I've got one hell of a temper. I'm much better these days. I've more or less learned to control it.' He raised an eyebrow. 'Maybe I've inherited it from you.'

Kate laughed and shook her head.

'I don't think so. You may be able to blame me for many things, but not that. So you accused him?'

'Yes. Well—' He corrected himself. 'I don't know exactly what I said. I'm afraid a good deal of it was probably unrepeatable. I know I told him he was a liar and a hypocrite, not fit to represent anyone, let alone an entire country. He aspires to be Prime Minister, you know.'

'No,' Kate said. 'I didn't know. How proud Sonia would have been.'

'Would she?' Jan looked at her consideringly. 'Yes, I suppose she would. I suppose they must have loved each other. They were never particularly demonstrative, though; never seemed close. They lived very separate lives, it always seemed to me. Sonia never wanted to travel far from Gramerci, and of course Christiaan had to spend half the year in Pretoria. Still, the marriage lasted and I don't imagine they argued any more than most married couples.'

Kate looked at him, studying his face. Like Guy, yet so unlike, she thought. The mouth was quite different, and the chin. It was stronger, firmer, leaner. And the eyes were remarkable, a dark, clear blue.

'Did Christiaan have any kind of explanation?'

'He seemed to be trying to tell me it was nothing to do with him. He shouted, "The bitch, the bitch,' as if he were blaming Sonia for everything, but I didn't hang around to pursue the matter. I didn't believe him, anyway. He must have known all about it. Afterwards, when I thought it over, I was pretty disgusted. There was Sonia, dead for less than a week, with Christiaan playing the part of the bereaved, inconsolable widower. Calling her names seemed in poor taste, to say the least.'

'I agree.' Kate frowned, thinking this over. 'It seems out of character. Or has he changed? When I knew him, saying the right thing seemed his guiding principle in life – though of course, he was running for office then. Perhaps that made a difference. Tell me,' she rushed on, a little diffidently, 'were you happy?' She hastened to answer her own question. 'Yes, of course you were! How could you not be in a place like that and a climate like that? It must have been a kind of paradise for a boy.'

'Yes, I suppose I was. I had a pony, friends, freedom. I went to the best school in the country—'

'I know. Sonia told me.'

'Sometimes, when I was young, I looked at friends' mothers and thought it would be lovely to have someone cosier than Sonia – someone who'd hug me and take my side about things and tell me how wonderful I was.' He grinned at her. 'But then, later, at fourteen and fifteen and sixteen, friends used to tell me I was lucky. Parents were thought of as a bit of a liability at that time. Sonia was a martinet and I was always wary of her, but she wasn't terribly interested in my day-to-day doings. I suppose it's true that I got away with murder. She always said so, anyway, when I started getting involved in activities she didn't approve of.'

'And Christiaan? How did you get on with him?'

Jan smiled and gave a wry smile.

'I hero-worshipped him when I was little. He was good to me. I suppose I was around fifteen or sixteen before I started questioning all the things he stood for. Still stands for.'

Kate looked at him. She ached with the effort it was taking to resist the urge to hold him close. I'm mourning all over again, she thought. Mourning all those lost years.

'You seem to remember the past very well,' she said.

He nodded.

'Yes, no trouble there at all. It's just this later part.'

'It'll come,' Kate said again. Decisively she stood up.

'I'm really going this time. We can't possibly cover everything in one go and you really ought to rest.' Still she stood for a moment, looking down on him. She touched his shoulder. 'I want to take you home soon,' she said. 'You have a little half-brother and sister. And there's Tom. You'll like Tom.' She paused, feeling suddenly that she had been assuming too much. 'If you agree, that is,' she added.

He reached for her hand and held it tight for a moment.

'I agree,' he said.

Elaine was sitting at her desk when Kate re-entered the main ward, but she rose at her approach.

'All right?' she asked briefly. Kate smiled.

'All right.' She laughed a little shame-facedly. 'I suppose I panicked last night,' she said. 'Thanks for moving him. I kept thinking about him lying helpless, and some intruder getting in under the noses of the staff. You know how my imagination runs away with me.'

Elaine turned and picked up a printed notice from the desk behind her.

'I've just received this,' she said. 'It's been rushed to every ward.'

Kate took the notice from her. It was headed SECURITY and went on to urge all staff to be on their guard.

> An intruder, dressed as an orderly, was apprehended last
> night as he tried to effect entry to the neurological ward.
> The introduction of security badges for staff members is being
> considered, but nothing can take the place of constant alertness
> to protect the property of staff and patients alike. PLEASE BE
> VIGILANT.

Kate read this with mounting horror.

'So someone did try to get in,' she said, when she had finished.

'Maybe your imagination wasn't so wild, after all. Or maybe he was just after drugs. That's what he said.'

'He's been arrested?'

'It seems so.'

'When can I take Johnny home, Elaine?'

'We'll want to keep an eye on him for a few days yet.'

'But I can keep an eye on him! You know I can. I want him home as soon as possible. I can get our GP to come in and look at him – you know him, he's a friend, he only lives a few doors away.'

'Well—' Elaine shrugged her shoulders, but she looked sympathetic. 'I can drop in too, from time to time, just to give him the once-over. If asked, of course.'

Kate laughed at that.

'You know we always love to see you.'

'Well, then, it's up to your Johnny. He can always discharge himself.'

For a moment Kate hesitated, as if she would go back to him then and there to sort the matter out. Then she shook her head.

'He looked tired,' she said. 'He needs to rest. I'll talk to him tonight.'

'And maybe talk to Tom?' Elaine suggested.

'Of course,' Tom said on the phone. 'Of course he must come. I said so, didn't I? Oh, darling, I'm so pleased he's OK.'

'Should we both come and see him tonight? I can lay on Mrs Nixon.'

'We must tell the children first—'

'I wonder how they'll take it? Oh, Tom – he's nice. You'll like him, I know.'

'I'm sure I will.'

Tom was thoughtful, however, as he put the phone down. Jan, he thought. We have to call him Jan. Hard to get used to after all these years of hearing him referred to as Johnny.

Not his fault, though. He's still the same chap. Still Kate's son. No reason, really, for feeling apprehensive about the outcome of all of this – and no reason at all why he should feel guilty at feeling apprehensive. Guilt seemed to be becoming a habit with him – which was crazy! He'd acted for the best all those years ago, always with her interests at heart. They'd married, had the children, prospered. Surely he'd been justified in encouraging Kate to put the past behind her? Dammit, she had been happy. She *was* happy!

Somehow none of this made him feel any better.

But I should have let her go back, he said to himself now, staring aimlessly from his office window. She needed to deal with it – exorcise the past. You can't bury things like that, not without damage.

He sighed heavily. Gross insensitivity, he thought. That's what he had been guilty of, no matter what his motives had been. He just hoped that the fates hadn't caught up with him, determined to make him pay, even at this late stage.

'Don't be silly,' Vicky said, indignantly.

Kate smoothed her hair and held her closer.

'Darling, I'm not being silly. I know it's a surprise – but it's a lovely surprise, isn't it? A big brother—'

'Mummy!' Mark was tugging at her skirt. 'You've got a sherbert dip in the cupboard and you said—'

'In a minute, Mark. Just wait! Daddy and I want talk to you.'

'You can't have a man for a brother,' Vicky said. 'Not a grown-up man.'

Mark was still tugging.

'Mummy, I want a little brother. Like Adam. Can't I have a little brother?'

'Mark, just *listen*. Both of you listen.' When Tom spoke in that commanding way the children usually did what they were told. Mark put his thumb in his mouth and leant against Kate. Vicky just glared, on the defensive.

'It was like this,' Tom said, moderating his voice. 'Mummy was married when she was very, very young, and she went out to live in South Africa. She had a baby boy whom she loved very much—'

Kate watched him and listened. This was the hard part, she thought. How could you explain it to any child? The years of separation, the silence. Tom, she had to admit, did it as well as anyone could.

'So now we're going to make up for all that lost time,' Tom said, winding up. 'Won't it be great? Mummy tells me he's longing to meet you.'

'Did he know about us?' Vicky asked.

'No. Nor about me. Nor even about Mummy.'

'Why?'

'The lady who was looking after him didn't tell him.'

'Why?'

'Well, maybe she was jealous. Maybe she didn't want him to think of anyone else as his mother.'

'Why?'

'Perhaps she couldn't have any children of her own. Look, I don't know why, exactly. You'll just have to accept that's the way it was. But now he's found us all and he's going to be part of our family.'

Mark took out his thumb.

'Can I have the sherbert dip now?'

Tom and Kate looked at each other and laughed.

'Perhaps he's got his priorities right,' Kate said. 'This is all a bit beyond their comprehension.'

'It's not beyond my . . . my composition,' said Vicky. 'But I wouldn't actually mind a sherbert dip, either. I wonder what Jan eats,' she added, following Kate to the kitchen. 'Do they have different things in South Africa? Elephants, and all that?'

'They do,' Kate said. 'But not to eat. Not on the whole, anyway. You'll have to get him to tell you about them.'

'I wonder if he likes sherbert dip, too?'

'I don't know. Maybe.'

She was conscious of a sudden feeling of panic. I know hardly anything about him, she thought.

*   *   *

It took Colin considerable time and effort to get hold of Gert Eksberg, but he finally managed it halfway through the morning.

'Hi,' he said, both cheerful and friendly – which, it had to be admitted, was in direct contrast to Eksberg, who sounded distinctly harassed. 'I owe you a beer. Can we meet tonight?'

'Any particular reason?' Eksberg asked.

'Just don't like being in anyone's debt.' Colin laughed, briefly. 'Well, it's as good an excuse for a drink as any. How about it?'

Eksberg appeared to be considering the matter.

'Can't make it tonight,' he said at last. 'How about midday? I could be at the Marco Polo around then. In fact,' he added, sounding marginally more cheerful, 'I could bloody well do with a break, now you mention it.'

'Well, I'm nothing if not flexible,' Colin said. 'See you in about an hour, then.'

He put the phone down, but sat for a moment without moving, chewing his lip. He was probably wasting his time, he thought, but what the heck? He wasn't particularly busy that morning and a word with Eksberg might answer some of the questions that refused to leave him in peace.

He looked at his watch. He'd have to leave in forty-five minutes. Meantime he reached for the file he had been reading before he had made his phone call, answering George Porter's suggestion that he write an exposé of a distinctly unsavoury property development company, currently running up apartment blocks in Sea Point. Nothing had been completed on time, and the savings of hopeful home-owners had been swallowed up, in some cases creating real hardship. There was homework to be done on the subject, George Porter had said, not at all to Colin's surprise. It was Porter's pet saying, a motto freqently mimicked by his irreverent underlings.

'Never let it be said that Vos doesn't do his homework,' Colin muttered absently to a passing colleague.

'What a hot-shot,' jeered the colleague, amicably. 'Be nice on the way up, man – you'll need us on the way down.'

Colin grinned, but feebly. It occurred to him that delving into le Roux and his affairs might make that day sooner than he would like. He still intended to go ahead, though.

'I expect you read about Jan Lampard?' he said, when he and Eksberg had sat down at a table in the corner of the bar, not yet as crowded as it would be in another hour. 'Mugged, they say, and left for dead in some London back street.'

'Do you mind?' Eksberg paused in the act of pouring his beer into the glass. 'I'm enjoying a break. I've had Big bloody Jannie up to *here*.'

'Oh? Sorry!' Colin grinned at him. 'It's just that you were pretty keen to get your hands on him the last time I saw you. At least, le Roux was keen, you said. I wondered if you'd caught up with him before he left the country.'

'No.' There was a note of finality in Eksberg's voice, but Colin continued to pursue the matter.

'Well, someone sure as hell caught up with him over there,' he said. 'The last I heard he was still unconscious. I rang the hospital. They said he was stable, though, and showing signs of coming round.'

'Look!' Eksberg banged the bottle down on the table. 'Can we change the subject? The less I have to do with le Roux and his bloody nephew from here on out, the better I'll like it.'

Colin managed to look sympathetic.

'Le Roux been giving you a rough time, has he? That's too bad! God knows you did all you could.'

'All I could, and then some.' Eksberg's voice was angry, his thin, dark face twisted. 'The man's mad. Believe me – I kid you not! I was up till the small hours listening to him raving on.'

'Mad? Le Roux? I thought he was going to be our next Prime Minister.'

'Then heaven help us! He's unstable. He drinks too much. He can't make a decision to save his life.' Eksberg seemed to have forgotten his wish to change the subject and leant forward eagerly, the bitterness spilling over. 'If he's the next Prime Minister, then I'll emigrate. Believe me.'

Colin looked at him thoughtfully.

'Strange. Whatever his faults, I always thought him competent. Ruthless, maybe, and heartless. But competent.'

'Well, he's not now.'

'Maybe the death of his wife—'

'No.' Eksberg brushed this aside as being of little importance. 'It's not that. He's crazy, I tell you. I'm sick to death of the man, so shut up about him and pray that Verwoerd stays healthy and in command for a long, long time. Tell me – who's going to win the game on Saturday?'

That was it, then, Colin thought as the conversation turned to rugby. Not anything to go on, really – except that the policeman's feelings about le Roux were running high. Because he'd received a rocket for not finding Jan before he left South Africa? It had to be more than that. At least now le Roux knew where to find his nephew if the only reason for wanting to contact him was to sort out a family matter; and even if Jan was as yet unable to deal with it, the signs were this was only a temporary condition.

Afterwards, he reviewed the words Ekberg had used. Le Roux was unstable, he'd said. He couldn't make a decision. In other words, he'd changed his mind about something. What?

He'd give a good deal to find out, he thought, as he walked back down Adderley Street to the offices of the *Courier*. Maybe he could devote a Saturday column to a feature on him. The man was constantly in the news, after all.

I'll speak to the boss, he decided.

12

'Has he come?' Vicky shouted eagerly from the top of the steps, earning a pained reproof from Miss Oates, who was the teacher supposed to be in charge of an orderly exodus from Moorcroft Close. Vicky spared her not a glance, but plunged down the steps at a dangerous speed, dragging Mark behind her.

'Careful,' remonstrated Kate.

'But has he—'

'Yes, he's at home, waiting to see you.'

Vicky, having slept on the news, had decided by morning that it was, after all, exciting and definitely unusual to have an elderly brother, long lost, appear suddenly on the scene. The trip to school that morning had been enlivened with non-stop questions and observations, and the passage of hours had apparently done little to curb her enthusiasm.

'Can I put my best frock on?' she asked as she climbed into the car. 'I usually do when we have visitors,' she added hastily, justifying the request.

'If you like,' Kate agreed. 'But you must be good, quiet children, though, because Johnny – I mean Jan – still isn't quite well.'

'Is he in bed, then?' Vicky asked.

'Well, he was when I came out. He had a long sleep after lunch, but he said he'd have a bath and get dressed so that he was up when you came home.'

'Miss Hill didn't believe me,' Mark complained. 'In news time I told her I had a new brother and she said no, I hadn't, because you hadn't been to the hospital to get a new baby, so I said it wasn't a baby brother, it was a big brother and she said I was making up fairy stories.'

'Miss Hill's silly,' Vicky said, backing him all the way. 'And Gaynor. She didn't believe me, either. She said Jan didn't sound like a boy's name at all. Yan,' she added experimentally. 'It is a bit funny, isn't it?'

'Yan, Yan, Yan,' shouted Mark, hanging on to the front seat and bouncing up and down. 'Hilly silly, hilly silly—'

'Calm down, both of you,' Kate entreated. 'I shall just have to drive round and round and not take you home at all if you can't be quiet and well behaved.'

'We will be,' Vicky promised. 'Won't we, Mark? We'll be quiet as mice.'

'Well, start practising now,' Kate said. She was beginning to experience early echoes of the familiar vague ache behind the eyes often brought on by the combination of heavy traffic and two ebullient children. Maybe it hadn't been such a great idea after all, bringing Johnny – Jan – back from the hospital. At least it was comparatively quiet there.

But really, she couldn't wish it otherwise. It was wonderful to know that he was at home, already in the house. Immediately she'd returned from taking the children to school that morning she'd cleaned the guest bedroom and made up the bed, switching on the electric blanket so that it would be warm for him. She'd bought flowers, too, and prepared a light but tempting lunch so that everything was ready by the time Tom brought him home from the hospital in the late morning.

He was wearing the clothes he had been found in. They had been laundered, but both the jacket and his trousers needed mending. I should have done that, Kate thought guiltily. All those hours I was just sitting and talking nonsense that he never heard!

He looked pale, apart from the fading contusions, and seemed quiet.

'Did you talk in the car?' Kate asked Tom when they were alone in the kitchen.

'A bit. Not much. Well,' he said in reply to a surprised look from her, 'I didn't want to tire him and he seemed happily occupied looking out of the window. I did say he was very welcome, though.'

She smiled at him.

'Good. Are you having a cup of coffee or getting straight back to the office?'

'I'd better get back. I shan't be late tonight.'

'Good,' she said again, reaching to kiss him, trying not to show

how glad she was to have Jan to herself. There was so much to talk about, she thought. But there was no doubt he looked tired, and as soon as he had eaten she encouraged him to go to bed, and only a few minutes later she looked round the bedroom door to see that he was sound asleep.

It was the best thing. The only thing, really. With plenty of rest he would soon be back to normal, remembering the details of the immediate past that remained so far forgotten.

The distant past had been forgotten, too, but for other reasons. He could remember nothing of his previous trip to England, he told her. Had never known, in fact, that he had ever been there. Home, to him, had always been Gramerci – the white house, the garden, the candlewood tree.

'It's still there, the candlewood tree?' Kate had asked him over lunch.

'Oh, yes. Sonia sold off the land, but they kept the house and the garden round it.'

'That must have been very hard for her.'

'I think she was glad to be shot of it, in the end. It had all got too much for her. She wanted me to go into the business, but I couldn't. That was another source of contention; she'd been determined on that for as long as I could remember, and when I put my foot down we had the mother and father of all rows. I held my ground, though. It would never have worked – we were chalk and cheese. And besides, there were other things I wanted to do.'

'What were they?'

'Law, initially.'

'Like Christiaan.'

'Well—' He laughed. 'I suppose so, at first. I rather fancied myself as a kind of Perry Mason, standing up in court to defend the innocent and unmask the villain – all glamorous stuff! But then Sir Randolph died and left me quite a bit of money and I began to think – why me? It shook me. I even felt guilty. I mean, I didn't even know the guy, and suddenly there I was, with no real need to earn a living like all my friends, and I couldn't see that it was right.'

'Sonia must have approved of that.'

'Well, no, she didn't. Not really. She said it was Gramerci money – that Sir Randolph meant it for the family business, and only left it to me because he thought I was going to carry on in the wine trade.'

'But you didn't see it that way?'

'Not really. I thought about it, of course. The Lampards have been in the wine business for a long time and I could understand how she felt. But the more I thought about it, the more I felt there were other things I had to do – and after all, the old boy did leave it to me with no strings attached. I had absolutely no flair at all for wine and I'd already embarked on studying for the law. I thought that if I were qualified, I could take up the cases of people who didn't have the means to defend themselves against some of the more monstrous charges that were brought against them by the government. That was around 1954 – a bad, bad period when *apartheid* was really beginning to bite. It was when the Nats finally deprived the Cape Coloureds of their voting rights, and when they started forcibly moving people out of their legally owned homes. Christiaan thought I was mad, of course. Not because I chose law over the wine trade, but because I intended to work for whatever people could pay rather than join some smart law firm in Cape Town.'

Just as he had done, Kate thought. But that wasn't enough for Christiaan. He had always wanted more recognition, more acclaim. More power.

Nineteen thirty-eight had seen his election to Parliament as a member of the Nationalist Party led by Malan, standing on a manifesto which called for separate residential areas and places of work, the abolition of all forms of African representation in Parliament and a halt to further land purchases for Africans.

Though Christiaan was elected, his party fared more poorly than it hoped and the United Party, an uneasy alliance of the old National Party led by Hertzog and the South African Party led by Smuts, was returned to power.

'It won't last,' Christiaan said cheerfully, savouring his victory with a glass of Cabernet Gramerci soon after the election. 'There'll be a split before long. Smuts and Hertzog are at daggers drawn.'

He was soon proved right, for with the situation deteriorating in Europe, talk of eventual war became more common. To oppose Germany, or support the Nazi regime? The issues in South Africa were not so clear cut as they were in Europe, and there were many who backed Hertzog's view that the Nazis were in the right. Smuts, on the other hand, took the opposite point of view.

Argument and discussion raged at every bar, every dinner table; even at Gramerci, Guy backed Smuts, while Sonia and Christiaan were totally at one in their support for Hertzog – not at all to Kate's surprise, for she had long since become resigned to the fact that whatever stance was taken by Britain, they were certain to oppose it. Guy's tolerant support for Britain, unexpected and unprecedented as it was, she regarded as little more than excitement at the thought of a scrap; not that he showed a great deal of interest in European politics or the moral questions involved. The politics of the golf club and the question of which horses were running at Kenilworth were far more pressing issues to his way of thinking.

Christiaan, still to declare his hand as far as Sonia was concerned, nevertheless remained a constant visitor, at least during the summer months. He had given up his Cape Town house in order to buy another in Pretoria for the six months of the year when the government carried on its business there, but in order to have a permanent base when it moved southwards he arranged to rent what Kate still thought of as Larry's cottage.

Whether Lilian approved or disapproved of this was never mentioned; in fact, Kate doubted whether her opinion was ever sought, for since Larry's departure, despite her best efforts, her mother-in-law had grown more and more withdrawn. Thinner, too. In the kitchen one day Evalina, muttering to herself and shaking her head, showed Kate the lunch tray which had been sent back with the meal hardly tasted.

'I worried about Oumissus,' she said. 'See here, all this good food. She ain't eatin', madam. She yust pinin' away. It was a bad, bad day when her friend left.'

Kate looked at the evidence unhappily.

'I know,' she said. 'What are we to do, Evalina? She won't come out with me any more, though I've asked her to.'

'I knows, madam.' Over Evalina's broad face there chased numerous emotions; anxiety, sadness, indecision. 'I say to Joseph, is a good thing she has you. Miss Sonia, she never had much to say to her mother.'

'I'll pop over to see her this afternoon,' Kate promised.

Evalina looked at her and looked away again, biting her lip, clearly wondering whether to say more. Kate watched her as she moved ponderously about the kitchen, scraping off the wasted meal into the pig bucket, stacking plates beside the sink, her mouth pursed, as if with indecision.

'Is . . . is there something else I should be doing to help her?' Kate asked hesitantly. 'Do tell me if there is, Evalina. You know her better than anyone.'

'Oh, I do, madam, I do.' Evalina picked up a towel to dry her hands, and turned towards Kate with her face now working with emotion. 'I don't know if I should speak, madam, but I so worried about Oumissus.' Still she seemed to hesitate. 'She . . . she drinkin' again. I don't know where she get it. Some *skelm* must go to the shop for her – someone who work outside, maybe. She been so good for years. Not a drop has she touched.'

'Oh dear,' Kate said, faintly. It was, she was well aware, an inadequate response, but she felt totally overwhelmed by this fulfilment of Larry's prophecy and quite unequal to dealing with it.

'I'll speak to my husband,' she said at last.

Evalina shook her head sadly and went about her chores, as if knowing in advance that this would bring no solution. For a moment Kate hovered indecisively, then, unhappily, she left. She would have to renew her efforts to befriend Lilian, she could see. Give her something else to think about. Involve her in some way.

But that, she realised, was the trouble. Non-involvement had been forced on her in her early years within this family, and now it had become a habit impossible to break so that even the art and the music and the handicrafts she had once delighted in now failed to touch her.

I know exactly how she feels, Kate thought; and as she did so, an icy breath of foreboding seemed to pass over her before determination took its place. No, she thought, tightening her lips. No, their circumstances were not the same. Larry had been wrong about that. Never, never, would she go the same way as Lilian. And strengthened by this resolve she crossed the yard to see her mother-in-law.

Unable to catch him alone earlier and having an instinctive reluctance to discuss Lilian in front of Sonia, Kate cornered Guy in the bedroom, sitting on the edge of the bed and waiting for him until he came in from the bathroom, a towel round his waist and his hair wet. There was a committee meeting at the club that evening, and afterwards he and a few of the boys were going out to dinner. Kate knew by experience that it would probably be the small hours before he returned home.

He pulled a comic face when he came into the room and saw her there, clearly waiting.

'What have I done?' he asked.

'Done?' Kate laughed. 'Nothing! Have you got a guilty conscience?'

He began towelling his hair, turning away from her.

'You look a bit ominous.'

She was struck anew by the beauty of his body – the wide shoulders tapering down to the waist, the long, powerful legs. She felt a pang of longing. It should all have been so different, she thought.

'It's Lilian,' she said. 'Evalina says she's drinking again.'

He spun round and looked at her. His mouth had thinned, his eyes narrowed.

'What do you mean? She doesn't drink. Have you seen her take a drop?'

'No. Not since I've been here. But she did, once.'

Guy resumed towelling his hair.

'Servants' gossip,' he said. 'You should be above that sort of thing.'

'Evalina's genuinely worried.'

'Evalina's an idiot where Mother's concerned.'

'She's fond of her.'

'Aren't we all?' Guy threw aside the towel and pulled on clean underpants. He went to the massive wardrobe where freshly ironed shirts were hanging. Most of them were white, some cream, but he had his favourites. He went through them slowly, finally choosing one of the newest.

'Which tie?' he asked her. 'I thought I'd wear the pale grey trousers and this check jacket. This blue one goes rather well with it,' he said, making his choice without waiting for her answer.

'You're taking a lot of trouble for a committee meeting.'

'Can't let the side down, can I?'

'Guy, what about your mother? There must be something we can do, though what it is, I really don't know. She needs company. Some sort of activity. That's where Larry was so good.'

Guy paused in buttoning his shirt and pointed a finger at her.

'Now don't get on to me about Larry,' he said. 'I did the right thing there. How could we have allowed a man like that to live in close proximity to our son—'

'But—'

Kate turned her head away, biting back her annoyance. Such recriminations were pointless, she knew, and she should never have mentioned Larry's name. Still, it angered her to think that Guy had somehow managed to redraw the character of this quiet, pleasant man in his mind so that now he was nothing less than a dangerous time-bomb threatening the morals of defenceless male children.

'All right,' she said at last. 'What's done is done. The question is, what are we going to do now? Evalina says someone is supplying her. She doesn't know who.'

Guy had finished dressing and was combing his hair, tilting his head to view the result.

'Very handsome,' Kate said dryly.

'Thank you, my darling. Look—' He came over and sat on the bed beside her. 'Don't worry about Mother. I'm sure Evalina's exaggerating the problem. They love to dramatise things, you know. Mother looks fine to me – and if a few drinks help her through the day, does it really matter? I mean, she doesn't allow herself many pleasures, does she? After all, she's not likely to disgrace the family by going out and keeling over in public. She hardly goes out anywhere.' He looked at his watch. 'Good Lord, is that the time? I must fly.' He bent to kiss her cheek. 'Don't know when I'll be back. See you in the morning. You're sweet not to kick up a fuss.'

She watched him go in silence. Should she have kicked up a fuss? Maybe she should. He seemed to be on so many committees and have so many outside interests these days that she was left alone several times a week. Lilian and I, she thought, once more feeling that same chill. Outsiders, both of us. Was it always to be so?

The newspapers had events other than Europe to occupy them during 1938; events nearer home. As an expression of Afrikaner solidarity and to commemorate the Great Trek, when hundreds of the Cape Dutch had packed their belongings into covered wagons and faced adversity and suffering to find a home away from British rule, there was to be a symbolic ox-wagon trek from Cape Town to Pretoria.

It seemed a brilliant, exciting concept and Kate's imagination was set alight by the idea. Almost for the first time she felt herself wholly in sympathy with the tough, stubborn, arrogant Boers who looked on South Africa as theirs by right. They had contended with inhospitable natural hazards: rivers to cross, mountains to scale, as well as drought and storms and floods. They had fought off the attacks of warlike Zulus, and pressed onwards in the search for land they could call their own.

They were brave, no one could dispute it; neither could anyone dispute the passionate love they had for their country, now as then. Though she still thought their attitude to race misguided, she could see that in their minds they had won this land fair and square and were proud of having done so; and proud, too, of their culture and language which they were determined to keep pure and untainted.

There were to be two wagons leaving Cape Town in August, trekking northwards, to be joined by others at the towns and dorps they passed through.

'We must see them set off,' Kate said one day when, over dinner, the arrangements had been mentioned. 'Johnny ought to see it.'

Sonia looked at her in astonishment.

'Well, of course,' she said. 'Guy and I are determined that he should. We hardly thought you would be interested, though.'

'Oh, Sonia, do we have to stay on opposite sides of the fence for ever?' Kate asked her, exasperated. 'This is my country now as well as yours. I have a terrific admiration for the Voortrekkers.'

'Really?' Sonia raised her eyebrows, her expression sceptical. 'And are you not the same girl who is so excited about going "home"?'

'Well, of course—'

'There you are, then.' Sonia smiled. 'All you Britishers are the same. Home is where the heart is and yours is hardly in South Africa.'

Afterwards, too late, Kate thought of a dozen different responses to this, but at the time she was struck dumb by a feeling of frustration and an intense longing to brain Sonia with the coffee pot which she was, at that moment, holding in her hands. For a moment she struggled with her anger.

'I still think it will be a thrilling sight,' she said stiffly at last. 'Of course I want to see it.'

'Well, if you're determined, David Nelson has invited us all to the balcony of his office in Adderley Street. It'll be impossible to see a thing from the pavement. I'm told there will be thousands of people there.'

'Honestly,' Kate said to Helen the following day. 'As if I wouldn't want to be part of it! Surely they weren't really thinking I'd stay behind?'

'Of course not,' Helen said. 'But you know Sonia. She was just making a point. Sticking the knife in.'

Kate shook her head in bewilderment.

'I simply don't know what to make of her. Sometimes I think that the fact that I'm reasonably fluent in Afrikaans annoys her, as if she feels that it's presumptuous for an English girl to attempt to speak it. I think she liked it better when she and Guy could natter away knowing I couldn't understand a word.'

'But if you'd made no attempt to learn it, it would have been another stick to beat you with. Better face it, Kate – you're never going to please her, so just ignore her.'

Which was, Kate thought, easier said than done.

The day when all Cape Town gathered to witness the departure of the two ox wagons was as thrilling as Kate could have imagined. One hundred thousand cheering *volk* had gathered on the Foreshore to see the trek start off after exhortations and prayers, and thousands more lined the streets along the route it was to take. Most buildings along the way had upper-floor balconies, and all were full for the occasion; not all, however, could boast such a genteel, socially acceptable gathering as that to be found on the balcony belonging to the offices of Nelson and Swart, Attorneys at Law. It was to be quite a party, with Cornelius Wenst, the Minister of Justice, present as guest of honour.

Kate had bought a new hat for the occasion and felt pleased with the reflection she saw in the mirror before setting out; however, she was ruefully aware that, having held Johnny on her lap all the way to town, her appearance was not quite so immaculate on arrival. And if she hadn't been aware, then Sonia was quick enough to tell her, stepping out of the front seat of the car where she had sat unencumbered throughout the journey to look at her with amused distaste and ask, with pretended innocence, if the hat was really intended to sit so far back on her head.

Grace Nelson, elegant as ever, came forward to welcome them, exclaiming rapturously at how Johnny had grown since she had last seen him.

'But no Lilian?' she said in dismay. 'I was so hoping she'd come.'

'I'm afraid she didn't feel up to it,' Sonia told her, a note of regret in her voice which Kate knew was totally false. It was, in fact, Sonia herself who had told her mother she would find the outing far too tiring and tedious.

'I'm so sorry,' Grace said. 'I must call on her, but somehow life is so full . . . Come along, all of you, come out to the balcony. Nothing's happening yet, but it's fun to watch the crowds. You'll find several old friends already there, and we've put a chair for Johnny by the railing so that he'll have a grandstand view.'

'Thank you, you're very kind,' Kate said. 'It's good of you to invite us.' Johnny, at that moment, seemed more interested in investigating the durability of a glass-topped table than going anywhere, so, with Guy and Sonia close behind, she scooped him up and bore him towards the balcony, aware even as she did so that he had tipped her hat to an angle the milliner never intended.

She turned in distress to Guy.

'Oh, Lor',' she said. 'Take him for a minute, will you, darling—?'

'Well, hallo,' said a sultry voice before Guy had made a move towards her. Kate turned and saw Greta, who, in dashing red and white, looked more like a fashion plate than ever. 'How lovely to see you.' Greta's smile was dazzling. 'It's been such a long time. How are you all? And how is this little man? My, how he's grown – and what a charmer!' She extended her red-tipped fingers (talons, Kate thought) to prod him, but Johnny drew back to lay his head on his mother's shoulder, looking at his assailant warily. Greta gave a merry laugh. 'He's probably been warned to beware of me,' she said, in great good humour. 'You haven't been talking to him, have you, Guy?'

'No,' said Guy shortly, unamused.

'I was speaking to Neil on the phone only this morning,' Greta went on. 'He's in Jo'burg on business, you know. He asked me if I'd seen anything of you and I said no, not for ages. I can't imagine where you've been hiding yourself!'

As far as Guy was concerned, it was as if she had never spoken.

'Come on, Kate,' he said. 'We're blocking the doorway.'

Kate smiled uncertainly at Greta.

'It . . . it really is nice to see you,' she said, not meaning it but uncomfortably aware of Guy's uncharacteristic rudeness. What on earth had got into him?

Wenst and Christiaan were already on the balcony, engrossed in earnest conversation that clearly was not meant for anyone else's ears. Kate felt cynically amused; only a few nights before she had heard Christiaan telling Sonia how important it was for him to cultivate Wenst. Get in his good books.

'Mark my words,' he'd said. 'Wenst is a coming man. A man worth knowing.'

In Kate's opinion, Wenst was a man worth avoiding. She had met him on several social occasions and had found him invariably unbending, if not downright unpleasant. Too damned virtuous for his own good, Helen said. In his book, if anything was enjoyable then by definition it had to be sinful.

Kate edged away from them, finding others more congenial to talk to. Guy joined her, happily enjoying his family man's role; and when afterwards she thought over the incident with Greta, she felt nothing but relief. If ever there had been anything going on between Greta and her husband – and she was by no means sure, with the passage of time, that there had been – then plainly it was over. He had barely given her a glance all morning.

'This Czech business,' Guy said one day, looking up from the newspaper with a frown. 'They're saying it's certain to lead to war.'

That the possibility had been under discussion for some weeks, even months, seemed to have passed him by.

'It may not,' Kate said, for the contemplation of such an outcome filled her with dread. 'We can always hope.'

'It puts your little trip in some doubt, though, doesn't it?'

This was something else that Kate had not been able to face.

'I suppose you're right,' she said miserably. 'Still, I'm determinedly looking on the bright side. The whole thing will surely be decided one way or the other by then.'

By the end of the month, Chamberlain had returned from Germany promising peace, and the fate of Czechoslovakia had been sealed. The moment Kate heard the news, she rushed into town to book her passage and apply for a passport, since previously she had merely been an addition to Guy's. When it arrived, she looked at it in delight, feeling that it symbolised the kind of independence that she had hitherto lacked.

She was to leave on 10 February 1939, and as soon as a calendar for the new year came into her possession, she ringed the dates.

'I just can't wait,' she wrote to Nancy. 'I'm really counting the days. Once Christmas is over, it will seem like no time at all. Yes, it is a pity that Guy can't be with me, but I knew from the first that it really wouldn't be possible.'

She came to a full stop, nibbling the end of her pen. Was it awful of her, she wondered, to be looking forward to a break from Guy and from Gramerci quite so much? It really wasn't something she could confess to anyone, not even Helen or Nancy, for wives of three and a bit years' standing weren't supposed to feel like that.

She was willing to bet that Nancy and Peter wouldn't – but then they knew each other and were friends as well as lovers. She and Guy – well, they hadn't known each other at all. And in a strange sort of way, though she knew his every expression and could foresee his reaction to almost anything, she realised that she still didn't know him and perhaps never would.

Christmas came and went. The Nelsons, once more, gave their traditional party. It had none of the drama of her first Christmas in South Africa but instead, for Kate, was a hugely enjoyable affair, made more so by the thought that she was so soon to be taking her trip to England. Home, she thought defiantly, metaphorically cocking a snook at Sonia.

Meantime, in anticipation of cold weather on her arrival, she was knitting frantically and had already made a small sweater for Johnny and, more ambitiously, embarked on one for herself.

One afternoon in early January, she was sitting in the depths of the candlewood tree puzzling over a pattern that was turning out more complicated than she expected, when she looked up to see her mother-in-law slowly approaching across the lawn, her arms held out a little at each side like one negotiating a tight-rope.

'Lilian!' she cried in relief. 'You're just the person I wanted to see. I'm in a desperate tangle with this jumper – please come and help! I was going to bring it over, but I thought you might be resting.'

Lilian paused and seemed to be looking at her, but then her gaze drifted away, unfocused. For the first time it occurred to Kate that she looked a little odd. She was usually so groomed and elegant, with pearls at her throat and ears, but now her hair straggled from a lop-sided knot on top of her head and her blouse gaped open. Kate put the knitting and pattern to one side on the seat and rose to meet her, worried by her appearance, thinking how frail and thin she looked.

'Lilian, is something wrong?' she asked softly, taking her arm.

With an irritated gesture, Lilian shook her off.

'I'm all right,' she said; but Kate knew that she was not. Her words were slurred and she staggered a little. Then her mood seemed to change, between one breath and the next. She gave a little, hiccupping laugh and put a hand on Kate's arm. 'I came to ask you a favour, darling,' she said in a bright, social voice. 'I need a drink. Rather badly. Bring me a bottle from the house, won't you?' For a moment Kate hesitated, and Lilian laughed again. 'I'd get it myself but they're all in there, on guard. They won't let me get to the cabinet.'

'No one's there,' Kate said. 'But I don't think—'

'You go, darling,' Lilian said. 'Just to please me.'

'The cabinet's locked.' There was a note of desperation in Kate's voice. This was true; the cabinet containing spirits was normally kept locked, but mainly to guard against theft from a chance burglar. Everyone in the household knew that the key was kept behind the beading on the top.

'Please,' Lilian said in a childish voice, putting her head on one side. 'Pretty please?'

'Oh, Lilian—' Desperately Kate looked around, hoping that someone – anyone – would come to her rescue. She could hear Rosie and Johnny playing somewhere behind the hedge, but there was nobody near at hand and she had no idea how to handle this. 'Look,' she said. 'Let's get you home. Then I'll see what I can do.'

Lilian withdrew from her again.

'You're going to tell Sonia,' she said coldly.

'No. No, I won't, really.'

'I thought I could rely on you.'

'You can. Really. I want to help.' Kate's assurance was perhaps more vehement because of the secret, shaming revulsion she felt. As if to deny it, she put her arm around Lilian's thin shoulders. 'Come,' she said. 'Let me take you home. I was hoping that you'd offer me a cup of tea.'

'Very well.'

Lilian's mood seemed to have changed again, and she was docile, withdrawn, content to be led back to her pretty bijou sitting room with its flower-patterned chairs and pale green carpet.

'Shall I make you some tea?' Kate asked, once they were there. Lilian said nothing in reply but smiled vaguely and Kate took this for assent. However, returning from the tiny kitchen, she found that her mother-in-law had fallen asleep and, with her head lolling sideways, was snoring slightly. Kate stood for a moment, looking at her. It was easy to see now how beautiful she must have been. She had fine bones and a kind of natural grace, even though she was emaciated and her skin was lined.

But she needed help, Kate thought. Guy simply had to take notice now. She couldn't go on like this.

'A home,' Sonia said crisply. 'Some kind of clinic. It's the only answer.'

Kate was prepared for this reaction, which was why she had contrived to get Guy on his own to tell him what had happened earlier, running across to the cellars to meet him at the end of the afternoon so that they walked back across the garden together.

'Couldn't we persuade her to come back to live in the house?' she had asked him. 'She ought not to be by herself. I spend quite a bit of time with her but from tea-time on she's quite alone and I'm sure it's not good for her.'

Guy refrained from answering directly.

'Did I tell you I'd found out who was buying booze for her?' he said.

'No! Who was it?'

'One of the estate workers. An old chap who came when he was a boy. She's known him for ages.'

'What did he say?'

'Just that she asked him to do it. He didn't have time to say much. He was out of here so quickly his feet hardly touched the ground.'

'Oh, Guy—'

'You're not saying I shouldn't have sacked him?'

'No. Not exactly.' Kate looked worried. 'It's just that he must have been put in a very awkward position. I mean – well, she's persuasive, you know. I didn't know what to do or say this afternoon, and it must have been far worse for him.'

'Well, he's gone now, and all the rest of the chaps will know why, so we shouldn't have any more trouble.'

'It's not as easy as that,' Kate said. 'It's a sickness, Guy.'

'Well—' He paused and with an imaginary golf club took a few swings at an imaginary ball. 'Sonia will know what to do.'

Kate opened her mouth to protest, then closed it again. The matter would obviously have to be discussed with Sonia; it was foolish to think otherwise.

Sonia, however, having delivered her judgment, was in no mood to sit and discuss the matter for Christiaan was collecting her in half an hour in order to attend some kind of official reception for a visiting dignitary.

Guy, too, was going out.

'I'm sorry, darling,' he said, full of regret. 'Honestly, I'd get out of it if I could. Heaven knows, I do enough for that club, but you know what they say. Ask a busy man—'

'What is it this time?'

'Oh, some kind of sub-committee about replacing the furniture in the ladies' lounge. The ladies have been complaining about it looking shabby.'

'Really?'

'Well, if you came more often, you'd see for yourself!'

'I know. I'm sorry. It's just not my sort of thing. You know where I would like to go, though, some time soon? There's a Fred Astaire and Ginger Rogers film on at the Majestic.'

'Sure,' Guy said. 'That'd be fun. Let's go tomorrow. By the way,' he added as he kissed her goodbye, 'it might be a good idea to look in on Mother in an hour or so.'

'I intend to, but she'd love to see you. Couldn't you just—'

'Sorry! No time.' And with a wave of the hand he left her.

She followed him out to the stoep, watching his progress as the black gleam of the car appeared at intervals through the oaks and was finally gone.

For a moment she stood there, leaning against the carved rail, arms wrapped around herself. What a funny life she had, she thought. Funny peculiar. Full of surface busy-ness; the clinic, the garden, social events, both major and minor. And Johnny, and Helen. What would she do without them?

During the day she could persuade herself that it was enough. Perhaps it was. Perhaps all marriages were the same. It was only at times like this, with Johnny asleep upstairs and the house and garden left to her alone, that she felt wistfully aware of her loneliness. And aware, too, of her wickedness, for she knew she should be counting her blessings, not wallowing in this unfocused discontent. How many girls would envy her, living here in these surroundings, with a little boy like Johnny and a handsome husband?

The birds were silent now and the crickets had begun their chirping. She could smell jasmine and wood smoke and hear Evalina's voice raised above the distant rattle of china, the slam of a door. In front of her, to the right, the evening sun was touching the treetops with gold, and to the left, beyond the vineyard, the hills were softened with wisps of cloud.

Peaceful, she thought. Just like heaven. Then she banged the rail with her clenched fist. She didn't *want* peace. She was too young for heaven.

Maybe she should have gone to the club with Guy. He was right – she hardly ever went with him these days; she'd had her fill of it. Had sat for too many boring nights waiting for him to be ready to leave. Nothing to say, not wanting another drink, longing only for bed and a good book to read.

She sighed, then stood up straight, squaring her shoulders. Not long now, she told herself. Soon she'd be on board ship, going home. She would go in now and make sure that Johnny was settled and sleeping, and then would go over to see Lilian.

It had been horrible, seeing her as she was that afternoon, and she could only feel sympathy for the worker who'd done what she asked of him. Was a clinic really the answer? She thought it over as she went upstairs to check on Johnny. Maybe it was, if Lilian agreed and the place was run properly and the people were kind. At least she would have company. The trouble was, she thought, as she pulled the light blanket over her sleeping child's shoulders and gently removed a toy truck from under his cheek, she didn't really trust Sonia to take the trouble to find the best. Or to act with any urgency. But perhaps she did her an injustice. When it came to the point, Sonia would want to do the best for her mother, however cool the relationship between them.

Surely, surely, she thought as she looked down at her son, there must be some kind of love between them, some concern. Did Lilian, in the past, ever look down on her daughter with the same swelling of emotion that she felt when she looked at Johnny? And did Sonia ever cling to her for comfort? She must have done! It would break her heart, she felt, if Johnny ever looked at her with the coldness she had seen in Sonia's eyes.

She closed the door and went downstairs, and as she did so, she remembered her knitting which Rosie had brought in from outside and left in the sitting room. She'd take it with her when she went to see Lilian, she thought. When it came to knitting and embroidery and all allied skills, she really was the expert. It was possible that a sleep and a meal had restored her to normality; the muddle her inept daughter-in-law had succeeded in creating with the wretched sweater would break the ice and give them something to talk about.

Evalina was in the sitting room when Kate went in, drawing the curtains against the night, mildly scolding.

'Mr Guy, he a careless boy,' she said. 'He left dat cupboard wide open to de four winds so any *skelm* could come in and help hisself.'

'Which cupboard?' Kate had picked up the knitting and was looking at it carefully, trying to pinpoint the place where she had first gone wrong. 'Oh, the drinks cabinet. Did he?'

'Wide open to de four winds, madam. You have to speak to him.'

'He takes much more notice of you.'

'You get away with you!' Evalina made a shooing motion with her arm, but she laughed and looked pleased.

'Did Oumissus eat her dinner tonight?' Kate asked.

Evalina's smile died and her face took on the creased, worried expression she habitually wore whenever Lilian's name entered the conversation.

'Not bad like sometimes,' she said. 'But oh, madam, dat poor soul—'

'I'm going across to see her now. I shan't be long, but ask Rosie to listen for Johnny, won't you?'

'Stay yust as long as you wish, madam. We take care of Yonny, Rosie and me.'

Having knocked at Lilian's door, Kate had to wait a little before she heard any response. She feared the worst, but at last she heard Lilian's voice telling her to go in and to her relief found that her mother-in-law looked just as usual. Her hair was dressed elegantly, her blouse was buttoned, the pearls in place; but more important, her manner seemed normal. She was sitting in an armchair leafing through a heavily illustrated book on Impressionist painters, the wireless beside her playing sweet music – Tchaikovsky, Kate thought, or Brahms, perhaps. Her musical education had been neglected along with every other aspect.

'How sweet of you to come, my dear,' Lilian said, smiling graciously, apparently no more distant than usual. 'Was there a special reason?'

'Not really. Well, I did wonder if you could help me with this wretched bit of knitting – I've gone wrong somewhere, and I can't quite see where – but most of all I came to see how you are. You were sleeping when I saw you last.'

'I was just a little tired.' Lilian shook her head, smiling ruefully. 'I'm not as young as I was, you know. I'm perfectly well, but I'm not sure I feel up to coping with knitting. My eyes, you know. Perhaps another time.'

'Yes, of course. It's not important.' Kate put her work aside and sat down on a stool close to Lilian, searching for a topic of conversation now that this one was denied to her. 'I've just noticed that wonderful clump of watsonias in the bed just outside your door,' she said. 'I had no idea when I put them in that they'd turn out such a gorgeous colour.'

'Really?' Lilian smiled again, but as if her mind was elsewhere. 'How nice, dear.' She hasn't noticed them, Kate thought in astonishment, knowing her mother-in-law's fondness for flowers. How could she not have done? They were staring her in the face the moment she opened her door.

'This is lovely music,' she said, after a few seconds' pause.

Lilian tilted her head.

'Yes,' she agreed. 'I listen every evening.'

Immediately Kate was struck by guilt.

'And I'm interrupting! I'm so sorry, but I was a bit concerned.'

She stood up so quickly that an unguarded movement of her arm caught the edge of the book which Lilian had put face down over the arm of the chair and it fell to the floor down the narrow gap between chair and wall. 'I'm spoiling your music! I'll come back another time. No, please—' For Lilian was diving down to retrieve the book. 'I'll get it. It was awfully clumsy of—'

The words died, for she saw, suddenly, that Lilian had not been so much concerned for the book but for the bottle and glass that she had clearly concealed when she had heard Kate at the door. The glass had tipped over, spilling its contents, but the bottle was safe.

'I'll get a cloth,' Kate said, and went into the kitchen.

When she returned, Lilian was still sitting in her chair, watching for her, her eyes wary. She said nothing.

'It's not very much,' Kate said, crouching down to blot up the spill. It was gin; she could smell it. The bottle was a fairly new one, with perhaps a tenth of it gone. 'No harm done.'

Lilian seemed to have decided to carry it off with aplomb.

'I do so like a little drink in the evening,' she said in a bright, social voice. 'There's nothing wrong in that, as far as I know,' she added, as if Kate had accused her of something.

'No, of course not.' Kate smiled up at her, trying to appear normal. She sat back on her heels. 'There, that's OK, I think, and there shouldn't be a stain. I'll go and wash the glass—'

'No, don't do that.' Lilian spoke quickly. She gave a nervous laugh. 'I didn't have much of that one, did I? You'd better give me another.'

Kate hesitated.

'Do you think that's a good idea?' she asked.

Lilian stared at her.

'Of course I do. What a foolish question. I wouldn't have asked otherwise.' Her manner had changed; she had become very much the *grande dame*. 'Give me the glass, then,' she went on, rising to her feet with enormous dignity despite a little unsteadiness. 'If there's one thing I cannot abide it's young people treating me as if I'm a fool with no mind of my own. I can look after myself perfectly well.'

Kate maintained her hold on the glass.

'It's only because we're worried about you, Lilian. You don't seem yourself.'

Lilian laughed at that.

'Myself?' she repeated, a note of wildness in her voice. 'I haven't been myself for the past forty years. Not since I came to this place. Now give me the glass!'

'Lilian, please—'

'Very well, keep it! There are plenty more in the cupboard. Now just leave me alone and go back to your part of the house.'

'Lilian, I'm on your side. Honestly. I want to help.'

'I don't need help, yours or anyone's. Now please go.'

But still Kate hesitated. Lilian was glaring at her now as if she were a stranger, and an inimical stranger at that. There seemed no memory in her mind of the restrained intimacy they had shared ever since Kate's arrival at Gramerci; of the drives, the shopping trips, the cups of coffee they had drunk together when the rest of the household were occupied elsewhere. Even so Kate felt that there must be something she could do, something she could say.

'Tell me,' she said conversationally. 'Where did you get the gin? Did someone go and buy it for you?'

By this time Lilian had picked the bottle up from the floor beside the chair and was cradling it to her as if it were her baby, infinitely precious. She smiled, but said nothing; and at once Kate knew. She must have come into the main house while she was upstairs with Johnny and fled back here, leaving the door open and unlocked.

We'll have to hide the key, she thought, her heart sinking. It seemed sad, such a retrograde step, yet what else was there to do? Perhaps Sonia was right after all.

13

The garden drowsed in the sun of late afternoon, the hills beyond shimmering a little in the haze. Christiaan le Roux leaned back in his chair under the shade of the striped umbrella, smiling faintly, legs stretched before him and hands loosely clasped; a man, it was clear, who was unfazed by tape recorders and had seen off more pressmen that he cared to count.

'You see, Mr Vos,' he said reasonably, 'we are not one country, are we? We are an amalgam of many, with problems quite unique to South Africa, which means that there are nettles which have to be grasped if we are to create a just society for all our peoples. Yes, there is bound to be suffering in the short term. I accept that. I hesitate to use the old cliché about the need to break eggs before one can make an omelette, but nevertheless it is undoubtedly true. In the long term the entire world will be forced to acknowledge that we in South Africa have got the right of it. It's already doing so, in its own way. We saw investment suffer after Sharpeville, but quite rightly the government clamped down on all subversive activity. Order was quickly restored, and already the internationals are showing interest again. There will be a boom in business by the end of this year, mark my words, and although we still have much to do, think of the distance we have already come! Already we have the Bantustans to give our Africans a place they can rightfully call their own. And Coloured voters have their own separate roll, with four constituencies—'

'Which have white representatives,' Colin said dryly.

'Now, Mr Vos.' Le Roux shook a playful finger at him. 'I am perfectly certain you understand the need for that as well as I do. It's not always easy for the Coloured population to act in a disinterested way, for the greatest good of the greatest number. Of all ethnic groupings, the Coloureds break down into more sub-divisions than any: Cape Coloureds, Cape Malays, Indians, Chinese. How can one speak for all? They lack the education, the cool judgment—'

Oh, sure, Colin thought with wry amusement. Like Verwoerd, you mean? He kept his mouth shut, however. It was, after all, le Roux's words he had come to hear.

'You must believe me, Mr Vos,' le Roux continued, his air of sweet reasonableness unabated. 'The aims of this government are not drawn out of thin air, dreamed up with no thought of what is good for other races. Yes, of course, we Afrikaners must have the good of the white population at heart – particularly, if I may say so, our own kind. The preservation of our language and culture is of paramount importance. I wouldn't dream of denying it. This is our country, and the world must recognise it as such. But the benefits of *apartheid* are not one-sided, you know. It can't, surely, be in the interests of our Bantus to live in squalid conditions in the townships, on the edge of white areas? It is my considered opinion, formed over many, many years, that there is a powerful desire in them for their own Bantustans where eventually there will be the same opportunities for work as they now find in our cities. Pass Laws and surveillance will be a thing of the past for them. They will be where they belong.'

Colin made no comment, which did not prevent a picture coming to his mind of despairing, unwilling people forcibly loaded into trucks with their pitiful possessions; old, young, mothers with babies, all surrounded by police who were deaf to any arguments or protests. He had not come to argue with le Roux, he told himself, no matter what his own opinions might be.

'If you'll forgive me, sir,' he said with a polite smile, 'your views on these questions are well known. It is more your background that our readers would find of interest – your childhood and upbringing. The things that shaped the politician that you have become.'

'Well—' Le Roux settled into his chair a little more, his smile broader. 'I was a country boy brought up in a godfearing, Afrikaner household, proud of my heritage. Need I say more?'

'With respect, sir, I think you should. After all, you are widely tipped as the next Prime Minister.'

With a modest laugh, le Roux brushed this aside.

'Well, let's not jump the gun on that one, Mr Vos! Dr Verwoerd will, I hope, lead us for a long time yet. It's an immense honour for me to be part of his government and I can honestly say I have no ambition beyond serving him for as long as he thinks necessary.'

And if you believe that, Colin thought, you'll believe anything. But still he smiled.

'Tell me about your childhood, Minister,' he said. 'Were you always interested in politics?'

Le Roux laughed again.

'Show me an Afrikaner who isn't! My parents were vitally interested, always, but at a local level.'

'That was in the Transvaal, I believe?'

'That's right. My family farmed there. It was always assumed that I'd follow on in the same tradition, but farming never really attracted me. I did well at school, passed exams, went on to Wits.'

Colin nodded.

'Much like myself, only our farm was in the Western Cape. I went to Wits, too. As a matter of interest, I was there at the same time as your nephew. Forgive me digressing for a moment, but I must say how glad I was to know he's on the way to recovery. It must be a great relief to you.'

'Indeed it is.' His smile dying, le Roux bit his lip and shook his head, as if the thought of what might have been was almost too much for him to bear. Then he sighed. 'It's no secret that Jan and I don't see eye to eye about any number of things,' he went on, 'but heaven knows, I don't wish him harm. I can't help being fond of the boy. Did you know him well?'

'No, not really. He was a personality, of course. A bit of a star on the rugby field.'

'And a fallen star off it! Can you imagine the mentality of a man who'd refuse to play for the Springboks? Refuse to play for his country? My wife was devastated.'

'I think most of the population felt the same way.'

'Yes, well—' He paused and sighed again, shaking his head. 'It was a great disappointment. But of course by the time the Springbok affair was spread all over the papers, I think we had become reconciled to the fact that Jan was never going to fulfil his earlier promise, in sport or anything else.' He seemed to be lost in thought for a moment. 'He was never the easiest of boys, Mr Vos,' he continued sadly. 'Always a rebel, kicking against authority. But all we wanted, really, was for him to be happy, follow his own star. In spite of our disapproval—' He

broke off, as if there were more to follow. Colin looked at him
curiously.

'Disapproval of what?' His voice was quiet, persuasive. 'His
politics?'

Le Roux shrugged his elegant shoulders, staring for a moment
into the middle distance without speaking. Slowly and regretfully, as
if, painfully, he were remembering past disappointments, he shook
his head yet again.

'Yes, of course his politics,' he said at last. 'The arguments, as
you can imagine, were legion. But there were other things—' He
appeared to pull himself up on the verge of a confidence. He gave
a brief, embarrassed laugh. 'What am I thinking of? Unburdening
myself to a journalist – I must have gone mad! But in any case, I
mustn't dwell on Jan's past misdeeds. They're best forgotten and
redemption is always a possibility. Leopards can change their spots.
I tried to convince my wife of it, but – and this is strictly between
us, Mr Vos – I'm afraid he lied to us once too often. I hope I can
rely on you to keep this off the record? I shouldn't, perhaps, have
mentioned it.'

'You haven't actually mentioned anything yet,' Colin pointed
out.

'Perhaps not, but I shouldn't even have hinted at our problems
with Jan. Such matters are better kept within the family. I know
my wife would disapprove strongly; she would never have let a
derogatory word about him pass her lips in public. But—' He
hesitated once more and sighed again. 'On the other hand, maybe
you should know the truth. For her sake.'

'And what is the truth?' Colin asked.

Again there was a hesitation.

'I assure you, Mr Vos, that it gives me no pleasure to say it,
but the fact is that Jan is a congenital liar. The truth simply isn't
in him. You never knew that? I'm surprised. What made him that
way?' He lifted his shoulders. 'How can anyone tell? He had a good
upbringing, a happy childhood. We were not his parents, but we
were as fond of him as if we were.' He appeared to make an effort
to put this sadness behind him, and did his best to smile. 'Forgive
me! This, I know, is not what you came to hear. I'm afraid I got
carried away. The whole matter is one that troubles me deeply, but
I had no right to inflict it on you and I trust you will respect my
confidence.'

'Of course, sir. In any case, I'll send a copy of the article for your approval before it's printed.'

Beneath Colin's ready reassurance the antennae were quivering. What was the old fox up to? All this about Jan – what relevance did it have to the primary reason for the interview? It seemed unlikely in the extreme that le Roux would get carried away unless he wanted to be; not at any time, and certainly not with a tape recorder running. He smiled reassuringly, however, giving no hint of his feelings. 'After all,' he continued smoothly, 'it's you the public wants to know about. Tell me, did you excel at sports, too?'

'Ah!' Le Roux settled himself back in his chair once more as if relieved to put unpleasant topics behind him. 'Yes, I did. I liked rugger and played for Wits a few times, but it was cricket that was truly my game. I was a spin bowler – a more than useful one, though I do say it myself. It was something,' he added, as if unable to leave the subject alone, 'that came in useful with Jan when he was a boy, I can tell you. Many a game of cricket have we had on this lawn in happier times.'

'I can imagine,' Colin murmured.

'I was tempted to take it up professionally at one time,' le Roux went on. 'I had offers, but by that time my mind was set on a legal career. I joined a law firm in Pietermaritzburg as a junior and I had to work damned hard, I don't mind telling you. Still, it paid off. Later I moved to a firm in Pretoria, much more prestigious, but there I dealt almost exclusively with divorce law which became a little tedious after a few years. I thought of moving on several times, but as the years went by I became more and more involved in local politics, as my parents had been before me.'

'Did you have ambitions then of branching out into a wider field?' Colin asked.

Le Roux gave his engaging grin.

'Oh, I thought of it, I have to admit. Dreamed of it, I suppose, but only to dismiss the idea as being impossible! Perhaps I was too modest.'

Colin thought this highly improbable, but kept his face impassive.

'What finally prompted you to take the step towards national politics, then?' he asked.

'I was offered a partnership by David Nelson in the firm of Nelson & Swart, here in Cape Town. But I'm sure you're aware of that. I hesitated some time before taking it. I felt my loyalties were elsewhere. I don't mind telling you, Mr Vos—' He leaned forward, serious now, and with that earnest, throbbing note that he often employed in his public speeches. 'I prayed about it, long and hard, asking for guidance. And I became convinced that this was the right thing for me to do, that the Lord wanted me to come to Cape Town. And oh, Mr Vos—' He sat back in his chair, at ease once more, smiling with satisfaction. 'How right that decision was! Not only did I meet my dear wife, but suddenly all manner of avenues opened up before me. In a few years I had achieved the ambition of a lifetime. I was the Member of Parliament for Wachsfontein – the constituency that I still have the honour to represent. Believe me, I had to pinch myself sometimes to make sure I was awake and not still dreaming.'

He was up and running now, Colin thought, nodding as he listened. Hardly any need to say a word – but this was all old material, known to most people already. The Saturday column was not meant to be controversial and he had no brief to rock the political boat; however, it wouldn't hurt to get le Roux on to something marginally less predictable. The desirability of introducing television to South Africa, perhaps, or the distant rumbles regarding excluding the country's teams from world sport. That would certainly get him going.

And what about prison reform? Helen Suzman had recently reported adversely on conditions in Pretoria prison, and it might be enlightening to know his thoughts on the matter – though come to think of it that might be straying into dangerous territory once more.

Would it, he pondered, be too intrusive to ask how he was coping with bereavement? On the whole he thought that it would, and since he had begun the interview by offering his condolences, he decided to say no more on the subject; however, it was le Roux himself who brought up the recent death of his wife when, all avenues explored and the interview over, they stood to walk back through the plumbago hedge to where the car was parked in front of the house.

For a moment he looked about him, smiling.

'A perfect evening,' he said. 'And if I may say so, a setting that matches it. This garden, Mr Vos, I regard as a memorial to my dear wife.'

'It's a very beautiful one,' Colin said, politely.

Still le Roux stood, noble head lifted, silver hair blowing a little in the faint breeze.

'It's . . . it's comforting, knowing that her jacarandas will go on blooming every spring. I'm very conscious of her presence here, encouraging me, wishing me well. Over there – see the candlewood tree?' He sketched the shape of it in the air. 'That was one of her favourite places. Sometimes I sit there in the evening, and I don't mind telling you, I can almost feel her beside me.' He chuckled engagingly as together they began their walk towards the house. 'I like to think the candlewood and I have much in common, you know. It's tolerant of different conditions, a born survivor; and useful, too. You probably didn't know that some tribes use the bark as medicine.'

'No, sir,' Colin said. 'I know very little about it at all. I like the analogy, though. I may be able to use it.'

'Sonia would like that.' Le Roux clapped a hand on Colin's shoulder. 'Forgive the sentimental maunderings of an old man.'

'You're not old, sir,' Colin said, as he was meant to say. Le Roux chuckled again as they resumed walking.

'Well, perhaps not as old as all that. Life in the old dog yet, eh?'

'You'll be enjoying this garden for many years to come, I'm sure.'

'I certainly hope so.'

'This must have been a wonderful place to grow up,' Colin remarked as he opened the car door. And was inspired to add, though he knew the answer already: 'Tell me, sir, did you manage to find Jan before he left for England? Gert Eksberg told me you were looking for him.'

Christiaan le Roux's smile was wiped away and for a split second he froze, eyes wide with sudden panic. His recovery was instantaneous, though his attempt at a light laugh was not wholly successful.

'Really?' he said. 'Eksberg told you? I'm surprised he thought it worth mentioning.'

'He said it was a family matter. You needed to contact Jan.'

Le Roux swallowed convulsively, but continued to smile.

'Oh, that!' he said. 'Yes, I did ask for Eksberg's help. No, I didn't catch up with Jan, but it wasn't important. It can wait.'

Colin smiled and nodded and thanked him again for graciously allowing the interview. He looked at the clock on the dashboard and, as if he had nothing more on his mind than the time, remarked that with luck the rush hour might be over.

But as he drove towards town he was on automatic pilot, barely noticing other traffic. What had caused that smiling, confident mask to slip? It had only been momentary. Le Roux was far too practised a performer to let emotion take over completely, but for that second it had done so, revealing a frightened man behind the public façade.

Why? Colin wondered. Was it the realisation that others knew he had been looking for Jan?

Whatever it was, he thought to himself, it would undoubtedly bear a little judicious investigation. He'd enjoy that.

Vicky had changed into the smocked tartan dress she wore on Sundays as soon as she came home from school, and had put on her best long white socks and black kid dancing pumps. She had brushed her hair so that, untrammelled by the usual pigtails and held only by an Alice band, it fell to her shoulders. On her face, Kate noted with amusement, she was wearing the prim, self-consciously well-behaved expression she usually adopted in church as with tiny, genteel bites she ate the grown-up afternoon tea of scones and two kinds of cake. Mark, on the other hand, having eaten his fill, was lying on his stomach behind the settee, playing with his Dinky toys, obeying his mother's instructions to be quiet but resolutely unimpressed by their visitor.

Kate looked at her daughter with affection, feeling a little guilty about her amusement – for was this not a case of the pot and the kettle? She, too, had changed into a better skirt and a new, pretty sweater, and had gone to the trouble of baking cakes and setting out the good china. Like Vicky, she was on her best behaviour.

I should have served up fish fingers and baked beans in the kitchen as usual, she thought guiltily. It'll be my fault if the children don't accept him as a member of the family. Still, he is an invalid and it's undoubtedly more restful and civilised like this. There would be time in plenty, she hoped, to introduce him to the less tranquil aspects of family life.

Jan seemed better for his restful day – his eyes altogether brighter, his expression more alert. Every time she saw him she was struck afresh by the incredible size of him. He seemed to dwarf the armchair he was sitting in; but now that, presumably, his vitality had gone some way towards being restored, it was more his personality that seemed to fill the room rather than his physical presence. No wonder the children seemed shy. She felt pretty shy herself.

He was being awfully good with Vicky, doing his best to draw her out about school and friends and general activities, to which she answered in barely audible monosyllables.

'Are you always this quiet?' he asked her at last; and only then did her face light up with its usual grin. She shook her head vigorously.

'Mummy said I had to be,' she explained. 'Because you're ill.'

'I'm getting better all the time.'

'You had a bang on the head.'

'That's right. And someone stuck a knife in me. Fortunately, they didn't make a very good job of it.'

'Does it still hurt?'

'Only a bit. When I laugh.'

'Well,' Vicky said, taking this seriously, 'you'd better not watch television, then, because some of it is very funny.'

'Popeye isn't,' Mark said, from behind the sofa. 'I don't like Popeye much.'

'There's no law says you have to,' said Jan.

'Mark hides behind the chair when he comes on television,' Vicky told him. 'I bet you didn't do that.'

'Well, no, I didn't,' Jan admitted. 'But then we didn't have any television.'

'Gosh!' Vicky stared at him. 'You must be awf'lly old. Mummy didn't have television when she was little, either.'

'We don't have television at all in South Africa, even now.'

'Gosh!' Vicky said again, unable to contemplate such a fate.

'And are probably the better for it,' Kate said briskly.

'Well, we do have the advantage where climate is concerned,' Jan admitted. 'Most of my childhood seems to have been spent outdoors. We had a pool put in—'

'Where?' Kate asked eagerly.

'Just beyond the hibiscus hedge.'

'Is the plumbago hedge as thick as ever?'

Vicky giggled.

'Plumbago's an *illness*, not a hedge. Mrs Nixon had it.'

'That's just where you're wrong, madam,' Kate told her. 'Mrs Nixon had lumbago. Plumbago is a bush with lovely blue flowers.'

'Well, sometimes they're white,' Jan said, 'but our hedge is blue. Yes, at the last sighting it was as prolific as ever.'

'And the jacarandas?'

'Still blooming every year.'

'What sort of a house did you live in?' Vicky asked. 'Is it like ours?'

'I think she's going to follow Tom into architecture,' Kate said. 'Houses fascinate her.'

'Hey, Vicky,' Jan said. 'Bring me some paper and crayons and I'll draw it for you.'

Vicky rushed to do his bidding, and as Kate cleared away the tea things he sat and drew, the big Dutch gable causing many questions and much comment.

'Don't tire yourself,' Kate begged. 'Please – the children understand they mustn't bother you.' She couldn't resist, however, taking a look over his shoulder. And there was Gramerci coming to life on the paper.

'Why, you're an artist,' she exclaimed in delight. He laughed at that.

'No I'm not! I've got a bit of a knack, that's all. Apparently my grandmother was the same.'

'You're right,' Kate said, remembering Lilian and her wishy-washy watercolours and Sonia's disdain of them. 'Yes, your grandmother did paint a little, at one time. She'd given up by the time I got there. I'd forgotten . . .'

But it had been the thought of Lilian's erstwhile interest in painting that had caused her to drive into town that morning towards the end of January that last year, she remembered.

She had lain awake worrying about Lilian – had been awake, she remembered, when Guy crept into the bedroom, shoes in hand, some time after two in the morning. Unwisely she had tried to tell him about the bottle his mother had taken from the drinks cabinet, but he had been totally unreceptive.

'Well, dammit, darling, it is her gin,' he'd said, half amused, half irritated. 'She's entitled to take it if she wants.'

'That's not the point!' Kate had switched on the bedside light and wriggled upright on her pillows, watching him as he got undressed. 'She shouldn't drink at all, Guy.'

Guy, about to hang up his jacket, turned and looked at her, his eyebrows lifted.

'Since when did you become so puritanical?'

In frustration Kate pounded the bed with her clenched fists.

'It's not that! Don't you understand? It's not just a question of her having a few drinks in the evening. I think she drinks all day, too, and once she starts she can't stop. She's addicted. An alcoholic.'

'And Larry told you this, I presume?'

'Yes, he did. But if you spent any time at all with her you'd see it for yourself.'

'I'll talk to her,' he said wearily, climbing into bed. 'Now for heaven's sake, go to sleep. It's been a long night.'

Kate's sigh was one of frustration, but she put out the light, and after a few moments lay down once more.

'What did you decide?' she asked. 'About the furniture.'

'Furniture?' Guy, half asleep, sounded mystified. 'Oh, the ladies' lounge! We decided to let things ride for the moment. It's not that bad.'

'It took a long time to come up with that conclusion,' Kate said dryly.

But Guy offered no explanation. He was already asleep. Kate, on the other hand, continued to stay awake, the question of what to do about Lilian going round and round in her mind. It was then she remembered those watercolours. Would it help if Lilian were to get interested in painting once again?

It seemed a pathetic remedy, bound to fail, but at least it was worth an effort and she made up her mind that the very next day she would go into town and buy some paints and brushes. A sketchbook, maybe. She'd have to ask in the shop what was needed, being totally ignorant about the subject. (Was there, she sometimes wondered, a subject about which she wasn't totally ignorant?) In fact, it might be a good idea to pretend to Lilian that she wanted to take it up on her own account. She could ask her advice, encourage her to give some lessons. She had no hope at all of success, but surely anything was worth trying.

Accordingly, she went into town next day and made a few purchases at a stationer's shop which also sold artists' materials. She followed this with a leisurely browse around Stuttaford's fashion department and would have extended the pleasure by going to the restaurant for coffee had it not been for the fact that she saw Marcia heading in the same direction. Relations between the two of them were no more cordial than they had ever been. Even so, Kate knew that should she enter the restaurant alone, Marcia would feel bound to wave her over to join her table, an unwelcome invitation she would reluctantly feel, in her turn, bound to accept.

It seemed far easier to forgo coffee at Stuttaford's and settle for having it somewhere else, or not at all. She consulted her list. Just as well not to waste more time, she thought; there were still a few practical things to buy – such as a potato peeler, for which Evalina had earnestly petitioned just before she left home.

The OK Bazaar was the place for that; which reminded her that she had not seen Dora for months. She looked around for her in the shop, but could see no sign of her, and as she paid for her potato peeler, Kate asked the woman behind the till where she could be found.

'She left, madam,' said the woman.

Kate felt no surprise. Hadn't she always said that Dora deserved better things? If there were any justice in the world, then she would have moved to a good dress shop where her expertise would be recognised; but when she asked if this was the case, the woman behind the till smirked unpleasantly and denied it with some satisfaction.

'She got in trouble, ma'am.'

Kate was mystified.

'What kind of trouble?' she asked.

'The usual. She having a baby.'

'Oh!' Kate was startled. 'Oh dear, I am sorry.'

The woman sniffed, pulling down her thin lips, reminding Kate of a particularly unpleasant spinster in Shenlake who was always the first to pass on gossip.

'She should be shamed,' she said. 'Her poor mother! How she feel, you tell me? She a real respectable, god-fearing lady, poor soul. Yes, madam?' And she turned to deal with a red-headed woman waving a colander, demanding attention.

Kate moved away, full of sadness. Dora was so talented and full of promise. Having a baby would undoubtedly mark the end of her career before it had begun. She could see it all – she would marry some oafish boyfriend just to give the baby a name, all her bright future blighted before it had ever had a chance to blossom. And the woman behind the till was right. Mama Lou would be devastated. On the other hand, did it have to be like that?

Her mind was working overtime as she went to get the car. Maybe if she drummed up some support, guaranteed some work, Dora would feel less pressurised. She could marry if she wanted to, stay independent if she didn't. Like this attempt at making Lilian take up painting again, it was worth a try. She could do with a couple of new dresses for her coming sea trip, and Helen, having given birth to her baby boy two months before, had been complaining only the other day that she was still finding her old clothes a tight fit. There were others, too, who had gone to her previously on Kate's recommendation, and none had been disappointed. She would go and see her right away, she decided. On her way home.

The door of the little house below the railway track was closed, and having knocked and waited, Kate was about to assume no one was at home. However, just as she turned away, it was opened by Mama Lou.

Kate's cheerful greeting faltered. The old woman looked twenty years older than when she had last seen her. She was shrunken, somehow, and her face had fallen in so that there seemed no flesh on her bones at all.

'Mama Lou! What is it? Are you ill?' she asked anxiously.

Mama Lou said nothing. She stood there, clinging on to the edge of the door as if for support.

'Please – may I come in?' Kate went on. 'I came to see Dora. I went to the shop, but they told me she's left.'

Still without speaking, Mama Lou opened the door wider and stood to one side. Kate went in and saw at once that something cataclysmic must have happened, for the room inside was untidy, even dirty, a used plate and cup still on the table, flies buzzing round rotting bananas. Mama Lou, a small, hunched, defeated figure, stood silent, her hands twisting a handkerchief she had pulled from the pocket of her overall.

'Mama Lou, are you ill?' Kate asked again. 'Is Dora here?'

At this the old woman collapsed into a chair and, covering her face with her poor, twisted hands, began to cry. Kate crouched down beside her, putting her arms around her.

'Tell me – oh, please tell me,' she implored her. 'What's happened?'

'My Dora's gone,' she said at last.

'Gone? You don't mean . . . surely she's not—' 'Dead' was a word Kate hesitated to use in connection with Dora, yet Mama Lou's excessive grief seemed to suggest that this was the case. There was a girl in Shenlake once who had committed suicide rather than face the shame of an illegitimate birth.

'Oh, Mama Lou, please tell me what's happened.'

Mama Lou blew her nose and wiped her eyes.

'She's gone, and I's de one who drove her away. I's de one.'

'Because she was having a baby? A woman at the shop told me,' she added. 'Surely, she'll come back.'

Wearily, Mama Lou shook her head.

'Not Dora. Not to live. She got big ideas, my Dora. Oh, she look sweet enough, but underneat' she like iron. She yust determined to get away.'

'It's not a crime to have ambition. Or even to have a baby.'

Mama Lou made no comment, but gave a bitter laugh.

'Maybe not, *mevrouw*, but sometimes it don't bring no happiness. My girl, she done wrong, and she know it. We argued, her and me, to beat de band.'

'There was no chance of her marrying?' In the face of this grief, Kate was reassessing the situation. Mama Lou blew her nose again and levered herself out of the chair without replying, clicking her tongue as she picked up the used plate and cup from the table as if she had only now seen the place through Kate's eyes.

'I'll make tea,' she said. 'De kettle's boiled. You sit, *mevrouw*.'

Kate did so, and in a short while Mama Lou was back carrying a tin tray on which was a china pot and two flowered cups and saucers.

'Young Joey from the garage, he would marry her tomorrow, baby or no baby,' she said as she poured the tea. 'A lovely boy, Joey is. He love Dora all his life. But Dora said she wasn't going to marry no grease monkey, not now, not ever.'

'Was he the father?' Kate asked. Mama Lou shook her head, sitting down in the chair opposite her. For a moment she stirred her tea without replying. Then she looked up, her mouth trembling.

'D'ere's something you should know, *mevrouw*. I should have spoke sooner. I told Dora I would, but I never did. I was so shamed, so very shamed.'

'What is it?' Kate asked, puzzled.

'Now, I am not blaming you, *mevrouw*, for all you did, you did from the goodness of your heart—'

'What is it?'

Mama Lou looked away from her, as if even now she could not bear the humiliation.

'That lawyer,' she said. 'Mr le Roux. He defiled my girl. He took her and used her and gave her ideas. He'd set her up in a fancy shop, he told her. Somewhere a long way from here.' She shook her head, beginning to cry again. 'I tell her she's a fool. A man like dat, what he care about her? He only want one thing. He was wicked, I tell her, and so was she. He'd never give her no shop, and if she had the sense she was born with she'd never see him again.'

'Christiaan le Roux—?' Kate stared at her in horror, unable to go on.

Mama Lou nodded.

'He the one. He took her out at night and bought her things. Scent and scarves and a powder compact. Enamel, it was. Black and yellow. And a fancy handbag, all shiny. Where dey went, I don't know, she never tol' me, I only know I tell her she's a fool. Oh, we argue and argue! And now she gone.'

'Did she tell Christiaan – Mr le Roux – about the baby?'

'She wrote me. Yesterday I get this letter.' Mama Lou went to the mantelpiece and from behind the photograph of the princesses produced a pink envelope from which she extracted a single sheet of pink writing paper which she handed to Kate.

'Read it,' she said.

Kate took the paper from her. Dora had written:

> I am sorry Mama. I have gone to Port Elizabeth to be with Dr Ryland, she will look after me I know you were right, Mr le Roux will not look after me or give me money I tell him about the baby and he say get out but he know the baby his. I told him and he know I tell the truth I wasn't going with no other man. But I cant marry Joey hes a good boy but I dont love him and one day I will have my shop and go up in the world. Also I dont want to shame you so I gone away. It is for the best. Maybe you come to me one day. I will write again. Forgive me and pray for me.
>
> Your loving daughter, Dora.

'Oh, Mama Lou, I'm so sorry,' Kate whispered. 'Oh, what an awful thing! And I *am* to blame! Without me, Dora would never have met him. But truly, I didn't know he was like that. It never occurred to me that he would take advantage—' She paused, shaking her head. She'd always distrusted Christiaan's easy charm, but this was despicable. Unbelievable, given his status and ambition – yet not, now she came to think of it, as unbelievable as all that. She had long ago recognised his arrogance and selfishness, his determination to take what he wanted from life without attempting to do more than smile charmingly in return. Look at the way he had treated Sonia – picking her up when it suited him, putting her down when it didn't, treating Gramerci as his home whenever it seemed convenient.

It wouldn't have troubled him – would never, even, have occurred to him – that by seducing Dora he could very well ruin her life. She was young and, for all her ambitions, innocent and unsophisticated; she was also Coloured, which, in his book, meant that he need feel no responsibility for any consequences.

'I'm so sorry,' she said again, her voice little more than a whisper. She took a breath and swallowed, desperately trying to think of words of comfort. 'Thank heaven she had the good sense to go to Dr Ryland. I didn't know they were still in touch.'

'She never forget us. She send a card every Christmas. She a good woman, that I know.'

'She is. She's just the kindest person in the world and Dora's right when she says she'll look after her.'

'She got no money, *mevrouw*. How she going to live? How she going to bring up that child?'

'Well, Dr Ryland is working at a prison hospital. I'm sure she'll be able to find Dora some kind of work and accommodation. I'll write to her and find out. When is the baby due?'

'Three months, maybe. She big already.'

Kate could barely speak, unaccustomed anger filling her head like a swirling mist.

'He can't be allowed to get away with this!' she said at last. 'He must agree to support her. And the baby.'

'Seems to me, he wash his hands of it.'

'Oh, has he?' Kate's jaw set stubbornly. 'We'll see about that! Look, would you mind if I took the letter? I'll bring it back.'

'Take it, take it. I don't want it.'

'You'll want the address, at least—'

'I don't forget it, if I want it. A prison, *mevrouw*. That where my daughter is. A prison. You take it. All that letter do is make me cry. You take it if you want, so's I never have to see it again.'

'You're sure? Really? Well, all right. I think it might be useful.' Kate folded it and put it in her handbag. 'Listen, Mama Lou.' Her face was set, her eyes hard. 'Try not to worry. I'll make that rat pay for what he's done.'

'He'll say he ain't the father,' Mama Lou said. 'That's what they all say. But I know my Dora. She a foolish, foolish girl who pay the price for sin, but there wasn't no one else, *mevrouw*. Not Joey, not no one.'

'I believe you,' said Kate.

She had always, in the past, been slow to anger, but on this occasion she could feel it burning and burgeoning as she drove towards home. She felt light-headed with it, almost euphoric. It was going to be such a pleasure to tell Christiaan le Roux what she thought of him.

It was a wicked, wicked thing he had done. Dora's innocence and vulnerability must have been crystal clear to him. Christiaan had used her, without thought, without respect – she could have been a *thing*, Kate thought, tremulous with rage. Something inanimate, without importance or feelings.

As she had been, at the same age? The thought made her catch her breath. Was this why Dora's betrayal was having such an effect on her? No, no, it couldn't be! The circumstances weren't a bit the same. Guy had loved her – *did* love her. It might not be a marriage made in heaven, they didn't agree on everything, but even so—

Her thoughts swerved back to Christiaan. He, on the other hand, had undoubtedly intended to drop Dora the moment she became a nuisance or another girl caught his fancy. How *could* he? she asked herself. He, a man of the world, a Member of Parliament, no less, who had made pious speeches, presenting himself as a concerned and responsible citizen, someone who was so far superior to all blacks and Coloureds that he could not sit down at the same table as them. He was a hypocrite of the worst kind, and she would make him admit his guilt if it was the last thing she did.

She parked the car in the back courtyard at Gramerci, and strode in through the kitchen, barely acknowledging Evalina and forgetting altogether to hand over the potato peeler, unaware of the curious glances that followed her. In the front hall she encountered Sonia, who apparently had come in from the office only moments before and was standing looking at the mail that had been laid on the hall table.

'Is Christiaan coming tonight?' she snapped. Sonia laid down a circular she had been reading and stared at her. This was Kate in a mood she had not seen before, not in the whole of the four years she had known her.

'I *beg* your pardon?' she asked, with amused outrage.

'Christiaan,' Kate said again. 'Is he coming tonight?'

'What on earth's the matter with you?' Sonia was frowning, no trace of amusement in her face now.

'I want to speak to him.'

'Not to ask for help for another of your lame ducks, I hope?'

'I wouldn't dream of it. I feel like marching into Parliament and shouting aloud the kind of man he really is. My God, if any of them knew what he's really like, he'd be out on his ear—'

'Have you gone raving mad?'

'I'm angry,' Kate said, coming a step closer to her. 'I'm so angry I can hardly speak. Do you know what your precious Christiaan has done?'

For a moment Sonia looked at her coldly, but Kate was sure there was a flicker of panic in her eyes.

'What?' she asked.

For a moment Kate hesitated. Whether her sister-in-law should be told was not a question she had considered; all her thoughts had been concentrated on le Roux – what she would say to him, how he would respond. Now, whether or not it was right to do so, she was too full of rage to assess. She dumped the parcels she was carrying down on a table in the hall and with trembling fingers took the single sheet of paper from her handbag.

'You'd better see this,' she said.

Gingerly – for it was, after all, cheap, lined paper of the kind she despised – Sonia took hold of it between thumb and fingertip. She read it swiftly, then looked up with a frown.

'What utter nonsense,' she said, crisply angry. 'You can't believe it. Christiaan wouldn't—'

'Oh, he would,' Kate said. 'Believe me, he has.'

'It's clearly an attempt to extort money—' Sonia paused, and read the letter again. 'Who is this Dora, anyway?'

'My dressmaker,' Kate said. 'A little Coloured girl. Daughter of the woman your mother used to employ. She's young and innocent and very pretty. She's the girl that I asked Christiaan to help over the deeds of her house. It seems,' she added bitterly, 'that he helped himself at the same time. Sonia, listen—' She was calmer now, more persuasive. 'Dora and her mother are respectable, hard-working people. I'm sure Lilian would vouch for that.'

'Really?' Sonia raised her eyebrows sceptically.

'I swear Dora's innocent – well, innocent of anything other than being young and silly and far too trusting. Look what she's written. She seems to have accepted the fact that Christiaan won't help her and she's left Cape Town, just so that she can make a new life for herself. Is that what she would do if she was simply out to make trouble for him? But he can't – he just *can't* – be allowed to get away with it.'

Sonia was staring at the letter, reading and rereading it, and as Kate saw the expression on her face as she did so, her anger was overtaken by a painful feeling of guilt. Poor, proud, barren Sonia! Maybe she should snatch the letter away – tell her it was a hoax, the events had never happened. How could she have been guilty of such cruelty? No one deserved this treatment. It was a terrible thing that she had done. What could she have been thinking of?

'I . . . I'm so sorry, Sonia,' she said hesitantly. 'I shouldn't have told you. And I certainly shouldn't have shouted at you. It's hardly your fault.'

Sonia said nothing. She was reading the letter yet again. Only when she had folded it carefully did she look at Kate. Her face was grim and her eyes glittered between narrowed lids. Still, for a moment she did not speak.

'Sonia—' Kate began again.

'I'll keep this,' Sonia said, interrupting her.

'No!' Kate's anger flared again. 'You'll only destroy it.'

Sonia gave a bitter little laugh.

'Oh, no,' she said. 'I won't destroy it. Don't worry – I'll make sure Christiaan faces his responsibilities.'

'I wish I could believe you.'

'I assure you, you can.' She looked at the folded square of pink paper and tapped it thoughtfully against her hand. When she looked at Kate, her lips were curved in a thin, sour smile. 'You're right,' she said. 'He must pay for this. Leave it to me. I can handle him better than you.'

Still Kate hesitated, a little puzzled. She had hardly expected Sonia to accept the truth quite so readily. She would have thought there would be more protests; instead there was no defence of Christiaan, no further accusations against Dora, no doubts. Just this apparent agreement that Christiaan was guilty as charged. Did she know something? Maybe this wasn't the first time she had heard such accusations.

'What are you going to say?' she asked.

'I don't know yet. Not exactly. I shall need to think; but believe me,' Sonia said after a momentary pause, her voice suddenly savage, 'I shall make him sorry he ever heard of this girl.'

Kate, for all her initial desire to confront Christiaan herself, now felt only relief. Undoubtedly Sonia was right – of the two of them, she was the more capable of handling him. On the other hand, Sonia's feelings for Christiaan were such that, when it came to the point, wasn't it possible that she might let him get away with a mere token payment?

'I don't know—' she began uncertainly.

'I'll make him pay,' Sonia said savagely. She was smiling now in a bitter, determined way. 'Don't worry. He'll pay through the nose for this.'

Kate took a deep breath.

'All right,' she said. 'I'll leave it to you. But you will do your best for Dora, won't you? He must be made to support her.'

'I've said I will. And he will.'

'All right,' Kate said again.

That seemed the end of it, and she turned to go upstairs to wash before lunch. Before she had gone more than a few steps she heard her name. She turned, one hand on the banister, to see that Sonia had come to the foot of the stairs and was looking up, her face as pale and set as if it were carved in ivory, her red lipstick a vivid slash of colour.

'Just one thing,' she said. Her voice was harsh as if to underline the fact that this momentary collusion between them was not to be taken as friendship. 'If you ever speak to anyone about this, I swear I'll kill you. Do you promise not to mention it? To Christiaan, or Guy, or Helen or anyone?'

She looked as if she meant it. Kate laughed uneasily.

'For heaven's sake, Sonia—'

'I mean it. Do you promise?'

'Everyone ought to know the kind of man he is.'

'Damn it, promise, will you?' Sonia's voice had risen. She lifted up the pink envelope, holding it between a finger and the thumb of both hands. 'I've said I'll sort it out, but I'll tear up this letter here and now if you don't give me your word.'

Kate lifted her hands in surrender.

'All right, all right,' she said. 'Just as long as Dora does well out of this, I won't say a word to a soul.'

'Not even Guy?'

'Not even Guy,' she confirmed. Least of all Guy, she thought as she turned and continued up the stairs. He would remember Dora as the girl who committed the unforgivable sin of invading his bedroom and drinking from his china, and undoubtedly would blame her for everything that had happened. He might even regard the whole episode as a joke and certainly wouldn't hold Christiaan in any way responsible. He might, she thought, even do the same thing himself if the opportunity arose.

No, she wouldn't mention it to Guy.

Lilian showed not the slightest interest in the painting materials Kate had bought. When she asked how she should set about attempting the view from the stoep, Lilian advised getting a book from the library.

'Or taking classes,' she said vaguely. 'I'm sure there must be classes. There's nothing I can teach you. I was never any good.'

'But you were! What have you done with those paintings you showed me? I liked them.'

'Which, my dear, simply reveals your lack of knowledge in the matter,' Lilian said. 'Now, if you'll forgive me, I'd rather like to have a little rest.'

Rather amused at her own naïvety in thinking they might provide even a momentary distraction, Kate took the paints away. Money down the drain, she thought. Maybe she ought to make some sort of attempt herself, just to justify the expenditure; it might, after all, be fun. But after half an hour's concentrated effort she threw down her brush and went to play with Johnny. Her mind wasn't on it – and even if it had been, she had a pretty shrewd idea that the end result would have been just as unsatisfactory. Better, far, if she'd spent the money on a new camera so that she could take some decent photographs of her son.

She would try Lilian with the painting some other time, she thought. In the morning, maybe, when she was feeling fresh. Or was she just being an awful, do-gooding busy-body, like Miss Ollerenshaw in Shenlake who visited the sick, insisting on shoving unwanted calf's-foot jelly down their protesting throats? She wished she knew. She wished Larry was still there. She wished there was *someone* who would listen to her anxieties about Lilian and take them seriously, but neither Sonia nor Guy did more than murmur platitudes about nothing being as bad as she thought.

'I just don't know what to do about it,' she confided to Helen when, late in the afternoon, she took Johnny round to visit her and pay his respects to Matthew, who was a source of infinite fascination to him. He stood for minutes at a time just looking at him in wonder, one little starfish hand lying gently on the baby's tummy. Helen had already remarked that it looked as if Jan would welcome a brother or sister. Kate, who was not at all averse to the idea, nevertheless brushed this aside. It was Lilian who was occupying her thoughts.

'I don't honestly see there's a lot you can do,' Helen said. 'If no one else acknowledges the problem—'

'Larry did. Larry kept her amused and occupied and she was all right while he was around. She's been so lonely since he left. I've tried to fill the gap but obviously I haven't been very successful.' Kate sighed. 'I just haven't tried hard enough, I suppose.'

'What about her friends?' Helen was dividing her attention between the pram under the terrace overhang and Kate's problems. 'She had any number in the old days. Grace Nelson was a particular buddy of hers. Couldn't you speak to her?'

Kate shook her head.

'I don't think it would help. I've suggested Lilian should ask her round for tea, but she won't do it, and she never accepts any of Grace's invitations. I think Grace has got a bit fed up with her, and I don't wonder at it. She doesn't want to go out for drives, either. She just isn't interested in anything these days.'

'Not even Johnny?'

'Not really. She makes the right noises, but she gets away from us as soon as she can. It's as if—' She paused, frowning. 'As if,' she continued more slowly, 'life has dwindled down to nothing more than where the next drink is coming from. I thought of asking the vicar to come and see her,' she added, striking a lighter note, 'but he tends to drive most people to drink at the best of times, so I can't think he would help very much. Evalina is just about the only person who treats the problem seriously.'

'Well, hooray for Evalina. At least she'll be there to keep an eye on her when you've gone.'

'Yes. Oh, Helen!' Lilian's problems faded from Kate's mind and she hugged herself and closed her eyes, the better to savour the prospect of her holiday in England. 'It's only another month. I just can't wait! What is it?' she asked, as Helen seemed to be on the point of saying something.

But Johnny had stopped standing passively beside the pram and was now, with undoubtedly the best of intentions, attempting to cram a toy car into the baby's hand, a move which was being greeted with a certain amount of noisy resistance. Both mothers leapt to their feet and the moment was lost.

Just as well, Helen thought later, when Kate had gone. Least said, soonest mended. On the other hand . . .

With the baby held to her shoulder, she stared out at the garden, seeing nothing, continuing the inward debate that had been going on in her mind for some time now.

To tell, or not to tell? What did a good friend do? Leave it, Paul said. Things would sort themselves out. It really wasn't any of their business, and she wouldn't be doing Kate any favours if she spilt the beans.

She hoped very much that he was right.

14

'I have never, *never* heard such nonsense in the whole of my life,' Nina said, pink with indignation. 'Jan has his faults, heaven knows, but lying isn't one of them. In fact he's sometimes too truthful for his own good.'

'I know. Calm down.' Colin risked a placatory touch on her arm, but prudently kept it brief. He had the feeling that she would run away like a startled fawn if he moved too rapidly.

She had agreed readily enough to go out to dinner with him, however, and, seen off by Hennie with many a wave and knowing smile, they had driven to Hout Bay, to eat crayfish in Colin's favourite restaurant.

He had saved the account of his interview with le Roux until they were settled at a table by a window with a view over the bay.

'I didn't believe it for one moment,' he reassured her. 'But why would le Roux be at such pains to impress on me that Jan is a liar? He tried to make out that he'd let it slip almost by accident, but I don't think for a moment that anything he does is by accident. He wanted to create the impression that no one should believe a word Jan says.'

'Or might say,' Nina said, after a minute's thought. 'Maybe he was simply covering his back, because he's afraid of something that Jan might tell the world.'

Colin looked at her thoughtfully.

'You might be on to something there. What, though?'

Nina shrugged her shoulders.

'I've no idea. Some family secret, maybe. Jan's never mentioned anything to me – well, nothing in particular. I gather there were a lot of terrible scenes when he began interesting himself in racial matters. In spite of the little-boy grin and the barrel-loads of charm, it seems that le Roux can be quite different in the privacy of his own home. It upset Jan a lot that they couldn't agree to disagree without so much bitterness and bad feeling, because they'd been close when he was young. Good old Uncle Christiaan was the one who provided any fun that was going. He used to go riding and swimming with Jan when he was at home, and play cricket, and that sort of thing.'

'Hmm.' Colin chewed his lip reflectively. 'Le Roux said as much.'

'Jan's never forgotten it. He always hoped that they'd come to some kind of accommodation one day.'

'What about Sonia?'

'Well, she was quite different. A cold fish, and a strange woman, by all accounts, quite unable to express any warmth or affection. He never doubted that she loved him, but it was an intense, possessive sort of love that insisted on him being the best at everything. Sports, school-work – it didn't matter what. He just had to come top. He told me that once, just before his eleventh birthday, she cancelled a party that had been arranged because he did badly in a geography exam.'

'It sounds grim.'

'It was, I think. He never felt he came up to her expectations for him; and then, of course, he began arguing with her over her racial attitudes and the fact that he had no intention of going into the family business, and they grew further and further apart. He felt bad about that. After all, Sonia was all the family he had. All that he knew about, anyway.'

'Le Roux speaks of her with great affection.'

'Mm – well . . . *de mortuis*, maybe. I certainly gained the impression there wasn't much love lost between the two of them. Jan always reckoned that Christiaan spent as much time away from home as he could, for the sake of a quiet life.'

'When did Jan start to rebel?'

Nina shook her head.

'I don't know. I don't think he could put a finger on it himself.' She smiled and her voice softened. 'You can't really explain Jan, you know. Anyone else brought up like he was would have accepted everything, just gone along with it. But he's so . . . so *passionate* about everything. No, not that sort of passionate, idiot. I mean he gets worked up about things – rages about injustice, throws himself heart and soul into lost causes. He was brought up by a Coloured woman called Rosie who still looks after him when he's here and keeps an eye on his house when he's away. She was more like a mother to him than anyone else, and he adored her. Still does. He grew up with her children – played with them, got into mischief, had fun. Later, he just couldn't buy this white superiority thing. He told me once that he respected Rosie more than anyone he'd ever met.'

For a few moments Colin looked out towards the bay, saying nothing, hearing the affectionate resonances in her voice. Then he gave a grunt of laughter.

'I ought to hate the bastard,' he said. Nina laughed, too.

'No one can hate Jan. Oh, you can be maddened by him, and you can rage at him, but you can't possibly hate him. And I promise you, he doesn't tell lies, whatever le Roux says.'

'I know. I believe you.'

'The boot's on the other foot, actually.'

In a few, succinct words she described Jan's last visit to Gramerci and the effect it had had on him.

'So you see,' she said at last, 'the story that his mother didn't give a damn for him was a pack of lies from beginning to end. She'd done all she could to keep in touch, but her letters never got to Jan. His loving aunt and uncle kept them from him.'

'And that's why he went to England? Because he found out?'

'That and other things. He wanted to meet up with some sympathisers over there – speak at a few meetings, and so on. Tell them the post-Sharpeville state of play. He'd been thinking of going for some time. It must be six or seven years ago that he'd planned to go and see some old uncle of his – a Sir, no less – but then the old boy died and everything was postponed. Then two years ago he arranged a trip, but had to cancel at the last minute. Some particular friend of his was held for months without trial and needed his help. Every year there seemed something to keep him in South Africa, but then when he found out all this about his mother, he was off like a shot.'

'Do you know her address?' Colin asked.

Nina looked at him for a moment without speaking.

'Yes,' she said at last. 'But I'm not going to give it to you. You'd only badger her for a story.'

Colin's grin was a little twisted.

'You're getting to know me altogether too well,' he said.

*　　*　　*

Jan was looking much better. Quite different, Kate thought, from the young man who had lain so silently in his hospital bed or slept so determinedly for his first few days at home. The knife wound had healed, making movement easier, more expansive; and he liked to move – liked to pace about and gesture as he spoke. His skin looked different, too, and his hair, which had been shaved over his temples, was growing back now at a seemingly furious pace, apparently crackling with life.

Kate had learned much about this stranger, her son. She learned that he filled the house; not just because of his physical size, but because his presence seemed to colour and dominate his surroundings. She had learned he had wit and found enjoyment and novelty in small things most would take for granted. He loved conversation, argument, sport, food and drink; could rage at a tale of injustice in the newspaper or on television, and roar with laughter at the children's jokes.

He was also untidy, noisy, and encouraged anarchy in the children; needless to say they adored him, hung on his stories of Africa, brought friends round to see him, and boasted of his exploits to anyone who would listen. He made Mrs Bishop giggle like a schoolgirl, even as she was picking up the clothes he scattered on the floor of his bedroom. He was a caution, she told Kate, and you couldn't really blame him for his untidiness.

'He's always had them blackies looking after him,' she said. 'He's not like us, dear.'

Kate, sometimes exasperated, nevertheless was entranced by him. She was beginning, now, to think of him as Jan quite naturally; and perhaps that was as well. Johnny, her own, lost Johnny on whose account she had shed so many tears, was gone for good, to be replaced by this young, ebullient, volatile stranger with whom she felt such an astonishing compatibility.

They talked all the time when the children were out of the house. Kate, chopping vegetables, would pause with knife in hand while he paced about the kitchen speaking of his beliefs and friends and occupations; and she would switch off the vacuum cleaner as she remembered just one more question, one more observation, that had to be voiced there and then. The realisation that she had given birth to this articulate and fascinating young man who preferred using his skill as a lawyer to help the dispossessed rather than achieve power in a white world was something that thrilled her to the skies. She could, she felt, not have asked for anything more, though it occurred to her to wonder what Guy would have made of him.

What Tom made of him she wasn't sure. He always treated him with a tolerance and joviality which Kate sometimes suspected was a little forced; but then Tom was busy just now – perhaps busier than he had ever been. He often came home later than usual after site meetings and discussions with the development company. It was natural, Kate thought, that he should seem thoughtful, even abstracted, and she did what she could to see that he should not feel excluded.

Strangely, though her conversations with Jan covered the past, present and even future, Jan showed little curiosity about his father and Kate had, from the first, avoided speaking about him as far as possible. She guessed they were both fearful – Jan, perhaps, of having a dream destroyed, she of alienating him by telling the brutal truth. There's no hurry, she told herself. Nothing would be gained by forcing information on him before he felt himself ready. It would be best if they could get to know each other first, so that he trusted her, believed her.

It was some days after his arrival that he asked for writing paper and an envelope.

'There's a girl,' he said. 'I must let her know I'm OK.'

Kate provided the requisite paper and asked no questions, even though she was full of curiosity and could not prevent herself reading the name and address on the envelope as she took the letter to the post. Nina Cambell, she read, trying to imagine the kind of girl that Jan would be attracted to. She would be intelligent, and would share his principles, of that she was certain.

'Won't you tell me about Nina?' she said to him eventually. He looked at her and grinned.

'You're sounding like a real mum.'

She laughed, unrepentant.

'I know. I refuse to apologise, though.'

'Nina.' He seemed to linger over the name, thinking private thoughts, serious for a moment before looking at her, smiling once more. 'Well, what can I tell you? We're friends. Best friends, I suppose you could say. She's put up with my erratic behaviour very well over the years.'

'Are you—' Kate began. 'I mean, will you—'

'Get married?' He laughed. 'I don't think she'd have me.'

'Why on earth not?' She sounded outraged on her son's behalf, and he laughed again.

'I know you don't know me very well, but can't you see how I'd drive a woman mad? I'm totally unreliable. I make dates and then something important turns up and I don't keep them. I don't honestly think I'm the marrying kind. But if I were—' His voice softened. 'If I were, then it would have to be Nina.' He paused for a moment. 'But it wouldn't be fair on her. I'm trouble, Kate. Trouble personified. Ask Christiaan – he'd tell you! Even here – look what happened to me the moment I set foot in London.'

'Could that really have had anything to do with South Africa?'

Jan shook his head.

'I don't know. It doesn't seem likely, I admit.'

The family doctor called to see him and pronounced himself satisfied with the progress made.

'You must have a head like cast iron,' he said. 'I don't think you were meant to be around to tell the tale.'

'Well, I may be around,' Jan said, 'but I haven't had much of a tale to tell. I'm still a total blank about where I stayed that second night and how I came to be down by the river.'

'It will probably come.'

'Sometimes I get the odd flash, like a partially remembered dream, and I think it's all about to come back, but it doesn't. It's frustrating, to put it mildly.'

'It'll come! Try not to worry about it.'

'All very well,' Jan said to Kate after the doctor had gone. 'I tend to travel pretty light, but even so, just about every stitch I own is in an unknown hotel somewhere in London. I just hope they're hanging on to it.'

'We can go shopping any time you want.'

He waved this aside.

'With what you bought me, I'm all right for the moment, but I must go to the bank and see about getting some money.'

'There's no hurry about that.'

'I'm not a pauper, you know, thanks to good old Sir Randolph.'

Kate set up the ironing board, plugged in the iron, picked up a shirt from the basket and began work. Idly, Jan watched her.

'You're good at that, aren't you?'

Kate laughed.

'Heaven knows, I ought to be, after all these years.'

'Did it come hard – after Gramerci, I mean?'

Kate thought this over.

'No,' she said. 'Nursing came hard, after Gramerci. Housework came easy after nursing. But hard as nursing was, I preferred it to the kind of life I had at Gramerci. Except for being without you, of course.' She dealt competently with the shirt, folded it and put it on the table, barely pausing as she picked up a small school blouse. 'At Gramerci, I was always conscious of long hours, waiting to be filled. Looking back, it seems to me I was only half a person. Which perhaps,' she went on, folding the blouse and beginning on yet another shirt, 'was half the problem. I was far too intimidated by Sonia, right from the beginning, though in all fairness it would have been hard to be any different where she was concerned. Tell me, what on earth did she do with herself after she gave up the vineyard?'

'Sat around. Wrote irate letters to the papers. She never took any interest in the garden when she had the vineyards to occupy her, but afterwards she'd be out there, day after day, driving the gardeners mad. She spent hours going through all the junk that she kept in her office, too. She was supposed to be getting her affairs in order.'

'I'm amazed that she didn't throw out my letters.'

'Perhaps she would have done, given time. The end came quite suddenly, which was really a blessing.'

'Poor Sonia,' Kate said. 'I can't pretend I had any affection for her, but life dealt her a pretty rotten hand.'

'Not being able to have kids, you mean? Yes, that was tough. Christiaan minded that like hell. He told me several times how much he wished things were different. I suppose neither of them had any idea of it before they were married.'

'Well—' began Kate; then fell silent. She had no wish to justify her own behaviour by blackening Sonia's character, nor Christiaan's; Jan still appeared to have a residual fondness for him. She hadn't even mentioned Dora. What was the point of raising all that ancient history now?

'What were you going to say?' Jan asked.

Kate folded the shirt, put it to one side and began on another.

'Nothing, really. Just that I think she adored Christiaan from the moment she saw him. She was determined to marry him, no doubt about that.'

Jan thought this over.

'Funny,' he said. 'And scary, really, to think that love can die so completely. I never saw any evidence of it, anyway. She seemed so . . . so scornful of him, most of the time. Proud of what he'd achieved, of course. In public, anyway. But privately there always seemed to be a kind of contest going on.'

'What about?'

'Oh, everything. Who had the upper hand. Who had the last word.'

'She was manipulative, always.'

Jan was silent for a few moments.

'I wonder why he married her?' he said at last.

Kate might have told him then – about Dora, and about her own suspicions that Sonia had used the letter as a weapon of blackmail – but the doorbell rang before she could speak. It was only the postman with a parcel, but somehow by the time she returned to the kitchen, as so often happened, another riveting subject had occurred to them and the moment had gone.

Perhaps it was as well, she thought, later in the day. She had no proof that marriage was part of the payment that Sonia had extracted from Christiaan in return for her silence. It had, however, always seemed odd to her that the engagement should have come so closely on the heels of Sonia's disgust at Dora's letter. Without doubt, that letter would have meant the end of Christiaan's career if it had ever been made public.

When Kate had asked Sonia what Christiaan had said and done about the letter, Sonia had smiled thinly.

'It's all in hand,' she said. 'He objected to the sum I considered suitable to send the girl, but in the end he paid in full.'

'I must say,' Kate said bitterly, 'that men don't stand very high in my estimation at the moment.'

Sonia had agreed whole-heartedly. Cads and bounders the lot of them, she'd said; yet only a week later she had hung on Christiaan's arm, looking up at him with a triumphant smile, wearing a large square-cut diamond on the fourth finger of her left hand. Her expression was one of satisfaction at having pulled off some kind of master stroke, Kate had thought. What Sonia wants, Sonia gets. Happiness, somehow, didn't seem to enter into it.

'Who did you play with when you were little?' Kate asked.

February had turned into March, and suddenly the weather had improved, pale sunshine encouraging them to walk on Hampstead Heath before going to meet the children.

Jan, adapting his stride to hers, smiled reminiscently.

'Rosie's kids, mainly. And Matt – Matt de Vries. He was a bit younger than me, but even so we were pretty inseparable until I went to varsity.'

'Really?' Kate turned to him in delight. 'His mother was my best friend, too. My only friend, really.'

'I never knew her. Not to remember, anyway.'

'No.' The light died in Kate's face. 'I just couldn't believe it when I heard she'd died – couldn't understand why she would risk having another baby. She knew the dangers, and so did Paul. They'd both been warned. She was a lovely person and she taught me so much. I couldn't have managed without her.'

'Paul married Penny quite soon afterwards, I believe. I'm told she's a very different cup of tea. Nice, though, in a bubbly, bird-brained kind of way. She's a good step-mother. Matt's very fond of her, even though he does rag her about never being out of the social pages.'

'Are they still written by Flick Masterson?'

'Flick—?' He frowned, then laughed. 'You must mean Flick Pleydell. I heard she was a journalist once.'

'Pleydell? What happened to Brian Masterson, then?'

Jan shrugged.

'Heaven knows. She left him, I think. No – that's not right. I seem to remember hearing that he drank himself to death, a long time ago. Anyway, she's married now to this fabulously wealthy night-club owner about four feet tall with a pot-belly. Well, maybe he didn't have that when she married him, but he certainly does now. She swans about encrusted with diamonds and owns racehorses and an awful lot of silly hats.'

Kate laughed.

'Well, well,' she said, amused. 'So I suppose it's her turn to be written about now.'

'Never out of the papers,' Jan agreed.

They walked briskly; the sun might be shining on the crocuses under the trees, but it was still cold. After a while, mindful of the time, they turned back. Jan had fallen silent and they were sitting in the car before either of them said anything of importance. She reached to put the key in the ignition, but before she could do so, he turned to her and put a hand on her arm.

'Kate,' he said softly. 'Tell me about my father.'

For a moment she didn't move. This was it, then – the moment she had known she would have to face eventually. She had tried to prepare herself for it but now that it had arrived she found herself at a loss.

'What, exactly?'

Jan looked at her steadily.

'What he was like. Why you left him. Why things happened the way they did. After all, I never heard your side, did I? Sonia always spoke as if he were some kind of super-hero, without spot or blemish, and you'd left him on the merest whim. I believed her when I was young, but later it occurred to me that this was unlikely to be the whole story. Now that I know you, I'm quite sure it wasn't.'

'No,' Kate agreed. For a moment she sat looking directly in front of her, seeing nothing. Then she sighed and turned towards him. 'No,' she said again. 'That wasn't all of it, not by any means, but I can see now that I was in some way to blame for everything that happened. I married him without knowing him – without knowing myself. Without knowing anything, really. The whole thing was doomed from start to finish. We were utterly different kinds of people . . . But Jan, there's no time now. It's a long story, and it can't be rushed.'

'But you'll tell me?'

'Of course I will. You have a right to know.'

Different kinds of people, she thought, as she started the car and drove off towards the school in silence. That had become clear, of course, from quite early in her marriage. His friends, his interests, his outlook on life – all were alien and incomprehensible to her. Would Jan understand?

At first she had thought it her fault, that Guy was perfect and that she was the one who had to change and adapt. But gradually her perception of marriage altered. She realised that, try as she might, she would never be able to change enough; and why should she, she began demanding – why should she? She was a person in her own right, with opinions and priorities that seemed justified. Even so, she regarded her marriage as a lifetime commitment – imperfect, perhaps, but as good as that of most other people.

Guy had his good points. He wasn't unkind; merely neglectful, thoughtless, quite oblivious to the fact that she was often lonely. He was always generous when it came to money, never grudging her new clothes and even buying her a small second-hand runabout which had made a great deal of difference to her life. She had, for a short time, won his approval by producing a son, and it had to be admitted that he was a proud and adoring father. She had always known that, always appreciated it.

And she would, perhaps, have gone on appreciating the good and putting up with the bad, had it not been for the terrible night when, having gone to bed early with a good book (Guy, as usual, being absent), she had been disturbed by Evalina hammering on her door.

'Madam, come quick!' She was panting with the effort it had taken her to haul her enormous bulk upstairs in a hurry. 'D'ere's a fire outside. Oumissus' cottage.'

In an instant, Kate was out of bed and running to the door, feeling for her slippers, pulling on her silk robe as she went. She could smell the smoke now – had been vaguely aware of it for some time, she realised, but had been too engrossed to take much notice, dismissing it as smoke from a *braai* somewhere, over towards the estate workers' village, blown towards Gramerci by the strong wind that had been rattling the windows all evening.

From the window halfway down the stairs which looked out on to the back yard, she caught a glimpse in her headlong flight of flames and smoke.

'Oumissus?' she asked, shrill with anxiety, looking back over her shoulder towards Evalina. 'She's not still inside?'

Evalina's face was blank with fear, her eyes wide. Barely able to speak, her breath laboured, she lifted her hands and shook her head.

'Joseph,' she wheezed. 'Joseph—' But she could get no further.

Kate paused in the hall.

'Has anyone called the fire brigade?'

Evalina shook her head again.

'We call you first,' she said, finally managing to speak.

Kate ran to the telephone and dialled the emergency number.

'Fire. At Gramerci. Come quickly,' she said. 'Yes, yes, just past Groot Constantia. Please hurry.'

Evalina was beside her, wringing her hands.

'Oumissus – she in dere! And Joseph, too. He go to find her—'

Kate ran outside, pressing her hand to her mouth as she saw the way the fire had taken hold. Joseph was nowhere to be found, but many of the estate workers were there, passing buckets, full of water taken from the kitchen, from hand to hand. Others had hoses directed towards the blaze, but still the flames, fanned by the wind, were growing in strength. Evalina, distraught with anxiety, uttered small, whimpering sounds.

'Oh, God!' Kate whispered. 'Oh, God – what are we to do?' Wildly she looked around. 'Where's Sonia?'

'Not home yet, ma'am.'

The flames had reached the thatched roof now. There were tongues of them leaping and flickering, first here then there, strengthening all the time; and as they watched in horror, they saw Joseph stagger from the cottage. He tore off his shirt, soaked it in a bucket and tied it over his nose and mouth before once more going inside. Rosie, hauling buckets with the best of them, moaned as she saw him and turned to Evalina, her mouth a square of misery, calling for her to stop him. But he was out of sight, beyond hearing.

Sonia and Christiaan arrived only a few moments after the fire engine, having followed it with increasing foreboding down the road.

'Where's Mother?' Sonia shrieked at Kate. In tears, Kate could only shake her head. 'She's still in there. Joseph has gone in, and two of the firemen – oh God, Sonia, it's a nightmare! If only this wind would drop.'

'Where's Guy?'

'Not home yet.'

But he should be, Kate thought. There seemed no threat to the main house now that the fire brigade had arrived, and little point, therefore, in disturbing Johnny. She had dashed upstairs to check on him and had found him fast asleep, totally oblivious to all the drama. To her, it seemed better to leave him in peace; but would Guy think this reckless? Oh, why wasn't he home? She needed him; needed his support. His mother needed him and so did the servants.

She ran back to the phone and dialled the country club. It took some time for the steward to answer and impatiently she waited, drumming her fingers on the table until at last the phone was lifted. The voice at the other end sounded half asleep. Kate had a mental picture of the poor man for whom she had always felt a certain sympathy. She could see his round, coffee-coloured face puffy with exhaustion, as she had often seen it on late, convivial nights when those at the bar were reluctant to go home. But this was no time for the niceties.

'Sam, it's Mrs Lampard here,' she said. 'I must speak to my husband. Please get him for me.'

'Who—?'

Her hysteria mounted.

'Mr Lampard. Please. It's urgent.'

'Who is it, Sam?' She could hear another voice now, light, amused, slightly slurred. 'Hallo, hallo – who wants what? I'm afraid there's only the hardest of cores left around the bar.'

Kate recognised the voice instantly.

'Flick? It's Kate. Fetch Guy. It's urgent.'

'Guy?' There was a momentary pause, and an odd, unfamiliar note of unease in her voice. 'I'm afraid he's not here. He left some time ago.'

She sounded unnatural, unconvincing, and Kate didn't believe her. He was there somewhere, she felt sure. Flirting, drinking, enjoying himself. Who knew what he got up to, all these hours he spent away from home? Her voice became shrill.

'It's an emergency, Flick. Lilian's cottage is on fire. We don't know . . . we don't know if she—' She was sobbing now, and the words refused to come. 'He ought to be here,' she said, pulling herself together.

'He's left. I'm telling you the truth.'

'Then where—?'

Flick said nothing and Kate sensed she was hesitating, wondering what to say, what to do. She heard her draw a deep breath, and when she spoke again she sounded guileless, almost childish in her innocence.

'Try the Carltons. I believe he went off with Greta.' Then she added, in a more normal voice, not disguising her relish: 'He usually does, after all.'

For a moment it was as if Kate couldn't understand – as if the words were spoken in a foreign language, quite unknown to her. Slowly, without speaking, open-mouthed with shock, she lowered the phone. Of course, she thought, staring blankly ahead of her, seeing nothing. Greta. Of *course*! All those nights at the club; all those committees; all those chance meetings with old friends that had kept him out so late. Anyone with an ounce of sense would have seen what he was about. Flick knew. Everyone must know.

What a fool she'd been! What a stupid, blind idiot!

'Kate? Kate?' It was Sonia calling her, coming through the kitchen, her voice wild. Kate put the phone back on its rest and went to meet her. 'They've found Mother,' Sonia said. 'She's burnt. Dead.' There were no tears; just a blank look of total disbelief. For a moment she covered her face with her sooty hands and, instinctively, Kate went to her, her arms ready to embrace her; but at the last moment she held back, satisfying convention by putting a hand on her shoulder. One didn't embrace Sonia. She would neither expect it nor welcome it, even at a time like this.

'Oh, Sonia, I'm so sorry,' she said.

Sonia lowered her hands, her face now streaked with soot.

'Joseph—?' Kate asked.

'He's all right. Where's Guy? He must be told. He should be here—'

'I know. I rang the club—'

'Thank heaven. He won't be long, then.'

Kate hesitated.

'He wasn't there. There's . . . there's another phone call I have to make.'

She felt strangely numb, as if all of this were a dream. She would wake up soon, find there had been no fire, no death, no lies, no betrayal. She looked up the Carltons' number, dialled it, and, when Greta answered, asked to speak to Guy in a voice that sounded, to her, quite unlike her own.

'Oh!' Greta sounded bewildered. She gave a little laugh. 'Is that Kate? You sound a little odd. My dear, Guy isn't here. What on earth made you think he might be?'

'Tell him his mother is dead. Tell him her house has burnt down. Tell him to come home right away.'

She put the phone down, not waiting for a reply. I may be a fool, she thought, but not that much of a fool. I know he's there. And still in this strange, trance-like state she went outside again.

'Music, music!'

Kate was holding an excited, bouncing Johnny in her arms, lifting him to see the band on the quayside, and the streamers thrown to

link the passengers and the friends and relations who had come to
wave them off for a few last precious minutes.

Helen was there. And Guy, just for the look of the thing. He had
thrown a streamer and she had wound it around Johnny's wrist, not
wanting, herself, to be bound to him in any way even though such
a fragile connection would be broken in only a few moments.

There was an air of jollity, of celebration and heightened
emotions; of holidays about to begin, of whipped-up excitement.
A girl close to Kate by the rail was laughing and crying at the same
time, joined to a young man on the quay by a long red streamer.
The young man was saying something, but his words were drowned
by the sound of the band and, shrugging helplessly, he contented
himself by blowing kisses. A lovers' parting, Kate thought; and
despite the girl's tears she envied her.

She was impatient to be gone. It was all she had wanted from
the moment she had realised how she had been fooled – how for
months, even years, Guy and Greta had kept up a show of being
indifferent to each other when all the time, at every opportunity,
they had been in bed together. And the opportunities had been many,
for Neil Carlton was often away on business trips without his wife.
The poor man had been as much of a dupe as she had, but perhaps
more understandably. She had, after all, been warned.

Guy had been a little shame-faced, but only a little – like a small
boy caught scrumping apples, secretly amused at the annoyance of
the farmer who was making a fuss over so little. He even seemed to
show a certain pride, Kate thought, for managing to bed the prettiest
girl in Cape Town. He'd pulled placatory faces, nuzzled her neck,
told her that there were husbands on their own doorstep guilty of
far worse crimes – and hadn't he always come home to her? Had
he ever given any sign of wanting to break up his marriage?

He seemed unaware of the extent of her hurt and humiliation. And it seemed to her, at that moment, that everything she
had thought that terrible day on board ship had been true; he
had never loved her, but had married her for what he could
get out of Sir Randolph. She was, as she had suspected then,
of no importance, without attraction, no good in bed or out of
it.

'You should have told me,' she said dully to Helen when she
had come to Gramerci a few days after Lilian's funeral. 'Still—'
She gave a bitter little laugh. 'They do say that the wife is always

the last to know, don't they? My God, how everyone must have laughed at me.'

'No,' Helen said. 'It wasn't like that. People were sorry. And as for telling you – well, I almost did, but I kept hoping that Guy would see sense, for Johnny's sake, if for no other reason.'

'He should have seen sense for *my* sake!' Kate's cry was one of despair.

'I think he would have done. He's sorry now. He told Paul.'

'Well, he hasn't told me very convincingly.'

'What are you going to do, Kate?'

'I was hoping Paul could help me there. I don't want to wait until next month to go home. I want Paul to find Johnny and me a berth on the next ship leaving Cape Town. I just can't bear being under the same roof as Guy at the moment. Maybe later it won't seem so impossible, but right now, all I want is to get away.'

'I can understand that. Don't burn your boats, though, will you?'

'You're about to tell me that time's a great healer.'

'Well, maybe. I have seen this kind of situation before, you know, and it's amazing what people are able to forgive.'

Kate made no reply to this, but smiled faintly.

'So you will ask Paul?' she said. 'I don't care what kind of cabin. I just want to go at the earliest possible moment.'

Helen nodded.

'All right. I imagine there won't be any problem. Europe is hardly at its most inviting at this time of year.'

'No. You're right.' Kate, despite the thought of cold weather, looked marginally more cheerful. 'By the way,' she said, 'I haven't told you about Sonia, have I? She announced yesterday that she and Christiaan are going to tie the knot at last. They're talking about being married at Easter.'

'And you won't be here!'

'I'll survive.'

'Well—' Helen looked suitably amazed. 'Imagine that! Did it have to take a tragedy like poor Lilian's death to bring him up to scratch?'

'Heaven knows.'

'It's not a leap year or I would have suspected it was Sonia who did the asking.'

'She's quite capable of doing that without waiting for a leap year,' Kate said dryly.

When, just before leaving Gramerci, she had a moment alone with Sonia, she wished her well.

'I do hope you and Christiaan will be happy,' she said.

'Of course we will,' Sonia said, as if there were no question of it. She looked at Kate for a moment, her mouth twisted a little in a bitter, secretive smile. 'We've a better chance than you and Guy ever had. We're two of a kind, Christiaan and I.'

'And you won't have a spiteful sister to deal with,' Kate snapped, her temper flaring at last before she turned to go.

'So maybe she did love him,' Jan said. 'Then, anyway.'

It was the day after the walk on the heath and they were sitting at the kitchen table.

'I'm sure she did. In her way.'

'Scary,' Jan said again. He was silent for a moment, thinking it over. Then he looked at her again.

'So – you went to England. What happened then?'

Hands clasped on the table in front of her, Kate looked into space, remembering.

She hadn't socialised on the ship, she told him; hadn't forced herself to play games or dress up. While the weather remained hot she played on deck with him, and in the intervals when he was being entertained in the ship's nursery, she had stretched out with a book which she used as a barrier to the rest of the world as much as something to read.

Later, when it turned cold, she remained in the saloon or the library. In the evenings she took a turn or two round the deck, and went to bed early. Afterwards, looking back, she could remember none of her fellow-passengers. It had been a blank, featureless time; a kind of half-life.

'It was so strange,' she said now. 'Being back home, I mean. Nothing much had changed. It was a pretty horrible winter – wet and cold and miserable. I'd forgotten how cold my mother's house could be. She was glad to see me, though, and of course she adored you and spoiled you terribly. It was a difficult time, though, because pride prevented me from telling her anything about Guy, and she did nothing but say what a wonderful husband he was to let me come on such a long holiday and how lucky I had been to marry him.

'The Coningsbys spoiled you, too. At least, Sir Randolph did.

Poor Lady Coningsby – Aunt Florence, as I did my best to call her – was in pretty poor health by this time and spent most of the day reclining on a day bed.'

'D'you know,' Jan said in surprise. 'I think I remember that, after all. There were tall windows, two sets, with a huge vase of flowers in between. And she had a tartan travelling rug over her—'

'That's it, that's it!' Kate was delighted at his feat of memory.

'I hadn't a clue who she was or what I was doing there.'

'And the pony?' Kate asked eagerly. 'Do you remember the pony? Sir Randolph bought an especially small one and led you round the estate on it. He was so proud of you. Said you were a natural.'

Jan shook his head, frowning.

'No,' he said. 'I've no recollection of that. Funny, though,' he went on, 'how I can remember poor Florence, at least in part, yet I can't remember where I left my clothes just a few days ago.'

As if on cue, the doorbell rang before Kate could reply to this. She went to answer it, and came back smiling, DS Baker in tow.

'Good news, Jan,' she said. 'Your belongings have been found—'

'Wow!' In his relief, Jan slapped the table with both hands as he got to his feet. 'That's wonderful! Where?'

'Burgundy Hotel, just off the Bayswater Road,' Baker told him. 'They phoned earlier to report you missing.'

'That's terrific news! They took their time, though, didn't they?'

'Well—' Baker looked apologetic. 'They gave you a few days' grace, but I'm afraid the main delay was at our end. In all fairness, though, you must agree that until just recently we didn't know who we were looking for. The officers at Paddington Green didn't put two and two together as quickly as they should have done.'

Jan dismissed this. What did such things matter now?

'What about my passport?' he asked. 'Is it there?'

'Yes. And the traveller's cheques. They're in the holdall. You'd left them in the hotel's safe.'

Jan shook his head.

'Amazing,' he said. 'I can't remember doing that.' He turned to Kate. 'If I saw the hotel, it might bring back other things.'

'We'll go and look. Right now.'

'If you don't mind, Mrs Newcott,' Baker said, 'there are still a few questions I'd like to ask your son before you do. May we sit down a moment?'

'Yes, of course.' Kate looked round at the cluttered kitchen, suddenly seeing it through a stranger's eyes. She had left Jan sleeping when she took the children to school. When she arrived home, he was just coming down the stairs, so she had made breakfast for him and coffee for both of them, and they had talked on and on, oblivious to the unwashed dishes and used coffee mugs still on the table. Normally she might have been a little embarrassed, but not now. Your son, DS Baker had said. Her son. What did anything else matter? 'I think more coffee all round, don't you?' she said, collecting the cups. Then, in view of the chaos: 'Go into the sitting room and I'll bring it in.'

Baker, already sitting, smiled at her.

'This is fine by me, if you don't mind,' he said. 'And coffee would be wonderful. Thank you. Now!' He fastened his gaze on Jan. 'We have this chap in custody. On remand. The one that was caught sneaking into the hospital. He may be just what he admits to being – a petty thief on the look-out for drugs and anything else he can find. He does have form. On the other hand, it's just possible that he might have been trying to have another go at you. We want you to come and have a look at him. See if you recognise him.'

'But—' began Jan. Then he sighed. 'Well, I suppose I can do that, but at the moment I don't see it would be much good. I still can't remember a thing.'

'Maybe when you've seen the hotel—'

'It's worth a try, I agree.'

'Does he have any South African connections?' Kate asked.

Baker shook his head.

'None that we've been able to find. I'd say he was pure Bethnal Green, myself.'

'I saw a man at the hospital,' Kate said suddenly. 'One night when I went to visit Jan. He was kind of crouching over the bed, but he went off very quickly when I put in an appearance.'

The policeman frowned.

'You didn't mention that before. What kind of a man?'

'He was dressed as a doctor. Maybe he *was* a doctor. It's just that . . . oh, I don't know! He just struck me as being not much like the doctors I used to know when I was nursing. But then very little is like it was then.'

'In what way was he not like them?' Baker asked.

Kate thought about it.

'Scruffier, I suppose. Not so well spoken.'

'What was he like? Tall? Short? Fat? Thin?'

'Average height,' Kate said, thinking back. 'Kind of . . . well, average, I'm afraid. He had a moustache and dark, rather greasy hair, a little longer than one might have expected.'

'You'd better come too, then,' Baker said. 'We'll have an identity parade. See if you can pick him out. If he was the same man that we're holding, then we may be on to something. I'll give you a ring to fix a time. But first, take a look at the hotel and see if that jogs your memory.'

'I'll do that,' Jan agreed.

His possessions were in the hall: a rucksack and a holdall, which he unzipped the moment that Baker had gone.

'Am I glad to see this again,' he said, taking out his passport. He held it up between thumb and forefinger. 'This was the cause of all the trouble – the reason I was rooting for my birth certificate in Sonia's desk. I was planning a trip later in the year, but finding out about you made me come as soon as I possibly could.'

'Do you feel up to dashing off to see this hotel?' Kate asked him.

'Sure I do. I'll do the washing up if you'll do the beds.'

Kate grinned at him.

'I do believe you're learning,' she said.

15

'There it is,' Jan said.

The Burgundy Hotel was set back from the road, on a corner, the side of it fronting the main road. Kate signalled a right turn and slowed down as she passed its main entrance, looking for somewhere to park. Only a few yards beyond it there was a quiet square in which were no fewer than three other hotels of varying sizes, and here she thankfully found a space for the car. Having parked, they walked back to the Burgundy, which had marble steps and two pillars on each side of the porch. For a moment they stopped on the pavement as if by mutual consent, looking at it intently as if willing it to give up its secrets.

'Nice place,' said Kate.

'Mm.' Jan's response was thoughtfully non-committal.

'Shall we go in?'

'Why not?'

The floor of the entrance hall and the wide staircase beyond it was covered in a grey carpet patterned with small red fleur-de-lis, widening to accommodate the reception area. The atmosphere was one of restrained opulence; the direct antithesis, Kate guessed, of the guest house where Jan had spent his first night.

There was no one in reception. Jan walked slowly through the hall towards the stairs, looking around him, gazing up at the two chandeliers, studying the huge oil painting of some ancient, foreign battle that adorned the wall. He stopped for a moment beside the panel on which were details of West End theatres. Did this mean something? Kate watched him anxiously, but his expression gave nothing away.

To the right of the stairs was a lift with metal gates which she saw was descending. It arrived at the ground floor, and two men emerged, darkly foreign, wearing identical pale raincoats, conversing in some unknown tongue as they made for the front door. They posted their keys into the box provided almost without pausing in their conversation or giving her a glance, but even so their passing appeared to encourage a girl to come from the office at the rear of the reception area. She was young and fresh-faced, dressed in a white blouse and neat blue suit with red facings.

'Can I help you?' she asked, seeing Kate standing there.

'I'm not sure.' Kate went over to her and indicated Jan, now standing at the foot of the stairs. 'You'll probably think this odd,' she said, leaning forward confidentially, 'but my son evidently stayed here—'

She got no further, for the girl's smile, politely professional, turned to one of real delight as she saw Jan walking towards her.

'Oh, it's *you*!' she exclaimed. 'I didn't think we'd ever see you again. Are you all right? I heard you were beaten up, but Peggy and me, we couldn't believe it. I mean, look at the size of you!'

'You heard right,' Jan said as he came to stand beside Kate. 'You remember me, then?'

'Remember you?' The girl still smiled, but she frowned, too, as if the question made no sense. 'Well, of course I do.'

'How much do you remember?' Jan asked her, urgently.

'My son has lost his memory,' Kate said, seeing that explanations were necessary. 'Just temporarily, we hope. He can't remember anything about staying here and we hoped coming back would bring things back to him.'

'Oh, I see.' The girl, clearly a little piqued that she had been forgotten so quickly, looked more sympathetic. 'That's terrible. Well—' She appeared to think back. 'I remember you because I took you up to your room and I don't do that very often. Don't you remember going up in the lift? There was a couple with us arguing in whispers. We laughed about them when they got out.' She went a little pink, as if this revealed her as guilty of unprofessional conduct. There had been, Kate guessed, a little flirtatious badinage somewhere along the way. 'You booked in some time after two,' she went on. 'I know that because I'd just come on duty, and because it was a change-over time and some of the staff were still at late lunch, Peggy held the fort down here and I took you up. You were in number thirty-two, which can be a bit tricky to find. It's on its own, up a little flight of stairs – a double, with bath. You wanted a single, but this was the only room we had available.'

Jan's expression was changing, his eyes narrowing as if this rang a bell with him.

'Is there a big mirror on the wall?'

The girl nodded.

'Yes, there is.'

'In a heavy gold frame?'

'That's right! But can't your friend fill in the gaps?'

For a moment, Jan looked at her, frowning, not speaking.

'What friend is that?' he asked.

She laughed and shrugged her shoulders.

'Well, I don't know his name, and I couldn't really tell you now what he looked like because we were busy when he came in, checking in a big party. He was quite a tall chap, I remember that. Tall and broad. He asked if he could see you and I told you you were in thirty-two, so he used the phone over there to speak to you and I think you must have asked him to go up because later I happened to see you going out together. I honestly can't tell you any more than that. It really was a very busy night,' she added, apologetically.

For a moment Jan said nothing and seemed lost in thought. Then he came back to the present.

'I must still owe you for the room,' he said. 'You must have wondered what had happened when you found I hadn't used it.'

The girl laughed again, flipping her hair back from her shoulders as if dismissing the vagaries of clients.

'Well, people do funny things. We could fill a book, really we could! When I heard you hadn't slept there, I thought, well, you must have decided to stay a night or two with your friend. Or a girl. I mean, it happens! I felt sure you'd come back because we had your passport, didn't we? But after a couple of nights without a word, Mr Gordon, the manager, said we'd have to pack up your stuff and put it in store. We needed the room, you see. And then, after a while, he said we'd have to tell the police in case anything had happened to you. And some time after that, we heard it had. You'd been mugged! Such an awful shame, when you'd only just arrived.' She was opening a filing cabinet as she spoke and riffling through it, finally producing a bill. 'There you are, then, sir. I'm afraid we have to charge for two nights.'

Kate blinked a little at the sum stated, but Jan, who had stopped at a bank to cash some of his traveller's cheques *en route*, paid without demur.

'Would it be possible to see the room again?' he asked. 'Just in case it helps.'

The girl looked doubtful and disappeared into an inner office to check.

'It ought to be good at that price,' Kate murmured.

'It was. I think. I seem to recall a superb bathroom. I only wish I'd stayed to enjoy it a little longer.'

Triumphantly, Kate pinched his arm.

'It's working,' she said. 'You're remembering.'

The room, it seemed, was booked but not yet occupied, and they went up to look at it – Kate surveying the muted Liberty prints and thick, pale grey carpet with a certain amount of amusement. They seemed to imply that Jan had his hedonistic side after all.

'Well?' she said. He shrugged his shoulders.

'I know I've been here. I remembered the pattern of those curtains as soon as I saw them. But more than that—' He looked around him, went to peer round the door of the bathroom, then came back to stare frowningly at the bed for a moment or two.

'I came up,' he said. 'And I seem to remember that I lay down on the bed and went to sleep. My sleep patterns were all haywire, I suppose. I didn't sleep much on the plane, or in the flea-pit where I stayed that first night. It was so damned noisy, and there was a light flashing on and off right outside the window. When I woke up . . .' His voice faltered a little, and his frown deepened. 'When I woke up,' he repeated, more slowly, 'it was dark. I must have slept for several hours. I was ravenously hungry and thirsty, so I rang down for room service to bring me some tea and ham sandwiches. Hey—' He poked a finger towards her, grinning wickedly. 'The girl didn't charge me for them, did she? Don't dare say a word!' He laughed, relishing the small coup. 'I turned on the radio and waited for the food, and when it came, the chap who brought it closed the curtains. I ate the sandwiches, drank the tea, felt much better. Then I had a hot bath.'

'And then?'

He took a turn around the room, briefly looking at the reflection of it in the gilt mirror which hung on one wall flanked by two flower prints. He ran a hand over the smoky blue velvet chair, one of a pair, that stood between the bed and the windows. For a moment, he studied it in silence.

'He sat there,' he said, pointing at it in a positive kind of way. 'I remember now. But who was he? How did he know I was here, and why did I go with him? I wasn't aware that I knew anyone in London.'

'He was a big man,' Kate reminded him encouragingly. 'Tall and broad, the girl said. Can you remember that? Was he taller than you?'

Jan narrowed his eyes, trying to picture him. Then he shook his head.

'It's no use,' he said. 'I can't picture him at all – except that I think he was wearing something brown. A suede jacket, maybe. But I can't see his face, Kate, or remember who he was. It won't come to me.'

'It will! You've done so well, remembered so much. Come on.' Kate took his arm. 'Perhaps we've done all the good we're likely to do here – and anyway, it's time I took you home for lunch.'

Jan stood his ground.

'Oh no,' he said. 'Not a bit of it. I'm in the money – remember? It's time I bought you lunch for a change. Shall we have it here?'

After lunch, they took coffee in a corner of the lounge, sitting side by side on a velvety settee in comfortable intimacy. Apart from a small group of American women on the far side of the room, animatedly swapping accounts of their various sight-seeing trips, they had the place to themselves.

'That was a lovely lunch,' Kate said. 'Thank you, Jan.'

'For heaven's sake, it's the least I could do. I keep telling you – I'm hardly on the bread-line.'

'I'm beginning to believe it. Jan—' Kate looked at him curiously. 'If you could afford to stay here, why on earth did you go to the other hotel in the first place?'

He laughed at that.

'Laziness, I suppose. Someone back home told me it was OK and I didn't look further. I'm not saying I don't like my comforts, but on the whole the lack of them doesn't bother me. It was the dirt and the noise I couldn't stand.'

'Did someone advise you to come here?'

He looked at her, his eyes narrowed in thought.

'Yes. Who could it have been? I know!' He snapped his fingers, suddenly remembering. 'I had the number of a kind of accommodation agency, so I rang and asked for something central, comfortable, middle range—'

'And they sent you here?'

'I spoke to a girl. She said there were several hotels in this area that might be suitable and suggested taking a cab to Collins Square.'

'That's where we've parked. Jan, this is wonderful. You couldn't remember any of this before.'

'No, I couldn't, could I? Well, that's what happened. I tried one of the other hotels first, but it was full so I came here. Even here, they could only take me for a couple of nights.'

'And what were your plans after that?'

'I was working myself up to get in touch with you. Believe it or not, having got to the point, I found myself suddenly terrified. I had your address but not your phone number, but I looked you up in the book as soon as I got into the room. That's something else that's just occurred to me. I remember staring at the name and address, hardly able to believe that it was there, that there really was somebody called Newcott living at 16 Cumbernauld Avenue, Highgate. Crazy, eh? I even lifted up the phone, but then I put it down again. I'd sleep on it, I thought. Think a bit more about what I was going to say.' He gave her a shame-faced grin. 'It was a cop-out, really. I was just plain scared.'

'What an idiot!' Kate leaned her head back against the soft upholstery and closed her eyes. 'I still can hardly believe you're here,' she said. 'It's just too wonderful to be true.'

She opened her eyes and saw that he was looking at her.

'What happened next?' he asked gently. 'In 1939, I mean. After you and I got back to England?'

She sighed. It wasn't, she knew, something she could put off for ever.

'You were a page-boy at my brother's wedding,' she said. 'But you know that. I showed you the photographs.'

'I haven't forgiven you for that yet. How could you possibly have dressed me up in that little Lord Fauntleroy suit? It was cruelty to dumb animals!'

'It was a sailor suit, and you weren't dumb. You were extremely talkative, just like you are now, mostly in the wrong moments. We'd promised you ice cream if you behaved yourself, and when the vicar asked if there was any just cause or impediment why these two people should not be joined in holy matrimony, you immediately started demanding ice cream at the top of your voice. Everybody laughed. Surely you remember it?'

He shook his head.

'I'm afraid not.'

'Well, it was a long time ago.'

'Momentous times.'

'They certainly were. Germany had marched into Czechoslovakia by then. I remember Sir Randolph jumping up and down and saying we should never have stood by and let them do it. One heard all kinds of war talk, though people still hoped it would never happen. To be honest, I was too preoccupied with my own problems to be fully aware of what was going on around me. The longer I stayed away from Guy, the less I wanted to go back to him. And yet – there was you to think about. I knew that in England, by myself, I couldn't give you half the start in life that you'd get back at Gramerci. And your father adored you, there was no doubt about that.

'On the other hand . . . Oh, Jan! Can you understand it? I felt so isolated there, so out in the cold. You were my son, but my wishes hardly counted. I was twenty-two by then – Guy's wife and your mother – but Sonia still treated me like a silly little schoolgirl without a brain in my head. And Guy went along with it. That was the awful part. By now, Sonia and Christiaan were married and I hoped against hope that maybe they would move out to live elsewhere – but no! As I feared, Guy wrote and told me that Christiaan had moved in. I couldn't see what kind of place there was for me there, and I was still smarting at Guy's behaviour. He didn't love me. He'd been unfaithful once, and I knew he would be again. And probably again and again and again.'

She paused, as if for reflection, while Jan, his elbow on the back of the settee, looked at her. What was he thinking? she wondered. How did *he* see her? It was hard to remember that this large and forceful character was her own son. His eyes were bright and direct, all his attention focused on her.

'So,' he said. 'What did you do?'

She sighed.

'I wrote to Guy,' she went on. 'I told him I didn't think I could go back with things still unresolved. I said I was prepared to try again if we could live somewhere on our own – Larry's cottage, maybe, or anywhere else he chose – just the three of us, a real family. I said I wanted other children and would try to be the sort of wife he really wanted.'

'What was his answer?'

'Just a letter saying he was coming to England on the next boat. It was the end of July by then, and his busy time was over. He'd be in Shenlake in time for your fourth birthday, he said. I . . . I thought that this meant he was prepared to make compromises himself, that we would have a holiday together here and go back to start all over again on a different footing.'

'But you were wrong?'

'Never more so! He told me in no uncertain terms that there was no question of his leaving Gramerci – the idea of going somewhere else was just a foolish whim on my part. And there was no question of Sonia leaving, either. It was absolutely essential that she was on the spot, he said; and anyway, Christiaan had to spend half the year in Pretoria, so what would she do then? No – I had to pull myself together, forget the past, stop dwelling on his little fling with Greta and go back to Cape Town to be a decent wife and mother.'

She gave a bitter little laugh.

'I pointed out that his little fling had lasted three years, if not longer, but he still claimed that I was making a mountain out of a molehill.' She sighed, paused for a moment. 'We had dreadful quarrels, Jan. All *sotto voce* in the privacy of our bedroom at Coningsby Hall. We'd moved up there, you see, the moment Guy arrived in England.'

She paused again, and her mouth thinned, grew bitter.

'Go on,' Jan said quietly.

'Well—' She paused once more, and sighed. 'Sir Randolph was the sort of man who was either totally for you, or implacably against. There were never any half-measures with him. All through my childhood he had a soft spot for my mother and consequently for Peter and me, too. He was kind to us, I can't deny it – but during the years I'd been away, things had changed. A widower came to live in the village, a man called Richard Agnew – a nice man, a retired banker. He wasn't wildly exciting, bless his heart, but he was kind and thoughtful and he took a great shine to Dotty. In fact he was just the kind of man she'd been looking for for the past twenty-odd years: solvent, eligible, the right kind of age.'

'And Randolph objected?'

'Apparently, yes. Having regarded her as some kind of romantic ideal, he now suddenly saw her as a scarlet woman and relations were icily polite by the time Guy arrived home. I was treated in much the same way.

'At some stage, Guy told him the marriage was in trouble – well, I'm sure he hardly needed to be told. It must have been quite obvious. Naturally, Guy told his uncle his side of the story, which I gathered afterwards portrayed me as a frigid, mean-spirited, argumentative harridan who had every intention of taking his son away from him.'

'And Sir Randolph believed all that?'

'He seemed to. He took me on one side and talked to me very sternly. I can't remember all the details, but I know the Empire came into it, and biting the bullet, and showing what I was made of. He'd had great hopes of me, he said. Thought I was just the girl for Guy, but he now saw that he had been sadly mistaken. But it wasn't too late, he said. I could still try to make amends.'

'What did you say to that?'

'I don't think I said anything much.' Kate smiled at him ruefully. 'The story of my life! I only think of what to say when it's far too late. Sir Randolph went to see my mother, too, for the first time for ages, and told her to talk some sense into me. It was, I don't mind telling you, one hell of a time. Can you wonder I was blind and deaf to what was happening on the international front? And when I did think about it, I still believed it wouldn't come to war. Like a lot of other people, I may add.'

'Did your mother attempt to persuade you?'

Kate gave a brief laugh.

'I'm afraid that ploy backfired rather. Dotty didn't mind criticising me herself, but she was very mother-hennish if anyone else did. Besides, Sir Randolph somehow succeeded in implying that my lack of moral fibre was her fault for bringing me up all wrong – and not only that, but also that as a family we were showing a distinct lack of gratitude for all he had done for us in the past. Boy, did that put the cat among the pigeons!'

'So she took your part?'

'Yes, she did – influenced a great deal, I must say, by dear

Richard, who was a tower of strength over that whole period; a
kind of calm centre at the eye of the storm. He really was rather
a dear.'

'Sad—'

'Yes, wasn't it? If they hadn't gone to Bath for their honeymoon—'

'Why did the Germans bomb Bath?' Jan asked, digressing
suddenly.

'Because it had three stars in the Baedeker Guide. York, too.
It was meant to break morale. It didn't, of course, but I'm afraid
poor Dotty and Richard were victims, just when she seemed to
have achieved happiness.' Kate paused for a minute, and sighed.
'Anyway,' she went on, 'that was all several years along the road
then. To my astonishment Dottie changed her tune completely about
Guy and said that if I couldn't bear to go back I should stay with
her. She would look after you, she said, and I could get trained for
something so that I could get a job to pay for our keep.'

'And that's what you decided to do?'

'No, no! Not then, anyway. I just didn't know what to do. It was
poor Florence who made me decide. She spent all her days reclining
on her *chaise-longue*, as I told you, and I'd taken to reading to her.
She seemed to like that. I got to know her better than I had ever done
before, and I was amazed to find how knowledgeable she was about
an enormous number of things. We had wonderful conversations
about – oh, everything. Politics, religion, art. She'd been brought
up in India as a girl and had travelled a lot. Yet she'd always lived
in Randolph's shadow and not only I but everyone else thought
her a complete nobody – yet all the time she had this wonderfully
sharp mind, full of original thoughts and insights and incredible
experiences.

'She had a wonderful turn of phrase! I said once that she ought
to write everything down, turn it into a book; and d'you know
what she said? She said she had written a book once and someone
had wanted to publish it, but Sir Randolph had been annoyed to
think that she was drawing attention to herself so she wrote to
the publishers and said she was very sorry, she would have to
back out of the arrangement. Can you believe it? That bouncy,
self-satisfied, *common* little man had squashed her completely and
kept her in subjection all their married life – a woman with ten
times his brain! And all the time he was having affairs left, right

and centre. Dotty was only one of many, I gathered from her afterwards.

'My goodness, it concentrated my mind wonderfully, I can tell you. Florence died quite soon after that. I remember standing in the churchyard at her funeral thinking what a wasted life she'd led and how mortality catches up with us all in the end. I remembered Lilian, too, and what the Lampards did to her, and it didn't take me long to make my decision. I told Guy that I wasn't going back and that I wanted a divorce. And custody of you, of course.'

'So what happened?'

Kate laughed softly; then she sighed.

'What happened? Fireworks are what happened. He shouted. I cried. I moved back to Chimneys and took you with me. He went up and down to London to see lawyers – and apparently was left with the assurance that even if he contested custody, I was likely to be the one that was awarded it. Mothers almost always were, then. Still are, I think. And all the time, events in the big world outside were moving on. And suddenly, August was almost over and even I became aware that it didn't look as if we were going to be able to avoid war, after all. Guy came to Chimneys to tell me he had to get back and had booked a passage on 2 September.

'He'd give me one last chance to change my mind, he said – speaking, I may say, with the air of a headmaster addressing an unruly and slightly retarded pupil, with not one expression of affection or contrition or willingness to change on his part. I told him I was very sorry, but I was staying. And I *was* sorry, Jan. Desperately sorry. I didn't want it to end like that, but I simply couldn't face the alternative. It wasn't simply that he'd been unfaithful. I might have come to terms with that. It was going back to the loneliness that I couldn't face. And Sonia, of course.'

'How did he react?'

'He was angry, but he seemed to accept this as my final decision. He asked for one favour – that you should spend one last day with him at Coningsby Hall on 1 September, the day before he was due to sail. He'd collect you early, he said, and bring you back before bedtime.

'It seemed a reasonable request and I had no objections. He came early, as arranged, but when bedtime came there was no sign of you. I phoned the Hall eventually to see what had happened, only to be told that Guy had lied to me. He – and you, of course – had already left for South Africa, on the flying boat service, and by that time were probably at Alexandria, in Egypt.'

The silvery chimes of a clock suddenly penetrated Kate's consciousness, and she grabbed her handbag in sudden panic.

'Oh, Jan, look at the time. I'll be late for the children.'

Hurriedly, they left, the present suddenly taking precedence over the past. Which was how it should be, Kate thought as they ran towards the car. Everything that had happened, everything that she had narrated to Jan, felt like fiction now, as if it had all taken place in another life, to someone else. And so, in a way, it had, for she could see nothing in herself now to remind her of the girl she had been.

'Shall we take Jan down to the farm to meet Mother on Saturday?' Tom said at breakfast, a few days later. Kate agreed readily.

'Yes, of course, if she doesn't mind. It'll be nice to get out into the country.'

'You know she'd love it. She's always saying she doesn't see enough of us.'

She was, Kate often told herself, very lucky to have a mother-in-law like Beatrice Newcott. She was, in many ways, an ideal granny; always happy to have the children to stay, or come and stay with them, yet with a busy and absorbing life of her own. Her distance from London was a further asset, for much as Kate liked Beatrice in small doses, she was perfectly aware that to have her on the doorstep would have probably spelled the end of their mutual regard. Beatrice was so full of energy that it was totally beyond her not to want to organise everything, up to and including other people's lives.

She was small and plump, reminding Kate always of a pouter pigeon; a no-nonsense, forthright countrywoman with a heart of gold. She was also, at times, the most infuriating woman it was possible to meet. She had been a widow for many years now, left on her own to run the small farm in Sussex on which Tom had been brought up. Some time ago she had needed a minor operation which curtailed her activities for a time, and Tom had persuaded her to employ a temporary manager. Three years on, George Pilbeam was still there, silent, stolid and uncomplaining. It wasn't, she was at pains to tell her family, that she couldn't manage on her own any more. She liked the company, that was all. Since George seldom spoke, it was hard to imagine how his company could be classed as entertaining, but then Beatrice needed no conversation from others. Having someone to talk at was her main pleasure.

'I'll give her a ring this evening,' Tom said. 'I hope things go well this morning.'

Kate sighed. This was the day arranged for the police identity parade.

'I'm not looking forward to it,' she said. 'Nor is Jan. His memory is still so patchy.'

'It's coming back, though.'

'Bit by bit. Tom—' Kate put fresh toast on the table and sat down opposite him. 'I just wanted to say I couldn't be more grateful.'

'Why on earth?'

'You're being quite incredibly forbearing! I know I'm a bit scatty these days, and the house is a mess, and you haven't always got a clean shirt—'

'When have I bothered about that kind of thing?'

She looked at him thoughtfully as he buttered his toast.

'Something's bothering you, though.'

'No it's not.'

'You can't fool me. What is it?'

Tom shrugged his shoulders.

'It's nothing. Honestly. I suppose I'm a bit *distrait* myself these days, what with one thing and another. I'm happy that you're happy. God knows, you deserve it after so long.'

'Thanks,' Kate said; but still she looked at him quizzically. There's something that doesn't ring true, she thought. He's not being totally straight with me.

'I love you very much, you know,' he said.

'Well!' Kate grinned at him. 'There's a nice thing to hear at the breakfast table. I love you, too.'

She stood up and leant across the table to plant a kiss on his nose, just as Vicky came in through the door.

'Yuk! You're being soppy again,' she said in disgust; but Kate denied this vehemently.

'It was just a reward for good behaviour,' she said.

Tom, in fact, felt far from virtuous. It wasn't that he didn't like Jan. Well, not exactly. He would probably feel the same ambivalence about any stranger who had suddenly taken over his home, he told himself; for that was what it felt like. It was simply that Jan was so . . . so *big*, his presence so dominating. Gone, now, were the peaceful evenings, the desultory conversations he and Kate used to enjoy, the joint concentration on the crossword puzzle, the long silences when both were lost in their respective books.

Instead, what did he come home to? Bloody sport, nine times out of ten. Why should Jan care about football? These weren't his teams, his country. But still he was riveted to television whenever a game was showing, cheering on the side he deemed the most deserving. And if it wasn't football, then it was something else. Anything involving a ball and competition of some kind.

Tom knew he had only to ask for the TV to be turned off. Invariably Jan asked if he objected, but so far he had said nothing, hiding his feelings, fuming in silence. In a way it was preferable to the endless discussions about South African politics which went on between Jan and Kate, inflamed day by day by the newspapers which were now full of the Commonwealth Prime Ministers' Conference, soon about to take place in London. It wasn't that he held any brief for the South African attitude towards race; just that he longed to urge them to give it a rest, for God's sake.

He was being unfair, and he knew it. It was only natural that Kate should want to devote herself to her son, talk to him all the time, learn all about his life, and he meant it when he said that he was glad to see Kate so happy. Part of his fear had been that Jan would prove to be a disappointment to her, and clearly this had been unjustified. Jan was everything she had hoped for.

For himself, he just wanted peace. Peace to relish this new and exciting project he was embarking on. Peace to enjoy quiet pursuits with his children again. (He wasn't jealous, was he? Surely it wasn't that! He ought to be delighted that Mark and Vicky had taken so whole-heartedly to their half-brother – and he was, he was!) Meantime, he hid his feelings and did his best to act normally, even though the question was always in his mind: how long, oh Lord, how long?

And yet, underneath all the petty irritations, he was conscious of guilt. If it hadn't been for him, Kate could have made the acquaintance of her son years ago.

To be honest, he felt surprised that she didn't hate him for it.

Much to DS Baker's disappointment, neither Jan nor Kate was able to recognise anyone likely to have been involved with the attack on Jan, but he had received the news of the unknown visitor to the Burgundy with interest, laced heavily with annoyance that no one had seen fit to mention him before, as if Jan had wilfully withheld information.

'You're sure you didn't see him in the line-up?' he persisted, unwilling to let the matter drop.

'No, I'm not,' Jan said. 'I'm not sure of anything. He could have been there, but if he was, I didn't recognise him.'

'It's awfully hard to be certain, isn't it?' Kate said, as they drove away from the police station. 'I'm pretty sure the man I saw at the hospital had a moustache, but there wasn't one to be seen in the entire place.'

'Moustaches are removable,' Jan pointed out.

'I know. I kept telling myself that and trying to imagine what he would look like without it, but the truth is I hardly registered his face. I was too busy looking at his off-white coat.'

'Maybe he really was a doctor.'

'Maybe he was. But you know what Elaine said when she was round yesterday. My description didn't sound like any doctor she could recognise. She seemed to think it all sounded rather suspicious.'

'You've been friends a long time, haven't you?'

'With Elaine? For ever,' Kate said.

But it only seemed that way. She hadn't known Elaine during those terrible first months of the war when she had felt she was going mad with grief over the loss of her son.

She hadn't believed it at first; hadn't been able to take it in. Looking back, it seemed that she had run around like a chicken with its head cut off in her efforts to get a passage back to South Africa.

There were mail boats still running, and the flying boats too, for a little while; the difficulty was finding space aboard them, for every South African in the country was besieging the shipping agents in a frantic attempt to get home, and people from East Africa were doing the same, even settling for those ships that went no further than Durban. They were willing to take their chances on finding other transport, by sea or overland, to reach other countries to the north. Bombs were expected to fall immediately; poison gas was a probability.

'Perhaps it's for the best,' Dotty said, trying to comfort her. 'At least he'll be safe. My advice is to wait. See how things go. They say it'll be over by Christmas.'

'They said that the last time, and it went on for four years!'

But perhaps she was right, Kate thought at times. The war couldn't last for ever, and maybe it would be wrong of her to attempt to bring Johnny back here where he could be in danger. Still she went on trying, until she was told, without hope of any reprieve, that there was no point in doing so any more. There would be no passages for civilians for the foreseeable future.

She received a cold letter from Guy. He was sorry to have had to resort to such extreme measures, he wrote, but she must surely see that he had no alternative. He was consulting his solicitors in Cape Town regarding a divorce, and suggested that she did the same from her end, though the whole thing might need to be put on ice until after the war. As for Johnny, he was perfectly well and happy and seemed glad to be back in his own home where he would be safe from bombs and gas and anything else the Germans might decide to throw at the British populace.

'You're no worse off than many other mothers,' Dotty told her, taking a more bracing approach. 'Look at all those little East End children sent away with labels pinned to their jackets.'

'At least their mothers can visit them,' Kate said bitterly. 'Anyway, they've nearly all gone back home now.'

'Not all of them. And some children have gone to America. Dr Grenville was telling me about his sister in London. Her husband has relatives in Baltimore, so they've sent their three children there for the duration.'

It was Kate's only comfort, that whatever happened Johnny would be safe. She disregarded Guy's instructions to consult her solicitor. For the moment she had no intention of instituting divorce proceedings, not before she knew what his intentions were regarding Johnny. Possession, it seemed to her, might well prove a good deal more than nine-tenths of the law in this case. It wasn't, after all, as if she had any intention of marrying again. At twenty-two, she had forsworn men for ever.

Winter came, bitterly cold, and grey with the absence of joy. The war, far from progressing towards a satisfactory conclusion, seemed to be stuck in some kind of time warp. Nothing was happening, and it seemed sometimes that it never would.

Everyone, however, was talking about war work. Twice in the

space of twenty minutes, having gone into the village to post a letter to Guy, Kate was asked if she'd managed to find something to do – and had been forced to admit, rather to her shame, that she had not.

'I ought to do something,' she said to her mother on her arrival home. 'I can't just hang about waiting for the war to be over. There must be some kind of war work.'

'You always liked first aid,' Dotty said. 'Remember all those lectures you went to? I never thought they were a lot of good, myself, but I suppose in wartime they might come in useful.'

Kate was staring at her, not speaking. There was a dawning light in her eyes which suddenly looked brighter than they had done for some time. Of course, she was thinking. Of *course*!

'Actually,' she said to Jan, 'I met Elaine in January 1940, at a convalescent home for officers in Surrey. It was the kind of place they sent VADs like us, who hadn't much more than a first aid certificate. We learned basics like making beds and taking temperatures, but it wasn't real nursing, which both of us yearned to do, so eventually we both upped and joined the Royal Army Medical Corps.'

'Was that more to your liking?'

For a moment, Kate thought about it, smiling to herself, remembering the cold, the meagre rations, the unremitting work, the poor pay – eighteen shillings a week, if her memory served her correctly. She felt again the chapped hands, the chilblained feet, the weariness when work in the wards was, of necessity, followed by hours of study. But she remembered, too, the bravery and the laughter of the men; the jokes, the ragging, the occasional tears.

'Oh, yes,' she said. 'It was much more to our liking. I even relished the hard work. It meant it was quite impossible for me to brood too much. Truly, I wouldn't have missed a day of it. For the first time ever I felt I was a square peg in a square hole. I never forgot you, though.'

'I know.' He reached out and touched her arm. 'I have the letters to prove it. There's even,' he added after a pause, 'the letter you wrote after you knew Guy had been killed.'

Kate took a long, slow breath. How strange it was that she should feel pain after all this time. She'd hated him, hadn't she? He'd hurt her more than anyone else in the entire world. Yet it was the vitality she had remembered now, just as she had when she had first heard the news. The vitality and the his extraordinary good looks.

'I don't think I could bear to read it,' she said.

Nina loved her work, but there was no doubt it had been a particularly tiring day. Inspectors, a prolonged and infuriating enquiry regarding a lost textbook, a staff meeting, all meant that it was later than usual as she let herself into her flat; but here all was peace – and, as an added bonus, a letter unmistakably from Jan was lying on the mat.

Her heart leapt a little at the sight of it; from habit, she told herself, as she bent to pick it up. From habit and friendship and relief, nothing more. The thought that the danger that she knew surrounded him in South Africa might have followed him as far as England had been a disquieting one, to say the least.

Any reports of my demise, [he had written] are a gross exaggeration. The Lampard head is clearly twice as thick as the usual variety and I'm now out of hospital and staying with my mother's family. I'm feeling much better and could even put the whole incident behind me were it not for the fact that I can't remember the smallest thing from the morning after my arrival to the time I woke up in hospital. A disturbing thought! Suppose I robbed a bank or ravished some passing English rose? They say all will come back to me in time, and I hope 'they' are right. No sign yet, though.

All the foregoing only adds to the feeling of unreality I'm experiencing here. My mother, whom I am to call Kate, bears no resemblance to me in looks, being small and rather beautiful in a quiet way, with dark hair and eyes. She has Italian blood, she tells me. It's odd, not knowing a thing about her. I'm learning, though. We talk endlessly, trying to catch up, and I find her molto simpatico. You would, too, I think. She hated the SA regime when she lived there, which is one reason, among many others, why she scarpered. I'll tell you more when I get back.

She's married to a guy called Tom, an architect, an amiable enough chap whom I catch from time to time eyeing me warily, determined to accept me cheerfully for Kate's sake but at the same time appearing a little bemused at the sight of this

*enormous cuckoo that has suddenly appeared in his nest. I
know he's wondering when the hell I'm going to get out of
it, and can't find it in my heart to blame him. I'm perfectly
aware that I take up a lot of space, in every way.*

*Did you suspect that I might be Good With Children? I
can't say that I did, but life is full of surprises. My small
half-brother and sister appear to approve of me and I have
become devoted to them. I am now a dab hand at Ludo
and have learned several ways of cheating at Snakes and
Ladders.*

*But I miss you, Nina. All right, all right, I know I'm an
unreliable bastard who can't be trusted to turn up on time,
or even turn up, period. I deserve all the accusations you
threw at me and the worst thing of all is that I can't see that
I'll ever be any better, not till I'm in my old rocking chair,
with all passion spent. Or till SA operates a just system of
government. Whichever is the sooner.*

*Write and let me know how everything's going – the literacy
classes and the women's centre, and everything. Is Daniel
out of prison yet? And did Naomi get off? I hated leaving
it unresolved, but I know she understood. Love to her, and
Dan, and and everyone. And to you. Especially to you. I'll
write again soon.*

There was a PS. 'Tell Dwane to do NOTHING until I get back.'

Nina read it, and laughed a little. Dwane was one of Jan's
protégés, a likeable rogue, recently released from prison, whose
talents included a facility for juggling figures. Jan, who was
conspicuously lacking in this area, employed him to do his accounts
and income tax returns, relieving himself of an onerous burden,
while giving Dwane much-needed employment and, hopefully,
a new start in life. The only snag was that alongside Dwane's
devotion to Jan, he possessed a fertile imagination and his wildly
imaginative tax claims had resulted, more than once, in unpleasant
attention from the authorities.

The laughter was brief. Thank God he's all right, she thought.
She read the letter again and, having done so, lay back in the chair
for a moment, staring at nothing. Life, she was thinking, was too
damned complicated by half.

She gave a sigh that was almost a groan; then tossing the letter aside, she got up. Get out of my hair, Lampard, she said bitterly, to no one but herself and the empty flat. She went briskly into her bedroom and began to strip off her working clothes, but then, down to her bra and pants, she paused and groaned again. Oh, *Jan*, she said.

Later, she rang Colin.

'I'll be home at the weekend,' she said, having given him a brief summary of Jan's letter. 'Let's do something nice. Get out into the country—'

'Great,' Colin said, with enthusiasm. 'I'll work on it.'

16

The interview with Christiaan le Roux formed the whole of Colin's Saturday column. By and large, he felt he had made the best of a bad job, even though he viewed his opening sentences with sardonic amusement. He had used le Roux's words regarding the candlewood tree as a kind of introduction and had laughed aloud at the sentimentality as he had written them; then he had paused, grimaced, almost torn the paper out of his typewriter to start the whole thing afresh. But in the end he had let it stand. What did it matter, anyway? He was prevented by the laws of libel from saying what he really thought about the Minister for Coloured Affairs. This anodyne piece was all that the editor would allow.

Saturday was free, and Nina was coming to Cape Town for the weekend. He'd had little room for any other thought all week, and now the day had arrived. Later it would undoubtedly be very hot indeed, but right now, Colin saw as he stood on his small balcony, it was fine and clear, with no wind – the perfect beginning to what he intended should be the perfect weekend.

It started well enough. They went to the beach on Saturday morning, and walked barefoot at the edge of the waves until the bungalows were left behind and they had the strand to themselves with only seabirds for company.

It seemed only natural to take Nina's hand. Such a simple thing, he thought, to take a girl's hand. Could anything be more innocent? Yet his heart was beating just as wildly as it had done when he was a schoolboy.

What was she thinking? It was hard to tell. She looked happy, carefree. They talked – not seriously, not politics, and not Jan, thank heaven; just everyday things. Books they'd read, films they'd seen, funny things that had happened. They picked up shells, and skimmed stones, laughed at very little, and stood for a few moments, like the good South Africans they were, gazing in appreciation at Table Mountain across the water.

'I wouldn't want to live anywhere else,' Colin said; and immediately thought, that's a lie. I'd go anywhere with Nina.

They had sat down, finally, in the shade of the granite rocks that formed a barrier between one beach and the next; and it had seemed the most natural thing in the world that they should kiss.

'We've been here before,' Nina said, a little huskily.

'I can't think why we ever left,' he replied. But of course he knew. She'd been dazzled by Jan. 'I never stopped loving you, you know.'

She laughed.

'You expect me to believe that? You've had thousands of girls since me.'

'None like you. I mean it, Nina.'

'Oh, sure, sure.' She was still laughing as he pulled her close, kissing her again.

'Is this a new beginning?' he asked, when at last they drew apart.

She reached up and ran a finger down the side of his face.

'Let's take it slowly, Colin. OK? It's lovely being with you again, but I'm a bit—' She paused.

'What?'

'Oh, at sixes and sevens.'

Colin looked at her, wanting her. Jan, he thought. Bloody Jan. He might be thousands of miles away, but he's here just the same.

He had the wit not to mention him, however.

That night they drove out to a new night-spot at Kloof Nek, and dined and danced in the warm air. There was nothing grand about the place, but below them the lights were strung out along the whole width of the bay from Clifden to Llandudno, making it seem as if they were suspended in some magical kingdom, far removed from reality.

'Dad's band plays here sometimes,' Nina told him.

Colin was glad that Les Cambell wasn't playing that night. He couldn't have held Nina so close, lips touching her hair, if he'd been aware of her father's eyes upon them. Among strangers, they seemed to be in a world of their own; but it proved to be a world that was shattered all too soon when he drove Nina home to find a brown Ford Consul parked outside the Cambell house and lights coming from the living room.

'That's Steve and Margie's car,' Nina said. 'I didn't know they were coming round tonight. Come on in and have a drink, or coffee, or something.'

Colin, who had been hoping for a protracted goodnight in a silent, sleeping household, sighed inwardly, but got out of the car and followed her to the front porch.

Hearing Nina's key in the lock, Hennie came to the door to meet them, opening it upon a scene that Colin knew was one of shock. He had been called upon to report too many such dramas to mistake the signs; the staring eyes, the stiff faces, the taut atmosphere. Steve and Margie were sitting together on the settee, holding hands, and Margie, clearly, had been crying. Steve sat woodenly, not smiling now, all the naturally upward lines of his face now drooping like a weeping clown.

'I'd better go,' Colin said, but Hennie reached for him and almost dragged him inside.

'No, no,' she said. 'You stay, Colin. Maybe you can help.'

'Mom – Margie, what is it?' Nina looked fearfully from one to the other. 'Dad, what's happened?'

'Oh, such a dreadful thing,' Hennie said. 'Such a *wicked* thing! I still can't believe it.' Tears came to her eyes, and she pulled a handkerchief from her sleeve to dry them. 'What we're to do I don't know.'

'Margie? Margie, what is it?' Nina crossed the room and crouched down beside the rigid, silent figure on the settee. 'What's happened? For heaven's sake tell us.'

'They say she married a Coloured man,' Steve said, looking away to the corner of the room.

'What?' Nina looked from one to the other. 'What are you talking about?'

'Now, just let's sit down and talk about this quietly,' Les said, bent on restoring calm. 'Steve, none of us believe it. You know that! You're like one of our own.'

'Will someone please explain?' Nina begged. She sat on the arm of the settee and put her arm around Margie. 'Please don't cry, Margie. Tell me what's happened.'

It was Steve who answered her.

'I've got to go before the Classification Board,' he said.

'I don't understand—'

'Nor do I,' he said. 'But someone at work has come up with a fantastic story. They say my natural father was a Malay, and the man I knew as my father just took pity on my mother when she was several months pregnant and married her just to make an honest woman of her.'

Nina looked at him, frowning.

'Is it true, Steve?' she asked quietly.

'Of course it's not true!' Margie could barely control her indignation. 'How can you ask that, Nina?'

Steve looked back at Nina, tightening his grip on Margie's hand but ignoring her outburst. He licked his lips as if they had gone suddenly dry.

'I don't know,' he said huskily. 'I honestly don't know, Nina. What I do know is that I was born only five months after my parents married. I worked that out when I was quite young. I thought it was a bit of a joke, actually, with my dad being such a pillar of the Church and seeming as old as the hills. He . . . he was certainly a lot older than my mom, even if she did die before him. They always seemed an unlikely kind of couple. Still, I was brought up as Edna and Michael Dwyer's son and as far as I know it was never questioned. Now both of them are gone and there's not a soul who knows the truth.'

'But who is it that's accused you? And what's the proof?'

Steve shrugged his shoulders.

'It can only be hearsay. An old rumour, maybe.'

'It's someone at work who's been passed over for promotion,' Margie said. 'It's jealousy – that's all it is. All it can be.'

'Is that possible, Steve?' Nina asked.

He shrugged his shoulders again with an air of hopelessness.

'Anything's possible. I know there are people who resent the way I've been put over them.'

'Man, you've lived all your life as white,' Colin said, joining in for the first time. 'No board is going to say that you're Coloured. That's the law.'

'I look pretty dark,' Steve pointed out. 'I've often been teased about it.'

'No darker than the average Spaniard. Believe me, they haven't a leg to stand on. You've nothing to worry about.'

'I think Colin's right,' Nina said.

Hennie, who had been sitting in uncharacteristic silence, her eyes going from one speaker to another, leapt to her feet.

'Oh, how can we help worrying?' she demanded. 'You must see what this means for Margie? What will happen to her and the baby—?'

'Look, man, why not get some coffee?' Les said soothingly. 'We could all do with a cup. We must try to keep calm. Tell me,' he said to Steve as Hennie reluctantly left the room, 'do you know who accused you?'

'I've got a damned good idea.'

'Does he say he has proof?'

'She,' Steve said bitterly. 'It's a she. The wife of an old chap who's done nothing but stir up trouble from the minute I got my promotion. He's been dropping hints for weeks that his mother-in-law once lived next to my mother and knew some secret about her past life. I took no notice. I just thought he meant that she had to get married. God knows, that was disgrace enough in those days.'

'Steve, listen,' Colin said persuasively. 'The Population Registration Act of 1950 states, quite definitely, that if you've always been accepted as white, and if your appearance and speech and education and demeanour are white, then you are to be regarded as white, no matter if you do have Coloured blood. I know this for certain, but even so I think you need some kind of legal representation. When's the Classification Board?'

'It hasn't been fixed yet.'

'Well, whenever it is, I don't think you have any cause to worry. If the accusation comes from who you think, then it'll be clear to the board it's only brought through spite and jealousy. They're used to those sorts of cases. They're not unreasonable.'

'*What?*' Nina lifted her head sharply and glared at him. 'Not unreasonable? You mean that it's perfectly OK to look at a man – any man – and say he's not fit to mix with whites, or marry the girl he loves? Is that what you're saying?'

'Nina, you know it's not!'

Her shoulders sagged as her anger dwindled into misery.

'What a world,' she whispered at last. 'What a world, when being Coloured's a crime.'

'That's what I feel,' Steve said. 'What the hell does it matter? Maybe the old woman's right and I am half-Malay. So what?'

'Don't even say that, Steve,' Margie implored him. 'You're white. I know you are.'

'Would it make you feel any different about me?'

For a split second, Margie hesitated.

'Of course it wouldn't,' Nina said, answering on her behalf. 'No girl worth her salt would feel any different.'

'Well, what's been decided?' Hennie asked, bustling in with the tray of coffee. 'What are we going to do about this wicked thing?'

'I've advised Steve to get a good lawyer,' Colin told her. 'But I honestly think he'll sail through this.'

'What about collecting signatures of everyone who'll say that they have always regarded him as white?' Nina asked. 'Just as a kind of back-up. How do you feel about that, Steve? Neighbours, school friends, people at work. There must be hundreds. And your boss, who appointed you to this job in the first place? And this wretched woman who's supposed to know the truth? Maybe she's acted like this before – made other accusations with equally small foundation. You never know. People do. Maybe we can discredit her – prove she's an unreliable witness.'

Had she learned all that from Jan, Colin wondered? But what a girl! What a wonderful, marvellous girl to have on your side.

'And even if I'm completely wrong and all that fails,' he said, 'you can always take it to the Appeal Court. Don't give up hope, Steve.'

Steve sighed heavily.

'It's made my mind up about one thing,' he said. 'When all this is over, we're getting out, Margie and me. Emigrating to Canada.'

Hennie stared at him in horror.

'Oh no, Steve! There'll be no need, once you're cleared. You can't go so far away. Tell him, Les.'

But Les, though he looked anxious, refused to say anything of the kind.

'Who can blame them?' he asked heavily. 'Who can blame them, Hennie? Sometimes I think there's no future here for any of us.'

The trip to Sussex on Saturday morning necessitated a fairly early start if they were to have a respectable amount of time with Tom's mother, and Kate came downstairs well before eight. Even so, Jan was in the kitchen before her.

'Verwoerd arrives for the Prime Ministers' Conference today,' he said, looking up from the paper.

'So he does,' Kate said. 'I'd forgotten. Would you rather be at Heathrow demonstrating than coming with us?'

Jan put the paper aside.

'Just as long as someone does,' he said.

'You might meet other activists there. You might even see this chap you went out with, the night you spent at the hotel.'

Jan thought this over.

'I suppose I might,' he said. 'But the main purpose of this trip was to see you. And I'd hate to upset Tom by ducking out of meeting his mother. Anyway,' he went on, picking up the paper again, 'there's another demonstration tomorrow, outside the Dorchester. Maybe I could go to that.'

Kate thought this over as she made preparations for breakfast.

'Maybe we both could,' she said.

Beatrice Newcott greeted them all with delight, hugging and kissing Tom, Kate and the children, then turning to take both Jan's hands, holding them tightly.

'You are *so* welcome,' she said, giving them a shake to underline her words. 'It must be wonderful for your dear mother to have you here at last. I couldn't be more pleased.'

'It's wonderful for me,' Jan said.

'Come in, come in.'

She tried to usher them inside the house, but the children demanded to go at once to see the pigs and the chickens. A confused few moments ensued as they leapt around excitedly, encouraged by an equally excited pair of cocker spaniels, all needing restraint while Kate produced Wellington boots. At last they were suitably attired and let loose.

'Look after Mark, Vicky,' Kate called after them.

'They'll be all right,' Beatrice said, watching them go. 'George is in the barn. He'll show them the puppies. Goldie's got a new batch, did I tell you? Heaven knows who the father is. Now, come in, do, and have some coffee. I've made some shortbread biscuits, Tom. His favourite,' she added, in an aside to Jan, who was still standing a little awkwardly in the middle of the room, looking bigger than ever in the low-ceilinged room, towering over Beatrice who came no higher than mid-chest level. 'My, you're a big lad, aren't you?'

Beatrice went on, looking up at him. 'Do sit down, dear. Over here, perhaps, would be best. Some of these little chairs are a bit rickety, I'm afraid. *Anno domini*, you know, like the rest of us.'

Kate regarded her mother-in-law with affectionate amusement as she bustled about, a very small ship in full sail, in her element now that she had guests waiting to be fed. The prospect of a visit from her son and his family invariably threw her into a veritable frenzy of baking, for Beatrice tended to measure hospitality by the number of collations she could cram into a day. This meant that the coffee and biscuits produced on their arrival would be followed in no more than two hours by an enormous lunch, hard on the heels of which would come tea, with fruit cake and gingerbread.

There could be no two women more unalike than Beatrice and Lilian, Kate thought, reminded of the past by all that had happened recently. Though she had celebrated her seventieth birthday a few months ago, Beatrice's formidable energy was unflagging, the day never long enough for her to accommodate all her activities. She was president of her local Women's Institute, chairman of a local gardening club, invaluable on the parish council. She baked her own bread, preserved her own vegetables, made jam from her own fruit. Now, dressed in her usual uniform of tweed skirt and lambswool twinset, a single string of pearls hanging a little lop-sidedly over the contours of her shelving bosom, she dispensed the coffee and biscuits while extracting from Tom every last detail regarding Shamley Hithe and generously giving her advice.

'I'm so pleased it's by the river, Tom,' she enthused. 'And with Georgian houses, too. What a wonderful chance to show what you can do! Of course, you must pay particular attention to the heritage angle. The river was London's main artery, you know, so that's an aspect you must play up for all you're worth. D'you know what I was thinking the other night? I was thinking that when it's all finished, you must stage a grand opening, in costume. Don't you agree, Kate? You'd look perfectly sweet dressed as a Gainsborough lady – yes, you would, no need to laugh. Tom, you could go as Pepys. Or perhaps Wren would be more suitable.'

'There's not a brick laid yet, Mother,' Tom said. 'Or a foundation dug.'

'I was just thinking ahead, dear, that's all. Oh, I am so proud of you! I have to admit I was disappointed when you decided not to take over the farm, but there was no dissuading you. There was no dissuading him,' she said to Jan, turning to him to pass the biscuits once more, shaking her white curly head vigorously as she did so. 'No, it was always architecture. And I must say, as the war went on and so much was destroyed by the bombs – not only here, but all over the world – I thought: "Yes. Tom was right all along. It's creating things that's important."'

'Generous of you to admit it,' Tom said, smiling.

'Of course, farming is creative in its own way,' she countered. 'Though I could never persuade you of that. He always had this dream, you see,' she went on, turning to Jan again. 'Even as a little boy. "I want to build things, Mum," he used to say to me; and oh, how he used to cry when his big brother knocked his bricks over or jumped on his sandcastle! Yes you did, Tom! Stand up for yourself, I used to say. Go and jump on *his* sandcastle! But he never would. He just couldn't bear to knock things down. I hope,' she went on, having satisfied herself that no one was without something to eat, 'that you're not going to use any of that nasty concrete that everyone seems to be going in for these days. I passed a new block of flats in Eastbourne the other day when I was going in on the bus, and I thought it looked quite soulless. Give me bricks any day.'

'There'll be some,' Tom admitted. 'Concrete does have advantages, you know. Everyone seems to agree it's the building material of the future.'

'But it hasn't the *warmth* of brick, Tom. You can't ever persuade me that it has the warmth of brick. Don't you agree, Kate? It simply hasn't the *warmth*.'

'I'm inclined to agree,' Kate said, 'but I suppose we mustn't be too conservative. The experts say—'

'Experts!' Beatrice's expression showed what she thought of such creatures. 'Saving your presence, Tom, I can't help thinking that these so-called experts are like St Paul's Athenians, always running after some new thing. New isn't always best, you know. There's much to be said for the tried and tested.'

Which thought led her on to the Cartwrights, newcomers to the village, who had bought one of those washing machines where you put the washing in, threw in some powder, and everything came out clean and rinsed.

'Well, I ask you,' she said. 'Why not ironed as well? I didn't think for one minute that it would work, and sure enough, they put it on and went to bed, and when they came down in the morning it had overflowed and they were ankle-deep in water. 'I'm sticking to my twin-tub and electric wringer, thank you very much,' I said to Mrs Cartwright. "That's quite new-fangled enough for me!"'

'No doubt that's what the Victorians said about their dolly-tubs,' Tom said.

Talk of Victorians led, inevitably, to news of ancient relatives unknown even to Kate. Jan, having listened in silence for a long time, refused a second biscuit in the face of a great deal of pressure from Beatrice and said that he thought he would go and join the children. He'd like to see the farm, he said.

Beatrice beamed with approval.

'What a nice young man,' she said, after he had gone. 'Isn't he a nice young man, Tom? Such good manners! You must be in your seventh heaven, Kate. And so *tall*! Is that from your side or from his father's? I know you never talked about him, but even so, it's my guess he was never forgotten. You can't, can you? Forget, I mean. I know I never forgot my little Maurice, though he only lived a few days, poor little soul. You keep thinking, what would they be like now? You know, you were wrong, Tom. I thought so then, and I think so now. You should never have stopped Kate going to get him when the war was over.'

Tom, sitting silent, found himself wishing that his mother had a sandcastle he could jump on. Jan, too.

'Tom didn't stop me,' Kate protested, reaching out to put her hand on his arm. 'It wasn't like that, was it Tom? We both thought we were acting for the best.'

'Well—' Beatrice stood up, collected plates and cups. 'It's all water under the bridge now.' She picked up the tray and bustled towards the kitchen. 'All's well that ends well.'

She left silence behind her. Kate knew she should follow her out to see if she could help, but for the moment she was more concerned about Tom's feelings.

'She's right,' Tom said, before she could speak, the words bursting out as if he had wanted to say them for a long time. 'You should have gone. I didn't realise. I mean, I hadn't had children of my own and had no real idea of what you were going through. I thought I did, but I didn't.'

'In the end it was my decision. You know that.' Kate spoke softly and persuasively, leaning towards him, gripping his arm more tightly. 'You know what Sonia wrote: that he was happy and doing well at school – a thoroughly well-adjusted boy who regarded her and Christiaan as his parents. He couldn't remember me, had never shown the slightest interest in me. I thought of what it was like at Gramerci – all that sunshine, and the wide open spaces, and this wonderful school they'd sent him to. He was going into the business, Sonia said. How could I compete with that? I thought I would only upset him.'

'Even so—'

'Well, it was wrong. I know that now, seeing Jan and hearing what he says about Sonia. But I believed her; and I loved you and I wanted to marry you. It seemed to make sense to put all that behind me and make a new life.' She gave his arm a shake. 'And it worked, didn't it? We've had a great life. We've been happy.'

'You put all your savings into the firm.'

'It was my choice. You didn't make me.'

'I thought,' Beatrice said, coming back into the room, 'that we'd have lunch about one, then afterwards we could, perhaps, walk into the village so that I could show you the new kneelers in the church. The WI made them, and they're really very beautiful. We have some wonderful needlewomen here, you know. I don't think there's anything they couldn't do, if they put their minds to it.' She warmed to the theme. 'You remember I told you about Mrs Perkins, Kate? Well, her quilting has been on exhibition in London. Which reminds me, I must show you the smocking I've been doing for a dress for Vicky—'

Kate experienced the feeling of being caught up in some all-enveloping tidal wave that was her normal reaction to Beatrice, tempered, as always, with real affection. You couldn't help liking her. On the other hand, there were times when her insensitivity made you feel like committing murder. One such occasion was when, having dealt with the subject of needlework, she returned once again to Tom's past mistakes.

'You should have gone, dear,' Beatrice said, picking up her knitting to fill in a few idle moments before she began seeing to lunch. 'Tom shouldn't have prevented it.'

'He didn't prevent me,' Kate said, barely able to hide her irritation at this second attack. 'He wouldn't have wanted to, or been able to, if I'd been determined.' She got to her feet. 'I think perhaps I'll go and have a breath of air, too.'

'That's right, dear.' Beatrice beamed at her, unabashed. 'You can borrow my wellies. They're in the porch.'

Tom made no move to accompany her. Fair enough, she thought. Beatrice would like to have him on her own for a bit – just so long as she didn't keep harping on about past mistakes. There was no point in it. Tom felt bad enough as it was, and as for herself – well, what about herself? She realised, suddenly, that between the pair of them she was beginning to feel that maybe, after all, she had some reason for feeling just the smallest bit resentful. For a moment she leaned on a gate, looking at the view and considering the question; then, impatient with herself and with Tom and his mother, too, she went on her way. She was being brainwashed, she decided.

Tom would never have prevented her going – she'd been right about that. On the other hand, he'd made his own feelings plain enough. It had seemed, at the time, a clear choice between the past and the future, and undoubtedly it was his attitude that had made it seem so. She had, she saw now, been manipulated. So maybe he was right to feel guilty.

Oh, forget it, she told herself as she came across Jan and the children in the barn, gazing delightedly at the tiny, blind puppies and their proud mother. All, as Beatrice had said in her somewhat less than original way, had ended well.

It was much later, as they were having tea just before leaving, that another awkward moment occurred. Beatrice turned to Jan, begging him to tell her all about South Africa.

'I'm very interested,' she assured him. 'I have a friend – you remember Elsie Parker, don't you Tom? She lived in one of those houses near the church for years and years, until her husband died, and then she went out to Durban to live with her daughter. Lovely girl. Blonde. Married a schoolteacher with a beard and glasses. Yes, you *do* remember them, Tom – you must do. Elsie and I still write to each other – she's a very good letter-writer – so although I've never been near the place, I feel I know it quite well. It sounds wonderful.'

Jan smiled.

'You'd hardly expect me to disagree with that,' he said.

'Of course,' she went on, in tones of amused disdain, 'you read a lot of nonsense in the papers about the blacks being oppressed. Elsie says that the foreign press likes to sensationalise everything, and I'm not to believe the half of it. We only get the bad news. The blacks are perfectly happy, she says. Her daughter has a little maid who sings all day! And it's wonderful the way the government is clearing the slums and moving all the blacks out to estates with brand-new houses to live in. You hear all these stories of unrest, but apparently it's not true at all, not a word of it! Do you know that every year thousands of blacks go there from other parts of Africa? Well, that tells its own story, doesn't it? Things aren't nearly so bad as we're led to believe.'

'They go to work in the mines,' Jan said. 'It's a matter of economic necessity for them.'

'But they go. That's the main thing. Elsie says that there would be no trouble at all between black and white if it weren't for the Communist sympathisers who seem to get some perverse pleasure in whipping up resentment.'

'I think you'd find,' Jan said, 'that not all sympathisers are Communists, though the government likes to dismiss them as such.' He was still polite, but all warmth had been withdrawn. Kate had never seen that look of scarcely disguised severity on his face before and it gave her a shock. She saw, dimly, that he might possibly be a formidable enemy if he set his mind to it. Beatrice, however, appeared to notice nothing.

'Well, I suppose you always get troublemakers, don't you?' she went on. 'Elsie says the police are wonderful.'

'Mother,' said Tom. 'Have you thought about when you could come for a weekend to look after the children? I told you we hoped to get away—'

'Elsie says,' Beatrice went on, ignoring her son's attempts to change the subject, 'that the police were quite right to handle Sharpeville the way they did. To say it was a massacre is simply ridiculous. They had no choice, she said. They had to act quickly and firmly to put down the revolt.'

'Of course there was a choice.' Jan's tone was cutting. 'It was meant to be a peaceful protest of the voteless, voiceless majority, forced by the government into the indignity of carrying passes. You can surely see—'

He seemed, suddenly, to become aware that he was not in court, or engaged in debate with a politician, and cut himself off short. Helplessly he raised his hands and let them fall again. 'I'm sorry,' he said after a moment. 'I don't want to argue with you, but it hurts when I hear the situation misrepresented so greatly. Believe me, there's much misery in South Africa, despite what your friend says – though I don't doubt that she sees nothing of it. That's the trouble. Whites live in one world, blacks and Coloureds and Indians in quite another.'

Beatrice was unwilling to leave it at that, and had gone pink with indignation.

'Elsie is not the sort of person to pass by on the other side when she sees wrongs that need righting,' she said. 'We used to do Meals on Wheels together, and she was instrumental in getting the roofs repaired on the old alms-houses. And far from living in another world, she says that people in South Africa are very good to their servants. They look after them very well and treat them kindly—'

'But they still can't vote, can they?' Jan asked, plainly clinging on to politeness only with the greatest difficulty. 'Their children can't be educated in decent schools, alongside white children. A paternalistic society is all very well, but what they want is freedom.'

Tom entered the fray.

'The people of Ghana aren't benefiting much from their freedom, are they? I gather that Nkrumah's government is as corrupt as hell. You can hardly blame the South African government from seeing it as a poor example of black rule.'

'It needn't be like that. You're not comparing like with like. No one's expecting South Africa to have black rule overnight, but one day it will come, one way or another, and I put it to you – what will serve the white community best? Partnership with an educated, sophisticated black majority, or the chaos imposed by an ill-educated, discontented underclass, united by their common grievances into exacting revenge?'

'That may be so,' Tom said, 'but it does seem rich that a country like Ghana is threatening to leave the Commonwealth if South Africa doesn't change its laws.'

'You don't think there should be changes?'

'I hate to break this up,' Kate said mendaciously, 'but I think we really ought to go. Don't you, Tom? It's been a lovely day, Beatrice, but I know Tom wants to get through all these country lanes before it's dark.'

'That's true,' Tom said, getting to his feet.

For a moment Beatrice stacked cups and saucers, her mouth still pinched. Clearly, Kate thought, she was busy revising her earlier opinion of Jan, whom she probably now regarded as an out-and-out troublemaker, if not one of those Communist agitators despised by Elsie Parker. Then, as if inspired, Mark begged to be allowed to go and see the puppies one more time, and Beatrice relaxed.

'Not now, my lamb. Daddy doesn't want to you get all muddy again just before you get into the car, does he? About the weekend,' she added, looking at Kate. 'I'll come any time you want me. Or why not let the children come to stay for a while in their Easter holidays? You'd like that, wouldn't you, Marky, love?'

'Yeah – yeah—' Both children leapt around, answering as one, while, excited by the noise, the spaniels leapt too, endangering a small coffee table and several plates of cakes. 'Can we, Mum, can we?'

'I don't see why not,' Kate agreed; and the awkward moment over, it was with renewed good feeling and many expressions of gratitude that they finally put on their coats and made their way to the car.

It was a long and tedious drive, made worse by the fact that Tom inexplicably missed a turning and found himself heading for Croydon, much to Kate's exasperation.

'For heaven's sake, Tom. How did we get here?'

'God knows!' Tom sounded mournfully fatalistic. 'The point is, how do we get out of it? I can't turn round here.'

'Pull up a minute, Tom. Let's look at the map—'

'I haven't got it. I took it out, if you remember, to look up Lyndhurst when I thought we might be going there.'

'Oh, Tom!' Kate's voice was weary. It had, she felt, been a trying day. The children were tired. *She* was tired. And heaven alone knew what Jan was thinking. On the outward journey he had kept the children amused with jokes and riddles and guessing games, but he hadn't said a word on this leg. She hoped he hadn't overdone things. It was hard to remember, sometimes, that he had been ill so recently.

'Maybe if we take this turn to the left we can get back to where we ought to be,' she suggested.

'Better to go right into Croydon and start from there.'

But Croydon, it seemed, was being dug up in its entirety and there were so many diversions that they merely became more confused, and Kate more tight-lipped, than before.

The light rain which had begun just as they left the farm had become much heavier and Tom leaned forward to peer through the windscreen.

'Maybe you should see about getting new glasses,' Kate said, a little waspishly. 'I'm sure we should have taken that turn to the left. There was a sign saying "Epsom".'

'We don't want to go anywhere near bloody Epsom.' Tom was tired, too, and his voice was sharp. 'If you can't be any more helpful than that—'

'We need the A24.'

'I *know* we need the bloody A24, but Epsom's too far south.'

'I didn't say we wanted Epsom. I thought if we went that way we'd get on to the A24, that's all.'

'Just shut up, Kate, will you? I'm taking this turning.'

'Well, don't blame me—'

'*Shut up!*'

Kate, astonished, shut up; and in the ensuing silence there was a thin, despairing wail from the back seat.

'You're quarrelling!' At Vicky's cry, Kate turned round to see the wide, anguished eyes of both her children accusing her from the back seat.

'No,' she said, guiltily. 'No, really, we're not. We're just tired, and it's very hard for Daddy driving in all this rain. Take no notice.'

'Daddy swore,' Vicky pointed out.

'Only a little bit. Daddies are allowed to sometimes, if they're sorely pressed. But look – we're on the right road now, so it won't happen again.'

'Want to bet?' Tom asked, under his breath.

'Well, don't quarrel,' Vicky ordered.

Kate reached over to the back seat and patted her knee.

'We weren't,' she said. 'Not really, anyway.'

But they had been, she admitted to herself. And not about wrong turnings, either. She stared out of the window into the rain-soaked darkness and was aware of danger lurking.

The children were asleep by the time they arrived home, and hardly woke as, in a joint effort, Tom and Kate undressed them and put them to bed.

'I think, if you don't mind, I'll turn in myself,' Tom said, when they had finished. 'I've got a splitting headache.'

Kate immediately was all concern, for he was seldom ill and always made light of it even when he was.

'Oh, darling, I'm sorry,' she said. 'It must have been that ghastly drive. I'm sorry I niggled. That can't have helped.'

'I expect I deserved it.'

'I'll bring you some aspirins,' she said, as he started towards the bedroom. 'Would you like a cup of tea?'

'That'd be nice.' He turned and looked at her. They hadn't switched on the main upstairs light for fear of waking the children, and his face was in shadow so that it was impossible to see his expression. 'Nothing to eat, though. I've had enough to last me a week.'

'I don't suppose I'll be very long coming up myself.'

'Don't hurry on my account.'

He did sound tired, Kate thought; and sad? Maybe not. It was probably just tiredness. She hoped so, anyway.

'You were a bit hard on Beatrice,' Kate said.

Jan had lit the fire in the sitting room while she was making tea, and they were sitting facing each other, one on either side of it. Kate had taken up Tom's tea and brought the tray in for them, and was feeling much better now that she'd drunk a restorative cup and had her feet on her own fender.

'Well—' Defensively, Jan eased his shoulders. 'Those kinds of people get my goat. They get a superficial account from some empty-headed friend, and suddenly they're experts.'

'She's old, Jan. She won't change now, and there's no point in getting mad about it. Her mind is closed on the matter. I should have warned you.'

'Well, I'm sorry if I upset her. I know I should have been more tactful. I have to admit I've heard a great deal worse than that rubbish she was spouting.'

'Her heart's in the right place.'

'I know. So many of them are. It's just that they fail to see what's under their noses. I've come across it so often in the likes of Beatrice's friend. Elsie, was it? Kind people, good people, charitable people – yet still totally myopic when it comes to government policies. I suppose you can't wonder at it. I mean, life is so comfortable for them, so pleasant in every way. The only blacks they encounter are those who work in their homes. I dare say Beatrice is right, and Elsie's daughter's little maid does sing all the time. She's in work, she probably has comfortable quarters. Maybe a boyfriend. Who's to say she's the kind of girl who asks for anything more? The trouble lies with all those who have nothing and who resent not having a voice, and having to carry a pass, and having to put up with sub-standard education, not allowed to use this facility or sit on this seat in the park or use that counter at the post office or swim from this particular beach. And if they do any of those things, or a thousand others, they're harried by the police and generally treated as less than human.'

Where did he learn this attitude, Kate wondered? He'd been nurtured by those who believed implicitly in white supremacy, yet, unbelievably, he had emerged from it all with just the beliefs she would have chosen for him, even if he did express them with all the arrogance of youth.

'What's going to happen, Jan?' she said at last. 'How long can they go on like this? Will it all end in chaos and bloodshed?'

Jan sighed.

'I hope not,' he said. 'It needn't. There's a lot of goodwill on all sides, really. There are thousands of whites, Brits and Afrikaans, who aren't at all happy with the way things are. It's just this bloody government that plays on people's fears and prejudices.'

'I suppose one day someone inspirational could emerge—'

'Yes!' He brought his clenched fist down on the arm of the chair in emphasis and his eyes blazed, alight suddenly with joyful certainty. 'I feel it so strongly. Feel it in the marrow of my bones.' He gave a self-conscious laugh. 'I actually wrote to Nina while I was on the plane, telling her I'd had some kind of inspirational vision that all would be well; and I did feel that, you know. As we took off, I looked down on the land and felt as if I was experiencing a glimpse of a paradisiacal future when all men would be brothers.' He laughed again. 'God knows what she thought of it. I expect she thought I'd been hitting the in-flight drinks trolley.'

'She'll be glad you wrote, anyway.'

'Yes,' Jan said. 'Yes, I expect she will. I hope she'll write back, one of these days.'

'She's sure to. You're good friends, you said.'

Jan flashed a smile, teasing her.

'My dear Mother – could you be fishing?'

'Never let it be said! I gather she shares your ideas.'

'Absolutely.'

'And you've known her a long time?'

'Since varsity.'

'And she's pretty?'

'As a picture.'

Upstairs, Tom could hear their low voices and their laughter, and felt ashamed of his emotions. Was he jealous? Was that why, all those years ago, he had encouraged her to stay in England and forget the past, even though that past had held her own child?

Restlessly he tossed and turned. This self-analysis wasn't like him. Jealousy wasn't like him, either, or the kind of petty irritation that he felt at Jan's constant presence in the house. It wasn't, he told himself, that he didn't like him. Admittedly, he was untidy and a bit noisy, and there was all that bloody sport, but he was a nice enough chap, amusing, popular with the children, anxious not to be too much trouble. It was hardly his fault that Kate fussed around him like a mother hen, protecting him from over-exertion, watching him to see that the children didn't take advantage of his good nature. She did her best to protect him from boredom, too. He'd caught the warning glance she'd cast at him the other night when she considered he'd been going on at too great a length about lightweight aggregates and the neglible risk of corrosion in reinforced concrete, just as if Jan hadn't asked questions on the subject. But of course, he was only being polite in showing an interest. You had to hand it to him – he had good manners. Usually.

It was more that he filled the house, as if he had this great aura around him, taking up space even when he was in another room. There seemed, these days, no room for anything or anyone else.

No room for me, Tom thought fretfully, recognising his childishness even as he did so and feeling ashamed of it. Jan wouldn't be there for ever. Praise the Lord, he'd said something about going up north somewhere to see some friends for a few days next week. Maybe he and Kate could catch up on things then. He could take her over to Shamley Hithe, show her the layout. He could wait until then with a good grace. He owed her that much.

And there was the guilt again; but what else was he to feel, when here she was, looking younger and happier every day, looking somehow different, and talking of different things that he had no way of sharing? He could hear them now, the voices rumbling, erupting now and again in laughter.

'Shall we really go to the Dorchester tomorrow?' Kate was, at that moment, asking Jan. 'I think we should, if Tom feels better and doesn't mind looking after the children on his own. I don't suppose he will. The weather forecast said it was going to be fine, so they could go to the Heath. We could go up by Tube. Unless—' She hesitated, and Jan looked at her enquiringly.

'Unless what?'

'Unless you'd rather go on your own. It might be a chance for you to meet other like-minded people. You could be invited to go on somewhere. I don't want to muscle in.'

'Don't talk such nonsense! You're not muscling in. I'd like you to be there.'

She felt he had handed her a present, but did her best to curb her smile of pleasure for risk of seeming to have blown his casual remark out of all proportion.

'Thanks. In that case I'd like to come. I'll see what Tom has to say about it.'

Tom, when asked the following day, raised no objection, and even offered to drive them to King's Cross so that they could catch a train direct to Hyde Park Corner. He had woken up feeling ashamed of his negative emotions of the night before, determined to do all he could to make the rest of Jan's stay happy. It couldn't, after all, last for ever.

17

Walking from Hyde Park Corner to the Dorchester, Kate began to feel a sense of rising excitement which had less to do with the demonstration than the fact that she was with Jan in this joint venture. There was a light-hearted air about it all, despite their serious objective. It felt, she had to admit, like a day out, an escape from routine.

There was, she saw, quite a crowd outside the hotel, most of whom had marched up Oxford Street and down Park Lane with anti-*apartheid* banners waving. Everyone seemed reasonably good-humoured, even the policemen who were in attendance. She recognised a few public figures among their number; Barbara Castle, the veteran campaigner; Fenner Brockway, always vocal on the subject of rights for the underdog. There was a scattering, too, of famous actors and actresses whom she recognised, and others who looked as if they ought to be famous whom she did not. Standing outside the hotel, she fell into conversation with a young woman beside her whom she knew at once by her accent as South African, born and bred.

'Yes, I've lived in Pietermaritzburg all my life, except for this last year,' she said, when Kate made conversational overtures.

'Are you going back?' Kate asked. The young woman – hardly more than a girl – shrugged her shoulders.

'Maybe. I don't know. My parents don't really want me to. My father's under house arrest.'

Kate looked at her in horror.

'That's terrible! What can he have done to deserve that?'

The girl laughed.

'Very little. You don't need to do much. He's a writer and lecturer, and he insists on writing and lecturing about things they don't agree with. And meeting people he shouldn't meet.'

'But—' Kate continued to stare at her, frowning. 'How does it affect him? It must be dreadful—'

'Oh, it is. My father's banned from writing anything, or having more than two people visit the house, or going out to any public place. We know the place is bugged. And you know something? He never hurt a fly in his whole damn life! All he ever campaigned for was justice and brotherly love.'

'It's no wonder he wants you to stay here.'

'Yeah.' She sighed. 'But South Africa's my country too, you know. I feel a bit of an alien here. Still, I do what I can.'

Kate jerked her head, indicating the crowd, the banners.

'Will all this do any good?'

She laughed at that.

'Of course not! It'll show our feelings, that's all. Security's too tight to do more than wave banners when Verwoerd emerges.' Her smiled died and her expression tightened. 'More's the pity,' she added savagely.

'But surely you're not in favour—?'

'Of violence?' The girl gave a bitter laugh. 'No, I suppose not. My dad would kill me. On the other hand, we're running out of choices. For almost eighty years, blacks and Coloureds have used peaceful means to get their voices heard. Their patience has been phenomenal. They've argued and persuaded, but where has it got them?'

'Nowhere,' Kate admitted. 'Even so—'

'Look,' the woman said, her attention caught by a sleek black limousine drawing up at the kerb. 'There's a High Commission car. Verwoerd must be coming out soon – they say he's going to Chequers for lunch. I don't know if that's right. I've heard Macmillan can't stand him – but anyway, it looks as if he's going somewhere. See those two men who've just come out, on each side of the entrance? They're South African security police, attached to the High Commission. I've come across them before.'

Seeing the signs that something was about to happen, the crowd grew noisier and the banners were raised higher. Kate looked around for Jan, who had wandered away somewhere to the rear to check the hangers-on for possible acquaintances of his own. She had lost sight of him for a moment, but now she heard his voice in her ear.

'Could we just ease away, very quietly?' he said softly.

He had turned with his back to the rest of the crowd, she saw, and looked as if he was doing his best to look smaller and less conspicuous. With a brief farewell to the girl, she took his arm and, skirting the side of the crowd, they walked swiftly away.

'What is it, Jan?' she asked.

'Did you see those goons beside the door?'

'They're security police—'

'I know! And that one on the right in the suede jacket is the chap who came to my hotel room. I knew him as soon as I saw him.'

Kate risked a look behind her, but the small crowd concealed a clear view of the doorway and she was unable to see the man in question.

'Jan – you're sure?'

'Absolutely.'

'He didn't see you?'

'I don't think so. I caught sight of him before he'd taken up his position, just as he was coming out of the door. And shall I tell you something?' he went on as the distance between them and the hotel increased rapidly. His voice was full of suppressed excitement.

'What?'

'Seeing that guy has brought everything back.' At a safe distance now, he turned and hugged her exuberantly. 'Everything! I'm better. I can remember it all.'

'Really? Everything?' Kate could hardly believe it. 'Oh, Jan, that's wonderful!'

She returned the hug joyfully, and for a second, oblivious to any danger, they clung together, laughing. Jan sobered almost immediately, however, and, releasing her, said quietly: 'You realise what this means, don't you? It's not such good news, actually.' He tucked her arm through his and resumed walking, a little slower now.

'Because he's a policeman? Jan, you are sure of this?'

'I told you – it's all come back to me. I can remember the whole sequence of events quite clearly now. He phoned up to the room, just like the girl said. I'd only just got out of the bath. He said that I wouldn't know him, but that his name was . . . what was it?' He screwed his face up in thought. 'Du Toit, that was it. Alec du Toit. His girlfriend was a friend of Nina's, he said, and Nina had told her I was coming to London. He'd phoned his girl the previous day and she'd passed on the news. God knows why I didn't smell a rat then. Nina never talks about me to anyone. He said he tried my original hotel first and they directed him to the Burgundy.'

'But you said they didn't—'

'I know! No one at the first place knew where I'd gone, but like an idiot, I accepted his explanation. I can't tell you how friendly and plausible he was. Someone had overheard me telling the taxi driver to go to Collins Square, he said, so he tried all the hotels in the area and finally hit on the right one. God alone knows why I was so gullible. I never would have been in South Africa, but I suppose being here, in London, I thought I was out of harm's way. My guess is that he probably had me under surveillance all the time. I didn't question him. I suppose the truth is that I was so glad to get his call, I didn't think straight. I know it sounds crazy, but it was a bit of a low point for me. Had I done right to come? Would you want to see me after so long? Somehow I didn't feel sure of anything any more, and hearing a South African voice again, particularly one asking me to go to a party, was very welcome.'

'So you went.'

'I went. It was a party being given by some Zulu friends, he said, where I'd be bound to meet some kindred spirits, so I said, 'Yes, great, love to.' What else do you say when people invite you to a party? He had a car parked just up the road. A Vauxhall Velox, I think it was. Whitish, not new, but not very old, either. We drove right through London, along the river, past the Tower. It seemed a long way, but we were chatting – you know how it is. He pointed out a few landmarks, said he worked in insurance and he'd been in London for six months, but otherwise he talked about . . . well, things I wouldn't have expected him to know about unless he was part of the anti-*apartheid* movement. Now I know he knew about them from the other side. The police side.'

'So what happened?'

Jan pulled her to a halt, and looked around.

'I don't know about you,' he said, 'but I could use a drink. Let's find a pub.'

They turned off Park Lane, found a hotel and settled for that, taking their drinks to a remote corner of the dimly lit and largely deserted cocktail bar.

'So what happened then?' Kate asked again.

Jan sipped his beer slowly, thinking back.

'We drove for what seemed a long way, and I began to worry

about whether he was going to be equally willing to drive me back. I asked him about it, actually, and he told me not to worry. It wouldn't be a problem, he said. I suppose that was his idea of a joke!'

'And you still weren't suspicious?'

'No. He was so bloody convincing. Obviously these Zulu friends weren't going to be living at the Ritz, and when we turned into a network of dismal-looking streets I still wasn't suspicious. It was only when he turned down between some buildings that looked like disused warehouses that I began to get worried. It all looked so grim and derelict. I could see that the windows were broken, and there were bits of plastic hanging on railings. We were close to the river. It was dark, of course, but you could see it gleaming, and there it was, right in front of us as we passed the warehouses and came out on to a bit of waste land.'

'Surely you wondered—'

'Yes, I did by that time. There weren't any houses around – just this pot-holed, litter-strewn bit of land, surrounded by ruined buildings on three sides and the river on the other.'

He drank again, clearly upset by his memories.

'You don't have to tell it all at once,' Kate said gently.

'Yes, I do. I want to. I knew something was wrong by that time. I asked him where the hell he was going, and in the middle of this bit of ground he stopped the car and turned round and said, 'Get out. This is the end of the line,' or words to that effect, and before I knew what was happening, the door was wrenched open on my side by some heavies who'd materialised from nowhere. There were three of them, I think. They pulled me out, and the first guy – this du Toit man – drove off like a bat out of hell as if his part in the proceedings was over. I started throwing punches, but then something hit me and I didn't know a thing until I woke up in hospital, nine days later. Strange, that is; existing, but not knowing a thing about it.'

'Thank God they didn't throw you in the river.'

'Baker seems to think they certainly would have done if the police car hadn't arrived at the crucial moment. He told me at the nick the other day that one goon had hold of my arms and one my legs – but the third guy shouted a warning and they dropped me and fled. 'Melted away,' was the way Baker put it. And I can imagine it, too – those old warehouses must have provided pretty good cover for melting away in.'

Kate shuddered.

'It doesn't bear thinking about. But that chap who took you there – he was taking a risk, wasn't he?'

'He can't have thought so. I wasn't supposed to be in any fit condition afterwards to tell anyone about it, was I?'

'We must tell Baker what you've remembered.'

'Yes.' Jan was looking down, fidgeting with the beer mat on the table. 'You get the unwelcome implications, though, don't you? Whoever beat me up and stuck that knife in me did so at the instigation of the South African High Commission. Or at least, that particular member of it. He looked up and met her eyes. 'In other words, some government official has to be involved.'

'Who?' Kate asked, after a moment. 'Not Christiaan—'

'No, no.' Jan rejected this completely. 'I can't believe that. It has to be someone in the police, I think. There are plenty of them who hate my guts.'

'Why?'

'Why?' he echoed. 'Because they take people to court and I get them off, among other things. You can take your pick of a dozen reasons – added to which I'm told I have an abrasive manner.' He grinned at her. 'And I'm arrogant. That's what Nina says, and she's usually right. But why should anyone move against me now? I'm out of their hair for the moment, so why go to these lengths?' He answered his own question. 'I suppose it was the perfect final solution. One troublemaker, removed for good, without any suspicion falling on anyone back home. On the other hand, I've never heard of such a thing happening before. Why me? If they were bent on keeping me quiet, they could have banned me, put me under house arrest—'

That reminded Kate of the girl in the crowd she had spoken to, and she told Jan about her. He looked interested.

'Sounds like the Van Meren daughter,' he said. 'Old Thinus Van Meren is a great character – either a saint or the Devil incarnate, depending on which side you belong. I go for sainthood.'

'I wanted to introduce you, but you'd nipped off somewhere. Did you see anyone else you knew?'

'Not a soul.'

He said no more, apparently lost in thought, miles away from her and from London.

'Jan,' she said softly, seeing that he was more shaken by this officially sanctioned violence than he wanted to admit. 'Do you have to go back? Can't you stay here?'

He put his glass down on the table, and looked at her with an expression of total astonishment.

'Stay?' he said. 'Of course I can't stay! I've got work to do.' Seeing her expression, he relaxed a little and smiled at her. 'Look, I know you think I'll be in danger there, but London hasn't exactly proved a safe haven, has it?'

'No,' she said, after a moment. 'Perhaps not.' She was silent for a moment, then looked up at him, smiling at her thoughts.

'You know,' she went on, 'I can understand how you feel about Cape Town. I really loved it when I was there. I used to drive back to Constantia along De Waal Drive, thinking I'd never seen a more exciting place. I wonder if I'll ever see it again.'

'Well, why don't you?' he asked. 'You could come back with me, just for a holiday.'

Kate laughed, dismissing the suggestion.

'On my own, you mean? Without Tom, or the children? Don't be daft! How could I?'

Jan smiled at her.

'Beatrice would have the kids,' he said. 'Didn't she say so? Why don't you think about it.'

All Christiaan's optimism had gone. He knew colleagues were talking behind his back once more, just as they had done immediately after Sonia's death, the only difference being that now he was supposed to be sufficiently recovered from his bereavement to be back to normal, at least where work was concerned.

He now saw that the half-baked plot cooked up by Eksberg had been a monumental mistake and instead of ridding himself of one problem, he had now added another even more frightening – the nightmare of being accused of attempted murder. No wonder that he was drinking too much, that he was incapable of concentration or of delivering the kind of speech for which he was justly famous. Had he lost his touch? Lost that famous political nous he had shown all his life?

Why hadn't he made more effort to throw himself on Jan's mercy? It might have worked. The boy was hot-headed and misguided, that was true, and one could understand, in a way, his anger that the same man who preached racial purity could once

have had an affair with a Coloured girl. Even so, he might well
have been persuaded to keep his mouth shut.

The fact was that the decision to rid himself of Jan for ever was
made when he wasn't himself; he'd been upset, recently bereaved,
grieving—

No, he couldn't play the grieving card. Not to himself. Grieving
was for his wider public. Any admiration or fascination he had felt
for Sonia had vanished a long time ago and her death was no excuse
for anything. It was the thought of the loss of his political career that
had sent him, momentarily, over the edge.

And with that journalist's remark about Eksberg, the day of
the interview, he was back there once more, thrown again into a
mindless panic. If Eksberg had been shooting his mouth off like
that, heaven alone knew what the morons in England had been up
to. None of them could be trusted.

He'd sent for Eksberg without delay and told him just what he
thought of him. He had considered withholding the money he had
promised – after all, the man had achieved nothing. Jan had kept
quiet so far, but who could tell how long that would last? There
was no doubt that the entire operation had been botched from the
beginning. On second thoughts, however, bearing in mind that he
was still dependent on Eksberg's discretion, he had paid him the
five thousand rand in addition to the two that was to be handed
over to Van Niekirk, cursing the day he'd ever met him.

But instead of being grateful and going on his way, Eksberg had
the nerve to ask that he should be put up for membership of the
Broederbond. He even went so far as to say that a promise had been
made, though Christiaan could remember nothing of the kind.

'I'm afraid,' Christiaan had told him coldly, 'you'll have to be
a little more efficient to merit an honour like that. You've had all
I'm prepared to give you.'

Sitting in his study at midnight after a busy day, tired, but knowing that his mind was too restless for sleep, Christiaan despairingly
surveyed the mess he had made of his life. An unsatisfactory
marriage, no child of his own, his political ambitions doomed—

At least Jan was alive. He surprised himself by feeling relieved
about that, and almost immediately was aware of a feeling of pride
in his own magnanimity. He wasn't, after all, such a bad chap.

Newspaper reports also said that Jan was recuperating in his
mother's home, of all things. This puzzled him. How could Jan

have known where to find her? He supposed it was through those relations in Oxfordshire, since he knew for a fact he had never received any of her letters or her new address. It was diverting to wonder how they were getting on. Kate would be . . . how old? Forty-four, forty-five? Maybe more. He'd lost count. She'd been a pretty little thing, too self-effacing for her own good, of course. It was no good being self-effacing in any dealings with Sonia. And full of ridiculous liberal ideas, now he came to think of it. She would probably get on well with Jan.

The telephone interrupted his thoughts. He picked it up.

'Le Roux,' he said. For a moment he could hear nothing but atmospherics. An overseas call. The thought that this surely was the British police made his stomach churn with renewed panic and he could hardly speak.

'Hallo? Hallo?' Desperately he tried to get his voice under control.

'Mr le Roux? Good evening. Can you hear me?'

'Who is that?'

'I must speak to Mr le Roux.' The voice was faint and distorted.

'Speaking,' shouted Christiaan. 'This is le Roux. Who is that?'

'Van Niekirk, calling from London.'

Christiaan spluttered with outrage.

'How dare you call me like this—'

'I thought you'd like to hear the news.' Van Niekirk's voice came in waves, as if being wafted by the ocean. 'About the unfortunate attack on your nephew. The investigation's been called off.'

'What? What?'

Christiaan could hardly make sense of it after all his fears.

'Lack of evidence. They'll never find out who did it now. Too bad, isn't it?'

Christiaan cleared his throat.

'How . . . how do you know? Are you absolutely sure?'

'Absolutely. I talked to the man in charge. They're not taking it any further. They've closed the book.'

For a moment Christiaan said nothing, the airwaves between them whooshing and crackling.

'Well,' he said shakily. 'Thank you. Thank you for letting me know.'

He put the phone down and sat for a moment with his eyes closed, unable to move. Thank God, he whispered. Thank God.

He reached for the brandy at last. He'd had two stiff drinks earlier in the evening and had been resisting the temptation to pour himself another, determined that he would go to bed sober for once, but now he poured himself a generous tot, his hand trembling.

It was over. He was not under suspicion after all. Was it possible? He could hardly believe that this particular cloud had lifted.

The other remained, of course, but confidence and optimism were flooding back even as he sat there, sipping his drink. When Jan came back, he'd make friendly overtures. Profess contrition. Offer a donation to one of the good causes Jan patronised so assiduously. They'd had worse rows than this in the past, and always managed to get over them. And after all, what had he been guilty of, when all was said and done? A young man's indiscretion, that's all it had been. Jan would surely understand. And it wasn't as if he hadn't paid for his mistake. The girl, after all, had been given a generous settlement and had made no complaint, then or later.

He threw back his head and laughed with relief. It was over. Everything was going to be all right. Lucky le Roux, someone had once called him, and by God, whoever it was wasn't far wrong. Someone up there was looking after him.

Undoubtedly it called for another drink.

Jan duly reported the recovery of his memory to Sergeant Baker, who invited him to come to the station to make a full statement. He did so, and was informed that he'd been most helpful. Nevertheless, he heard no more on the subject.

Both he and Kate read every comment printed in the papers about the Commonwealth Prime Ministers' Conference, now in session in London. South Africa was getting a rough ride from the other states, and it seemed more than likely that she would be asked to change her laws or leave the Commonwealth.

'Maybe Verwoerd will see sense,' Kate said. Jan shook his head.

'He won't,' he said. 'He'll stick to his guns and take us out before he's thrown out. Mark my words. He'll see any suggested reform as the first steps towards total integration and he'll fight it tooth and nail. It'll be interesting to see what Ben has to say about it.'

Ben was his Birmingham friend. Jan had come to England armed with his address and telephone number but had lost it in the attack. Having resorted to Directory Enquiries he had found it again and had now made arrangements to visit him. He refused to let Kate take him to the station. He'd go on the Tube, he said. He was quite recovered now. He'd ring and let Kate know when he was coming back.

The house seemed unnaturally quiet when he had gone. Tom, clearly, felt nothing but relief, though he refrained from commenting on it; the children, however, bewailed Jan's departure and demanded to know when he was coming back.

'Soon,' Kate promised. 'He's only gone for a few days.' She caught Tom's eye and grinned, knowing how he felt, understanding it. Tom had laughed, too, and it had been a good moment, proving that normal life would return. And indeed, for the first couple of days, she had to admit that she, too, enjoyed the peace.

It was after that she grew restless, and began to look forward to his return. Verwoerd had, as Jan had predicted, announced that South Africa was leaving the Commonwealth and had returned home to Johannesburg to a hero's welcome. Not so, she read, in Cape Town, where there were fewer Afrikaners. She longed to talk the whole thing over with Jan. He made her feel alive and involved; not a has-been, which was the effect those women outside the school had on her. Not just the housewife and mother, sunk in domesticity, that she had become.

She had lunch with Elaine one day and told her of Jan's suggestion that she should go back to South Africa with him, just for a holiday.

'I think you probably should,' Elaine said. 'If it can be managed. What would Tom say? And what about the children?'

'The children break up for Easter in a couple of weeks' time. They could to go Beatrice. And Tom has a trip to Stockholm planned. It's only for a few days, but he's terribly busy. He might welcome some peace and quiet.'

'Have you talked to him about it?'

'No,' Kate confessed. 'No, I haven't. I've been ducking it.'

Elaine finished her salad, laid down her knife and fork and sat back, looking at her thoughtfully.

'I think you should go,' she said again. 'I always thought you should.'

Kate groaned.

'Don't you start! Tom's mother went on and on at the poor man, as if it was all his fault. And it really wasn't.'

'I'm not blaming Tom. Well, not altogether. I merely think it would do you a lot of good to see it all again and face the past. Face your ghosts.'

'Jan says he'd like me to go. He's mentioned it several times. I just feel that maybe I ought not—'

'That's what you said the last time,' said Elaine.

She wouldn't mention the matter to Tom until Jan came back, Kate thought. He might have changed his plans, having seen his friend; maybe opted to stay in England longer, or something. As it was, he'd phoned to say he'd be home in a couple of days, so it wasn't very long to wait.

A letter arrived for him the following day, Nina's name and address on the back of it leaving no doubt who had written it. For a moment Kate studied it. The writing was neat, cursive; a pretty hand. Did that upward tilt to the last letters of each word indicate optimism, or determination? She had no idea; and suddenly feeling intrusive and rather ashamed of herself, she put the letter on the mantelpiece.

'It's today Jan's due back, isn't it?' Tom asked at breakfast the next day. 'How – er – how long do you think he intends to stay after that?'

'For ever and ever and ever and ever,' Vicky said, before Kate could say a word.

'Hardly,' Kate said, smiling at her. 'He has work to do in South Africa.'

Was now a good time to let Tom know she was thinking about going too? she wondered. She saw Tom looking at her.

'What's up?' he asked.

'Nothing. Well, I do want to talk to you some time.'

'I think,' Tom said dryly, 'that with Jan coming back this afternoon, we've probably missed the boat.'

Jan came back with a holdall full of dirty washing, looking full of vigour and apparent pleasure at being back in Cumbernauld Avenue. The children flung themselves at him and demanded to know what he'd been doing, and he was sitting at the kitchen table drinking tea and eating toast before Kate remembered the letter. She went to get it for him, but he put it on one side while he finished his tea, only opening it when Vicky and Mark went into the sitting room to watch children's television.

Tactfully, Kate took herself off with them, and ten minutes or so elapsed before he put his head round the door. His expression was sombre.

'Kate,' he said. 'Could I have a word?'

The news from Cape Town wasn't too good, he told her when she joined him in the kitchen. Nina's sister's husband had been called before the Race Classification Board. Someone had denounced him as Coloured.

'It's someone with a grudge,' he said. 'The government's laid itself open to this kind of thing with these daft laws. I don't really think he's in any danger, but Nina's obviously worried about it. You can't blame her. If he's declared Coloured, then his marriage will be invalid and he'll lose his job and his home – and what will happen to Margie and the baby is anyone's guess.'

Kate was staring at him, barely comprehending.

'But is he Coloured?'

'No one's ever thought so before.'

'Does he look Coloured?'

'Well, he's darkish. Kind of swarthy. Nothing remarkable. A nice chap.' Jan looked down at the letter he held in his hand and skimmed through it once more, frowning. 'Nina seems to have things in hand. She's recruited an old friend to help her – a journalist. Still, I'd like to be there.'

'Well, you would, of course. When, Jan?'

'The board's on the twentieth. If I went earlier I might be able to help a bit.'

'You said he's in no danger.'

'I don't think he is, but you never know. It's as well to be prepared.' He sighed and shook his head. 'What a bloody country,' he said bitterly. 'God, it makes me sick! Just a bit of paper, just letters on a document. W for white and C for Coloured. Change a W for a C, and there you are – your life ruined, a second-class citizen for the rest of your life.'

Kate looked at him for a moment as he stopped pacing and once more read through the letter.

'Jan,' she said hesitantly. 'Jan, does this mean I'd be in the way if I came too?'

He looked up in surprise. 'No, of course not. Have you decided?'

Kate took a deep breath, conscious of the hurdles she felt quite sure she would have to surmount.

'I think I have,' she said.

There were no hurdles.

Jan removed himself to his room that evening to write a reply to Nina's letter, thus giving Kate an opportunity to raise the subject of her proposed trip to South Africa.

'Darling,' she began tentatively, 'you know perfectly well, don't you, that I've never, ever blamed you for the fact that I didn't go back to Cape Town after the war—'

'But you want to go back now,' said Tom.

She stared at him, astonished.

'How did you know?'

Tom grinned.

'Intuition? Or is that a woman's prerogative?'

'Well, what do you think?'

He looked at her, serious now.

'I think you should go,' he said. 'The Easter holidays are almost upon us. Mum would have the children for two weeks, and I've got this Stockholm trip. It seems a good time.'

'Oh, Tom, that's what I thought. You really don't mind?'

'I don't think I have the right. Do you? I stopped you going before—'

'Oh, Tom, *please*! Stop agonising.'

'I intend to,' Tom said. 'From this day forward, I declare an end to agonising. It's an extraordinarily wearing kind of occupation. I shall shed ten years when my conscience is clear.'

Kate laughed, and kissed him.

'I'll go and phone Beatrice,' she said.

It occurred to her as she went out to the hall that, if true, this was a pretty easy way to shrive oneself of fifteen years' guilt and feel ten years younger into the bargain, but she dismissed this thought as unworthy.

A break will do us both good, she thought.

Arrangements were made, flights booked.

'You will come back, won't you?' Vicky asked. She was excited at the thought of two whole weeks on the farm, but still needed reassurance on this point. Kate hugged her.

'Yes, of course. As if I wouldn't!'

'And Jan will come back,' Mark stated firmly.

'Well, one day.' Kate had put him straight on this point more than once and now had the distinct impression that he was harping on about it merely to annoy. 'I told you, Mark. Cape Town is Jan's home. I'm just going for a holiday, just like he came on holiday here, but he's going to stay.'

'Why can't we go?'

'Because it costs a lot of money, and because you're going to stay with Granny. You'll have a lovely time. Those little puppies will have their eyes open now.'

'Can we have one? Mum, can we have one?'

'I don't know. Maybe. You'll have to ask Daddy – look, Vicky, take Mark away and play with him, there's a good girl. I've got so much to do.'

There were summer clothes to find, skirts to shorten. Why, Kate demanded, did hems go up and down so much? And yes – in answer to Tom's query – yes it *did* matter! She looked an absolute freak in most of last year's clothes. Everything was shorter this year.

There were the children's things to go through, and the store cupboard to be stocked for Tom's use. Mrs Bishop had consented to do extra hours—

'Though heaven knows why she needs to,' Kate said. 'Without the children, the house should stay like a new pin. Still, she'll do your washing and ironing, and even cook a bit if you ask her.'

'I'll be fine,' Tom said, without a great deal of enthusiasm. 'Don't worry about me.'

Kate sighed at this response with its faint echo of martyrdom; but then, she thought, her moods went up and down a bit and Tom could hardly be blamed if his did the same. There was, undoubtedly, excitement at the thought of seeing South Africa again; of feeling the sun, warm on her winter skin, and glorying in the incomparable scenery. But as the time of departure came ever nearer she could not avoid a certain amount of anxiety over the wisdom of raking up the past.

Elaine, of course, said that she was doing the right thing; that she'd suppressed too much and wouldn't be free of the burden of all that had happened until she had faced it and put it behind her once and for all. It was a theory to which Tom, now, paid lip service, even though he had dismissed it out of hand in the past.

She felt far from certain, though, that he was wholly convinced. It had seemed, these last few days, as if he had withdrawn from her, become remote, only going through the motions of being an understanding, co-operative husband. It was as if politeness had taken over from the loving harmony they had always enjoyed; politeness with an edge of doubt.

Well, she thought, perhaps she should be thankful for that and accept his apparent co-operation at its face value. Not all husbands would have even pretended to understand, let alone agreed to the trip so readily.

'She's coming back, Dad,' Vicky assured him at the airport, seeing his mournful expression.

Tom said nothing, but smiled bravely – almost as if he knew better, Kate thought, seeing his expression. What sort of nonsense was this? She was a little irritated by it, and their leave-taking, overtly loving, seemed somehow to lack any real feeling.

She said nothing about missing him or wishing he could come too – mainly because it wouldn't have been true. She wanted this time to face the past with Jan and felt she needed a break from everything else, a period to put everything into perspective.

Jan bade the children an affectionate goodbye; had promised to write, promised to send them pictures of lions and elephants and every other animal to be found in Africa. He shook Tom's hand and thanked him profusely. He had given him a giant-size bottle of malt whisky as a parting present, as well as a case of wine. Kate only hoped that he wouldn't find it necessary to drown his sorrows too liberally in her absence.

Jan looked happy to be going home, in spite of the fact that, for all any of them knew, he could be going into danger. He had phoned DS Baker a day or two before leaving, to let him know of his departure. The case had come to a dead end, Baker had said. The intruder they'd found in the hospital was no more than a petty thief who'd offended before and no doubt would again.

Kate had looked surprised when this was reported to her.

'They've stopped looking? Really? I thought Baker was anxious to catch those thugs.'

'Well, he says there are no leads to go on—'

'But you gave them a lead. You told them about that security man we saw at the Dorchester.'

'Yes.' Jan crossed the room and sat down without speaking. 'Yes, I did. I asked him what happened about that.'

'And?'

'Oh, he says I must have been mistaken. The chap I saw at the Dorchester wasn't called Alec du Toit at all. His name's Van Niekirk, and he has a cast-iron alibi for the night in question.' He was silent for a moment or two. 'And, d'you know,' he added, 'I don't believe a word of it. You know what I think? I think Baker came to the conclusion the whole thing had political overtones and he was better off not knowing. There was something in his voice – something guarded, something less friendly than before. My guess is that he and this du Toit-Van Niekirk man got together over a drink or two, just a couple of coppers together, and Van Niekirk told him I was trouble, the entire government of South Africa wanted my guts for garters, and that I probably deserved all I got.'

Kate had been shocked.

'Oh, I can't believe—'

'Well, I can.' Jan gave a breath of laughter. 'I'll bet any money it happened that way. Forget it, Kate. It doesn't matter. I dare say he's right.'

Now, walking across the tarmac towards the plane, Jan turned round and gave an airy wave.

'Goodbye, London,' he said. 'On the whole, you've been great.'

'Really?' Kate, remembering all the bad things, looked at him quizzically. 'Was it really all worth it?'

Jan grinned down at her.

'You bet,' he said.

18

When Christiaan le Roux came back from spending a few days in his constituency, he found that Colin Vos had been trying to get in touch with him.

'Too bad,' Christiaan told his secretary. Marie Potgeiter, efficient as any secretary could be and well into her forties, was nevertheless susceptible where nice young men were concerned and had rather taken to Colin.

'But Mr le Roux,' she protested. 'He's the journalist who wrote that lovely article about you in the—'

'I know perfectly well who Colin Vos is,' snapped le Roux, who had long since stopped being charming to Miss Potgeiter. 'I have no wish to speak to him. And what's this?' He consulted the list on his desk. 'Helen Suzman? I don't want to speak to that little troublemaker, either. What does she want this time?'

'I don't know, Mr le Roux. Some problem with a constituent, I think.'

'Tell her I can't spare the time.'

'Yes, Mr le Roux.'

Miss Potgeiter turned to leave the office, Christiaan eyeing her back view with disaste. She'd do for now, he thought, but when he was Prime Minister he would choose someone else. Someone young and bright and pretty. Someone who lifted the spirits.

What could Colin Vos want with him? Full of renewed confidence, he'd enjoyed himself in Wachsfontein; been fêted and dined, had kissed babies and flirted with their mothers in a decorous kind of way. His speeches had gone down well, too, and all in all he had come back feeling on top of the world. Now, hearing that Colin Vos wanted to see him again, some of the euphoria of the past few days ebbed away. What more could they have to say to each other? Surely they'd covered every conceivable angle in the interview?

It had resulted in a pretty good write-up, he had to admit; far
less abrasive than he had expected, though admittedly editorial
constraints might have accounted for that. George Porter, the
Courier's editor, was not one who would want to offend powerful
politicians.

Even so, Vos had managed to get in a few digs, a few remarks
that could be taken two ways. Reading it a second time, Christiaan
detected a satirical note which had not come as a total surprise.
All through the interview he'd had the impression that Vos had
been putting on an act; all politeness on the outside, disparagement
within. And then, right at the end, he'd mentioned Eksberg.

Maybe he should see Vos after all. It might keep him sweet –
keep him on side. For a moment he sat deep in thought, tapping
his teeth with his silver pencil.

Then he threw the pencil on the desk. He'd been right the first
time. He wanted no more to do with the man.

'He won't see me,' Colin reported to Nina on the phone. The schools
had broken up for their Easter vacation, and she was back in Cape
Town at her parents' house.

'It wouldn't do any good, anyway,' Nina said. 'He never inter-
venes in cases like this. It's been tried before.'

'It wasn't only about Steve that I wanted to see him,' Colin
said. 'I'm working on a theory that it was le Roux and Eksberg
together who organised the assault on Jan through some contact
in London. I was hoping to get some idea if it was feasible.
Oh, it may be nothing – I suppose it seems a bit far-fetched,
but I have this hunch that something of the sort was going on.
I wish I could talk to Jan. See how much he knows about what
happened.'

'Well, you'll have your chance,' Nina said. 'He's coming home.
Arriving the day after tomorrow. Sunday.'

'Oh,' Colin said, after a moment's silence. He hadn't expected
his wish to be answered quite so soon. Feeling, however, that this
reaction was somewhat inadequate, he added: 'That's good.'

'I'm meeting him at the airport, with his car, and then going up
to the cottage. You could join us there.'

'I don't want to be an unwelcome third—'

She had shown signs of impatience at that.

'Oh, Colin, don't be silly! We'll need to talk. Anyway, you won't be an unwelcome third, or any kind of third, come to that! He's bringing his mother with him. Isn't that incredible?'

'Incredible,' Colin agreed, trying to inject some enthusiasm into his voice. 'Has Steve heard anything more? You sound so much happier!'

'No. Nothing. I'm getting a huge list of signatures, though, so I'm really optimistic. Have you found anything out about the woman who's accused him?'

'Only that she's a miserable old bat who loves to think the worst of everyone. I can't get any evidence that she's done this kind of thing before.'

'The race laws are tailor-made for someone like that,' Nina said. 'The sheer stupidity of them makes me want to weep.'

Nevertheless, she sounded buoyant. Colin didn't pursue the reason for such high spirits. There really was no need. She clearly felt that everything was going to be fine, now that Superman was flying to the rescue.

They'd had to change planes in Johannesburg. The flight from Heathrow had been smooth and uneventful, but was less so on the Johannesburg to Cape Town leg of the journey. Never having flown before, Kate was nervous, not knowing if these bumps and lurches were perfectly normal or if they heralded an immediate plummet to the earth below. Other passengers, including Jan, appeared unconcerned, however, so she did her best to relax, and when they began to lose height she was so excited by the sight of Cape Town and its surroundings coming closer by the minute that nervousness was forgotten altogether.

The warmth when they left the plane was like a welcoming embrace, and she stood for a moment on the tarmac and lifted her face to the sky in homage.

'Home,' Jan said, doing likewise.

Kate smiled, rather surprised to find that it seemed strangely like home to her, too.

Nina was there to meet them, and Kate took to her on sight. She liked her looks and her smile and her unstudied friendliness.

'It's wonderful that you could come, Mrs Newcott,' she said as they walked to the car.

'Oh, Kate, please. Yes, I think it's wonderful, too. I still can't quite believe it.'

'Do sit in front with Jan, so you can see everything.'

Echoes of the past! But such altered echoes, Kate thought, as she took her front seat.

Much had changed since that first journey. There were new roads, more buildings, more traffic. But other features were timeless and just as she remembered; the warmth of the air, the quality of the light. And the mountain – oh, the mountain! She felt a rush of emotion. Ridiculous, really. For much of the time she hadn't been happy here, yet somehow, now she was back, it felt as if happiness had been there all the time, just out of reach.

'Will Rosie be at the house?' she asked Nina, turning round to speak to her.

'No, not today. I phoned her a few days ago and asked her to make sure it was clean and aired and the beds were made up, and she did that yesterday. She said she'd report for work tomorrow.'

'I'm dying to see her,' Kate said.

'She's excited about seeing you, too.'

'I've brought her a present – a cardigan in a sort of cherry red. She liked bright colours.'

'She still does,' said Jan.

Jan's house was on the southern slopes of Table Mountain. Once they had left the suburbs of Cape Town behind, the road turned upwards, snaking through trees.

'Oaks,' Kate said. 'Just like the ones at Gramerci.'

'Well, I trust you're not expecting a similar kind of house,' Jan said. 'It's just a cottage, really. A *pied à terre* – somewhere to sleep and park the car. You have been warned.'

'The view is gorgeous,' Nina said. 'But better at night, really, when you can see all the lights of the town.'

She sounded almost proprietorial, Kate thought, looking for clues that might help her understand this relationship.

There were other, imposing properties in the neighbourhood. Glimpses of houses, green lawns, tended flowerbeds, could be seen through the trees as they climbed upwards. But Jan's cottage, she found as they drew up outside, was a simple, low stone building with a thatched roof, a stoep running the length of it, the garden little more than a tangle of flowering shrubs gone wild.

'It could be worse,' Jan said, as if he felt an explanation was called for. 'Walter cuts the grass from time to time. Rosie's husband,' he added, for Kate's benefit.

But Kate was smiling.

'Look – plumbago,' she said. 'And hibiscus. And, oh – smell the jasmine! It's *lovely*, Jan.'

From the stoep, she could see Devil's Peak, and the long line of the mountain; and the same view, she found, could be seen from her bedroom.

'I'm afraid it's a bit spartan,' Nina said, looking a little anxiously at the bare room, furnished with nothing more than a bed, a wooden chair, and a chest of drawers with a mirror over it. 'There's a built-in cupboard in the corner. You'll need hangers – I'm willing to bet there aren't any! Don't worry – I'll find some. And I feel quite sure there must be a rug I can filch from somewhere else. Jan just doesn't notice such things.'

'Don't worry. It's fine,' Kate said, reassuringly; but, a little amused, she thought of the Burgundy Hotel and wondered if there was a side to Jan's nature that even Nina hadn't suspected.

'I'm really glad to meet you,' she said. 'I want to meet all Jan's friends.'

Nina looked amused.

'That would be a bit difficult,' she said. 'He has so many. Sometimes I think—'

'What?' Kate asked, when she hesitated.

'Well – too many, I was going to say, but maybe no one can have too many friends.'

Kate considered the question.

'I don't know. You can spread yourself too thinly, maybe.'

'Oh, Jan never stints himself.'

A hint there, Kate wondered? A suggestion that in being so generous with himself and his time he might neglect those nearer home? It was possible.

Nina had bought provisions for them, and the makings of a cold lunch which was to be shared with this journalist she had spoken about – Colin somebody. Jan had greeted the news of his imminent arrival with a distinct lack of enthusiasm, but Nina had said he was as much involved in Steve's campaign as any of them and wanted to help, at which Jan said no more.

They were sitting on the stoep in canvas chairs having cooling drinks when he drove up. There seemed to Kate something a little guarded in the way he greeted Jan, though on the surface all was friendly enough. He smiled very nicely when he was introduced to her; a pleasant, polite young man, she thought. What was his relationship to Nina? A family friend, maybe. But when Jan disappeared to bring Colin a can of beer from the fridge she happened to catch sight of his expression as he looked across at Nina, and all doubts were immediately dispelled.

He loves her, she thought, with a slight sinking of the heart; and from the odd clues he's given, so does Jan, even if he doesn't know it. Someone was bound to be hurt, sooner or later. It was a depressing thought – but one, she told herself firmly, that did not concern her. The mother-hen role was one she refused to play; though with all the partisanship of motherhood, it seemed hard to believe that this pleasant but modest young man could rival her son in physical attraction.

Jan's first act, on arriving home, had been to change from the clothes he had worn in England to shorts, open-necked shirt, and flip-flops, the lack of formality merely succeeding in increasing the impact of his physical presence, undimmed by his spell in hospital. It seemed hard to imagine that this vigorous man could ever have lain unconscious and immobile in a hospital bed. Kate had always thought him a fine specimen, even before she knew for certain that he was her son; now, in his home setting, in the kind of clothes in which clearly he was most at ease, he looked magnificent; glowing with vitality and several times larger than life. Guy would have been so proud of him, she thought. Whether he would have been proud of Guy was quite another question.

Jan listened to all they had done to strengthen Steve's case, and agreed with them that on the face of it he had a strong one.

'But I agree with Nina,' he said. 'There's nothing to be gained by trying to involve Christiaan. He never interferes.'

'But maybe if you asked him—' ventured Kate.

Jan laughed at that.

'Me? I'm the last one to have any influence with him. The last time we met I called him every name under the sun.'

'Well, I knew there wasn't any love lost—'

'How could there be? I hate everything he stands for.'

'You don't think,' Colin said, speaking hesitantly after a short silence, 'that le Roux might be the man behind the attack on you in London?'

'No, no, not at all—' Jan waved this aside.

'He was looking for you, just before you left. He used a cop called Eksberg to try to find you.'

'Really?' Jan frowned, thinking this over. Then he shook his head. 'No, I can't believe he'd do a thing like that. As I said to Kate, there are plenty of others who'd like to see the back of me. Are you sure this cop wasn't just using Christiaan's name as an excuse for making enquiries?'

Colin shrugged.

'It's possible, I suppose. But I mentioned it to le Roux and just for a moment he looked terrified. I swear I didn't imagine it.'

'You did have an awful row with him, Jan,' Nina reminded him.

'Hardly! A row involves two people, whereas I simply told him what I thought of him, and he just stood there gaping like a fish out of water.' He turned to Colin. 'Did Nina tell you why? Well,' he went on, as Colin nodded, 'I admit I was upset, and I probably upset him, but it hardly seems enough for him to put a contract out on me. My opinion is that some members of the police cooked the whole thing up between them, possibly unofficially. What do you know about this Eksberg man?'

'Not much,' Colin said. 'What I do know, I don't like. Even by police standards, he's very right-wing, it seems. A ruthless bastard was how he was described to me by another policeman. And another thing – he's also said to be strapped for cash. He has an expensive wife, I'm told.'

'You mean he might have been open to offers?'

'It seems possible.'

'What about a chap called Van Niekirk? Have you come across him? He's big and burly, with a round head. Fair hair, going grey. He'd be a policeman too, I imagine, seconded to the High Commission in London.'

Colin shook his head.

'Can't say I have – but that doesn't mean much. He could have served anywhere in the country. I could make enquiries in Pretoria.'

'Why Pretoria?'

'That's where Eksberg comes from, and where he worked before he was posted down here. It might possibly be that they were friends, or worked together.'

'Well, that could link Eksberg and Van Niekirk, but I'd still take a lot of convincing that Christiaan was involved. You're on the wrong track there, man.'

The atmosphere between the two young men seemed to have thawed a little, Kate thought, but at this point she seemed to detect exasperation on Colin's part.

Nina rose to get lunch; cold chicken and salad. Jan went with her, Colin looking sombre as he watched them depart from the stoep.

'I think he's dismissing le Roux too lightly,' he said.

'Do you? Do you really think he's involved?'

'He and Eksberg were in cahoots about something, I'm pretty sure of that. And I'm fairly sure it was something to do with Jan. I told you, I saw le Roux's expression when I mentioned that Eksberg had been asking questions. Still, Jan seems to know better . . .'

He thinks Jan is big-headed, Kate thought. And possibly pig-headed, too. Even Jan himself admitted to arrogance; was this an example of it? But then she thought of Christiaan playing with Jan on the lawn of Gramerci and she shook her head.

'It's awfully hard to believe he could mean Jan any real harm,' she said. 'He was always so fond of him.'

Colin continued to look sceptical, but said no more.

Over lunch, the conversation turned to less controversial matters, and soon after it was finished Colin announced that he had to leave. He was driving out to see his parents, he said. It was his mother's birthday.

'Did you buy her that picture we saw?' Nina asked him.

'Yes, I did.'

'Oh, good! She'll love it, I'm sure.'

Jan stood up and began stacking the dirty plates on a tray, affecting not to hear this exchange. He abandoned this to go to the top of the steps to bid Colin goodbye, but stayed behind when Nina went down and across the grass to where he had parked the car where, for a while, she and Colin indulged in a few moments' private conversation.

'Far be it from me to intrude upon the sweet sadness of parting,' Jan said acidly to Kate. She had taken over his task of clearing the table and gave him a brief, amused glance as she did so. He picked up the laden tray and, as their eyes met, he grinned at her, a little shame-facedly. 'Well,' he said, 'Nina deserves better things.'

'What did she say to you, back there in the kitchen?'

He laughed as he headed for the kitchen. It seemed the only answer she was likely to get.

The reunion with Rosie took place the following morning – shyly, on Rosie's part, but with shining eyes and every evidence of goodwill. She had grown into a sweet-faced woman, not as large as her mother had been, but plump and matronly.

'I do my best by our boy,' she said earnestly to Kate. 'He a good, good boy.'

'I know. He's told me. He thinks the world of you, and I'm so grateful.'

The cardigan Kate had brought for her was received with delight, and a bunch of roses given in return.

'My Wally, he a great gardener,' she said. 'He tend the garden at Gramerci for years, till we both feel it time to move on. Now he work at Kirstenbosch, and I do a little work around.'

'You had a big family, Jan tells me.'

'Five children, three grandchildren. They all think the world of our boy.' She was tying an apron around her as she spoke. 'Now I must get on, madam. Sorry there is no comfort here!'

Kate laughed.

'I wouldn't say that! I slept very well.'

'Our boy need a good wife. Miss Nina, she the one.'

'Maybe you're right,' Kate agreed. 'But I don't think our wishes enter into it, do you?'

Jan had left for town early. He had a tiny office somewhere in Woodstock, he told Kate, and needed to check on how a number of things had gone in his absence, as well as going to see Steve, who had waited for his return before seeking any legal representation.

Kate didn't mind. Nina had offered her services as a chauffeur and was coming to collect her at ten thirty to take her into town.

'To see the changes time hath wrought,' Nina said. 'Though actually I imagine it's much the same as when you knew it.'

Not long before she was due to arrive, the telephone rang. Kate answered it.

'Oh—' Apparently her voice was causing a little hesitancy at the other end of the line. 'May I speak to Jan, please?'

'I'm afraid he's not here just now. Can I take a message?'

Another hesitant moment elapsed.

'Just say that his uncle called—'

'Christiaan? Is that you? This is Kate.'

'Kate? Kate Lampard?' One would think from the delighted surprise in Christiaan's voice that they were the best of friends. 'My dear, how amazing! You've come back after all this time.'

'Only for a holiday. Jan and I arrived yesterday.'

'And he's dashed off and left you already? That's too bad!'

'No, no. Not at all. He has work to do, and I'm perfectly happy. A friend is coming soon to take me into town.'

'Revisiting your old haunts.'

'Yes. It's a strange feeling. Christiaan, I was so sorry to hear about Sonia. You must be lost without her.'

'Indeed I am.' His voice throbbed with feeling. 'But life goes on.'

'And you're keeping well?'

'Fine, thank you. Yourself?'

'Oh, very well.' Kate hesitated a moment. 'Christiaan, I don't want to be a nuisance, but this seems a good opportunity to ask if you'd mind if I came to see Gramerci again. Just to walk round the garden. There would be no need to bother anyone.'

'My dear, of course you must come! Come to tea, or drinks, or something. Jan must bring you.'

'Well, thank you. That's very kind – but as for Jan bringing me, he's really awfully busy catching up after his time away. I can't answer for him.'

'Let me see—' Christiaan sounded as if he were consulting a calender. 'I appear to be free on Wednesday afternoon. No caucus meeting or anything, as far as I can see. Why don't I send a car to pick you up and bring you here for tea? Jan can come too, if he's free. Shall we say four o'clock?'

'Four o'clock it is,' Kate agreed. 'But I happen to know Jan has an important engagement on Wednesday afternoon.'

'That's a pity.' Christiaan's regret sounded genuine enough, Kate thought. But then he had always sounded genuine, even when he was lying through his teeth. 'I'm really very anxious to talk to him. Well, some other time,' he went on smoothly. 'In the meantime, I shall look forward to seeing you and having a good old chin-wag about old times.'

Kate smiled wryly to herself as she put the phone down, her imagination immediately supplying several topics of conversation that were better left in oblivion. Then her smile died. Was she crazy to be going back to Gramerci? She was curious to see it again, that was true, but she was undoubtedly frightened of the memories it would awaken. But wasn't facing ghosts what this trip was all about? Elaine would certainly say so.

Nina arrived just then and she dismissed the matter from her mind, eager to see the town again. She found it little changed. The flower ladies still sold their blooms in the shade of the old bank, and Adderley Street was as wide and white as ever, Greenmarket as bustling.

'Stands Stuttaford's where it ever was?' she asked. 'I think I have to go there for coffee, just for old times' sake. Do you mind?'

'I had the same idea myself,' Nina said. 'Anyway, a browse would be nice. For all its charms, Paarl doesn't have much to offer in the fashion line.'

So they browsed and drank coffee, and window-shopped all the way up the street until they reached the Botanical Gardens and the Lion Gateway, and traffic-free Government Avenue where squirrels frisked under the oaks.

'Such a lovely place,' Kate said, looking back the way they had come. 'I always felt it was a crime not to be happy here.'

'And now you are.'

Kate didn't answer immediately. They had sat down on a bench under the trees, all around them Coloured nursemaids with their charges, and the sound of children's laughter.

'Yes,' she said at last. 'Yes, I'm happy – and in this poor, misguided country that almost seems a crime, too. Christiaan le Roux has asked me to tea on Wednesday,' she went on, going off at something of a tangent. 'He wanted Jan to go, as well.'

'Steve's board is on Wednesday,' Nina said.

'I know. I said he wouldn't be able to make it. Afterwards I wondered if I should have mentioned it – asked for his help.'

Nina shook her head.

'There'd have been no point. He wouldn't have done anything.'

'It must be a worrying time for you all.'

'Not so bad now Jan's here,' she said. 'It'll be OK, I'm sure of it.'

'Yes,' Kate said, after a moment. 'He does rather have that effect, doesn't he?'

'I'll bet you anything you care to name that you'll have an

argument with him,' Jan had said on hearing of her date with Christiaan.

She'd laughed at him.

'Nonsense,' she said. 'I shall stay calm at all times and let any political talk wash over me. Actually, he's threatening to talk of old times, which could be much worse.'

'Don't you believe it,' Jan said lazily. 'Nothing in this world is more maddening than hearing Christiaan explaining just why the blacks and Coloureds are so much better off under *apartheid*.'

'I'm going to be nice and not rise to any bait,' Kate assured him. 'It's Gramerci I want to see. What's going to happen to it when Christiaan's gone?'

'It's entailed,' Jan said. 'It'll come to me.'

'Back to the Lampards!'

'Don't know that I'll welcome it. It's a bit too much of a responsibility.'

'You might feel differently by then.'

'Perhaps. It's hardly likely to happen soon.'

'It's strange to think of seeing it again,' Kate said.

The prospect, she found on Wednesday as four o'clock approached, made her inexplicably nervous. Calm down, she told herself. Christiaan was no threat.

She had hoped to hear the result of Steve's board before she left for Gramerci, for it began at two o'clock, but by the time the driver came for her, there had been no word.

She forced herself to relax against the soft cushions of Christiaan's car. Rather to her annoyance, she had spent far too much time wondering what to wear for this occasion. Why it was so important for Christiaan to see her at her best, she hardly knew. Pride, she supposed; not wanting to appear to have done less well for herself than if she had stayed a Lampard – which she was the first to admit was far from laudable. What did his opinion matter anyway? She'd never admired him, never cared what he thought of her.

In the event she had few suitable dresses to choose from, having travelled as light as possible, and was more or less forced to wear a pink linen suit which she had always thought flattering and could foresee being brought out on many more occasions during her stay.

Calm down, she told herself again. Take deep breaths.

She was conscious from time to time of the Coloured chauffeur's eyes in the driving mirror, full of curiosity. It was hardly to be wondered at. He must be speculating who she was. All Christiaan's staff must be concerned about what he would do without Sonia and what would happen to them.

They were approaching Constantia Nek now. How many times have I driven this way, Kate thought, with the trees on each side and the wine country ahead and the blue sky above seen through the lattice-work of the leaves?

They'd soon be passing Helen's house – *there*. But it looked different. Wrought-iron gates instead of the wooden ones, and white gate-posts with some kind of stone creature sitting on the top of each. She experienced no desire to turn in between them. Without Helen there, what would be the point?

They'd reached the fork in the road now. There were vines on each side, the harvest over. And here was the entrance to Gramerci, not changed at all, and the drive with the oak trees meeting overhead. Slowing down, they drove between them. She could feel her heart fluttering. Was it Christiaan that was making her so nervous? Or was it Gramerci itself?

There had been changes, Jan had told her, but at first sight they were not noticeable. All the vineyards had been sold, but the entrance to them and to the new owner's house was in another road, leaving Gramerci looking just as it had always done; and sure enough, there it was, much as she had first seen it, with its white walls gleaming and the flowers surrounding it as bright as ever, the shutters folded back and the two ridgebacks – descendants, surely, of the dogs she had known? – alert and listening as the car approached.

She wasn't eighteen any more, she reminded herself, and this place had no more than historical interest for her. Even so, her throat was dry as they came to a halt, just as if the past threatened her in some way.

She straightened her back and lifted her chin, forcing herself to breathe deeply as the driver came round and opened her door. Stepping out on to the stony drive, she smiled and thanked him. I'm dreaming, she thought. Sleepwalking. On autopilot. It seemed impossible to believe that Guy wasn't somewhere on the estate; that Lilian wasn't in her bijou little cottage across the back courtyard, and Sonia working in her office.

There was only Christiaan, silver-haired now but instantly recognisable, dressed in sage-green linen trousers and a paler shirt, a green and red silk cravat at his throat. He was smiling his old, charming smile, coming down from the stoep with his hand outstretched.

'Kate, my dear!' Had she ever been his dear? She couldn't imagine so. Nevertheless, he repeated it. 'Kate, my dear! What a wonderful surprise! You haven't changed a bit. Welcome back at last.'

What they talked about during those first few minutes she could never remember. The view, probably, and the garden. She was glad to be seated at last, with tea being served on the stoep by a thin, Coloured girl, dour and unsmiling

'Quite a contrast to Evalina,' Kate said when she had gone.

'Ah, Evalina!' Christiaan smiled reminiscently. 'What a character she was – but never quite the same after we heard that Guy had been killed.'

'He was always her boy.'

'As Jan was Rosie's. Rosie stayed on for a long time, but both she and her husband—' He paused, and Kate looked at him questioningly. He shrugged his shoulders. 'Well, it's no secret that Sonia and Rosie had many differences over the years. When Jan grew up and left home she and Walter took themselves off.'

'She still looks after Jan's little house. I met her yesterday.'

'Oh? Then I'm sure you will have heard her reasons for leaving Gramerci.'

'Actually, no. She said nothing about that. We just talked about . . . oh, all kinds of things. Jan. Her family. And Walter – he seems to have found himself a good job at Kirstenbosch. He loves it there, she says, and has had quite a bit of promotion.'

'Really? Risen up through the ranks, eh? He always did push a pretty lawn-mower.'

Kate looked at him, smiling a faint smile, determined to show no sign of the irritation caused by this amused, dismissive patronage. The changes in him were more obvious now that they were at close quarters. There was a blurring of the jaw-line and puffiness under the eyes, and the eyes themselves were not the clear blue she remembered but were faded and bloodshot; more than that, they seemed wary. He smiled readily enough, just as he had always done, but there was no warmth in his eyes.

'Apparently, Walter's very knowledgeable,' she said. 'And Rosie's brother, Bokkie, he's done awfully well. He's a lawyer

– did you know? He was always a studious little boy. I remember him doing his homework in the corner of the kitchen.'

Christiaan's laugh was brief and unpleasant.

'If you call it doing well to whip up unrest among perfectly contented black workers, then he's succeeded beyond anyone's wildest imaginings. You've been away a long time, my dear. Things are not always what they seem, you know.'

'Things have changed, that's true.' She did not enumerate them; he would know that she meant the notices that abounded, directing whites in one direction, blacks in another. Beaches, buses, parks and post offices – nothing was exempt. Separate amenities, they called it, but in no way did that imply that the amenities were equal. 'Changes that include Verwoerd's decision to take South Africa out of the Commonwealth,' she said, forgetting to be non-controversial for a moment.

'My dear Kate, what alternative did he have? It's intolerable that the Afro-Asian block should tell us how to run our country. No self-respecting representative of South Africa would have accepted it. Did you see the pictures in the paper of the hero's welcome Dr Verwoerd received in Johannesburg on Monday? His decision was popular enough here.'

'Among Afrikaners.'

'Well, of course! They have always identified more with this country than the British. It's a known fact. Naturally the British are uneasy about severing the ties that bind, but since we become a republic at the end of this month they will have to resign themselves or get out. That is the stark choice that's in front of them.' He had been speaking coldly, but now, suddenly, he smiled and leant forward to pat her arm. 'But my dear Kate, we haven't met to fight old battles, have we? It is a great pleasure to welcome you to Gramerci after all these years.' He waved his arm, indicating the garden. 'What do you think of it?'

'It looks as lovely as ever.'

'It does, doesn't it? The garden's a constant joy to me – as it was to Sonia, too, particularly after we gave up the vineyards.' Smilingly, he looked out at the lawn and the flowerbeds, savouring the joys of ownership. 'You know,' he went on, glancing at her shyly as if diffident about showing his emotion, 'I regard it as her memorial. Sometimes, in the evening, I sit here or in the candlewood tree, and I look at all the beauty spread out before me, the garden and the valley and the distant hills, and d'you know, Kate, I could swear that she's with me, putting a hand on my shoulder, keeping me company, encouraging me in my endeavours.'

Kate reflected that Sonia must have changed a great deal if this were the case, but naturally made no comment.

'You must miss her,' she said.

'Twenty-two happy years,' Christiaan mused. 'Not forgetting those carefree years before we married. We met one Christmas at the Nelsons' party, you know—'

'Christmas 1934,' said Kate. 'I remember it well.' Oh, the agony of seeing Guy and Greta together, circling the floor like dancers in a dream! She'd left the terrace unable to bear the sight any longer and had fled to the drawing room to see Sonia talking to this handsome stranger. 'Another life,' she said. 'I married again, you know.'

'Happily this time, I hope.'

'Very. Tom's an architect, and we have two children; a boy and a girl.'

He looked at her, his face suddenly bleak.

'I would have loved children,' he said.

'You had Jan.' The words were out before Kate could prevent them. She looked away, reining in her emotions, and was calm when she turned to him again. On the whole she felt she was doing very poorly in the politeness stakes. 'You were good with him,' she said, making amends.

'Only when he was very young. Later . . . well—' He laughed, shrugged his shoulders. 'Your son is a headstrong lad, you know, with one hell of a temper. It's no secret that we didn't get on, after he grew up.'

'Your views are so different,' Kate said, but pacifically, uncontroversially.

It was, undoubtedly, the right thing to say. He poured tea, offered cakes, looking after her needs with a great show of attention, and as he did so he talked with charmingly self-deprecating humour, of himself, his activities and his achievements.

'Coming back like this,' Kate said at last, 'makes me realise what a very complicated society this is. It's quite unique, isn't it? It's no wonder that outsiders fail to understand it.'

'Exactly what I've always said! To hear the comments of the fools in London you might be forgiven for thinking it would take no more than a snap of the fingers to do away with *apartheid*. They are wrong. It would be the end of civilised society here – if not for us, then certainly for our children and grandchildren. In fact, it is not for us but for the future generations that we are determined to stand like walls of granite against dilution of *apartheid*.'

Kate smiled at him.

'You're addressing me like a political meeting!'

'I'm saying nothing I haven't said a thousand times, and will say again. It is, after all, the truth. The world thinks we are considering only our own comfort and convenience, but that is not so. How much easier it would be for us to allow a few small concessions here and there, little by little – say yes, this black man is a good lawyer or that black man is a talented writer, of course they may come and live in Constantia, or take their seats in the House! All of this we could allow, in the hope that their selfish satisfaction in their own advancement would encourage these people to leave us in peace to pursue the kind of life we have always lived here. But don't you see how we would be letting down our children, Kate? The children yet unborn? What kind of a country would they have as their inheritance?'

I have been here before, Kate thought, fighting to keep silent, knowing that any argument she might put forward would be a waste of breath. Why did I ever imagine that I could sit happily and have tea with this man?

'You don't think,' she said calmly at last, 'that all these Africans who are so selfishly eager to have some kind of representation will eventually turn to violence, if they are for ever thwarted in their ambitions?'

'There will be hot-heads,' Christiaan admitted. 'But just as at Sharpeville, they will be stamped upon. And in time, everyone – black, white, the whole world – will see that we are right. Separate development is the only answer.'

She could take no more, but continued smiling.

'You're such a busy man, Christiaan, I really ought not to take up your time. I wonder if I could just take a look around the garden—?'

She was interrupted by a servant, who came to tell Christiaan that Dr Verwoerd's office had phoned and wanted to speak to him. Immediately he rose.

'Please excuse me,' he said to Kate. 'I must obey my master's voice.' He waved towards the garden. 'Go anywhere you wish. I'll join you there in a few minutes.'

Kate puffed out her cheeks as he left, feeling that she'd done
well to restrain herself.

It was with mixed feelings that she went down the steps and
turned towards the garden beyond the plumbago hedge which she
had always felt was more her own place than anywhere else on
the property. She had momentarily forgotten the existence of the
swimming pool, new since her day. There it was, a translucent blue
glimmering through the hibiscus hedge at the end of the lawn.

Here, this side of the hedge, all was as it had been before, with
the exception of the table and the chairs to one side, the striped
umbrella unopened, the chairs tipped up against the table to keep
them dry in the event of rain.

A memorial to Sonia? It was more, she thought with a touch
of amusement, a memorial to herself. There was the bed she had
planted, full of mature plants now, a huge clump of agapanthus
ragged and wilting in the hot sun, the pink watsonias apparently
thriving. There were the small gladioli, the galtonias, the strelizias
Sonia had shown no interest in the garden while she had the
vineyard to think about. Still, perhaps she was doing her erstwhile
sister-in-law an injustice for certainly she – or someone – had
devoted much time to it more recently.

And there, across the grass, was the candlewood tree. Kate was
ill prepared for the strange lurch of her heart as she looked at it.
Nothing she had seen up to this moment – not the oak-lined drive,
not the house, not the view of the valley or the flowerbed – had
brought back the past as this did. It was as if she could see herself
sitting in the shelter of its branches, alone and forlorn and longing
to be happy.

Slowly she walked towards it, and sat down as she had done so
many times before, running her hands along the smooth wooden
seat, looking up into the branches. She picked a leaf, feeling its
leathery stiffness, breaking it with the remembered snap; and
suddenly, without warning, she was weeping – for Guy, who
turned his back on so much, for herself, who had loved him once,
and for Jan, who had grown up so far from her in a home without
warmth or affection.

What a fool she had been! How could she have denied herself,
and him, when not a day had passed without her thinking of him
and wanting him back? How could she have persuaded herself that
he was better off here?

Better off? With Christiaan and Sonia? She must have been mad! She, of all people, should have known that beauty and comfort weren't enough for a happy life. If only she had received one word from him over the years – not when he was small, of course, she hadn't expected that, but later – then she would have acted differently. But he never spoke of her, Sonia said. Never thought of her. Never asked questions.

Tears poured down her cheeks, ruining the careful make-up she had put on for Christiaan's benefit – this hateful man whom now she saw must have been just as much a party to this deception as Sonia. He must have known about her letters. He lived here, didn't he? He couldn't possibly have been totally ignorant of her efforts to reach Jan.

He had wanted children, a son. He had said so himself. Jan must have seemed the next best thing.

'Kate, Kate—' Christiaan had come into the garden and, aware of her tears, he hurried towards her. 'You mustn't distress yourself.'

She shrunk away from him, not wanting to feel the touch of his hand, rummaging in her bag for a handkerchief.

'This must be such a nostalgic trip for you. It's bound to be upsetting.' He sat down beside her. 'But cheer up, my dear. This old tree is meant to be comforting! I know I find it so. Some say it has medicinal properties, and I always say it gives me inspiration. It's a survivor, you know, rather like myself. Sometimes I sit here in the evening, and I feel—' He paused, suddenly remembering that he had used the line already that day.

Kate had her face turned from him, struggling for calm, and she made no comment on this.

'Tell me,' she said at last, her voice hard. 'How was it that Jan never received any of the letters I wrote?'

'I . . . I don't know what you mean.'

She looked at him directly, not caring that her eyes were red and forgetting all her resolutions to stay calm.

'Yes you do. You must have known. You were here, as well as Sonia. You all lived in the same house, at least for part of the year. How was it Jan never saw them? Not once, in all the years! Did you bribe the Post Office in some way?'

He forced a laugh, but Kate guessed from his expression that she was not so far from the mark.

'No, of course not. Well, not exactly.'

'What does that mean – not exactly?'

'My dear Kate, it was all done from the best possible motives. Sonia felt it would be unsettling for a little boy—'

'And you went along with it. Come on, Christiaan. How did you manage it? Jan didn't stay a little boy, did he? There must have been times when he picked up the post or saw it on the hall table. Did you have a little arrangement with the Post Office?'

'Well, Sonia felt—'

'You bastard,' Kate said. She felt light-headed with anger. 'You know something? You're weak, Christiaan. You can't even take responsibility for something like that, even though I'll bet anything it was you who leaned on the post office. Sonia wouldn't have had the authority. Well, I hope you never make Prime Minister, because you're feeble and indecisive and just plain evil – the very last thing this country needs.'

He leapt to his feet as if stung, his face suddenly white with fury.

'How dare you?' he demanded. 'I've invited you here in good faith, welcomed you to my home.'

'It was my home once!'

'And you turned your back on it. You left your husband and child.'

'My child was taken from me.' She stood up, facing him. 'It broke my heart. Don't you understand that? I wanted him back – always, always! I wrote to him and said so, over and over. And never once, over the years, did I have a word from him. Only from Sonia who told me that he wasn't interested – that he never asked about me, never wanted to see me again.' She had begun to cry again, tears pouring down her cheeks. 'I thought the fact that he never wrote back when he was older meant she was right. I didn't want to force myself on him, so I gave up trying. I tried to forget the past and make a new life for myself. But it was all lies, all of it! He did ask questions, and he did want to know me, but he was told I had no interest in him. He never saw my letters and birthday cards. She stole them – *you* stole them!'

'I did no such thing!'

'At the very least you turned a blind eye. You must have known.'

'If I may say so, my dear,' he said nastily, 'you gave up very easily, didn't you? You made no effort to find out the truth for yourself.'

'Because, fool that I was, I thought it was best for him. This was his country, his world.'

'Well, so it was. And you've had other children, after all—'

'So one more or less didn't matter? There speaks a man with no children of his own.' She drew a deep, shuddering breath. 'I'd better go.'

'I think you had.'

'He found them, you know.'

He had turned as if to leave but paused at this and, with a look of weary patience, looked at her once more.

'What are you talking about?'

'My letters. He found them. He has them now. All the letters, all the birthday cards. I'll never know why Sonia didn't burn them, but then she always kept everything, didn't she? Jan found them in her desk—'

Once more he had started to walk away, but at this he stopped and turned sharply to face her.

'He found *what*?'

'My letters. All of them. He told you.'

He took a step towards her, staring at her as if she had taken leave of her senses.

'He told me? What on earth do you—?' Slowly the look of anger left his face as realisation dawned, to be replaced by first bewilderment, then an expression of dawning delight. 'You mean that's what he was shouting about that day?' He threw back his head and laughed with unashamed relief. 'My God, is that what caused all the fuss? I thought . . . I thought—' He shook his head, still laughing. 'What a crazy boy he is! Well, he found you at last, didn't he?'

For a moment Kate said nothing.

'What did you think, Christiaan?' she asked, falsely mild.

'Agh, never mind, never mind.' He waved the question aside, still chuckling to himself. 'Just say I got the wrong end of the stick, eh?'

Kate continued to look at him, frowning. An idea had sprung to her mind as he spoke, the merest whisper of a doubt which seemed to grow by the second. What else did he think Jan might have found among Sonia's archives?

Perhaps Colin's suspicions weren't so unthinkable after all. There was a coldness at this man's heart; she had always known it, though time had dulled the memory. He was capable of anything. There was nothing he wouldn't do to gain his own ends. Doubt hardened into certainty. She was sure that Colin was right.

'I think I'd like to go home now,' she said stiffly; and without another word, she walked past him towards the gap in the hedge.

19

Kate returned from Gramerci to find something of a celebration in progress. Colin and Nina were there as well as another couple whom she assumed were Steve and Margie Dwyer.

'It seemed like touch and go at one time,' Nina told her, hurrying to meet her as she got out of the car. 'The old crone had assembled quite a lot of evidence – all circumstantial, but there were one or two assessors who seemed inclined to take it seriously.'

'In spite of your petition and all the signatures?'

'The majority were swayed by that, and Steve's work record and everything. Jan was marvellous—' She broke off quickly. 'Come and meet Steve. I don't think he can take in the fact that the nightmare's over. It's been one hell of a time for him – and Margie too, of course.'

Steve received Kate's congratulations with a smile and a few words of gratitude, but he seemed subdued – unlike his wife, who was bubbling over with joy.

'He's been hit hard by this,' Jan said to Kate in a quiet moment. 'He's usually the life and soul.'

'You can understand it, I suppose. To go on for years and years, never doubting your birth or status, and then to have the whole foundation of it put into question—'

'He's leaving, he says. Emigrating, as soon as he can arrange it. That's something that's happening all too often these days, I'm afraid, but who can blame him? He says he'll never feel safe again. Tell me – how did you get on with our worthy Minister for Coloured Affairs?'

She didn't smile as he expected.

'There are things I have to tell you, Jan,' she said. 'When everyone's gone and we have a minute.'

He looked at her with interest.

'Something serious? We're supposed to be moving on to the Cambells' house any minute. We were only waiting for you. Hennie and Les are looking after the baby, but we phoned them with the news and Hennie insisted on a party. Can you face it?'

'Sure! I'd like to meet them.'

'This thing you have to tell me—'

'It'll keep,' she said.

They sat, much later, on the stoep looking down on the lights of the town.

'Fairyland,' Kate said, knowing it wasn't.

'Mm. All squalor hidden. Come on, then – tell all! What is this dark secret of yours that you've been hiding from me?'

'It's not my secret at all.' Kate paused for a moment, as if choosing her words with care. 'Actually, I can't imagine why I haven't told you before, except that it all happened a long time ago and I cherished a ridiculously quixotic notion that it wouldn't be right to make relations between you and Christiaan worse than they already are.'

'Go on,' Jan said, all attention.

'Well, there was this girl,' Kate began. 'A pretty little Coloured girl called Dora who made dresses for me.'

Jan listened, not moving; and when she had finished he sat still for a moment, only the crickets breaking the silence.

'My God,' he said softly at last. 'You do realise this is dynamite, don't you?'

'I do now,' Kate said. 'Colour was an issue then, of course, and as a new Member of Parliament it would have damaged Christiaan if it had all come out, but it's even more important these days. What made me furious at the time had very little to do with colour, really. It was the fact that Dora was young and innocent and bright and talented. Christiaan used her without a thought as to what it might do to her. It seemed a kind of *droit de seigneur* kind of thing. He wanted her – he had to have her.'

'And Sonia wanted him and had to have him. Do you really think she blackmailed him?'

'Yes, I do. And Jan – this is what I wanted to tell you. I think that maybe Colin was right, that the attack on you was set up by Christiaan. I think that he misunderstood you, that day you found all my letters. He thought you were talking about something quite different, that was perfectly obvious. I think he thought you'd found the letter from Dora that Sonia used to blackmail him.'

'For heaven's sake, I *told* him! I made it clear—'

'Apparently not. Maybe it was a subconscious kind of thing. Perhaps he'd lived all his married life with the threat of exposure and in a strange kind of way had always expected it.'

'Then why didn't he destroy the letter the minute Sonia died?'

'It could have been a momentary lapse of memory – something he hadn't got round to doing. I expect he had a lot to think about. Anyway, I told him the truth this afternoon – that you had found my letters – and he was obviously surprised and relieved. Overwhelmingly so. I'll bet anything that letter still exists, though, knowing Sonia. Or that he believes it does.'

'She destroyed a lot of papers.'

'But does he know which ones?'

Jan had no answer to this, but for a moment sat looking straight ahead of him, staring bleakly into space.

'You really think,' he said at last, clearly reluctant to believe it, 'that Christiaan employed this Eksberg guy to find me and bump me off?'

'It's a horrible thought, but I do honestly think he's capable of it. Oh, forget cricket on the lawn and happy days on the beach, Jan. Christiaan le Roux is a selfish, ambitious man. You know that. Certainly, I'm convinced of it. I always knew his charm was surface deep, but I never realised until today how ruthless he could be. Do you know that he had an arrangement with the Post Office not to deliver my letters to you? All Sonia's fault, of course, according to him, and perhaps it was, in part. He went along with it, though. He wanted a son, so he had to have one. And what really got to me was that he appeared to see nothing wrong in that, nothing to apologise for. He's a cold, cold man.'

'Well—' Jan sighed. 'It's hard to take.'

'Will you believe Colin if he finds some link between Eksberg and this Van Niekirk man?'

He gave a wry laugh.

'Circumstantial evidence,' he said. 'Which is what scuppered the case against Steve, remember? You can't trust it an inch.'

He was forced to take a more serious view, however, when on Saturday Colin phoned to say that he had some interesting information.

'Can't tell you over the phone,' he said. 'OK if Nina and I come over tomorrow morning?'

'We'll see you then,' Jan said. He put the phone down, but stood for a moment without moving. Kate watched him a little anxiously, but made no comment. She was still no wiser about the situation concerning the triangle displayed before her almost daily. The last few days had been spent in sight-seeing trips, sometimes with Nina, sometimes with Jan, sometimes with both. She had been up Table Mountain, walked in the Kirstenbosch Gardens, driven up to the clean, fresh air of Franschoek once settled by the Huguenots from whence had come the Lampard ancestors.

The friendship between Jan and Nina was plain to see, but there seemed a growing edginess, too; the occasional snide remark from Jan eliciting a frosty reply from Nina. Like Tom and me, Kate thought on occasions. They wouldn't do it if they didn't care. She was assiduous in appearing not to notice, however.

She had written postcards to Mark and Vicky every day, and had spoken to Tom once on the phone, on the eve of his trip to Stockholm. All was well, he told her. The children were happy. He was busy.

'But missing you,' he said.

'I'll soon be home,' Kate assured him.

Home seemed unreal; but then, so did Cape Town, just as if she were back in some kind of recurring dream. Sitting in the sun, enjoying the incredible scenery and the friendly bustle of the town, she was aware only of her delight in being here once more. Yet all too frequently she was reminded of the darker side of this wonderful country – its inhumane laws, its poverty.

On Saturday morning she had gone with Jan to visit a particular friend of his, a Coloured priest, down on the Cape Flats, and had looked in horror at the *pondokkies* – the shacks made of beaten petrol cans and pieces of corrugated iron, where perhaps several families lived in crowded squalor. The hopelessness was heavy in the air, the contrast to the magnificent homes in Constantia or Newlands too great to contemplate.

'It can't go on like this, can it?' she said to Jan as they drove towards home. 'Not realistically. These people may have little education, but they're not daft. They know what's going on in the rest of Africa.'

'And they're beginning to know their power,' Jan said. 'Why

industrialists and captains of industry can't see that we're all dependent on each other, I can't imagine. If unrest develops to the point where the workers go on strike, then heaven help us all. It's happened on a small scale already. If they really joined forces and stuck to their guns, they could hold the country to ransom.'

'If only—' she began, then sighed.

'What?'

'I was going to say, if only that charismatic leader you envisage would emerge right now—'

'No one in this government would recognise him. He'd be gunned down, thrown in prison. That's what makes me feel so hopeless, sometimes. In their blindness, they're destroying the very men who could show them the answer.'

'Jan,' Kate said, after a few minutes' silence. 'You can't let Christiaan be Prime Minister! He's an evil man, I'm certain of it.'

For a moment Jan said nothing. Then he sighed.

'You're right,' he said.

Colin and Nina came, as arranged, on Sunday morning, exactly a week after Jan and Kate had arrived in South Africa.

'You've simply got to take this seriously, Jan,' Nina said as they came up the steps to the stoep. She walked up to him and took hold of both his arms, looking up into his face, giving his arms a shake. 'Promise me you'll stop being so damned pig-headed, and you'll pay attention to what Colin says?'

Jan grinned at Colin over the top of her head.

'Listen to the girl! When have I done other than pay attention to Colin?'

Colin didn't return the grin.

'This really is pretty serious, Jan. I don't know what you'll think you ought to do about it.'

'Sit down,' Kate said, getting to her feet. 'I'll bring some coffee.'

'Let's hear what Colin has to say first,' said Jan.

Kate subsided again, and chairs were dragged up for the others.

'A couple of nights ago,' Colin said, 'Nina and I were at a party at a hotel in Sea Point.'

'It was Jackie Pienaar's birthday,' Nina said. 'You remember her, don't you, Jan?'

'Why wouldn't I?' Jan asked lightly. 'You and I went together to her last.' He looked at her, and their eyes held for a moment.

'Shall I go on?' Colin asked pointedly. 'As we walked through the foyer, we passed the bar, and who should I see slumped on a stool but Eksberg, looking very much the worse for wear. I'm afraid I deserted Nina and went back to talk to him. He was on his own and throwing down whiskies at a rate of knots. Apparently his wife has left him – gone home to Momma because he's been posted to some dorp at the back of beyond. He's convinced that this is le Roux's doing – that he's leaned on the Chief of Police to get him moved because of the sensitivity of some job Eksberg was supposed to carry out on his behalf. Le Roux just didn't want him around any more, he says. It's broken up his marriage and ruined his life and the gist of it all was that he'd like to kill the bastard.'

There was silence on the stoep, and all eyes were on him.

'Go on,' said Jan.

'I kept the whiskies coming and he became even more loquacious. As well as all his other grievances, Le Roux had welshed on a promise to get him into the Broederbond, he said. I asked if this job had anything to do with you, Jan, and he said of course it had. Le Roux wanted you taken out – who wouldn't?' Briefly Colin permitted himself a flicker of amusement. 'I said, all innocent, that Van Niekirk must have been a useful contact once he'd found that the bird had flown to England – and he clammed up then. Mumbled something about loyalty and friendship and not landing a good buddy in the—' He paused and looked at Kate. 'dirt,' he finished, hastily censoring what had clearly been a more colourful expression.

Jan said nothing but sat looking at Colin, his face giving no clue as to his feelings.

'I knew it,' Kate said softly. 'I just knew it, that day I was at Gramerci.'

'Jan, he must be brought to justice,' Nina urged. 'You can't let him get away with it. What I don't understand is why he should do such an awful thing.'

'Kate thinks she knows,' Jan said. 'Tell them, Kate.'

Once again Kate recounted Dora's story.

'So he thought Jan was about to expose him,' she finished. 'That's what I think, anyway,' she added with a touch of defiance, seeing that Jan still seemed sceptical.

'Well, for whatever reason, I'm sure le Roux was behind the attack,' Colin said. 'It all hangs together. The way he looked when

I mentioned Eksberg's enquiries to him. The association between Eksberg and Van Niekirk. Look the facts in the face, man!'

Jan got to his feet.

'I'll get that coffee,' he said. 'Unless anyone prefers a beer? OK, coffee it is.'

The other three watched him go.

'Give him time to come to terms with it,' Nina said. 'He's not at all a good hater.'

'Nor am I,' Kate said. 'But I'll make an exception for Christiaan le Roux. He must never, never be allowed to lead this country. OK – others may be just as bad, but he can't be allowed to profit from something as horrendous as this.'

'His stock's pretty high right now,' Colin admitted. 'He made a superb speech in Parliament the other day about the advantages of being out of the Commonwealth. It was a total load of baloney, of course, but utterly convincing to those who wanted to be convinced. Everyone was commenting how he's back on form now after a bad patch.'

'The natural successor to Verwoerd, the *Cape Times* said.'

Colin shot a teasing grin in her direction.

'Maybe you're reading the wrong paper,' he said.

'The *Courier* wasn't much better!'

He pulled a wry face.

'You're not wrong there. Poor old Porter's far too timid.'

Jan returned with the coffee.

'All right,' he said. 'You win. I've summed up the evidence and find the defendant guilty.'

'I'm so sorry, Jan,' Nina said softly. 'I know what you must feel.'

'Yeah, well . . .' Jan sat for a moment, saying nothing, his coffee cooling in his cup. 'Christiaan and I haven't agreed about anything for years, and we've certainly had some cataclysmic rows in our time. Even so, I was misguided enough to think there was some basic affection left. More fool me . . .'

His voice trailed away. Kate looked at him, sympathy in her eyes, in spite of her avowed hatred for Christiaan. He was taking it hard.

'So what are we going to do about it?' Colin asked.

'Well—' Jan seemed to rally his resources. 'I also came to the conclusion that we haven't a shred of evidence. Nothing that would stand up in court. Eksberg and Van Niekirk would obviously deny everything—'

'But you saw Van Niekirk,' Nina said.

'It would still be his word against mine. He had an alibi, the police in London said. And who would you choose to believe? A policeman or a known troublemaker?'

'Especially one who has been a congenital liar from the cradle,' said Colin. Jan looked at him, unamused, and Colin lifted both hands, as if in surrender. 'According to le Roux,' he said hastily. 'I did but jest.'

'Couldn't you simply publish the Dora story, Colin?' Nina asked. 'There seems a kind of poetic justice about making it the cause of his downfall after all.'

Colin shook his head.

'I'd never get it past George Porter. Anyway, without the letter or any other evidence, le Roux would talk himself out of it somehow.'

'There's evidence,' Kate said suddenly. 'There's Dora! Well, it all might seem a long time ago to you babes, but it wasn't the Dark Ages, you know. Dora was about my age – certainly no older. The child would be about twenty-two now.'

'But where is she? Do you know? Is she still in Cape Town?'

Kate's sudden euphoria subsided.

'I've no idea,' she said. 'Her mother lived in Gysbert Street—'

'That doesn't exist any more,' Jan said. 'All that part was redeveloped. It's a kind of industrial area now.'

'Dora left, anyway. She went up to Port Elizabeth, to a friend of mine—' Kate came to a sudden halt. 'Of course! What an idiot I am! Jane might know, and she would be easier to track down, if she's still in the country, because she's a doctor. There must be medical registers—'

'There are,' Colin said, taking out a notebook in a professionally efficient way. 'Give me her name and I'll look her up.'

'Dr Jane Ryder,' Kate said. 'Of course, she might have married—'

'Where was she last working when you knew her?'

'In the women's prison at Port Elizabeth. Dora went to her for help when she was pregnant, but that was over twenty years ago. I left very soon afterwards and I've had no news since.'

'Right. I'll get on to that as soon as I can.'

'So what's the plan?' Nina asked. 'Say we find Dora – what then? Do we get her permission to tell her story? Or simply confront le Roux with the facts and say resign or else?'

'No!' Jan roared his denial, thumping the table with his clenched fist in such a contrast to his previous subdued manner that they all jumped. He got to his feet and began ranging around the stoep, as if his disillusionment and anger had been simmering slowly and had now come to the boil. 'To hell with that! I'm damned if I'm going to let him get away with giving some feeble excuse – ill-health, or some such – and bowing out of public life without a stain on his character. He tried to kill me, remember? His politics are vile, his morals non-existent. The man's a mongrel, a menace to society, a Grade A bastard, and he's got to be exposed – not just because of what he tried to do to me, but because he could do it again if anyone else happened to get in his way.' He whirled round and faced Colin, pointing his finger. 'You find out about this Jane Ryder,' he said. 'And tell me as soon as you know anything. Kate, your job will be to talk to Dr Ryder and then, once we've located Dora, to persuade her to confront him, with as much publicity as possible. I'll try and think of a suitable occasion.'

'He's addressing a meeting in the City Hall next Friday,' Nina said. 'I saw a poster.'

Colin confirmed this.

'That's right. He's talking about the Commonwealth issue again – explaining it to the faithful.'

'Jan, do sit down and stop flailing around,' Kate said. For a moment he looked astonished, then amused, but he did as he was told. He was used to giving orders, she saw, not taking them.

'What exactly is it that you have in mind?' she asked him. 'I can't see Dora getting up in a hall full of whites to announce she was once seduced by the Minister for Coloured Affairs. Not the Dora I knew, anyway. She was much too shy. Well, anyone would be!'

'Honestly, I don't know what I have in mind,' he said, more temperately. 'You're right. Much depends on what Dora is like now – or what her son or daughter is like. Maybe he or she would be only too willing to give evidence.'

'Maybe she had a son who's turned out the spitting image of le Roux,' Colin said, only half-facetiously. 'Hey, that would be a good twist, wouldn't it – suddenly producing a look-alike out of the crowd?'

Jan ignored him.

'I'll work on it,' he said. 'It needs some thought.'

'Five days,' Nina said, bringing them all down to earth. 'That's all we've got, if you're going to make use of that meeting.'

They left before lunch, and Jan saw them off, standing for a moment looking after the car as it drove away. He had a thoughtful expression on his face when he returned to the stoep.

'I can't quite work out what Colin's angle is,' he said to Kate.

Kate frowned.

'What on earth do you mean? He wants to help, that's all.'

'Oh yeah?' Jan laughed briefly. 'Well, maybe. He wants to please Nina, anyway.' He turned to go into the house. 'But who does Nina want to please, I ask myself?' he murmured absently as he went inside.

It took less than one day to find that Jane was still practising, not in Port Elizabeth, but at a mission in Namibia. That afternoon, Kate phoned her. Dr Ryder was busy in surgery, she was told. Maybe if she phoned after five o'clock.

At five o'clock, she was busy on the wards.

'Perhaps if you gave me her home number . . .' Kate suggested.

'Sorry, madam, this is not allowed,' said the voice on the other end. 'But if you leave your number I can ask her to call you.'

Kate thought this over.

'Tell her it's Kate Lampard,' she said. She spelt it out carefully and gave Jan's number for the return call. 'Tell her I need to speak to her rather urgently.'

She felt little confidence that the message would be passed on, and was delighted when, at about nine that night, Jane was on the line, happy to speak to her after so many years, and sounding the same as ever.

'I was really hoping to hear news of Dora,' Kate said, after all the pleasantries and personal news had been dealt with. 'I don't suppose you're still in touch with her?'

'Dora? No, not for many years now. She stayed in Port Elizabeth for a while after the twins were born—'

'*Twins?*'

'Of course – you wouldn't have known that! Yes, she had twins, a boy and a girl. She found work in a hotel in P.E. at first, mending linen and so on, but then she got married and moved back to Cape

Town. Her husband had a job in a factory – now what on earth was his name? I should know. We exchanged Christmas cards for a few years, but then I went to England for a course and somehow lost touch. It's maddening – I just can't think of it.'

'Oh, Jane – please try to remember! It's desperately important that I should get in touch with her.'

Jane accepted this without comment. As she was the kind of person who had devoted her life to others, Kate assumed that she probably thought it quite natural that she should be concerned about Dora, even after so many years.

'Give me some time,' Jane said. 'I really don't know where she is now, but if I find my old address book I can at least tell you her married name and where she was about ten years ago, if that's any help. I'm sorry I can't do more.'

Kate thanked her profusely, impressed on her how little time she had in Cape Town, and rang off.

'She said she might ring later tonight,' she told Jan, reporting the conversation. 'But she has no information later than ten years old. Goodness knows if that's going to be good enough.'

'It would be a start,' said Jan.

It was only an hour later when the phone rang again. Jane had found her old address book. Dora was now Dora Petrus and was last known living in Woodstock.

'Where my office is,' Jan said, happily surprised.

'I've often wondered why.'

'Because (a) it's cheap, and (b) it's close to most of my clients. What was the name of the road?'

'Point Street. Number sixty-five.'

'We'll go there first thing tomorrow.'

The house was one of many, set back a little above a narrow street that climbed a steep hill. It had a miniature gable and stoep as if the original inhabitants of Point Street had ideas above their station in life. Now the houses had, almost without exception, fallen into disrepair – the plaster scarred, the wooden rails broken and badly in need of paint. Ragged children swarmed over stoeps and played in the road and emaciated dogs foraged in the gutters.

Number 65 was no better and no worse than the others. Their arrival caused a stir among the children and a dozen pairs of eyes watched Jan and Kate as they went up the steps to the front stoep.

An old woman with a face like a walnut was sweeping the stoep. She paused and lifted her head as they approached, toothless jaws working, an expression of wariness on her face as if she suspected some kind of official interference.

Jan greeted her in the *taal* and explained their mission but she was unresponsive to his smile. When he had finished she continued to look at him for a few moments, saying nothing. Then she nodded her head a few times as if, at last, she accepted he meant her no harm. Her reply was lengthy and largely incomprehensible to Kate, but she nevertheless recognised the name of *Mevrouw* Petrus, repeated several times.

'Well?' she demanded after Jan had peeled off a note to give her, and they had descended once more to the street. 'What did she say?'

Children, happily engaged in swarming over the car, climbing on the bonnet and the boot, ran away at their approach, shrieking with laughter, and for a moment Jan was too busy shooing away the tail-enders to speak.

'She knows her,' he said at last. 'She said that the Petrus family lived there before her two sons and their families moved in, but now *Mevrouw* Petrus has a little clothing store round the corner and they live on the premises.'

'That sounds like Dora,' Kate said, smiling. 'She always wanted to own a dress-shop.'

They would have missed it, had it not been for the rail of cheap and shoddy clothes outside. What Kate had expected she was not quite sure; she only knew it was nothing like this, for in the old days Dora had possessed taste and refinement. Perhaps taste and refinement were not marketable commodities here; or perhaps her customers had no money to indulge in such niceties. Certainly there was no sign of it in the garish, tawdry, thrown-together garments that were on sale.

A girl was behind the counter, but there were no customers. She was quite young, not more than fourteen or fifteen, and her expression was wary and her eyes wide at the sight of the two Europeans coming into the shop.

'Good morning,' Kate said, smiling at her. 'We're looking for *Mevrouw* Petrus. Is this where she lives?'

'She gone to market, *mevrouw*,' the girl whispered shyly.

'Will she be back soon?'

The girl hunched her shoulders.

'I don't know, *mevrouw*.'

Jan was standing a few paces behind, and Kate looked over her shoulder for further instructions, but before she could speak someone had approached and was standing in the doorway. Kate's jaw dropped. It was Dora – and yet it couldn't be, for this girl was young, not many years older than Dora herself when Kate had known her in the past.

The shop girl had seen her too, and spoke to her in the *taal*. Immediately the second girl smiled pleasantly and came forward.

'You want to speak to my mother?' she asked.

'Of course! You're Dora's daughter. You couldn't be anyone else.'

'I'm Louise. Yes, we are supposed to be rather alike.'

'You certainly are,' Kate said. 'I can vouch for that. I live in England now, but I knew your mother when she was younger than you. She made lots of beautiful clothes for me before the war. I'm Kate Newcott, by the way, and this is Jan Lampard, my son.'

'Jan Lampard?' Louise Petrus looked at him with interest. The name was clearly not unknown to her. She shook hands, first with Kate and then with Jan; a remarkably self-possessed young woman, Kate thought, and lovely to look at, just as Dora had been. Her skin was the shade of milky coffee, her eyes a dark and lustrous brown.

'My mother doesn't do sewing any more,' she said.

'It's not that. I just wanted to see her – to talk—'

Well, please come inside and wait. I've just come off night duty at the hospital,' she added. 'I'm a nurse.'

'Yes, of course.' For the first time, Kate registered the fact that her blue checked dress was some kind of uniform. 'Well, you must be tired. We won't keep you up, will we, Jan? We'll come back—'

'No, no, don't do that. Mom will be here soon, I'm sure.'

Kate glanced at Jan and saw his all-but-imperceptible nod.

'Well, thank you,' she said. 'That's very kind.'

Louise led the way towards the room behind the shop, but stood back at the door to allow them to go first. There was, Kate saw, a thickset young man sitting at the table, dressed in cotton trousers and a greyish singlet, once white. His powerful shoulders were hunched over a bowl of cereal and as they went in, he looked at them, mouth gaping open, bloodshot eyes cold with sudden hatred.

'Oh – Theo!' Louise seemed surprised. 'I didn't know you were home.'

He gave a wolfish grin.

'Nor does Mom,' he said, as if this thought gave him pleasure.

He added something in Afrikaans, picked up his spoon and bowl and disappeared through a door which appeared to lead to the back of the premises, without a word to Kate or Jan, or any acknowledgment of their presence. Louise looked embarrassed.

'I'm sorry. I apologise for my brother,' she said.

Her *twin* brother? Kate was astonished. If indeed this was so, he looked like another breed altogether – uncouth and unpleasant, to say the least.

'We apologise for disturbing him in the middle of his breakfast,' Jan said. 'Are you sure it wouldn't be better if we came back another time?'

'No. Please stay. Would you care for some tea?'

She filled a kettle at the sink and put it on the battered stove which stood in a corner, inviting them to sit down on the two hard, wooden-armed plastic chairs set against the wall. Jan engaged her in polite conversation during which they found that they had several friends in common, while Kate looked around her.

The room was even smaller that that in which Mama Lou had entertained her so many years before, and showed little more sophistication. Even so, it was spotlessly clean and she knew it was a palace compared to many other places where Coloured families were forced to live.

She was amused to see that the family's patriotic tendencies still flourished. In place of the old pictures of the little princesses, there was a large framed photograph of the Queen and the Duke of Edinburgh hung on one wall, flanked by numerous family portraits, including one of Louise and her brother as two engaging toddlers, smiling for the camera. What had happened, Kate wondered, to change that happy little boy into the vaguely sinister figure that they had seen here only a few minutes before?

'You seem to have a number of brothers and sisters,' she said, with a nod towards the photographs.

'Yes. Seven in all. Dawn – my sister in the shop – is fifteen, and next to me in age. The others are all small. And all out, thank goodness. They got up early today to go on a Sunday school outing.' She looked up and gave a quick grin as she poured the boiling water into the teapot. 'To be honest, I dread coming off night duty in the holidays, there's always such a racket going on. I can never wait until school starts again.'

Kate smiled in sympathy.

'I know just what you mean. I was a nurse myself, once. I never could get used to night duty.'

Louise poured two cups of tea and gave one to Jan, one to Kate.

'Aren't you having one?' Kate asked, when she had sat down beside the table, her hands folded. Louise looked uncomfortable.

'I . . . I'll wait,' she said.

Jan got up and took his cup over to her.

'Have this one,' he said. 'I'll pour myself another. You can't imagine we'd mind.'

'I don't know, sir,' she said, her voice very low. 'There are those who would—'

'Not me,' he said. 'And not my mother. Please drink a cup of tea with us. Your need must be a damn sight greater than ours, if you've just come off duty.'

'Thank you.' She sipped her tea in silence for a moment before settling the cup back on its saucer and looking at Jan. 'I knew I'd heard of you,' she said. 'You're the lawyer from Victoria Road. You help people.'

'I try. Not always successfully, I'm afraid.'

'And you quit the Springboks.'

Jan laughed.

'There you are,' he said to Kate. 'It's the only thing people remember about me.'

Their laughter had just died when Dora came in. She stood on the threshold looking from one to the other, on her face a look of fear.

'Is it Theo?' she asked. 'Is there more trouble?'

Kate put her cup down and got to her feet.

'Dora – it's me, Kate Newcott. Kate Lampard, as I was then. Don't you remember? You made clothes for me a long time ago. This is my son, Jan.'

Still wary, Dora came in and put her shopping bags down on the table. She was plump now, but still pretty. There was even something of the old style about her, dressed as she was in a plain navy blue shirtwaister, with a red scarf at her neck.

'Yes,' she said. 'Yes, I remember. I don't do no sewing now. I have de shop.'

'It's not that. We wanted to talk to you.'

Dora looked at Louise, who at once got up.

'If you'll excuse me, I'll take this to my room,' she said. 'I was glad to meet you, Mrs Newcott. And Mr Lampard.'

'Goodbye, and thanks for the tea,' Jan said.

'And sleep well,' Kate added.

Louise went, but in a second was back again.

'Theo is home,' she told her mother. 'He must have come early, just after you went to market. He's out the back somewhere.'

This time she disappeared for good, leaving the other three looking at each other in a somewhat awkward silence. Dora did not sit down and made no suggestion that they should.

How do we begin? Kate thought. It had seemed so simple in theory – speaking to Dora, explaining the situation, asking for her help. Now it seemed a monstrous imposition. How could they imagine it was right to push their way into her life like this, reminding her of a past she must surely have forgotten long ago and would wish to be forgotten for ever? Why would she want to rake everything up again, just to help them?'

'Dora—' She went over to her and took her hand. 'Dora, I know it's been a long time. And I know you must hate the sight of me.'

Dora looked at her, frowning.

'Why I do that, Mrs Lampard? You helped us.'

'By introducing you to Christiaan le Roux! Some help that was.'

Her round, self-contained face gave little away. Without expression, she stripped off her red lace gloves and put them down beside her shopping before reaching for another cup, and pouring herself some tea.

'Please sit down,' she said at last. They did so.

'What a charming girl Louise is,' Kate said.

For the first time Dora smiled, briefly.

'She a good girl, Louise. Always good. At school, she work hard and pass exams. Now she doing real good at the hospital.'

'You must be proud of her.'

'Yes.' The shutters had come down again. For a moment there was silence.

'I spoke to Dr Ryder,' Kate said. 'It was she who told me your name and where to find you. And that you had twins.'

Dora looked at her sombrely.

'Louise and Theo,' she said. 'Two children more different you couldn't find.'

'Well, of course, non-identical twins can be as unlike each other as any other brother and sister, can't they? Louise looks just like you.'

She was talking too much, Kate recognised. Chattering, just to cover the awkwardness. She felt nervous, intrusive, and looked pleadingly at Jan for help. In response, he leaned towards Dora.

'Mrs Petrus,' he said. 'I'm sure you must be wondering why we are here, and I hope you'll forgive us for coming into your home like this and talking about things you'd probably rather forget. The thing is—' For a second he hesitated, biting his lip, before going on. 'The thing is, Christiaan le Roux tried to kill me. Have me killed, anyway. And the reason he did this was because he thought I knew about you and the way he treated you in the past. We want to expose him, so that the whole world knows what kind of man he is.'

Her eyes widened with sudden fright.

'You don't tell him I here, Mr Lampard. Don't you tell him. I don't want nothing to do with him.'

'We know that—'

'I promise him I stay away. I promise I don't say nothing to no one, when he give me the money. He say he do something bad if I break my word. Ten years, we stay in P.E., but then my Piet lose his job. A friend tell him, there's work in a factory in Cape Town if you come right now. So we come. We got more children by that time, and there were six of us to feed. De twins, Dawn, Lennie and another on de way – what else we do, you tell me? All de time, I afraid. I don't tell no one who de twins' daddy, not even Piet.'

'They don't know?'

'I never tell.'

'They think it's Piet?'

She bent her head, giving it a small shake.

'No,' she whispered. 'They know it ain't Piet. But I never tell. Now you want me to tell everyone? Well, you can just forget it, Mr Lampard. I never going to tell.'

'Dora,' Kate said persuasively. 'Don't you agree with us that a man as hypocritical as le Roux shouldn't hold high office? Think of it – he's the Minister for Coloured Affairs. He's the one who says that Coloureds can only live in this place, or do this job. He's the one who says marriage between whites and Coloureds is a criminal offence. And he tried to kill my son.' Her voice shook a little, but she quickly recovered herself. 'Doesn't he deserve to have the truth told about him?'

For a moment her emotion seemed to make Dora pause and think the matter over. She looked at Jan.

'What you want me to do?' she asked.

'Just stand in front of him and tell the truth, with witnesses to hear—'

'No, sir.' Vigorously she shook her head. 'No, I not saying a word. You better go.' She stood up and went over to the door as if to show them out.

'Will you think it over?' Kate asked. 'We'll make sure there's no danger.'

Jan produced a card and pressed it upon her.

'Just in case you change your mind,' he said.

'I not saying a word,' she repeated stubbornly.

'So that's that,' Kate said, when they were on their way to town. 'I suppose we were on to a loser, when you think about it. It was a monstrous thing to ask, really. I felt terrible in there.'

'I know what you mean,' Jan said. He sighed. 'Well, we'll have to think of something else. If Colin won't print it, maybe we can leak it to one of the less prestigious papers.'

'Without Dora's permission?'

'Can we afford to be too finicky about it? Or are you in favour of just telling him we know all and trusting to luck he'll resign? God, that would stick in my craw. He'd retire to write his memoirs, with everyone saying he was the best Prime Minister we never had!'

'It would be better than nothing,' Kate pointed out. 'He'd have given up his career.'

'To become a venerated elder statesman.' Jan's face, seen sideways, looked forbidding, seemingly carved out of wood like those of his Boer ancestors. 'I won't have it,' he said. 'He must be exposed.'

He dropped her in town so that she could shop for presents to take back to the children. And something for Tom? She looked for a long time at the window of a gentleman's outfitters, attracted by a shirt in a shade of dark mossy green. She could imagine him wearing it – and could imagine the neighbours remarking on it, too. It would suit him, she thought, and look good with that green tweedy tie. Or was it a little too daring, too Bohemian, even for him? His mother would hate it. Perhaps this new contract would change him. Maybe he would start going to the office in the kind of Edwardian collar and natty suit that were now the trend, even here in Cape Town.

She'd think about it, she decided, as she drifted on.

A loud voice attracted her attention. A thin woman in a white silk suit with a Jackie Kennedy pillbox hat on her head was emerging from a side street, accompanied by a stout, middle-aged lady in royal blue with a pearl choker and a strangely immobile face, heavily made up. Incuriously, Kate looked at them, then, suddenly realising their identity, she turned, startled, to study the nearest shop window, as if it contained objects of enthralling interest.

The woman in white was Marcia; and unbelievably, the stout party was Flick. She could see them now, reflected in the window. Go on, Kate urged them silently. Go on.

They went on, and she breathed again.

It was unsettling, though, knowing they were in town. She did not analyse the reason why she was so anxious to avoid them. Maybe Elaine would say they were two of the ghosts she ought to confront.

Well, too bad, she thought. She wasn't going to. And seeing them dawdling down the street away from her, she, too, retraced her steps and sought sanctuary in the gentlemen's outfitters. She'd buy that shirt for Tom after all.

Later, she took a taxi home, arriving there just as Rosie was leaving to catch the bus which stopped in the lower road.

'Mr Jan phoned from de office,' she said. 'He says, tell you to call right away. I left a note. Can't stop or I miss de bus.'

Kate thanked her, and immediately dialled Jan's office number. He had sounded dispirited when they parted earlier that morning, but now she could tell that his spirits were soaring.

'You'll never guess,' he said. 'I had a visitor, not long after I got back here.'

'Not Dora?'

'No. Not Dora. Louise!'

'Dora told her about Christiaan?'

'No – Theo did. It seems he was listening outside this morning and managed to get the gist of what we said. He confronted Dora after we left and got the truth out of her. She was upset – Louise heard the fracas and came downstairs to see what was going on and check her mother was OK. Theo, it seems, has a reputation for violence.'

'So what's going to happen?'

'Louise hates Christiaan's guts. He's done nothing but tighten the screws against Coloureds from the moment he took office. Life for them has got harder and harder over the years, and this – how he used her mother – is just about the final straw. She'll go along with almost anything we decide, just so long as it's not illegal. She doesn't want to risk losing her job.'

'No, of course not! She mustn't do that. So what's your plan?'

'I'm working on it,' said Jan.

20

The south-easter was blowing so hard that there was no question of sitting outside that night. The four of them, gathered together once more to discuss strategy and to eat a dinner cooked by Kate, were sitting inside, in Jan's somewhat bleak living quarters. Kate, on seeing then for the first time, had thought it a good thing that books were said to furnish a room, for certainly, in Jan's case, precious little else did.

'I assume,' Jan said to Colin, 'that your Mr Porter isn't averse to covering newsworthy stories, even if they do have an anti-government slant?'

'No, not at all,' Colin assured him. 'I don't mean to imply he goes along with everything they do. Far from it! It's just that he's more cautious than some of us think desirable. He tends to pussy-foot around things, but news is news, even to him.'

Jan grinned.

'Then we'll just have to see that news is what we make,' he said. 'Factual, corroborated, and photographed. What are the chances of your being detailed to cover Christiaan's meeting on Friday?'

Colin pursed his lips, considering the matter.

'Well, it wouldn't normally be my job, but I could probably swing it.'

'Doesn't matter if you can't, now I come to think about it. Better, perhaps, if you're outside on the steps with a camera – or a photographer – at the ready, waiting for the man himself to emerge.'

'What have you got in mind, Jan?' Nina asked.

'Well—' Lazily Jan tilted his chair back and gazed at the ceiling. 'I dreamed up a fantastic scenario where we put Louise in the front row so that as soon as Christiaan came on to the platform he would see her, whereupon she would leap up and cry "Daddy, Daddy!"'

He came down to earth, bringing the chair down with a bang. 'Only unfortunately I could see a number of drawbacks. Like the fact that, being Coloured, she'd never get past the man on the door and anyway would be manhandled out of the hall before anyone would take it in.'

'And dismissed as either mad or a troublemaker or both,' Nina pointed out. 'So what's Plan B?'

'I thought,' Jan began slowly, 'that we could prepare a question to be asked after Christiaan's spiel is over – there's bound to be time allowed for discussion afterwards.'

'What kind of question?' Nina asked.

'Something that elicits the kind of answer that sums up his beliefs concerning the evils of miscegenation. I haven't worked out the wording. It'll take a bit of thought, but I'm sure that between us we can think of something. Maybe it'll be best if we sound sympathetic to his views; tell him what a jolly good chap he is for keeping the races apart, then hit him with the question, whatever that may be.'

'Then?'

'Then the party's over and he leaves. He'll go off at the side of the platform, of course, but his car will be drawn up outside the front entrance of the City Hall, and he's bound to come out that way, down the front steps – where Colin and Louise will be waiting for him, camera at the ready.'

'And she steps forward and says "Daddy, Daddy"?'

'Words to that effect.'

'But why would that be any better than your previous idea? She could still be manhandled off the scene—'

'Maybe – but not before he's had a good look at her and fallen back in surprise.' Jan gave an exaggerated, eye-popping impression of Christiaan, falling back in surprise.

'You see,' Kate broke in, turning to Nina, 'Louise really is phenomenally like her mother was at the same age. It gave me quite a turn, I don't mind telling you. We're hoping that Christiaan will be so flabbergasted at the likeness that he'll looked shocked and guilty – which is the moment for the photographer to snap him. And Jan thinks – and I must say I agree with him – that if Christiaan's all over the papers looking shocked and guilty, then even if he denies it, people will think there's no smoke without fire. Louise says she's perfectly prepared to give chapter and verse, and I'm equally prepared to back her up.'

'What about Dora?' Nina asked. 'Does she agree to all this?'

'Louise says leave Dora to her. She'll come round to it, she says.'

'I wonder!'

'Any better ideas?' Jan asked her.

Nina shook her head.

'Not really. What about this question, though? Who's going to ask it, and what will it be?'

'Well . . .' Jan smiled at her, very innocently. 'It can't be me, can it? However much I wave my hand in the air, Christiaan is hardly likely to invite trouble by kindly asking me to state my views. The same goes for Kate, too. And Colin, of course, will be lurking on the front steps.'

'So no prizes for guessing who you have in mind!' Nina sounded amusedly resigned.

Colin frowned.

'Is it really necessary to involve Nina?' he asked, a little stuffily.

Jan laughed.

'Actually, it's too much of a risk having only one person who could be overlooked,' he said. 'And a woman, too. Nats tend not to approve of women raising their voices at political meetings. So I thought I'd plant a few sympathisers at strategic points all over the audience, primed with the same question. That way we'd hedge our bets, and Nina needn't really be involved at all if she doesn't want to be. I just thought she might like it.' He looked at her, smiling into her eyes. 'She always used to.'

'Do you mind, both of you?' Nina's amusement was now tinged with outrage. 'I'm perfectly able to speak for myself. Of course I don't mind being involved.'

'Well, that's all right, then,' Jan said smoothly, trying not to look too pleased with himself.

One point to him, Kate thought, observing. She gave a small, sympathetic smile in Colin's direction, but he looked away. Had he thought she was gloating? She hoped not. He was so nice, and so crazy about Nina that she ached for him.

'I do think it's important for us to get him to make a definite commitment about no sexual contact being possible between the races, don't you?' Jan said. 'It'll make a much better story, when only minutes later he's confronted with his love-child.'

In spite of himself, Colin laughed.

'You'll have me lying awake all night thinking of suitable headlines,' he said.

'How about "Le Roux's Secret Sin"?' suggested Nina.

'Or "Minister's Misdeeds"?' said Kate. '"Do what I say, not what I do, says le Roux."'

'"Secret Sex with Stunning Seamstress!"'

'I think we ought to get "love-child" into it,' said Jan. 'Readers love a love-child.'

'Surely the word "Coloured" should figure somewhere, for maximum impact?' said Nina.

'It's all right for us to make a joke of it,' Kate said, sobering a little. 'But think of Louise! Did you ever know anyone braver? This isn't going to be easy for her.'

'She knows that,' Jan said. 'And she's determined to go through with it. I gather she's always been pretty active in the anti-*apartheid* movement, and knowing Christiaan's her father has hardened her feelings about everything, if that's possible. Now – the question. What are we going to say? We'll butter him up first – congratulate him on the government's stand against the unworkable demands of the rest of the Commonwealth.'

'Which, if accepted, would only lead to the kind of miscegenation that was anathema to all right-thinking Nationalists,' Colin added.

'That's not exactly a question,' Kate said. 'He could just say "Thank you very much" and leave it at that.'

'Anyway,' Jan said, 'I'm not at all sure that some of the people I'll have in the audience can pronounce "miscegenation", let alone "anathema". I think we'll have to stick to "sex between the races."'

'We could ask him to confirm his views,' Nina said. 'Ask him to spell out exactly where the Nats stand on the matter.'

'At which he might ask where you've been living all these years,' said Colin.

'No, he won't,' said Jan. 'He'll get carried away. He gets euphoric after a good speech and likes nothing better than to expound basic principles. Oh, wow, I think we've really got him by the short and curlies on this. He'll walk right into it. And it couldn't happen to a better man. More wine, anyone? We ought to drink to this.'

He filled everyone's glasses and raised his own.

'To the unmasking of the Minister,' he said.

'Not a bad headline,' Colin said, following suit.

Kate and Nina went swimming at Sea Point the following day, Tuesday.

'Three more days,' Nina said, as they drove across town. 'I'm getting quite nervous. I hope this comes off as planned. I don't know what Jan will do if it doesn't.'

'I'm afraid something quite simple will happen to upset things,' Kate agreed. 'Like Christiaan coming out of another door. Or Louise getting cold feet.'

'I don't think she will. Well, Jan doesn't seem to think so.'

Kate glanced in her direction.

'You still think a lot of him, don't you?'

'Jan? Yes, of course I do. Shall we have lunch in Sea Point, or do you want to go home for any particular reason?'

'Oh, let's have lunch out,' Kate said, recognising a determined change of subject when she saw one.

Nina returned to it, however, once they had enjoyed their swim and were sitting in the sun by the side of the swimming pool.

'Kate,' she said, a little hesitantly. 'You do know, don't you, that Jan and I were very close for quite a long time?'

'Yes. He told me,' Kate said. She pondered her next words. What should a mother say in these circumstances? Probably nothing, she thought; but she couldn't resist the opening thus offered. 'I think he wishes you still were.'

'Does he? Really?' Nina looked at her. 'Oh, I know he makes unpleasant comments to Colin from time to time, but that doesn't mean anything, except that he's always been slightly jealous of him. I used to go out with him before I met Jan, you see. And then our paths crossed again, just after Jan and I had parted, and he seemed so nice and familiar and on the same wavelength.'

'I like him enormously.'

'Do you?' Nina wrinkled her brow. 'Well, I do, too. But you see . . .' She broke off and sighed. 'Why is life so difficult?' she demanded. 'When I gave Jan his marching orders, I honestly thought I couldn't put up with him any longer. I never knew where I was with him – if he'd turn up for dates, or leave me suddenly when something more important turned up. And it always was important, I know that. He's just so . . . so *committed*.'

'I can see the difficulties,' Kate said. 'I think he's great – well,

I would, wouldn't I? And I'm wild with happiness that we've discovered each other. But having said that, I have to admit that he's not the easiest person to live with. He does tend to take over so.' She laughed suddenly. 'I was thinking of Tom,' she said, in explanation. 'He made such valiant attempts to adapt to Jan, but it was hard for him. He likes order and a bit of peace when he comes home at night.'

Nina laughed too.

'I can see the problem.'

'Don't misunderstand me – he likes Jan a lot. It was just that he seemed—' She hesitated.

'All over the place,' Nina said, supplying the words. She laughed again. 'I know all that. I know everything about him. And you know something? I'm still crazy about him. I don't think there'll ever be anyone else for me.'

'Poor Colin,' Kate said, softly.

Nina sighed.

'I know. I feel awful. I really thought he might be the answer, you know.'

'Have you told him he's not?'

She shook her head.

'Not yet. I'll have to, of course, but thankfully he's busy tonight and tomorrow, and Thursday night I've promised to sit in for Margie and Steve because their girl's sick and they've booked to see that dance troupe at the Opera House. I really don't want to say anything until after Friday, just in case—'

'Just in case he's too shattered to perform his role?'

'It seems so calculating, doesn't it? I've never felt so guilty about anything. Listen,' she said, suddenly grasping Kate's arm. 'You won't say anything about anything to Jan, will you? Promise?'

'Of course I promise.' Kate patted her hand. 'I'll be as silent as the grave. I have no doubt whatever that you'll work it out for yourselves. And I expect Colin will find someone else, you know. Eventually. People do.'

'I know,' said Nina. 'It is hell, though, isn't it?'

'Hell,' agreed Kate, suddenly longing for Tom.

Dr Verwoerd's request to Christiaan that he should address the meeting in the City Hall since he himself was otherwise engaged was the cause of great gratification, most of all because the

Minister for External Affairs, who might, perhaps, have been a more obvious choice, had clearly been passed over. The exit from the Commonwealth, hailed in Johannesburg as some kind of victory, had been far less warmly received in Cape Town and nobody discounted the importance of explaining the benefits to the doubting populace.

The Prime Minister had clearly decided that Christiaan le Roux was the man for the job, which showed, Christiaan thought, a highly satisfactory degree of confidence and surely implied that he considered him a worthy successor.

Christiaan was aware that his stock, so recently in decline, was now surging upwards again. His speech in the House concerning the extension of the Group Areas Act had been the occasion of congratulations from the rest of the caucus, while his witty response to a question by his arch-enemy, Helen Suzman, on the subject of the Separate Registration of Voters Act had sent the Nationalist members into paroxysms of such delighted mirth that even now, two days later, he felt a glow at the thought of it.

He woke early on Friday morning, filled with a pleasurable sense of anticipation, hearing already the plaudits he felt sure would be forthcoming after he had made his speech. In conjunction with Boris Cloete, his PPS and adviser on such matters, he had worked hard on every line of it. Every speech was important, but speaking in front of the public carried a different kind of responsibility. It was an opportunity to enhance his appeal to the people he soon hoped to lead. Gravitas was essential, of course, and a demonstration of total commitment to the Nationalist ideal, as well as a sure knowledge of South African history. Mention of the heroic struggles of the early settlers as they affected today's rugged individualism always went down well; but on the other hand, there would be occasions for a lighter touch. Ghana's insistence on civil rights, for example, had proved a fruitful field for this and Boris had surely outdone himself in this area.

He was pleased with the speech. Boris was a good man. It was a pity, he thought, that he wouldn't be able to script answers to the questions that would come after; still, he rather prided himself on being good at coping with that kind of thing. He couldn't, actually, remember an occasion on which he had been lost for words – as Helen Suzman had cause to know, he thought, as the memory of Nationalist laughter once again rang in his ears.

He lay in bed for a while, going over his commitments for the day. There seemed no reason why he should not leave his office early in the afternoon, in time for him to come back to Gramerci and have a few quiet hours before it was necessary to drive back to the City Hall. He'd have a small siesta, take a shower, have a drink, sit in the garden a while, getting his thoughts in order.

It wasn't all bullshit, he reflected – all that business about sitting in the candlewood tree, feeling Sonia's presence. Well, that bit was total nonsense, of course, for when had she ever been any kind of inspiration? However, as if to give verisimilitude to his public statements, he had of late taken to this routine, and there was no doubt that he found it beneficial. Calming. He could collect his thoughts, go through his speech. If there was one thing he hated on this kind of public occasion it was having to consult his notes.

Breakfast was served on the stoep. The wind that had blown up earlier in the week had died away, only a shadow of its usual self this time, and the past two days had been pleasant, the morning still and warm, holding the promise of heat to come.

It was going to be a lovely day; and why, as he drank his coffee feeling at peace with the world, the thought of Kate's visit should come into his mind to spoil it, he couldn't imagine. He still felt aggrieved that such an occasion, intended only as an opportunity for her to see again the property she had thrown away so lightly – and, perhaps, to admire the way his career had advanced – should have been taken as an occasion for such unwarranted rudeness.

Still, he had learned through her that he'd misunderstood Jan entirely, so it had all been worthwhile. Jan didn't have the incriminating letter. Had never had it, and never would. It had been, quite obviously, among the papers that Sonia had burnt, all the worry and aggravation a total waste of emotion. Why hadn't she told him? Well, he knew the answer to that! She was probably still jeering at him, wherever she was.

Forget it, he told himself. And forget Kate. He need never see her again, and whatever her opinion of him, it would affect nothing.

The sugar-birds had already started fluttering around the red-hot pokers below the stoep, and somewhere a warbler was singing. The coffee finished, he put down his cup and relaxed in the warmth, the scent of jasmine drifting towards him.

It really was a perfect day.

*   *   *

'I came here once to hear an organ recital,' Kate said, as she and Jan went up the steps of the City Hall. 'That was in the Grand Hall, of course.'

'With my father?'

'No – with Helen. Neither Paul nor Guy were very appreciative of Bach. I was ignorant, too, but I loved it and I vowed to come to classical concerts more often. I didn't, though. I left Cape Town soon after.'

The meeting was in a lesser hall, which was filling fast.

'Are all your friends in place?' Kate asked Jan. Before taking his seat, he looked around.

'Yes,' he said, as he sat down beside her. 'I can see quite a number of familiar faces. Not Nina, though.'

'Who's the chap fussing around at the front?'

'Some big-wig Nat. I don't know his name.'

'Who's going to sit on the other chairs on the platform?'

'Other big-wig Nats, I suppose. Or the mayor. I dare say he'll be here.'

For a few minutes Kate looked about her silently. The audience was predominantly male, but there were a few women, mostly middle-aged, sitting beside their menfolk. She nudged Jan as Nina came in, taking her seat a few rows in front of them. She was wearing a yellow and white silk suit and looked outstanding, a bird of paradise among sparrows.

'She's gorgeous,' Kate whispered. Jan smiled but said nothing.

Kate wondered if she were nervous – whether she would be the one who would be invited to put her question to the Minister, or whether it would be left to the various unknowns that, according to Jan, were dotted about the audience.

For her, the tension was building, becoming acute. She looked at her watch. Four minutes to go before the meeting was due to start.

They had seen Colin outside. Louise was not there, but he said everything was in hand. He had seen her only minutes before and had arranged that she should wait in a café for everyone to go in and the meeting to start. She'd promised to arrive very shortly, he assured them.

Kate looked at her watch again, annoyed with herself on seeing that only a minute had elapsed since the last time. People were chatting, leaning back to talk to friends in the row behind, the

woman in front of her nodding earnestly in response to a monologue
from her stolid husband.

'Two minutes to go,' breathed Jan.

'I couldn't bear it if he was late.'

'He won't be! He never is. He'll be geeing himself up behind
the scenes somewhere, raring to go. He loves this kind of thing.'

Kate said nothing, but looked instead at the increased activity of
the big-wig Nat at the front of the hall, now talking to a grey-suited
young man who had emerged on to the platform.

'I know him,' Jan said. 'That's Boris Cloete, Christiaan's assist-
ant, or private secretary, or whatever ministers have. He writes all
his speeches.'

'Well, maybe you're right, then, and Christiaan is backstage
somewhere.'

Kate had deliberately resisted looking at her watch, but now did
so and saw that it was past the hour. More than five minutes.

'You're wrong about him not being late,' she said.

'Maybe he had a puncture or something.'

The hall was full now, with a number of men standing at the back.
Everyone was looking expectantly towards the platform, which was
now empty, the two men who had previously occupied it having
exited stage left, still talking.

'There's obviously some kind of delay—' Kate looked down and
saw that she had twisted her handkerchief so vigorously that it had
fallen apart. 'God, I can't stand much more!'

'It's only ten past. Not so late, really.'

Jan was chewing his lip, however, less calm than he sounded.
Kate looked anxiously towards the platform, willing something to
happen. She thought of Colin waiting on the steps. And Louise –
would she be there yet, or was she still in the café? There was a
strange sensation in her stomach. Come *on*, she urged Christiaan
silently.

She glanced in Nina's direction, and as she did so, Nina turned
round and raised her eyebrows in enquiry. She couldn't possibly
be as cool as she looked, Kate thought. She must be longing for
the proceedings to start.

At twenty past seven, the big-wig Nat, followed by Boris Cloete,
came on to the platform once more. He looked uneasy.

'Something's up,' Jan whispered.

Slowly the buzz of conversation died and all eyes were directed towards the man on the platform. Still he waited, saying nothing, until there was total silence.

'I very much regret to tell you that Mr le Roux is unable to attend this meeting tonight as he has been suddenly taken ill. We're assured it's nothing serious, but unfortunately he's unable to come here tonight to speak to us. His Personal Private Secretary, Mr Boris Cloete, has agreed to step into the breach, and since he has been involved in all the government deliberations on the withdrawal from the Commonwealth of Nations, I know that while sending sympathy to Mr Le Roux, you will welcome Mr Cloete—'

Nina twisted round to look at Jan and Kate, half rising from her chair. Helplessly Jan shrugged his shoulders, implying that they had no option now but to stay. Then, as if such a thought was too much for him, he seemed to change his mind and, signalling to Nina to leave, he took Kate by the hand and pulled her to her feet. There was an embarrassed and embarrassing silence while, watched by the entire audience, the three of them walked out, followed, after only a moment's hesitation, by Jan's supporters, five young men and two women, from various points in the hall.

'Jan – this is awful! We should have stayed.' Release of tension made Kate want to giggle. 'That poor man—'

'I'm not having you spend your last night listening to a bloody Nat,' Jan said.

Nina joined them.

'That was a horrible experience,' she said. 'Oh, Jan – I'm so sorry! It seemed such a foolproof plan.'

Jan put his arm around her shoulders.

'There's no such thing,' he said, putting as good a face on it as he could. 'We'll just have to try again another time.'

'What do you think is wrong with him?' Kate asked.

'Heaven knows,' said Jan. 'He has the constitution of an ox, so I can't imagine it's anything serious. Why? Do you want me to send him flowers or something? Come on – there's only one thing to do when you fall flat on your face like this—'

'What?'

For a moment Jan didn't answer, but looked up to greet his friends, now joining them in the corridor.

'Have a party, of course,' he said. 'Come on, you lot. Back to my place.'

*   *   *

Driving back home, Kate detected he was less dismissive of Christiaan's illness than he had appeared.

'I've never known Christiaan to be ill,' he said.

'There's always a first time.'

'I've got a feeling there's something wrong.'

'Well, of course! They said so—'

'Really wrong, I mean. Or,' he added after a short silence, 'could he have got wind of it somehow?'

'How? Would any of your friends have warned him?'

Jan gave a short laugh.

'They'd die first. I can vouch for all of them.'

'You mean he might not be ill at all, but just prudently keeping away?'

Jan thought this over.

'That doesn't ring true either,' he said.

There was another, more mundane concern that was bothering Kate.

'Do you think this party of yours will go on a long time?' she asked anxiously. 'You do remember I'm flying to Jo'burg at the crack of dawn? I mustn't miss my plane.'

Jan laughed.

'Don't worry. I'll turf everyone out at midnight, or when we run out of booze, whichever is the sooner.' He glanced down at her. 'Have you enjoyed it, Kate?'

She laughed.

'Well, it's been different,' she said. Then she sighed. 'It's been wonderful, Jan,' she amended, putting her hand on his arm. 'I've loved seeing it again. It's confirmed everything I thought, really – that this is a beautiful country, but I couldn't live here. Not yet, anyway. Maybe one day, when sanity takes over.'

'It'll happen,' Jan said. 'Believe me.'

When midnight came, Kate hadn't wanted the party to end. It had been riotous and raucous and as unlike anything she had ever known before as she could possibly imagine. Maybe this is what being young is like, she thought, realising, not for the first time, that this period in her life seemed to have passed her by. It was gratifying that no one present appeared to treat her as middle-aged, but merely accepted her presence as normal. It seemed that she, too, had found a way of shedding ten years, if not twenty.

She wondered, briefly, what the mothers outside the school gates would have thought if they'd seen her dancing the Charleston, or joining in the rugby songs roared out by Jan and his friends. Undoubtedly they would have thought it unseemly in one of her great age. Well, to hell with them! She hadn't enjoyed herself so much in years.

Tom would have been surprised too, she thought, before dropping off to sleep. He might have enjoyed it, though, and would certainly have agreed with her that it was a complete contrast to parties in Highgate, with the obligatory finger buffets and carefully arranged flowers and meaningless social chit-chat about children and schools and the doings of the au pair. At least Jan's party had been cathartic for all concerned, leaving the participants feeling philosophical about their disappointment and looking forward to another attempt to corner le Roux.

But perhaps, she thought, conscious that the morning might find her with a headache she would regret, it wasn't something she would want to do too often.

Louise had been disappointed at the lack of success of their plans.

'Another time, eh?' Colin said, as they had all been saying. She had agreed. Yes, she'd do it another time. A hundred times, if necessary.

He had given her a lift home before going up to Jan's house, so that she could change and get to the hospital for her spell of night duty. When she heard that an important man had been brought in, she guessed at once that it was Christiaan le Roux.

'What's wrong with him?' she asked the nurse who was about to go off duty.

'No idea,' the nurse said. 'Some kind of accident, I think. The girl who told me didn't know. It's nothing to do with us, anyway. He's over in one of the VIP rooms.'

Suppose I'd had to nurse him? Louise thought. Suppose I had to administer drugs? She was glad such temptation was not to be put in her way.

Christiaan was conscious when they brought him in. Half conscious, anyway. He came and went, as urgent faces bent over him, probed the wound, spoke to each other in words he didn't understand, the pain all the time like a fearsome monster squeezing him between two giant claws.

They told him they were going to operate; asked him for the name of his next of kin.

'No one,' he said, in a voice that seemed to fill his head, but which the nurse seemed to have difficulty in hearing.

There was Jan, of course. No one else. Such a lovely boy, he thought. Admiring. Companionable. He'd come.

But then the mists cleared and he knew he was wrong. Jan hated him. He couldn't remember why. Something to do with his mother's letters . . . ? Nothing made sense any more. Eksberg. His face seemed to swim before him. Where did he come into things?

'Am I dying?' he asked the nurse. He lost consciousness immediately and didn't hear her answer, and when he next was aware of anything he was being wheeled along a corridor. It seemed a long, long way. Cream walls, white ceiling, trundle trundle, trundle.

Suddenly he saw that other face, with the wide, malevolent grin and the staring eyes. The Coloured man, coming towards him in a running crouch, over the grass to where he sat within the candlewood tree, pondering his speech. He had looked up and tried to shout – but there was no time, no time. He couldn't move. That damned tree – it was almost like being in a cage.

The trolley had come to a halt. He was lifted, put down again, given an injection, gowned figures all around him. And as consciousness slipped away he seemed to hear the sneering words howled at him by his assailant as he plunged the knife in, again and again and again.

'Daddy, Daddy, Daddy, Daddy . . .'

Jan had wanted to fly with her as far as Johannesburg, but Kate had talked him out of it. It would be a waste of money, time and effort, she said. It was only a case of walking from one part of the airport to another, following the signs. There was only a little time between planes and her baggage could be checked straight through.

They stood beside the check-in desk, looking at each other a little awkwardly.

'There's really no need to hang about,' Kate said. 'I hate goodbyes, don't you? And we have kind of said it all, haven't we?'

'Maybe. I'll see you through the gate, though.' He picked up her hand luggage and took her arm, and slowly they walked across the concourse together.

'Perhaps all parents and children should meet as adults,' Kate said.

'It certainly gives the relationship a new perspective.'

'You will write?'

'Of course. You too.'

'Of course. And you'll come over again soon?'

'Could Tom stand it?'

'You know he could. And the children would be ecstatic.'

'Give my love to them.'

For a moment they clung together. In the departure lounge she found the plane was already boarding and she set off down endless corridors, away from Jan, away from the past, away from Cape Town.

Later, as the plane took off, looking down on it, she thought it still the loveliest city she had ever known, and was grateful to have had the chance to see it again.

She'd be able to tell Elaine that she had laid ghosts; that she'd been to Gramerci and left her old unhappy self behind there. And she'd tell Tom—

What would she tell Tom? That they'd both been wrong; she most of all, for giving up so easily.

But none of that was important now. Only the present mattered, and the future, and loving each other, and being friends—

Like Jan and Nina? It would happen, she felt sure of it, and on the whole felt confident that there would be a happy ending. It might not be her kind of happy ending, but that hardly mattered. They were the new generation.

The telephone was ringing as Jan came back from the airport. He hoped it was Nina. It might be. They hadn't said a lot last night for there had been no opportunity, but there'd been a moment when he'd gone into the kitchen to open another bottle of wine and she had followed, and she'd said – or he thought she'd said – something about having told Colin—

Or had he dreamt the whole thing? She hadn't had time to say much because someone else had joined them and insisted on telling them all about his trip to Durban and the girl he'd met there, and after a while she had slipped away, saying something about talking to him later. Perhaps she was phoning to explain further. He hoped, very much, that she hadn't told Colin that she'd marry him. She wouldn't, would she?

But it wasn't Nina; it was Groote Schuur hospital.

'Mr Lampard? We understand you're Mr le Roux's nephew.'

'By marriage,' Jan said cautiously. 'We're not exactly close. Is he there? Does he want to see me?'

'I'm afraid I have bad news for you. Mr le Roux was brought in here last night having suffered a knife attack. It was necessary to operate. It really was his only chance, but I'm afraid he never regained consciousness. I'm so sorry.'

'He's . . . he's dead?' Jan couldn't take it in. 'But they said he was unwell, at the meeting. I thought—'

'It was thought best to soft-pedal the seriousness until he'd been properly examined. I'm so sorry. There are formalities. Perhaps you could come?'

'Of course. I'll come at once. Tell me,' he added, before the hospital official could hang up, 'do they know who did it? Was it at Gramerci? His home?'

'Yes, I understand that it was. And a Coloured man has been held. Someone called Theo Petrus, I believe.'

Jan drew in his breath.

'I see,' he said. 'Thank you.'

Slowly he put down the phone, went out to the stoep, and stood for a few moments with his hands on the rail and his head bent.

Christiaan. Gone. It didn't seem possible. Why was he experiencing grief? It wasn't, surely, for the vainglorious politician. It had to be for the smiling man with the cricket bat who had cheered immeasurably the life of a lonely little boy.

Ripples in a pool, he thought. One action setting off another, and all to end in Groote Schuur hospital. Poetic justice? Perhaps – but he hadn't ever wanted it to be delivered like this.

He drew a deep breath, and straightened his back. There would be much to do, arrangements to make, undoubtedly the police to deal with. An ordeal, all of it. And at the end, Gramerci. What was he to do about that?

What else but share it with Nina? All of it – the good and the bad. For a moment he continued to stand there, staring at nothing, seeing a future that contained commitments other than that which had so far dominated his life.

The struggle would go on. That went without saying. But was it too hopeful to think there was room for other things as well?

He lifted his hands and brought them down sharply on the rail, as if suddenly he had made a decision. Then he went inside to phone Nina.

BARBARA WHITNELL

CHARMED CIRCLE

THE ROSSITERS lived just over the garden fence –
and inhabited a completely different world.

Rachel was lonely, missing her parents, forced to live
with her disapproving, strait-laced grandmother.

The family next door was noisy, colourful, careless of
convention: bubbly Alannah, sensitive Barney, Diana,
so casually beautiful and clever. And Gavin, who she
could only adore from afar.

Invited into their charmed circle, yet never quite part
of it, the Rossiters became the emotional centre of her
life.

But as the shadow of terrible events begins to loom
over their seemingly secure pre-war life, Rachel finds
her relationships with the Rossiters becoming more
complex, more adult – and more disturbing.

'Here is a strong story, well told, with an abundance
of real feeling and a winning spice of humour. Above
all, characters that live, and live on in the mind (and
dare I say the heart) long after you finish reading.

 Warmly recommended'

Sarah Harrison

'A compelling read'

Dee Remington, *Family Circle*

HODDER AND STOUGHTON PAPERBACKS

JENNIE FIELDS

CROSSING BROOKLYN FERRY

Zoe Finney's wealthy in-laws think she's crazy, leaving her expensive wedding-present Manhattan apartment for a house in Brooklyn. But it's supposed to be a fresh start. If Zoe can't have a simple, ordinary marriage, at least she can have a house that is truly her own, a place to wait until something changes.

Zoe's six-year-old daughter, Rose, isn't content with simply waiting until something changes. She doesn't see much point to a father who lies in bed all day and doesn't talk to her. She cannot remember ever being touched by him. Rose wants a proper father, and Keevan, their new next-door neighbour, seems to fit the bill very nicely.

Keevan's a part of the old Brooklyn, pre video stores, muffin shops and sun-dried tomatoes. He wants to be a father to Rose as much as she needs him. But Zoe is married to Jamie, and she is convinced that one day he's going to be himself again. Nothing is going to make her forget how much she loves him . . .

HODDER AND STOUGHTON PAPERBACKS

ELIZABETH SHORTEN

A NEW WOMAN

When Becky Carlyle unintentionally becomes the family breadwinner, she thinks she knows the risks. If she doesn't work hard enough, she won't be able to support them all. But no one's warned her that if she works too hard, she may lose the child she adores.

At the moment six-year-old Adam is seeing more of his nanny than his mother. Her husband Rupert, an out-of-work actor, resents Becky's success and spends his evenings in nightclubs. The trendy British art film she's producing seems to be spinning out of control when one of the stars hits the bottle and the young director develops a desperate crush on her.

The strain of seeing to everyone's needs except her own is starting to take its toll. None of the people who rely on her feel they're getting their fair share of Becky's attention, and the one who gets the least is Becky herself.

Something has to change in Becky's life, but she's not sure what. And the decision may be taken out of her hands . . .

HODDER AND STOUGHTON PAPERBACKS